THE CHAPLAIN'S ASSISTANT

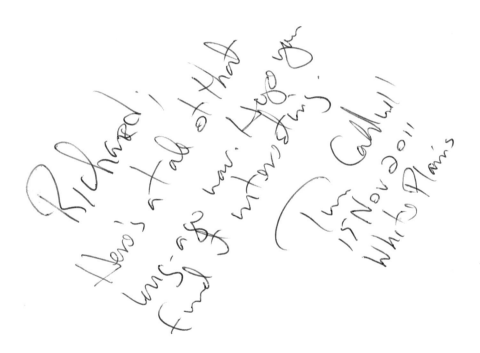

THE CHAPLAIN'S ASSISTANT

GOD, COUNTRY, AND VIETNAM

A Novel

JT Caldwell

Glenn Street Press
Mount Pleasant, Michigan

THE CHAPLAIN'S ASSISTANT
GOD, COUNTRY, AND VIETNAM

Copyright 2009 by JT Caldwell

For permission to reproduce selections from this book, write to

Permissions, Glenn Street Press
2020 S. Mission, #135
Mount Pleasant, Michigan 48858
www.GlennStreetPress.com

We live in a society that demands disclosure: this is mine. Most of what is described in these pages happened to the author. However, certain events described in the first person happened to other soldiers but not to him. The chronology of the events has been altered for the purpose of coherence. Most of the characters are real, but a few are composites of several people. No real names were used for the characters with the exception of the late Maynard Klein, a beloved choral conductor and professor of conducting at the University of Michigan. And, finally, no helicopters were damaged in the writing of this book.
JTC

ISBN: 978-0-9841964-0-1 (pbk)
ISBN: 978-0-9841964-1-8 (ebk)
Library of Congress Control Number: 2009933841

Printed in the United States of America

To the real Liz with all my love

3:00 AM, September 1970

The walls shook.

Howitzers, I thought. *Wonder if they're ARVN or ours? If they're ARVN, I might be safer back in the bunker.* I swiped at a mosquito that buzzed near my ear, shrugged my shoulders to relieve my aching muscles, and continued playing the miserably tuned upright piano. My fingers felt like waterlogged pulpwood as they moved across the keys. I tried to feel the sway of the music. Finally the notes that had seemed to stumble over themselves began gliding quicker and faster until they were skipping and running. Bach. *Preludes and Fugues.*

The walls shook again.

I played on, louder, softer, as my eyes scanned the score. The music curved, turned corners, and arched as it penetrated the dust-filled air of the empty chapel. The notes danced, sometimes with slow grace, sometimes jigging. The sounds flowed into me, calming the rapid-fire images in my head.

But the images kept coming, seeping around the edges of my mind and through the silences of the music, and with the images came the questions.

What could I have done for those guys?

I played on, trying to drown the voices in my head with music.

I was scared.

Howitzers rumbled in the distance. The walls shook again. Was the sound closer? Was the enemy closing in?

Still, I played on. The musical lines rose and fell, luring me into worlds where musical patterns ruled with soft forms. An unexpected harmony broke through like the smile of a mischievous child. "Come play with me," it said. Bach said. *Prelude* led to *Fugue*; *Fugue* to another *Prelude.*

The Meat Wagons arrived at the morgue across the street. Ambulances—signs of hope in the World, but there was no hope here. Not tonight. Not from the bloody horror that drove me here to this place where I searched for solace in the embrace of music.

The music became clearer, more vivid; the dilapidated piano more resonant. Here were harmonies, shapes, colors, sonorous dreams that moved through the turbid heat, echoing across centuries: Bach to me.

So I sat at the piano in the chapel with shuddering walls, as the tropical night dragged itself toward morning, wanting the music to encircle me, to hold Vietnam at a distance for a few brief moments. Here, in the circle of melodies and rhythms, the long-dead master communed with his distant child, ushering him into a small sphere of tranquility and order amid the ordnance of war, teaching him that even in the midst of chaos and insanity, beauty could survive. Music would endure.

CHAPTER 1

▼

Greetings from Your Friends and Neighbors

August 1, 1969

Spoleto, Italy. Images of ancient buildings; graceful aqueducts spanning deep, green valleys; piazzas laid by Roman slaves centuries before Christ was born; opera houses filled with music; the melodious language, the magnificent cathedral: All of this vanished as I opened my eyes in the dark room.

I think I'm back in Michigan, I told myself. As if on cue, the woman next to me in the bed turned over and snuggled up against me. She threw a leg over my legs, and an arm across my chest as she put her head on my shoulder. She took a deep, contented breath as her body relaxed onto mine. I smiled in the darkness and pulled her even closer. Karen, my high school sweetheart and my wife of three years.

"God, I missed you," I whispered.

I had spent the summer singing opera in Spoleto and had arrived at the Detroit Metropolitan Airport around nine o'clock the night before. By ten o'clock my ears had unblocked, and the sharp, shooting pains in my sinuses had receded. By eleven o'clock I was in bed with Karen, proving that having sex really was like having learned to ride a bike.

There is a six-hour time difference between Italy and the United States, and my sleep patterns would probably be a mess for several days. I had awakened well before dawn, but gone right back to sleep with Karen beside me. When I woke up the second time, it was mid-morning. My sinuses were still recovering from the plane trips: Rome to Paris, Paris to New York, New York to Detroit—up and down, high pressure to low pressure. My head felt so puffy that I could have given the Pillsbury Doughboy competition for "Yeast Head of the Month."

I also felt like a displaced person. I looked around and saw nothing that was mine—or ours. We had moved in with Karen's parents at the beginning of the summer, and my in-laws' home—as comfortable as it was and as kind as they were to have us plop down with them for the summer—was still my in-laws' home. I missed the old, small apartment where we had lived since marrying the summer before my senior year at the University of Michigan. It hadn't been much, but it was ours as long as we forked over the rent to Old Man Thomas.

I looked around the house stuffed with furniture and years of living that came with raising a large family. Compared to the open, sparsely furnished room I had shared with a friend and fellow singer, Frank, that summer in Spoleto, the house seemed to be closing in on me as it warmed in the August sun. It was even hotter outside, and the humidity was climbing. My head was throbbing, the air felt heavy and oppressive, and I had the attention span of a two-year old. Everything was out of joint.

I wandered out the screened door and onto the small stoop that faced the street. I kept reminding myself that as hot as it was going to be that day, it didn't feel as hot and steamy as Rome had felt when I had visited there just two weeks earlier.

Karen appeared with coffee. Even on the hottest of days, she preferred hot coffee. "How are you doing?" she asked.

She handed me her coffee cup and swept her shoulder-length, dark brown hair into a ponytail. I looked into her blue eyes and felt the same tingle I had felt when I first dated her in high school.

I touched her cheek. "I missed you so much. It was a very long summer away from you."

"I missed you, too," she said, taking back the cup and sitting it on the porch rail. She put her arms around me and laid her head on my shoulder. I'm five foot nine—only a couple of inches taller than her—so we always fit well together. As I held her slender body next to mine and felt her arms around me, my body started reminding me how good it felt to hold her. One part of me in particular remembered just how well we had fit together the night before.

"I don't ever want you to go away again," she said.

"I won't," I said. "We have that nice little apartment waiting for us in Dubuque, and all I want to do is go there with you, teach those Iowa kids to sing, and live happily ever after."

She raised her head and smiled. "I can hardly wait. I didn't unpack most of our stuff when we moved from Ann Arbor, so it really won't take a lot of time for me to get us ready to move. If you would take care of the U-Haul, I can start—"

"Hang on," I interrupted. "I'm still feeling kind of foggy. Let me see if I can clear my head, then I'll start pitching in. We have a lot of decisions to make about the move, but I'm not thinking too clearly right now."

She signed. "I know. I guess I'm impatient. You were off being a star all summer, while I just drove to Ann Arbor for work and classes. I'm tired of the drag." She was finishing her teaching degree and working part-time in a university office, something she had done since we were first married. I had been the full-time graduate student with a small Fellowship and church job that paid some of the bills, but she had earned more than half of what we needed while also taking classes. It was a drag, and I would be forever grateful for what she did.

I pulled her to me. "I know. I wish we could have been together, but...."

"That's old stuff. I'm glad you went. It's just that now I'm ready to get on with things. You know, moving, being the wife of the most talented singer and conductor in all of Iowa, and making babies. Those kind of things."

"Yeah. And now that you're a University of Michigan graduate, too, you should be able to find a teaching job, at least for a couple of years. Then we could think about having our three children—"

"I think four sounds better," she said.

I kissed her cheek. "You know." I kissed her neck. "We could get started on Baby Number One right now." I kissed her ear.

She looked at her watch. "It's only eleven o'clock in the morning. And besides, didn't we do something like that last night?"

"Yes, we did. You were wonderful."

"Thank you. You weren't so bad yourself, except ..."

"Except what?" I asked.

"Well, what is the last thing you remember from last night?" she asked with a smile.

"I remember making love, then, the next thing I remember is waking up early this morning and you snuggling into me." I paused. "Oh, no!"

She laughed. "That's right. You fell asleep on top of me."

I blushed. "I can't believe I did that," I said. "But that was hours ago, and I had just arrived after a very, *very* long trip from Italy. I'm much more rested now that I've had a good night's sleep, so I bet I can stay awake for at least ten minutes after … you know." I looked at my watch. "It's about four in the afternoon, according to my body clock. It's the end of siesta time in Spoleto, and you remember how I get when I'm waking up."

She smacked me playfully on the chest. "I'd be embarrassed. I mean, Mom and Dad are here, and we disappear into the bedroom for an hour?"

"For several hours," I teased. "After all, it was a long, hot summer, with me in Europe with all those attractive, single girls in the choir and you back here. I have a lot of catching up to do."

She stepped away from me and crossed her arms. "You wrote me a lot of nice, torrid letters, but you didn't say anything about those girls. So, is there anything you would like to tell me?" Her tone was still bantering, but a subtle note of seriousness had crept in.

"You mean besides all the long walks and cold showers? Hmmm, let me think. I was glad that Frank was there as my roommate. He made those long nights so much more bearable." I smoothed an eyebrow with my little finger.

She chuckled and hugged me again. "Oh, Ted, you're never serious. I missed you so much."

"I missed you too. I really did … theriouthly."

She shook her head, kissed me, and then went inside to help her mother with lunch. I was finishing my coffee when the mailman arrived.

We chatted briefly about the weather, and I mentioned that I had been a substitute carrier the previous summer as I was finishing my master's in music. We commiserated about life in the postal service as he handed me the mail.

I sorted through it and then put it on the small table in the entranceway. One envelope immediately caught my attention: it was from my draft board. My fingers shook as I opened the letter. I had sent Dubuque my deferment forms months earlier. I was "essential personnel," the Dean had said, and the university would make sure that I would be deferred.

This is my deferment, I assured myself as I opened it. I was wrong. Under the letterhead of the Draft Board were three words: Notice of Induction.

Time stopped. I stood in the small alcove, reading and rereading the letter. My legs felt shaky, and the domestic noises from Karen and her mother dulled to silence. My universe was focused on just three words: Notice of Induction.

Karen found me a few minutes later, sitting on the sofa, staring at the letter. "What's the matter, Ted?"

I handed her the letter. She read it once, then again, slowly. "What does this mean?" she asked softly.

"It means I've been drafted." I was barely able to talk.

A flush crept across her face; her eyes teared. "What'll we do?"

I stood up. "I'm going to call Dubuque to see if they can do something." I made for our bedroom, bounding up the dark stairwell that led to the second floor. I was looking for the papers from the University of Dubuque related to my employment.

"Remember Dean Anderson said the university would take care of the draft stuff?" I said when I returned, papers in hand. "They'll straighten this out."

I called the university and was told that Dean Anderson was on vacation. There was an associate dean, but he was out of his office at the moment, the secretary said. I should call back in an hour.

I was on an emotional rollercoaster as Karen and I talked about what to do next. Karen's mother, Emily, found us sitting on the sofa. Karen told her about the letter. Emily had dealt with many a crisis as she had raised her six children, and she dealt with ours with equal calmness. "Call our congressman," she suggested. "I bet he can do something. It will at least give you something to do while you wait for the person in Dubuque."

It took a series of calls for us to track down Representative Bill Carson's phone number for his office in Washington. Of course, he was not there. One of his aides took my information and said he would relay it to Congressman Carson.

It was time to call Dubuque. My call was put through to the associate dean, Dr. Harry Wilson. Dubuque was a small school, so he remembered me from my interview, he said. He was looking forward to being in the town-gown choir that I would be conducting.

I tried to explain my situation, calmly, deliberately, trying to sound as professional as I could under the circumstances, so he would not think they had hired some inexperienced kid fresh out of graduate school, which was, of course, exactly what they had done. We talked for several minutes. He asked questions as he tried to understand the situation. He said he would investigate.

"I think we can work this out," he said, bolstering my hopes. "After all, we could make better use of a conductor than the army, right?"

I was elated and grateful. I was drowning, and he had thrown me a life preserver. "He thinks he can work things out," I told Karen. I wanted to call my parents but remembered that they were out of town. My father, the Southern Baptist minister, was holding a revival somewhere; Mom was with him.

I told Karen that I wanted to go to my parents' house even if they weren't there. I couldn't find the words to explain to her that I needed to be in the house where I had spent so much of my childhood. She wanted me to stay for lunch, but my stomach was in such a knot that I couldn't eat. I didn't think I could keep anything down. I needed to get outside, to move around. I needed to go home.

"I told Mom I'd help with shopping this afternoon," Karen said. "We need food for dinner, and we can't act like we're staying in a hotel."

"I know," I said. "It's okay. You stay. I'll be fine. I'll walk over and check the house out. The exercise will help get my mind off ... this." I gestured toward the letter.

Down College Street—Karen's street—to Fort Street, turn right on Fort, then one mile to Lincoln. I knew the route like the back of my hand from the years I'd walked Karen home from high school. As I turned onto the tree-lined street, I saw the two-story, red brick house that Dad's church had selected as the parsonage.

The house was closed of course. Every shade was drawn, and I knew that every door and window would be locked, and every light turned off: Dad was always meticulous about that. The house had been closed for several days, so it was stuffy, but not the oven it could have been.

This house was special to me. As I was growing up my father had moved us from coal mining towns in eastern Kentucky, to West Virginia, to Florida, and then to Lincoln Park, Michigan, all at the Lord's behest of course. This house had been our home all through my high school years. This was the first house I had lived in for more than two years, and it was the last house I shared with my parents and sister. I would miss it when Karen and I moved to Dubuque—*if* we moved to Dubuque.

I wandered up the stairs to my old bedroom. There were three bedrooms and a half-bath on the second floor. My bedroom was at the end of the hall with double windows that faced the street. Mom had kept it just like I had left it: a desk, a bed, a small radio, a bookshelf, and a record player with built-in speakers. I had listened to a lot of operas and symphonies on the radio and the record player.

I wandered down to the kitchen. Mom made iced tea in the Southern way—meaning with lots of sugar—and always kept a full pitcher of it in the refrigerator. I poured a glass and then went out to the swing on the porch.

The swing had been a gift from Dad to Mom. He never made much money from the churches he pastored, so he had very little to give her in a material sense. Fortunately, Mom cared very little for material possessions, so she never complained. But Dad often tried to do something special for her to show how much he loved her.

He knew she had loved to swing from the time she was a young girl, so he had asked a parishioner to build a swing for him, one that was wide enough for two adults. I had helped him put it up one Saturday when Mom was attending a meeting. He loved the surprised look on her face when she came home and saw it.

The swing had quickly become her favorite retreat. From the first days of spring until the cold winds of winter blew in, Mom would sit in it in the early morning, drinking coffee, reading the Bible, and sometimes singing her favorite hymns in her pure, soft voice. She was a woman who found satisfaction in small pleasures.

My bedroom window looked out over the roof that covered the porch, and I often left it open in the springtime, so there had been mornings when the sound of her singing would come drifting softly through my open window. Sometimes in the peaceful transition between sleeping and waking, I would hear her.

I always loved the sound of her voice. Her singing would bring back childhood memories of warm summer days in Kentucky. Even if I was playing outdoors, I could hear her voice coming through the open windows when she sang as she worked. I never stopped to listen, but her singing tied my heart to her in ways that I could not understand and would never find words to express.

So I sat in her swing in the cool shade of the porch, drinking the tea she had made as my emotions tumbled over themselves. As I gazed up and down the shady street, I tried to think of what Mom might say about "the Lord's will," but couldn't find much comfort in those words. After a few minutes, I hauled myself out the swing, washed my glass, locked the door, and walked back to the house on College Street and Karen.

I called Congressman Carson's office the next morning and asked for George Arnold, the aide who'd promised to relay my message to the congressman. The receptionist informed me that it was Mr. Arnold's day off, so he wouldn't be in.

"What? I spoke to him yesterday. I have an urgent problem—I received my draft notice. It's a big mistake; I'm not supposed to get drafted. I have a job, a teaching job at a university. I'm essential! The president of the University of Dubuque said I am essential! Arnold said he would talk to Congressman Carson about it."

There was a brief silence, then: "I'm sorry. I do not control Mr. Arnold's schedule. I'm just a secretary. However, I noticed that he has left me a message. Your name again?"

"Bertson. Ted Bertson." I was fighting to control my temper, but my temper was winning.

"Okay. This is for you, then." She paused again. It occurred to me that she was enjoying my discomfiture. "The message reads, 'Tell Bertson sorry. Carson cannot do anything.'" She cleared her throat. "I'm afraid that's all it says … Hello? Are you still there?"

"Yes," I croaked, "I'm still here."

"If you have any questions, I suggest you call Mr. Arnold tomorrow. Good-bye." She hung up.

Karen spoke first. "He couldn't help?"

I shook my head. I was trying not to give up—after all, we still had Dubuque. Karen put her hand on my arm but said nothing. I walked out the front door to stand on the small porch. I was afraid to call the university. As long as I did not call, I could convince myself that there was hope.

I called Dr. Wilson late the next morning. It was not good news.

"The paper work for your deferment was found on a secretary's desk," he said. "It was never sent to your draft board."

"What do you mean, 'never sent'?"

His tone was conciliatory, and his words seemed to come in bits and pieces. "Well, you see, the regular secretary was on maternity leave … several replacements … work piled up … somehow misplaced…. President Jordan called your draft board … refused to reconsider their decision. I'm very sorry. Have you considered calling your congressman?"

"Yes, but he can't help either."

"Well, then, again, I'm sorry. I'm sure you understand that we must fill your position, as it would not be possible to hold it for you."

"Yes, I know."

He seemed at a loss for words. "Best of luck," he said after an awkward silence. "Perhaps we'll see you when you get back from the service. Good-bye." The dial tone droned in my ear.

"That's it," I told Karen. "That's all."

CHAPTER 2

▼

My Mother Didn't Raise Her Boy for a Soldier

August 13, 1969
7:00 AM, Fort Wayne, Detroit

The sun had been up only a short time, but the air was already sticky with humidity. I parked our white Ford Fairlane next to a No Parking sign and looked over at Karen. We had held hands like nervous children and said very little on the half-hour ride; now, there was no time to talk. We got out of the car and stood on the curb on Fort Street.

Traffic whizzed by, the drivers oblivious to us. I ran my hands through her hair, looked into her eyes, and kissed her. I didn't want to let her go, but after a few moments I grabbed my small suitcase, kissed her one last time, and then walked away from her and through the iron gates for my pre-induction physical.

Signs with various combinations of letters were everywhere: USARHQ, NCO, NARQUARK. I found one that wasn't in this peculiar gibberish: "INDUCTEES REPORT HERE" was over a double-door that led into a building that was as long as a football field and about as wide.

Other signs directed me to a high-ceilinged locker room painted the color of bleached seaweed. I entered the room, along with several other men. A sergeant immediately ordered us to strip down to underwear and shoes.

Are they drafting them out of high school now? I wondered. *Those guys look barely eighteen. I'm twenty-four and I look old, like I'm thirty.*

The sergeant was leaning against one of the lockers, smoking a cigar as he surveyed the room.

"Should we wear socks with our shoes?" I asked.

Squinting through a cloud of blue smoke, the sergeant slowly turned his head toward me and looked me up and down. "I said, 'Strip down to your underwear and shoes.' Nothing else, asshole! Get it?" It was not much of a recruiting tactic.

We put our clothes and suitcases in lockers, and then we were given small paper bags for our valuables. We wandered out into the hot building, with locker keys hanging from thick, white strings around our necks, wearing only our underwear and shoes, and clutching our paper bags with sweaty hands.

The induction center was, I would discover, typical of large military buildings. The design was classic army—brick exterior and an interior that was probably drafty in the winter and hot as hell in the summer. The interior walls seemed to have been erected as an afterthought and painted one of those military colors that could pass for gray, green, or blue. Overhead, large fluorescent lights hung at the proper intervals to ensure that everybody would look as if they had spent the last year living in Carlsbad Caverns. A thousand nearly naked male bodies in a building without air-conditioning on a hot August day meant we smelled as bad as we looked.

Twenty of us were culled from the herd and escorted into a room that held twenty school desks. We were apparently going to take a test. I was good at tests, although I had never taken one dressed only in my underwear and shoes.

I learned one lesson quickly: On a hot day, never ever lean against a hard plastic surface without a shirt. At first, it froze me; then, as I continued to lean against it, my skin stuck like glue. I left at least two layers of my epidermis on the chair as I pulled away from it to sit up straight when another overweight sergeant entered the room.

He looked slowly around in a manner, I supposed, that was intended to appear menacing. It worked. In fact, he was probably trying to remember what he was doing there. Eventually, he said, "Looks to me like each of you got two arms, two legs, one head, and, maybe, one dick, so you'll all prob'ly be inducted. You'll be done here today about seventeen hundred hours." A couple of young gung-ho types with muscles and tattoos nodded their heads in understanding. "Five o'clock to you civilians. At that time, you'll know whether you've passed the physical. Those of you who did not pass will be free to go; those of you who pass will remain on this base. You will be told what will happen to you at that time."

The test we then took while sitting at the school desks was, of course, almost impossible to fail; a slow six-year-old could have passed it. Ignorance, it seemed, was not an excuse whether in a court of law or to keep from being inducted into the military.

By late afternoon, I was standing before a sergeant who was seated behind a beat-up gray metal desk. My paper bag was rumpled and soggy from my hands that had sweated as I had endured being poked and prodded by various military personnel, some of whom might have even have had medical training. The sergeant moved his lips as he silently read my answers on one of the numerous forms I had completed during the day. One of the questions had asked how many years of education I had completed.

Because I had just received my master's degree at the University of Michigan, I had written "eighteen."

The sergeant looked up at me, scowling. "Bertson, I don't want to know how fuckin' many years old you fuckin' are. I want to know how many fuckin' years you've been to fuckin' *school*."

"Eighteen," I answered.

"Bertson, I'll goddamn say it again: I don't want to know how fuckin' many years old you fuckin' are. I want to know how many fuckin' years you have been to fuckin' *school*."

"Eighteen. Twelve years through high school, four years as an undergraduate, two years for my master's degree. That makes eighteen."

His eyes glanced up and down the form, over to me, then back to the form. Finally, he understood. He scowled as he looked at me. "What the fuck are you doin' here?"

"Hell if I know."

The physicals were completed around five o'clock. We dressed and were then led out of the sweat-permeated building. Once out in the open air, we trudged across the street to another undistinguished building to sweat some more. No announcement had been made as to which of us had passed our physicals, but I noticed there were armed military police posted at all the doors of the building. I had a sinking feeling that the poking and prodding we had undergone had proven all of us to be healthy enough to die for our country. I was in shock: I was about to be inducted.

Do they let us go home again to say good-bye? I wondered. *Do we have a week?* Canada or Sweden was looking more appealing with each passing minute.

A sergeant entered the room where about two hundred of us stood like cattle in the stockyard of a slaughterhouse.

"Men, you have all successfully passed your induction physicals." He paused almost as if waiting for applause. There was none. "All branches of the military services are presently inducting. The Marines have been taking all draftees for the last two days."

There were several groans, and someone muttered in the crowd muttered, "Oh, shit!"

"However," the Sergeant continued, "the Marines have filled their quota today, so all of you will be inducted into the United States Army."

Sighs of relief filled the room. *Hurry! Take us before the Marines get us!* An officer stepped into the room and swore us into the army. We mumbled words about duty, service, and protecting something. He then told us we had twenty minutes before boarding the buses for Fort Knox where we would enter basic training, so we should say our good-byes quickly.

Our families had appeared. How had they known we would not be allowed to go home? I spotted Karen in the crowd, and then saw my mother and father. I squeezed through the hugging, crying clumps of people to reach my family. I hugged my father first, then my mother. Karen came to me, and I held her tightly as she buried her face in my neck and cried. I felt her tears on my skin, and I inhaled the familiar fragrance of her hair. I felt numb, as if my brain had locked up inside my skull.

The twenty minutes passed in an instant, and we were herded into waiting buses. The military was living up to its legend: After making us hustle, we sat waiting for about an hour. I guessed that it took that long for the driver to figure out that Fort Knox was in Kentucky. As dusk descended, we finally left.

Everything was a blur from the time I got on the bus until the next afternoon. The bus drove through the night and arrived at Fort Knox in the wee hours of the morning. I was groggy with fatigue as we were yelled off the bus and directed into a large, brightly lit room, filled with school desks. We were expected to sit in these desks and stay awake while a parade of sergeants lectured about the joys of army life. The lectures were punctuated with the crack of a yardstick against the wall and the *thunk* of books dropped on desks as the patrolling corporals tried to rouse slumbering inductees.

During the early morning, we were told to dump the contents of our suitcases and bags on the floor so the contents could be inspected for weapons and drugs. I fell asleep during the inspection, but was awakened by the sergeants yelling at us to stuff our belongings into our bags and "fall out" in front of the building. We were then marched—herded was more like it—to an unlit barracks and told to choose a bunk. None of the bunks had a mattress, but none of us cared.

I fell into an exhausted sleep only to be awakened an hour later. I staggered to another part of the base where I was issued clothing, shaved nearly bald, given more tests, filled out more paperwork, and finally served food that I suspected had been left over from the Korean War.

Later, about thirty of us stumbled onto an olive green school bus. The driver was a skinny, acne-scarred corporal (we had learned the meaning of the stripes on the sleeves) who looked about fourteen years old—a junior-high reject. As soon as the last limping draftee was aboard, the driver pulled the handle that banged the doors closed. Then he jammed the transmission into the lowest gear with a grinding noise that sounded like he had forgotten to use the clutch. The bus lurched forward, snapping me against my seat, then throwing me forward. I felt like maybe I had been drafted to serve my country as a crash-test dummy.

We rode to various locations, where we sat while the driver got off, smoked a cigarette, talked to other fourteen-year-olds (who often were holding clipboards), climbed back into the driver's seat, swore as he slammed the door shut, and then hauled us, lurching and bouncing, to the next stop. Meanwhile, the sun had risen and had turned the bus into an oven.

By late morning, the oppressive heat and the rocking of the bus had lulled me into such a stupor that I felt like I was becoming numb from head to toe. My newly issued fatigues stuck to me, my legs were asleep, my butt had stopped signaling its whereabouts in the early morning hours, and I was not sure I would ever walk again. Somehow, it didn't matter, as I was on the verge of a not-unpleasant out-of-body experience.

Reality broke into my trance in the form of the ugliest, most distorted face I had ever seen. That was my first sight of Drill Instructor Ernest Wiley. I would learn that this was his pleasant look.

Sergeant Wiley stood five-foot-seven, with a lean, slender build. He wore a short-sleeved khaki uniform topped by a brown, flat-brimmed drill instructor's hat. His army-issue glasses magnified his brown eyes so he looked as if he were peering at the world through Coke bottle bottoms. He spoke in a nasal baritone that rattled my fillings when he stepped onto the bus and shouted us off into the heat of the morning.

Wiley let us know that he was personally offended that we were having difficulty dragging our newly acquired, three-hundred-pound duffel bags off the bus. The fact that it was one of the hottest August days in the century and that we'd had two hours of sleep in the last forty-eight was not a problem to him.

"Why are you pussies having so much trouble?" he drawled. (All the drill sergeants had a southern drawl, even if they were from the Bronx). He looked around at us as we stood at attention—or at least, our civilian version of it. "Maybe I should just have you drop your pants and see if there are dicks on any of you." Silence. Sweat rolled down our faces, and our shirts stuck to our bodies. We were melting in the sun like human Popsicles. "Shee-it! I probably wouldn't find enough dick meat to fuck a duck!"

While Wiley was engaged in his anatomical discourse, four other buses pulled up and four other drill sergeants called the riders out with similar verbal artistry. We were separated into platoons of fifty men; I was one of the fortunate ones assigned to Sergeant Wiley's platoon. He marched us (as only civilians can march) to our barracks through the scorching Kentucky sun. Kentucky gravity tugged at our baggage as we stumbled on.

At least, I thought, *we'll be able to rest a few minutes when we get to the barracks.* Wrong again. As soon as we arrived, Wiley ordered us to run inside, drop our fucking bags on the first fucking unoccupied bunk, then get our fucking dicks back out-fucking-side by the fucking count of twenty, whereupon he loudly proceeded to count.

Fifty sweaty male bodies tried to squeeze through one door at once. We pushed and jostled as we exploded into the room. Having been near the front of the mass, I flung my stuff onto the first empty top bunk I saw, and then looked around for a way to get back outside quickly. Bodies were still hurling in through the door, so I looked around for another way out and saw a door at the far end of the barracks. Unfortunately, so had all the other recruits. It was a mad scramble out that door and around the building. Meanwhile, we heard Sergeant Wiley counting: "Fifteen, sixteen, seventeen...." Of course, not everyone made it back into formation by the count of twenty.

Wiley kept counting and had reached forty by the time the last recruit arrived. Astonishment filled Wiley's magnified eyes as he surveyed our crooked lines. "I see that some of you assholes didn't fuckin' believe that I was fuckin' serious that you had twenny counts to get the fuck back here. Now, all of you git down and push Kentucky away."

I, along with most of the others, looked mutely at Wiley. I didn't have any idea what he meant. He looked in my direction because, unfortunately, I happened to be standing in the front line. He took two long steps until his nose was three inches from mine and, because I had two inches on him, he looked up into my left eye.

"What's a matter wid you, shit-for-brains? Don' you understand English?" I made the mistake of looking at him. "Keep your eyes straight ahead when yer at attention, motherfucker. You understand *that?*"

"Yes, sir," I croaked.

"No, boy. You will *not* address any sergeant as 'sir.' You *will* address any sergeant as 'sergeant.' You *will* only address commissioned officers as 'sir.' You got that, dickhead?"

"Yes, sir, Sergeant."

"How old are you, fuckface?"

"Twenty-four."

"Twenny-four? Twenny-four! What are you, some kind o' draft-dodgin' hippie?"

"No sir!"

"Twenny-four, *what?*" he snarled.

"Twenty-four years old."

"Twenny-four years old, *Sergeant*, dipshit!" he yelled. He was very careful to enunciate his "T." Drops of saliva spotted my glasses.

Even though a little voice in my head said I should think before I responded, fear and exhaustion overrode my good sense.

"Twenny-four years old, Sergeant Dipshit!" I barked with all the resonance I could muster. I had been, after all, a voice major in college, and resonance and projection are the name of the singing game. My response could be heard at least one military block in any direction.

As a result of my resonant indiscretion, I am probably the only University of Michigan graduate who has ever cleaned out a Dempsey Dumpster. By the time I crawled up into my bunk that night, my confederates had been sleep for several hours.

As I drifted off, I heard music in my head. An imaginary orchestra lulled me into sleep as the smell of the dumpster wafted into my nostrils. Forty-eight hours had passed since I first entered Fort Wayne in Detroit. God help me, I was in the army.

CHAPTER 3

▼

Home of the Free and the Brave

August 15, 1969

Lights! WHAM!

"Alrigh', chew motherfuckers, ge' chur asses outta those beds! You ha' fi'teen minutes ta ge' chur fuckin' uniforms on an' fall in fo' chow!"

Dear God! What was that? Was someone beating on a trash can lid? I'm blind! No, wait. My eyes aren't open. Ow! There's a naked light bulb dangling over my bunk. Maybe if I turn over and open my eyes while I'm face down in my pillow....

WHAM! "Didn' chew fuckin' hear me, boy? I said *git up!*"

I glanced at my watch: four-thirty.

WHAM! "Boy, if you're not outta that bunk in one secon', I'm gonna throw you out."

I sat up, and hung my feet over the edge. The floor appeared to be somewhere between six and twenty feet straight down. I took a deep breath and jumped, landed hard, and staggered against the next set of bunks. When I turned to see who had been yelling the obscenities, I saw a kid with a buzz haircut and two stripes on the sleeves of his fatigues holding a trash can lid in his hands. He looked like he was about seventeen years old.

He stood for a moment, scowling at me. Then he turned and slammed the lid against a metal post. He took two steps across the wooden floor of the barracks (this was the floor I would grow to know intimately over the course of Basic Training, as I scrubbed it, waxed it, and pushed Kentucky away on it), grabbed the mattress of a lower bunk and dumped its sleeping occupant on the floor. The dumped trainee sat up, rubbing his eyes and looking around in a daze. The corporal turned and headed toward the exit at the other end of the long wooden barracks. He slammed the lid against a couple of posts, uttered a few "fucks," and disappeared through the door into the pre-dawn darkness.

I was considering lying down on the floor to catch a couple of winks when Sergeant Wiley stepped through the door that the corporal had exited.

I guessed that he had stood outside, counted to ten ("one, uh, three ... no, wait, four, no....") and then that sucker came in.

Wiley surveyed the room. It was full of young men wearing their army-issue white boxer shorts, many of which were being extended, tent-like, by youthful early-morning erections, known as pee-hards. Wiley took a breath and began his oration: "All right, you pussies, you will now gather 'round while I demonstrate how you *will* dress your bunks."

A trainee tentatively raised his hand as if he were in a schoolroom. "Sergeant, sir, I have to go to the can. May I be excused for a minute?"

Wiley looked at him for a moment, and then began his demonstration. The trainee cleared his throat, raised his hand again, and repeated his request. Wiley stepped over to him until his face was about three inches from the trainee's terrified face.

"You will hold your piss until I dismiss you. Is that clear?" Wiley growled.

"Okay," the trainee replied.

"'Yes, Sergeant!'" Wiley snapped.

"Okay, I mean, yessir, Sergeant," the trainee stammered.

Nature began sweetly calling me during this exchange. Much more delay and the call would become a shrill scream, but I decided there was no point in bringing it up; one excursion in a Dempsey Dumpster was enough.

Wiley went through the demonstration, step by step, talking as if he were reading the instruction book. There were instruction books for everything in the army, all written by some of the best military minds for use by the semi-literate, such as Sergeant Wiley.

Eventually, Wiley had made the bunk according to the highest military standards. Then he turned and asked if there were any questions. By then, my hand kept drifting down to squeeze my dick, the kind of gesture a small boy makes when he "has to go." In fact, most of the platoon was shifting from one foot to the other. There were no questions.

Wiley then turned, jerked the bedding from the mattress, and threw it on the floor. "You will now go to your bunks and dress them as I have demonstrated," he said.

There was a small, collective groan as we walked back to our bunks. In a few minutes, walking upright without leaking would require a major effort, so we all wanted to hurry through the routine. Of course, very few of us were able to grasp the complexities of bunk dressing on the first attempt, and Sergeant Wiley felt obliged to dump several mattresses on the floor to express his indignation over having to work with a "bunch of fucking *re*tards."

Finally, he growled that we were dismissed and that we had twenty-five minutes to assemble in front of the barracks in fatigues and helmet liners—or else. He didn't elaborate on what "or else" might mean. None of us cared to ask, because at that particular moment our teeth were floating.

All fifty of us scrambled to the latrine located at the end of the barracks. It was a room made of cinderblock that had been painted a shade of green that, under the glare of the naked light bulbs, was the color of wilted lettuce. Six white porcelain sinks jutted out of a wall. A stainless-steel shelf ran the length of the wall over the sinks—we set our shaving kits on it—and a mirror over each sink hung above the shelf. A long, white ceramic-lined pissoir ran along the wall next to the sinks, and six toilet stools lined the wall opposite the sinks.

Somehow, all of us were standing in front of the barracks by five thirty. The sun would not rise for another hour, and we stood shivering in early morning dampness, doing what we would do so often in the army: waiting. I kept telling myself this was not a bad dream. I was tired and damp and shivering. Memories of hot, sunny mornings in Italy, the strolls through Spoleto in the evening, breathing the fresh mountain air; the nights performing the opera—all of this came to me, trancelike. The memories pulled me away from the quiet swearing of the men who stood beside me, as well as from the sound of my breathing that was amplified in my helmet-liner.

Wiley and the lid-banging corporal eventually appeared and told us to form two lines. The dim glow from a streetlight silhouetted his drill instructor's hat and slender form. The hat reminded me of Mr. Ranger's hat in the Yogi Bear cartoons.

Wiley barked at us to join him in a series of jumping jacks. After that, the corporal led us on a brisk run around—and around—the mess hall. Gasping, sweating, wheezing, we finally stopped at the foot of a short flight of stairs that led into the mess hall.

Another sergeant emerged from the mess hall and yelled at us to line up in a single line. We *would* enter the mess hall, we *would* move through the line quickly, and we *would* find a table and eat as quickly as possible—*without talking.* Anyone caught talking *would* have his food thrown away and *would* receive extra duty.

The line slowly entered the steamy mess hall. Trainees, wearing aprons and looking as miserable as the food they served, slapped scrambled eggs, soggy toast covered by some sort of gravy, and pieces of unidentifiable meat onto our plates. Several weeks later, I had my first taste of KP and understood why these trainees looked miserable.

The mess hall was too small for so many troops. It was filled with trainees eating at twenty-odd picnic tables, complete with bench seats. Three large fans circulated the sultry air, and three sergeants moved between the tables, shouting at us to "eat faster, eat faster" and "no talking. Eat, you fuckers!" There was a sudden uproar as one trainee, who had apparently spoken to someone, was suddenly jerked from his seat and half pushed, half carried from the hall by two sergeants. A smirking corporal picked up the trainee's tray and dumped the uneaten food into the trash.

I was surprised at how quickly I was able to stuff down the mystery meat, tasteless eggs (I was not about to ask someone to pass the salt and pepper), and gravy that had congealed into lard as soon as it had touched my plate in the serving line. I bussed my tray to the kitchen window and walked out into the cooler air. The food sat in my stomach like lead.

Most of us who had finished eating were sitting on the ground, trying to catch a few winks of sleep, or talking to guys we would be living with through the next ten weeks. Wiley appeared from around the corner of the mess hall and called us to our feet. *Did he ever eat?* We lined up again.

"Now that you swinging-dicks have had some good army food, we will now work it off before it turns to more lard on yer fat asses. Leh-uuuhft face! Left face, you stupid asshole! Yeah, you, in the second row. *That* is yer left. On the ruhhhn. Harch!" Wiley yelled. So began our first two-mile run of the day.

Within the first mile, about twenty of us were on the side of the road losing our breakfasts. Easy come, easy go. As I shambled along to rejoin the runners—escorted by the corporal who had lingered over me yelling about my pussiness—I kept thinking this couldn't be happening. I prayed to God that I would wake up from this stupid dream. And soon.

CHAPTER 4

▼

Be All That You Can Be

To understand Basic Training, you have to have some insight into military logic.

Military Logic Premise No. 1: Shiny boots keep democracy safe.

A great deal of time in Basic Training is spent polishing things—boots, shoes, brass (a substitute for brass had been available for the last 150 years, but this *was* the military, and polishing brass apparently built character), windows, and floors, but most of all, boots. Not just the part everyone sees but the soles as well. The reason behind this was apparently to let the enemy, who had just shot us, see we were good soldiers from the ground up.

Military Logic Premise No. 2: Enlisted personnel, unlike the rest of humanity, respond well to abuse and, in fact, come to prefer it to humane treatment.

This was the same argument the slave owners used before, during, and after the Civil War. As far as we know, the owners never asked the slaves for their opinions. Neither does the military.

Military Logic Premise No. 3: An army lives on its stomach.

This is because the army just ate at the mess halls, so it can't walk. The army doesn't waste money on food for the trainees because (1) the cooks won't know how to prepare it, and (2) the trainees will probably just throw it up anyway during their *après mange* running. The true purpose for the mess hall in a Basic Training unit is to provide KP opportunities.

Military Logic Premise No. 4: Don't train the inductees with up-to-date weapons, as they will not appreciate them and probably will break them. Train them, instead, with the weapons their grandfathers used.

Early in Basic Training, we were issued our rifles—M14s that had been used in World War II and Korea. It was 1969; the Vietnam conflict had been on our televisions for years, and "M16" had become a household word. So what were we doing with M14s? Learning how to take them apart (the military term for this is "disassemble," as in: "Each of you swinging dicks will now disassemble your fucking weapons in one fucking minute"), how to hold them for inspections so the officer can check the barrel for cleanliness (officers were very concerned that we kept our barrels clean), and of course, how to march around the field with them in precise formations so the officers could look at a lot of clean barrels all at once.

Military Logic Premise No. 5: Save money by killing the trainees early.

This is accomplished by putting out-of-shape bodies through torture under the guise of physical conditioning. Death-by-training saves the government money on food, clothing, and housing.

Somehow I managed to survive Basic Training, but I wondered about those fellows who didn't. There weren't many of them because the drill instructors made examples of them to the rest of us, and it took a certain bravery (or foolhardiness) to buck the system. I imagine those poor souls wandering through life with the DI's succinct character analysis tattooed on their foreheads: "Commie lover" or "fag puke."

I have wondered, particularly, about the gentle soul I saw for the first and last time one hot August afternoon during bayonet drill. We had been struggling for several hours to eviscerate straw-filled dummies while the DIs made remarks about our ancestry.

Eventually, the platoon had formed into a large circle with the DI in the center. He shouted, "What is the purpose of the bayonet?"

We lunged toward him with our weapons while shouting, "To kill, Sergeant!"

"What?" he shouted. "I can't hear you."

"To kill, Sergeant. To kill!"

"What is the purpose of the bayonet?" the DI shouted again.

"To kill, Sergeant!"

Then it happened. One lone voice continued, "… and destroy what God has created."

The pause, as the novelist wrote, was pregnant. The DI, dumbstruck, froze for an instant then growled, "Who said that?"

"I did, sir."

We all looked at the ashen-faced, burr-headed kid who had spoken. It took the DI three steps to reach the offender. He jerked the rifle out of the trainee's hands, grabbed him by the collar, and stalked out of the circle, pushing the slender young man in front of him. They both disappeared around the corner of a barracks.

I don't know what happened to the young trainee. Rumors circulated that he was transferred to the Marines, or that he pulled KP for the next forty-three years. I imagine he is walking around today trying to explain to his children why the words "fag puke Commie lover" are tattooed on his forehead.

My first contact with a chaplain occurred when one visited the platoon on a hot August afternoon. We had just finished a grueling physical training session that was followed by a four-mile run. Three men were overcome by the heat and carried off on stretchers, and those of us to made it back to the staging area—a sandy open area devoid of shade—were drinking water from large coolers that had been left there for us. We were a sweaty, smelly, sore, and surly bunch when we were called to attention as the chaplain approached us. He quickly put us at ease, and had us sit on the ground.

He remained standing as he went through his spiel about the various religious services the army offered to soldiers of all faiths. I hoped such services included rituals such as last rites, which I would probably be requiring shortly. The chaplain mentioned that he would like to talk to any interested personnel about becoming a chaplain's assistant.

I had assumed that I would be heading for Vietnam as a member of an infantry platoon. I didn't relish the thought of becoming a walking target. But how many chaplains' assistants had I heard of being killed in combat? Zero. Zip. Of course, I had not heard of chaplains' assistants until that moment, but at the time I was not troubled by that small oversight. I made an appointment with the chaplain.

Captain Bonnard, the chaplain, was very cordial during my interview. He seemed surprised that with my education I was in the army as an enlisted man, rather than an officer. I assured him that I was loving every minute of my time in the service. But I had a wife and career, and I wanted to return to both as soon as possible. Being an officer meant that I would have to enlist for at least three years. I was not sure the musical world could survive so long without me.

He told me I would do very well as an assistant, and because of my musical training, I would probably be assigned to a base chapel in the states or in Germany. I gladly signed the appropriate forms to volunteer for the training, assuring

Captain Bonnard that I would be happy to serve the Lord and the army. What I didn't say to him was that I would be particularly happy if I could serve them both in Germany.

We shook hands, and I returned to my platoon feeling as if my future in the service might not be quite so odious. I was very innocent in those days. A few days later, I was notified that I had been selected to fill the honorable position of chaplain's assistant, and the hopes of a European assignment rose before me.

The end of Basic Training finally arrived, and Sergeant Wiley notified us about the date and time of the ceremony. He said that after graduation, we new E-1s (otherwise known as "privates") would be given forty-eight hours of leave before reporting back to Fort Knox. After the leaves, we would be sent to other units for Advanced Individual Training, known in the army as AIT. I called Karen as soon as I could so we could make out plans.

The graduation took place on Friday, October 17th, in the afternoon. Friends and families who wanted to attend were invited to arrive a couple of hours before the ceremony, so I went looking for Karen as soon as we were allowed to leave the barracks.

I wandered through the milling crowd of trainees and their families looking for her, and, to my surprise, I found my parents. There had been a slight change of plans, Mom said, and they had come with Karen. Dad said that Karen was looking for me.

I was happy to see them, but I had a twinge of disappointment that I tried to keep from them. I had been hoping to spend all my time with Karen engaged in passionate and strenuous physical endeavors since we had not seen each other since the day I was inducted. Since we had very little money, I had even reserved a room for us—for no charge—in a housing unit on the base, a place where army personnel could stay with visiting spouses.

Karen appeared and came into my arms. For a moment, nothing else in the world mattered as much as kissing her. Our kiss ended, and the world came rushing back. She stepped away and gave me an appraising look.

"He looks pretty good in a uniform, don't you think?" she said to my parents.

Mom clasped her hands in front of her. "He's my handsome son," she said.

"That's right. You've never seen me in uniform have you?" I said. The last time you saw me was at Fort Wayne before they hauled me off to this zoo," I said.

Karen brushed her hands through my short hair. "This takes some getting used to."

Mom took Dad's arm. "We'll go find something to drink while you two get reacquainted," Mom said. "Karen, we'll find you in the bleachers before the ceremony," she said as she led Dad away through the crowd.

Karen apologized for not letting me know they were coming. I said it was okay, but I wondered how we could spend much time together.

"Here's what I thought," she said. "Patty and John (my sister and her husband) moved to Louisville last week—"

"I didn't know that," I said.

"They keep you kind of isolated from the world here," she said. "So it's hard to reach you quickly. Anyway, they're in Louisville, so I thought Mom and Dad could stay with them and we could stay at that place you found. We could see them for lunch and dinner and have the rest of the time to ourselves."

"That's perfect," I said, and kissed her. "You're beautiful and smart. Will you marry me?" I asked.

"No."

"No?"

"I'm already married to a brilliant conductor. I just like to make out with men in uniform," she said.

"Mmm. Well, I'm wearing a uniform, and I'm free this weekend," I said, and kissed her again.

Just then I heard a whistle like DIs used in our training. It was our signal to return to our units. I told Karen we would work out the details of the plan after the ceremony. I kissed her and walked back to my barracks.

The ceremony was simple. Each company (a company was made of three platoons— a platoon consisted of approximately forty to fifty men) was paraded across the field in front of the viewing stands, thus demonstrating that we could march in straight lines while being reviewed by officers who probably had nothing better to do. All of this took place before our assembled families, who snapped away with cameras of various shapes and sizes.

By the end of the parade, the companies were lined up side-by-side, facing a speakers' stand where the officers stood. The sergeants of each company put us at "parade rest," and the commander of the training battalion spoke. He talked about the excellent soldiers we had become—he apparently had not talked to any of our drill instructors—and lauded the excellent training we had received, which led me to believe he had not seen any of our drill instructors in action.

He ended by congratulating us on completing our basic training then dismissed us. With that, four hundred soldiers cheered and ran off the field and into the arms of their families and friends. About five minutes later, a whistle blew, and we returned to our various barracks for final inspection.

All the men in my platoon had all been hard at work that morning cleaning, checking in bedding, returning any equipment that had been assigned to us, and packing our duffels. We were to leave the barracks exactly as we found it nine weeks earlier when we came crashing through the doors looking for bunks while Sergeant Wiley attempted to count to twenty. Ah, the memories.

We waited about thirty minutes for our inspection. A second lieutenant arrived, and we stood at attention as he and Sergeant Wiley walked through the building. He finished the inspection, and then put us at ease.

We had passed the inspection, he said. Then he told us that all leaves had been cancelled.

I was stunned. I missed his next few words, but I recovered in time to hear him say that we would be given passes to leave base for a few hours. However, we had to be back for reassignment by 2300 hours (11:00 PM to the civilized world). After all the weeks of separation, Karen and I had only a few hours before I was shipped out again. I was furious. I was also learning how the army operated.

We were restricted to the barracks as we waited for someone to bring our passes. There was non-stop bitching about the unfairness of the situation, particularly since it took almost two hours for the passes to arrive.

As soon as I received mine, I raced to find Karen and my parents and give them the bad news. My father—who was always eager to be where he wasn't—immediately decided that he, Mom, and Karen could "visit" with me for an hour or so, and then they could drive back to Michigan.

Mom, bless her, convinced him to wait. She said we could all go to Louisville and spend some time with Patty and John, then have dinner in a restaurant near the base.

"It's important that Ted and Karen have some time together without any of us around," she said. "After that, we could drop Ted off at the base and spend the night at Patty's."

Neither Mom nor Dad was ever able to talk about anything of a sexual nature when I was growing up. So Mom seemed a little embarrassed when she talked about our having "time together." I was pleasantly surprised that she had even thought of it.

Karen and I both knew what she was talking about; I'm not sure that Dad did, though. He looked at his watch several times, fidgeted with his pant leg, then said okay, but he would still like to leave early so he could drive straight back to Michigan.

So off we went to Louisville to see Patty and John. After a couple of hours with them, we drove back to Fort Knox. The sun had set by the time we found a restaurant near the base. Dad was more fidgety than ever during dinner, and Mom would occasionally put her hand on his shoulder, as if he might float out of his chair if she didn't keep him there. Karen and I had not had one moment alone, and I was becoming despondent.

As soon as Dad had taken his last bite of food and looked like he was ready to ask for the check, Mom, double-bless her, suggested that Karen and I take the car and disappear for a while. She and Dad could stay at the restaurant and have a long dessert.

Dad, still not catching Mom's drift, looked at his watch a few times, handed me the car keys, then said that he would like to leave in thirty minutes or so. Mom, putting her hand on his shoulder again, told us to take our time.

We almost ran to the car. But when I started to leave the parking lot, I realized I didn't know where anything was on or off the base because I had not driven since being inducted. It was almost eight o'clock, so I only had three more hours of freedom. This was not turning out well.

"Ted," Karen said. "We can't afford a motel. But I want to make love to you even if we have to do it in a ditch. Can we find some place where we'll not be disturbed?"

"The only place I can think of that has a lot of space is Fort Knox, but I don't know where anything is," I said.

"It's Friday night, so won't most of the soldiers be off the base? I bet we could find a deserted parking lot."

I drove to the main entrance as quickly as I could. I produced my ID for the guard who waved me though with hardly a glance. We drove around the base aimlessly for what seemed like a long time. Finally we found a parking lot that was out of the way and had very few cars in it.

With all its drawbacks, this situation did provide the occasion for a sexual first for both Karen and me. We had entered marriage as virgins—a rather unusual state, I know, but given my religious background I was afraid my dick would fall off if I used it for anything other than pissing before I was married. So we had not had many of the typical experiences of adolescents in heat, such as fornicating in a car.

As soon as I parked the car, the physical tension and passions that had been suspended for three months erupted. I don't remember many of the details, but I recall banging my head against the roof of the car, being jabbed by a doorknob, having a muscle cramp in one of my legs, trying to look casual when a military police car shined its spotlight on us ("We're married, for Chrissake … to each other!"), and getting my head wedged between the steering wheel and the seat at a particularly crucial moment. We never did figure out how I got in that position.

Only after the passions had passed and every window in the car was steamed over did we stop to think how much easier everything would have been if we had used the back seat. We started laughing when we realized Mom and Dad had been having dessert for two hours. Dad was probably walking back to Detroit.

My parents were very understanding when we returned, which meant that Mom had probably had a quiet talk with Dad. They took me back to my company area where we said our good-byes, and Dad, still looking at his watch, drove away into the night with Mom and Karen. Karen wrote me later and said Dad had, indeed, driven back to Lincoln Park that night.

I changed back into my fatigues, stuffed my civvies into my duffle, and hauled it to the staging area in a parking lot by 11:00 PM. At 5:00 AM, shortly before sunrise, I heard my name called. I had been sleeping on the ground, half on and half off my duffel bag, so I was stiff and groggy as I trudged over to the sergeant in charge.

I took the papers he thrust toward me, then I climbed onto the truck he pointed to. I sat on an uncomfortable bench with my duffel bag between my legs. Dew had fallen during the night, my clothes were damp, and my army-issue glasses fogged over repeatedly. I took them off and, once again, tried to dry them on my fatigue shirt. When I put them back on, the lenses were smeared. In the half-light, bouncing around as the truck drove over bumpy roads, I found my destination in the mass of jargon on my papers: Fort Dix, New Jersey.

CHAPTER 5

▼

Merrily We Roll Along

The truck drove through the dawn to the Louisville airport. After an hour of swaying back and forth like a drunk and being launched off of the hard wooden benches that lined the back of the truck whenever the tires rolled over anything larger than a matchstick, we lurched to a stop. Everyone was ordered off the truck and into a large military-looking room where, of course, we waited.

Two hours later, an ugly, dark green air force transport arrived, and we trudged over the tarmac, up the stairs, and onto an ugly olive drab plane. Air force enlisted men greeted us by yelling for us to put our asses in the mesh seats, strap ourselves in, and make sure our duffels were pushed under our seats. They were obviously not destined for careers as flight attendants.

The plane seemed to taxi for miles before taking off, and we sat for almost three hours in the windowless fuselage, swaying in the mesh seats as the plane beat its way to New Jersey. The plane landed with three hard jolts.

We half-walked, half-staggered off the plane, boarded a military bus, and then were driven through New Jersey to Fort Dix. That particular section of the state was composed of highways, junkyards, and assorted ugliness. Fort Dix, it turned out, was uglier yet.

I was sent to a processing building, where I shuffled through several rooms in which clerks completed forms that told other clerks that I had, indeed, arrived. I eventually arrived in a room where three other newly minted privates were sitting. There we sat, in our new army dress uniforms, all of which looked as if they had been slept in, which was true, and stubble on our heads where hair once grew. We looked like death warmed over.

After a long silence, I asked, "You guys coming or going?"

"I don't know about these guys," said one, an overweight, long-faced fellow with a prominent nose, "but I haven't come in months." His name, I soon found out, was Rich Hindeman, and he had also come for training as a chaplain's assistant.

A sergeant entered, told us to gather our gear, and led us to our barracks, where we were placed in four-man rooms. Compared to the forty-man rooms of the Basic Training barracks, this seemed like a private suite.

We were unpacking our duffel bags when the sergeant reappeared. "You men are to report in your fatigues to the Arms Room of the building across the street, ASAP," he said, and then he disappeared.

"Damn," Rich said, "they probably have us on toilet detail already."

We arrived at the Arms Room and found ourselves in line with about fifty other men. After we were issued helmets, flak jackets, and rifles, the sergeant in charge appeared and called us to attention.

"Okay, men, listen up. We have received word that peace demonstrators will be attempting to enter Fort Dix sometime this afternoon, and we have orders to stop them. You will be formed into squads and taken to several entrances where you will join up with other squads already in place. An officer will tell you about the final procedures when you arrive. Okay, fall in."

Twenty minutes later, my squad arrived at one of the gates. A sergeant formed our ragtag squad into lines, called us to attention, and then stepped aside for the officer in charge. There we stood, twenty newly minted soldiers, wondering what the hell we were doing there.

The officer, a captain who looked younger than I did, looked us over, shook his head, and said, "Men, we have had reports that demonstrators are converging on Fort Dix with the purpose of entering the fort and disrupting normal routine. We are ordered to stop them at the gates and patrol the perimeter to ensure that only authorized personnel enter and exit. You will be positioned behind the military police at the gate and used as backup to them. You will not, I repeat, *not*, in any way respond to anything you may see or hear from the demonstrators. Sergeant, move the men to the side of the entrance and put them at ease until further notice."

Jesus, what will we do if they come through? I wondered. *None of us has been trained for this kind of thing. We've only been trained to use bayonets, hand grenades, and rifles. I can see the news reports: "Depraved bloodthirsty soldiers shoot, stab, and blow up defenseless flower children, who were just trying to be nice! When asked why he had committed such heinous crimes, Private Bertson shrugged his shoulders and answered, 'That's all they taught us.'"*

Wonder if I'll recognize anybody. These are the same kind of people who demonstrated so often at U of M. Let them take over the damn base! They would at least use more colorful paint on the buildings.

We waited three hours; no one came. I wondered if the person who had alerted the military to the demonstration was off in the distance, enjoying the spectacle of an entire base going onto alert.

I thought about the demonstrators, both imagined (here) and real (like at U of M). Exactly why did they demonstrate? Was the war really immoral? I believed our government was well intentioned and was fighting for what seemed to be a just cause.

I had been raised with very conservative values, such as love of family and country, and I believed in the basic justice of our system. I also believed that right would eventually triumph over wrong, as would good over evil and reason over insanity; I believed that the universe was essentially just. God was in his heaven, and all was right with the world. Occasionally things went awry, and evil would wreak havoc for a time, but good people always would set things right. My thinking was shaped by the liberal 1960s, when we were taught that everyone could be educated to make better choices and to live better lives. Or so we thought.

The initial phase of training at Fort Dix centered on developing the skills to be a dutiful army clerk. That is, how to type, what forms to use, and when.

We were then introduced to the off-road vehicles known as jeeps. We were first taught how to recognize them ("This is a four-wheel-driven, gasoline-powered, small, personnel transport") and then how to drive them ("This is the clutch; this is the gearshift"). We also learned which trucks to sleep in while waiting for the sergeants to decide what they would teach us next.

One morning, we were roused out of bed just before dawn, rushed through breakfast, and then rushed to the supply room, where we waited in line for about an hour for someone to arrive with a key to open the door. We waited outside in subfreezing weather—winter arrived early that year—so we were nearly frozen by the time we were allowed inside. There, we were issued unlined field jackets, gloves, helmets, and rifles (the old M14s again) and clips of blanks.

Eventually, we were told we were going to be put through maneuvers in battle conditions that were exactly like those we would experience in Vietnam, only colder. I was quite sure I would be sent to Europe, but I decided to go along with the drill, just in case.

We were trucked to the staging area, where—as our teeth chattered—we were given classes on recognizing and treating heat stroke and heat exhaustion. At some point during the lecture, I realized that I could no longer feel my fingers or feet. I began stomping and clapping as quietly as possible—until it became clear that everyone else was stomping and clapping, too. We looked like a scene from an old western, as if we were Indians dancing around the campfire. The sergeant droned on with his lecture, oblivious to the cold and, apparently, us. At Fort Dix, such a display of ruggedness by sergeants was seldom an example of stoicism; rather, it was because there was enough alcohol in their blood to serve as anti-freeze.

After the lecture, we were led through what we were told was a simulated Vietnamese village. As I looked around, I wondered how many huts in Vietnam had twelve inches of snow on the roofs.

We arrived at a pine forest (another touch of authenticity) beyond the "village," where we were divided into squads and were told to prepare mock ambushes. None of us had been trained to set up ambushes. In Basic Training, we were led *into* ambushes by the corporal. The ambushers were other corporals and NCOs, who enjoyed showing the trainees how many ways they could get killed. None of us ever survived an ambush. It was, perhaps, a small gap in our training that while we were regularly killed as we walked into an ambush, we never had been taught how to set up an ambush ourselves. However, now my squad was the attacker, so we were moved into the pine trees, given our orders, and told to hide. We were not to shoot until we heard the "pop" of the flare gun being fired.

I found a soft, warm patch of ground under a large pine tree where I lay down and waited. As soon I was out of the wind, I began to get warm. The forest was quiet except for the whisper of the pines as wind moved through the upper branches and the occasional cawing of a crow. In no time, I dozed off.

I woke up with a start. *How long have I been sleeping?* I wondered. *Five minutes? An hour? Did they have the battle yet? Darn, I didn't hear anything. I don't know where I am—how will I get back? If they find I'm missing, boy, will I be in trouble. I had better start walking. But what if the patrol hasn't come through, and I mess up the ambush? Boy, will I be in trouble. I'll be on KP for the rest of my stay here. Maybe I should stay here for another thirty minutes, then move …*

Just then the flare gun fired and startled me. I fired my first round without looking. I fired off all my ammunition without seeing anyone, since the patrol had hit the ground at the sound of the flare gun. From the sound of the firing, though, I guessed I wasn't the only one firing blind.

When we stopped firing and crawled out from cover, I realized that we would have more likely killed each other than the enemy. Going to war was making less sense all the time.

We were marched back to the trucks, frozen, tired, and hungry. I met up with Rich and discovered that he had missed the entire exercise. He had wandered off into the bushes to urinate during the lecture and when he returned, he discovered that we had all left the area. So, being ever resourceful and suspecting that we would probably not be having much fun doing whatever it was we were going to do, he waited in one of the warm trucks. When he heard us returning, he slipped into the bushes and back into the ranks when we reassembled.

The next day, we were taken into the fields again, this time to experience the joys of shooting the M60 machine gun. Learning to shoot the M60 accurately was like serving soup while wearing roller skates: It could be done, but it would be messy at first. We all had several turns to attempt to solve the mystery of hitting a stationary target. During a lull in the shooting, a deer walked onto the range. A sergeant, needing to kill something, jumped into one of the shooting pits, pushed a private out of the way, and began firing at the deer.

Every fifth round was a red tracer which was to assist the shooter in finding the target. We watched the red line of bullets leap out toward the deer. The deer began running parallel to our line. Everyone froze as the deer ran, bounding lightly across the field as the deadly red line swept toward it, yet it managed to stay in front.

The deer ran toward the tree line and then veered off into the woods. Rich and I cheered. The echoes of the gunshots and our cheers died away. In the stillness that followed, the men around us stared at us as if we were aliens from another planet. Perhaps we were.

CHAPTER 6

▼

Ein Feste Burg

Fort Hamilton was a walled fortress sitting in Brooklyn, New York, on the Verrazano Narrows. Its original purpose—defending against enemy ships—was long since superannuated with the invention of planes and missiles. So the army, having an obsolete fort to dispose of, decided to turn it into a training facility for men whose obsolescence was debatable. Fort Hamilton was the school for chaplains and chaplain's assistants.

We had learned to kill in Basic Training at Fort Knox, to type the proper army forms and to drive jeeps at Fort Dix. Now the men and officers at Fort Hamilton would complete our training by teaching us how to serve the men ministering to the men who would be doing the killing for us.

Rich and I, along with forty other future assistants, arrived at Fort Hamilton late on a Sunday afternoon in early November. Our military bus passed through the gate guarded by MPs and stopped in front of one of several red-bricked buildings.

A thin, nervous, forty-year-old sergeant of medium height met us. "My name is Sergeant Vales," he announced. "I will be in charge of this platoon, and I want to make myself perfectly clear: I will not, repeat, not put up with any shit from any of you. So if any of you swinging-dicks figure you can fuck around with me, you better pick some other place to do it, or your ass will be in deep shit before you can say motherfucker. Also, since this is the training school for chaplains, swearing and foul language will not be fucking tolerated. Is that clear?"

Training days at Fort Hamilton began with breakfast and, occasionally, physical training before breakfast if Sergeant Vales was not too hung-over. Then we moved from class to class for the remainder of the day, much like we had in college. The classes consisted of learning to arrange altars for Catholic mass ("The chalice goes here. Be sure you have the correctly colored cloth for the season, and drape it here"), the Lutheran service ("The chalice goes here, the opposite of where you place it for the Catholics. A lot of times, the Lutheran chaplain will prefer to arrange his own, so ..."), as well as for the Baptists, Methodists, and others ("Take everything off the altar ..."), but not for the Jews ("Ask the rabbi"). We studied which special liturgical holidays each denomination celebrated and what our general duties would be.

Most of this was new information to many of the assistants in training, as few had ever darkened the door of a church or synagogue. The qualifications required to become a chaplain's assistant were basic: some college education and a desire not to be cannon fodder. Chaplains, or so we reasoned, always stayed behind the lines in more civilized quarters, probably in the United States or Europe.

We had our first inspection on the Saturday morning of our first weekend. The men who had been through these inspections before seemed nonchalant about the event, but we "newbies" had very recent memories of the rigorous inspections of Basic Training and of being restricted to barracks when we didn't pass. Rich and I wanted to pass this inspection so we could see New York City, which was only a subway ride away. Like me, Rich had been raised in a small town in the Midwest. New York was beckoning us.

The time for inspection arrived. We were called to attention, and each man stood beside his bunk. The commander of the school, Major Robert Jenkins, entered behind the large, pot-bellied company sergeant, Jack Danielson.

For those of us who had arrived that week, this was the first time we set eyes on our commanding officer, known in the military as the CO. I had heard some interesting rumors about Major Jenkins and his proclivity to drink. Having a company sergeant whose name so closely approximated the well-known whiskey probably did not help the Jenkins situation.

I occasionally wondered what it might have been like to be the CO of a bunch of chaplains and their military-hating assistants. I would eventually learn about the army system for promotions of commissioned officers. It was quite simple: Your superior officer recommended you, or didn't recommend you, for promotion, based on a rationale known only to God. Higher-ranking officers then considered the recommendation. They discussed you in terms of personality ("He's a nice guy"), command potential ("Can he find his own ass with both hands while blindfolded?"), and performance. Performance—this was the operative word. In an organization designed for warfare, performance in warfare became the basic standard for all performance. "Outstanding performance" was, obviously, hard to prove if the officer in question was desk-bound; combat, then, was the way to go. If you had combat experience, which usually meant sending other people into combat while you followed from a safe distance, then your chances of rapid progress were greatly increased. Sometimes, or so it seemed to the personnel under your command, your rating improved a bit if the number of your own troops killed was less than the number of enemy troops killed.

If you were recommended for promotion three times but turned down each time, you were expected to resign "for the good of the service." It was never clear what you had to do to be passed over repeatedly, but fornicating with the general's dog in front of the general's house was mentioned as one possibility. If you did not resign but chose to remain, for example, at the rank of major, you were then called a "career major" by your fellow officers, meaning that was the highest rank you would ever achieve in your whole damn life and possibly any life that followed. Major Jenkins was a career major.

He entered the room as Sergeant Danielson called us to attention, each man standing in front of his bunk. Major Jenkins was short, with a thickness to his body that suggested a man past his physical prime and tending toward puffiness. He nodded to the sergeant and then began to slowly make his way down the rows of bunks. That was when I noticed he was wearing white gloves. White gloves! I had heard about "white glove inspections" but had never undergone one.

As he passed through the room, he would occasionally stop, mutter something to Danielson, and then continue. Once or twice, he walked between the bunks, bent down to the floor, and ran his white-gloved hand under the bed. He then rose with a smile and would display his smudged glove to the sergeant, who was writing on a clipboard. This ritual was repeated several times as the duo made their way around the room and out the door. Sergeant Vales, who had been standing by the door, then shouted, "At ease!" and told us to stay by our bunks. Then he left the room, too.

Vales returned a short time later and announced that no passes would be issued for the weekend because the room was a fucking pigpen with enough dirt under the fucking beds to start fucking gardens. We also had fucking contraband in the fucking lockers that we had damn-fucking-well better get rid of. We would spend the rest of the fucking day cleaning the entire fucking room for another inspection sometime late in the fucking afternoon. This was all said in a loud but rather calm voice. I often wondered how sergeants expressed themselves when they were really angry.

I noticed that the fellows who had been at the fort for several weeks seemed to take all of this quite stoically and were apparently unconcerned about being confined to base for the weekend. Meanwhile, we newbies were scurrying around, cleaning furiously, still holding on to the hope that if we passed the second inspection, we still might be given passes.

One problem remained: what should we do with the contraband? "Contraband," according to the army, was anything stored in an army locker that was not army-issue. Our contraband was quickly jammed into our duffel bags (duffel bags, being army-issue, were stored in army lockers), once again proving the old tenet: out of sight, out of mind.

After we cleaned all morning, Sergeant Vales announced another inspection would be held immediately. Once again, Major Jenkins entered and began rounds, this time without Danielson. When a corporal from the office called Vales out of the room, the major continued alone.

Jenkins was not convinced the room was clean, and to prove his point, he knelt down beside one of the bunks opposite from where I stood and crawled under it. We heard a small chuckle, a chortle that let us know he had found the remnants of someone's garden still lurking under a bunk. But when he tried to back out from under the bunk, he snagged his coat on one of the wires that supported the mattress. He was stuck.

We heard the commotion under the bunk but, because we were "at attention" and being well-trained soldiers, none of us moved. The profanity coming from under the bunk increased in both volume and complexity. I had never heard a commissioned officer swear; I thought that was the privilege of the NCOs.

Major Jenkins' exertions caused the bunk to shake. Rich leaned over to me and muttered, "Think we should tell him to take off his coat or to try crawling forward?"

"No. He's an officer and a gentleman. He'll figure it out, maybe."

Sergeant Danielson arrived. He immediately saw what was happening. Out of the corner of my eye, I saw him cover a smirk with his hand. He quickly composed himself and looked around the room, as if deciding what to do. I was hoping he would call a fire drill.

He walked over to where the major was enmeshed in the mattress wires, suggested that the major remove his coat, and then lifted the light bed frame. Jenkins stood up, put his coat on, and stalked out of the room with Danielson following.

Seconds later, Vales, who had been elsewhere during the major's ordeal, entered and announced we all had passes for the weekend.

During the next week of training, we discovered that (1) we would be confined to the fort for most of our training, and (2) we could easily leave the fort without passes by simply walking through the gate. MPs manned the gate, but because we didn't bother them, they didn't bother us. The training passed fairly quickly and was done each day by five o'clock, so Rich and I spent most of our evenings in New York City.

During the third week, I was reminded once again of the twists and turns of Fate. The national draft lottery had begun. The concept was simple: There are 366 days in a year (including the extra day for leap year). Write each date on a piece of paper, put all the dates into a jar, and have a pretty girl pick out the pieces of paper, one by one. The first date drawn becomes number one; the second, number two, and so on. All able-bodied men under the age of twenty-five who were born on the date of the first-drawn date are drafted, and then the finger of Uncle Sam moves to men under age twenty-five who were born on the second date drawn, etc., etc., etc., until the military ranks are filled. The longer the war continues, the farther down the list the draft will move. This continues until the end of hostilities or until the government runs out of able-bodied men. Simple.

My birth date number was 341—341! I read the news on a dreary Saturday afternoon while sitting in the mess hall in Fort Hamilton. The Department of Defense was estimating that the draft would eventually reach 145 to 150.

My first impulse was to cry. If only the government had begun the lottery earlier; if only I had ducked and dodged the draft a couple of months more; if only, if only. Loneliness settled on me like a blanket. Karen was hundreds of miles away, and there I sat in my fatigues, in a cold, graceless military post, looking at the chartreuse walls, cement floors, and the long tables where we ate tasteless army chow. Autumn rain was falling, washing away the variegated fall colors and turning the world into a depressing study in grays.

I walked back to the empty barracks and flopped down on my bunk. The wind blew the rain against the high, drafty windows that allowed the dull outdoor light to pass through. My spirits felt as dreary as my surroundings. As I listened to the rain hitting the glass, I faded into the comfort of an afternoon nap.

The days seemed to accelerate as we neared Thanksgiving. We had two more weeks of training after Thanksgiving, during which time we would receive our orders for our next duty station. Several days before the holiday, Rumor Central began passing along news that of the forty-three of us who were in training, forty were to be assigned to Vietnam. The lucky three would be sent to stations in the United States or Germany.

Rich and I tried to keep our hopes up, so we joked about the poor schmoes who would be languishing in 'Nam while he and I were learning German. We also knew, though, that hope was fading.

Karen was coming to New York, and we would celebrate Thanksgiving there, or so we hoped. Sergeant Vales had told us officially that we would receive passes for the holiday, but I was wary of promises the army made since the fiasco at the end of Basic Training. Our letters to each other were full of plans of how we might use our time together. She kept writing about her eagerness to see various parts of the city, while I wrote of my eagerness to see various parts of her body. It had been so long since we had seen each other that I was having trouble remembering what she looked like. I was sure it would all come back to me quickly, though.

Karen was scheduled to arrive in the early afternoon, the day before Thanksgiving. In my eagerness, I arrived at the Port Authority almost an hour before her shuttle bus from Newark Airport was due. A cold front had moved in following several days of rain, so to ward off the chill, I was wearing my dress uniform and the army-issue dress coat that went over it. I always felt uncomfortable wearing my uniform off-post, particularly since antiwar protestors were scouring the streets of New York City, trying to find soldiers to engage in arguments about the morality of the war. I had witnessed several such episodes, but it was unclear if the protestors were trying to convince the soldiers to go AWOL (Absent Without Leave) or if they, the protestors, simply wanted an excuse to noisily proclaim their beliefs on the crowded streets.

I felt sad as I watched the looks of fear and confusion on the faces of those young soldiers as they were berated by the protestors as being baby killers and Nazis. They were just kids, perhaps drafted straight out of high school, but they were being told that they were immoral scum by the very people they were supposed to be fighting to protect. Sometimes, the soldiers would yell back, although to little avail since the antiwar folk had their arguments prepared and were intent on browbeating anyone who disagreed with them.

On the other hand, there were times, when we had to be in uniform while off-post, that people would stop me, look at my nametag, and say, "Thank you, Bertson."

I never did understand why it was necessary to be in uniform at certain times but not at others. Rich and I assumed there was a lieutenant somewhere in the bowels of the Pentagon whose sole function was to determine when we should or should not be forced to wear our uniforms when off-duty.

So there I was, eager to have Karen arrive, but walking around the cavernous building, watching the ebb and flow of people. Time passed slowly. Eventually, I wandered out of the building, looking for one of the ubiquitous street vendors who sold my newest gastronomical passion, warm pretzels with mustard.

The smell of diesel fumes mixed with the aroma of roasting chestnuts, hot-dogs, and various other treats as I strolled around the outside of the Port Authority. The sun was out and its light raised my spirits even as the chilly wind snapped around the corners of the building. It was a beautiful day, but there was a constant nagging feeling—an underlying uneasiness, inside me. It was a shadow that hovered at the edge of my vision even on the brightest of days. It was a feeling of powerlessness, of not having control over my life, of imminent danger. The war was thousands of miles away, but it still threatened me.

I pushed those thoughts away as I returned to the building, chewing on a fairly tough pretzel. I had grown fond of spreading a thick coat of mustard on the pretzels, but it tended to be messy. I was attempting to bite off a particularly chewy piece while simultaneously trying to keep the mustard from splashing on my uniform, when I heard, "Hi there, soldier. Looking for a good time?"

I turned, intending to tell the hooker to go away. It was Karen. Her plane had arrived ahead of schedule, and she had managed to arrive at the Port Authority almost twenty-five minutes early.

"I'd kiss you if you would get rid of that mustard mustache," she said with a laugh.

I grabbed her hand, scrambled over to the nearest trash can, dumped the pretzel, furiously wiped my mouth, and then, for the first time in two months, I kissed her. Even through her coat, her body felt warm. Her familiar scent, the softness of her mouth, the feel of her arms around me made my heart race and my eyes water.

"Would you mind if we just laid down right here and made love?" I asked into her ear.

"Mmm, I'd like that, very much," she said. "But I don't want to spend the holiday in jail."

"Why would they put us in jail?" I asked innocently.

"Let's see, how about blocking traffic? Or indecent exposure? Or just having too much fun?"

"Okay, you have a point."

"No, I think you have the point." She smiled as she nudged me with her hips.

"Good thing I'm wearing a coat," I said. "Is that all your luggage?" I pointed to a medium-sized suitcase.

"Uh-huh. I didn't bring a whole lot to wear, actually."

"How come?" I asked. She usually had at least a couple of suitcases, even for overnight trips.

"I guess I expected that you would want me out of my clothes more than in them."

She was right.

I had reserved a room in one of the older hotels—the Carlton—near Times Square. It had taken some effort to find one that offered a military discount, and the Carlton fit the bill. I had to be wearing my uniform when we checked in, hence the uniform when I met Karen, but after that I could shed the olive drab clothes and wander around in my civvies.

Our room was small but clean. Not that we noticed much on the first day—we were preoccupied with each other. We checked in around three in the afternoon and emerged again that evening around nine, satiated with each other and ravenously hungry. We spent Thanksgiving morning snuggled in bed until almost nine; then, after a late breakfast, we set out on foot to see the sights. We strolled around the city until four o'clock, stopping occasionally for hot dogs, pretzels, of course, and coffee. The sky was overcast, as it would be for the entire weekend, but the city seemed bright and alive. I was like a child showing off new toys as I led her to places that I had discovered on my journeys into the city. I had fallen in love with New York, and I hoped she would too.

We had Thanksgiving dinner in a small restaurant in Greenwich Village. It was a mom-and-pop place where many of the diners recognized each other and schmoozed from table to table.

The waiter, who looked old enough to be my grandfather, chatted with us when he came to take our order. He asked the usual questions: Where were we from? Was this our first time in the city? Karen told him that I was in the army, and she was visiting me.

The waiter said that he had seen action in the Big One, WWII—the South Pacific, Guadalcanal. It wasn't anything, he said, like the Rogers and Hammerstein musical.

"You mean Ezio Pinza wasn't there singing 'Some Enchanted Evening?'" I asked.

He smiled. "Nah, no Ezio Pinza."

Later, I noticed he was glancing in our direction as he spoke quietly with some other locals. One of them, on his way out, stopped at our table. He said that Joey—apparently the waiter's name—had told him to say hello to a fellow vet. I said I had only been in the army for a few months, so I didn't think I qualified as a vet yet.

He said that in the army, making it through Basic Training qualified a person for vet status. A faraway look crept into his eyes as he talked about being in "the Big Red One." I smiled at Karen as I imagined him sitting around the VFW Club, eyes misting, drinking beer with other old farts and talking about the good old days. I shuddered to think that I could become like him.

The man leaned on the table, resting his weight on his knuckles. "One thing I'll tell ya, buddy. Your time in the service will give ya some of your best times, and your worst." He patted me on the shoulder, said good-bye and good luck, and then left.

Karen's friendly smile disappeared quickly as the man walked away. Something was bothering her. I had been living in a military setting, preparing to go to war since August, and as unsettled as I had been, I was getting used to the idea. I asked her if anything was wrong. She shook her head, but her eyes filled with tears. I paid the bill, and we left.

There was a small park across the street from the restaurant. Karen gripped my hand as we walked over to it and found a bench. She snuggled next to me, crying softly, and I put my arm around her shoulders.

"I'm sorry," she said, wiping her face with her gloved hand. "I didn't want to spend our time together crying."

I pressed her to me. She curled her legs up onto the bench. "It's just ..." She wiped away fresh tears. "It's just that I've missed you so much, and I've been so lonely, and I'm afraid, and that old man talking about the war.... I've not wanted to know anything about what's been happening to you because I'm afraid I'll just worry more."

She turned to face me as she cradled herself in my arms. I rocked her as she cried, my face resting on the top of her head.

As I held her, I noticed the passersby on the sidewalks, many with shopping bags in their hands. Pigeons fluttered among them looking for food while avoiding being trampled. Impatient drivers blew their horns; busses growled and belched black exhaust. Life flowed around us like a river that rolls over small stones, wearing them down until they disappear, just as we would soon disappear into the lives that lay before us.

She looked up and wiped her face with a tissue she'd dug out of her pocket. "I must look a sight," she said. "Also, I'm about to freeze, and I need to pee."

We stopped in a coffee shop and warmed ourselves with flavored coffee as I told her about the rumors I had heard. It was likely that almost all of my class would be going to Vietnam. I was quick to add that there was still the chance that the rumors were wrong, that I might be sent to Germany or a stateside post. Hope dies hard.

So we indulged each other by living in a fantasy. For the rest of the weekend, we pretended we could escape the war, that our lives would be untouched by the killing and wounding that flooded the news media. It was easier to keep up an optimistic front than to talk about the fear that was growing in me like a malignant tumor.

Even with a discount at the hotel, we could only afford to stay for two nights. On Friday morning we moved to a guesthouse in Fort Hamilton, where we could stay for free. The guesthouse really was just that: a comfortable, red brick house, set on a military base. Snow had fallen overnight, dusting the pine trees that surrounded the house, as well as the neatly trimmed bushes that flanked the cement steps that led to the house. The front door, made of dark wood, opened onto a large living room-like area, complete with a baby grand piano and fireplace.

A middle-aged woman—a civilian—greeted us. She told us that we would be the only couple there for the weekend, so we could have our choice of rooms. The similarity to a cozy home ended when we stepped into the bedroom wing.

The rooms were military Spartan: The smaller room, the one we took, had a row of four military bunks lined up side by side, lit by harsh, overhead florescent lights. There was no furniture other than a chest of drawers that looked as if it had been around since colonial times. The communal bathroom was down the hall.

"It looks like the basic barracks design is a little hard for the architect to overcome," I said as we set down our suitcases.

The uncomfortable feeling of the room gave us incentive to continue our roaming in the city, which we proceeded to do right away. Karen had bought a new pair of shoes for the trip, and on Saturday night, she pointed out that we had walked so much that she had holes in the soles.

Sunday, the day when Karen was scheduled to return to Michigan, arrived all too soon. Rain had returned during the night, and the sky was still dark with clouds when we awoke that morning. The atmosphere matched our moods.

We made love one last time and were lying in bed, my arm under her head, when she said she had been meaning to tell me something.

"What?"

She hesitated as she looked up at me. "I haven't been on the pill since you left in August."

I was silent as I thought back to all the times we had made love that weekend. "Why didn't you tell me?" I finally asked.

"I wanted to, but I was afraid that it might spoil our time together, that you would be mad."

I looked at her. Tears shimmered in her eyes. *If I go to 'Nam, I'll be killed*, I thought. *Now, maybe I'll leave behind a widow and a child.* My stomach screwed itself into a knot. I sighed.

"Tell me what you're thinking," she said.

I rolled onto my side, my arm propping up my head. "It's just, well, if I *do* go to Vietnam, I mean, well, I thought that if something happens to me, you could make a fresh start with your life. But if you have a baby—"

"Ted. I don't want a fresh start. I want you. I don't want anything to happen to you, but I guess that I thought that in case, you know, in case something *did* happen, I could have your child—our child—a part of you, with me forever." She rolled away from me, onto her side. "I'm sorry. I should have told you." Her voice was choked with tears. I touched her shoulder, and she turned toward me, put her arms around me, and cried.

There was so much to say, so much that we both feared, but neither of us could find the words. We had been married three years; ever since we'd dated in high school we had been each other's best friend. But at that moment in the guesthouse, it seemed that we had been children playing house. And now, life had caught up with us.

The questions about our future—like what kind of job I might have or where we might live; the mundane, everyday kinds of questions that young couples talk and dream about—those questions were suddenly unimportant. We faced a future that I might not share with her.

I held her, rocking her gently; I felt hollow inside. My wife wanted me to live, to share her life, and yet she had contemplated my death. And she wanted something, someone, to remember me by. How could I make her understand a feeling that I didn't really understand myself: a child—our child—was not *me*. I would still be dead, my future gone, my dreams, the dreams we had for us, vanished. A memory.

I would be just a memory, like the photographs I had seen in so many homes of so many old people that my father ministered to—the photographs they would point to and shake their heads, saying, "He was killed in the war. He was so young." A memory. A fading photograph.

I spoke softly to Karen, trying to comfort her that morning. But as I spoke, it seemed that the room grew darker, colder. I held my wife in my arms, and I felt strangely alone.

One week later, I received my orders for Vietnam.

Training at Fort Hamilton ended shortly before Christmas. We went through a military graduation ceremony that was the army's way of letting us know that we were still members of that organization ("Your soul belongs to God," a drill instructor had screamed at us once in Basic, "but your ass is mine!"). So, once again we starched and pressed our olive drab greens, donned our helmet liners and tried to remember how to march in a straight line.

We left Fort Hamilton as official U.S. Army-trained killers, clerk-typists, projectionists, and chaplain's assistants. We were certified as being able to type bulletins, file papers, arrange altars, show movies, and slay the enemies of the Free World.

We were all given furloughs for the Christmas holidays. Shortly before I was to leave for the airport, I went looking for Rich to say good-bye. I found him packing his duffel and musing aloud about the kind of food he was going to cook for his Last Meal.

Rich considered himself a gourmet cook and had spent a lot of time talking about his ability to detect the subtle aromas of various herbs and spices in his food. He would tap his large nose, saying it was his second-best sexual organ. Preparing and eating a good meal, he had said, was second only to a full-blown, oh-my-God-the-top-of-my-head-is-exploding orgasm. He had said that the form of verbal foreplay that turned his wife on the most was describing the aromas of exotic herbs and spices. My knowledge of herbs and spices was very limited, as was Karen's, and I doubted that she would become aroused by hearing me recite my very short list of salt, pepper, garlic, cinnamon, nutmeg, and oregano.

Rich and I sat on the bare bunks, bunks that would soon hold another class of chaplains' assistants-in-training. We talked about where we might end up in Vietnam ("Anywhere, so long as it's not North Vietnam"), and wondered if we would run into each other. Rich speculated that he would end up with some heroic rabbi who loved working the troops near the DMZ (although neither of us was sure that there *was* such a thing as a Demilitarized Zone in Vietnam), where the action was. I, on the other hand, would probably wind up on hospital duty in Saigon, surrounded by beautiful nurses. I was too depressed to even speculate.

We laughed about Sergeant Vales, recalling how, after weeks of his harassment, we had taken our revenge one night by simply locking him in his room and having a wonderful evening in the city.

And about the night some guys, drunk out of their heads, returned to the barracks after midnight. One of them decided he had to piss, so he just whipped it out and proceeded to pee on a bunk. The guy sleeping in the bunk woke up to find hot liquid splashing on his head, soaking his pillow. World War III almost began that night in Fort Hamilton.

We walked to the gate of Fort Hamilton, me hauling my duffel and a small suitcase. I would catch a taxi, courtesy of Uncle Sam, that would take me to the Port Authority, where I would catch a bus to Newark Airport. Rich and I hugged each other and said our farewells. We had grown close over the past months at Fort Dix and Fort Hamilton. I knew I would miss him.

CHAPTER 7

▼

Home for the Holidays

Our living situation in Michigan was as it had been that summer: Karen was living with her parents. We would live with them during my final leave.

I had called Karen as soon as I knew I was being sent to Vietnam. She had cried, not so much for being surprised but because our last hope of escaping the war was gone. She had told her parents but had promised that she wouldn't say anything to mine until I had told them. On the evening I arrived back in Lincoln Park, I said hello to Karen's parents, and then we went to my parents' home for dinner.

It felt strange to drive our car again after having driven nothing but jeeps and trucks since August. The snow-lined streets of Lincoln Park were festooned with Christmas decorations, and the stores were busy with customers as Karen and I rolled along Fort Street. She sat close to me—her arm threaded through mine, her head on my shoulder—as she had done so often on our dates.

A gentle snow was falling as we pulled into the driveway of my parents' home. The porch light was on, and I could see my mother moving around the living room. The wooden porch swing was unmoving in the cold December air.

As we climbed the stone steps to the porch, I remembered that this was the place—this porch, this swing—where I had retreated in my mind when I had been knocked unconscious during a pugil-stick bout in Basic Training. In my trauma-induced dream, I had been sitting in the swing, drinking iced tea, and reading a book on a leafy, sun-filled summer day, when the sound of a strange siren intruded. I stood up and leaned against the black wrought iron railing, peering toward Fort Street for the source of the approaching sound. The siren became a man's voice yelling, "Hit him again, goddamn it! Hit him again, you motherfucker!" His words were punctuated by the shrill screech of a drill sergeant's whistle. I had opened my eyes to see a young soldier standing over me, a boxing helmet on his head, waving a pugil stick over my head. Although the sergeant yelled at him to hit me again, the soldier wavered, not wanting to hit me while I was down. The sergeant pushed the soldier out of the way, and the corporal pulled me to my feet, asking me if I was okay. I was physically okay but also very disappointed to find myself in Fort Knox and not on the porch where we now walked.

My mother's eyes teared, and my dad shook his head when I told them I was heading to Vietnam. We sat in the living room, drinking tea, as Mom asked about Fort Hamilton and told me what my sisters had been up to. Dad said I looked like I was in good physical condition and asked if I had been eating enough. My father, being an eastern Kentucky boy and the youngest of twelve children from a relatively poor family, was fixated on food. He would ask, "Are you getting enough to eat?" whenever he didn't have anything else to say. I had once heard him direct the same question to a four-hundred-pound woman.

Karen and I left after an hour or so and went to our favorite high school necking spot, a run-down pastry shop called Carol's Donuts. Carol's had been a good place to go in high school because, as a good fundamentalist Christian PK (preacher's kid), I was not allowed to drink, dance, play cards, or go to movies, and I had very little money for anything else. Eliminating all the other teenage activities left necking and heavy petting as the entertainment of choice. Had my parents known what was going on, they might have preferred us to be on the unholy dance floor.

We had learned to drink coffee at Carol's. We would buy a large cup of coffee, take it to the car (which I had parked in the rear of the unlit parking lot), and make it last for a long, long time as we talked and made out. On cold nights, our breath would fog all the windows, so that we would have to air out the car so I could see to drive Karen home. Once, during one of our steamy sessions, we heard someone giggle close to the car. We straightened our clothes, and I rolled down my window—and discovered that the entire car had been "TP'd." We got out of the car, just as my younger sister and several of her friends drove out of the parking lot, shrieking with laughter.

We had not been to Carol's for years, so it was nostalgic for us to see the place. That night, the first night of my pre-Vietnam furlough, the coffee was not very good, and the donuts were tasteless. The coffee and doughnuts had probably always been tasteless, but when I was younger and in heat, I just didn't notice. The store looked tired and rundown, its once-bright lights yellowed and dim. The "girls" behind the counter had become sour-faced, middle-aged women. Life had changed—people had changed—at Carol's. Now our lives were changing too.

My furlough brought me home during a typical Michigan winter: gray day after gray day. Moisture from the lakes pierced our warmest clothing, making the wind feel like it cut to the bone when it whipped up. As soon as snow fell, it turned to a thick, brown sludge in the streets, making them as dingy as the sky.

The dreary winter atmosphere, which matched the faces of my friends and relatives, made me feel like I was attending my own wake. When people found out I was leaving for Vietnam they did not know what to say, so they said nothing. Instead, they talked about family visits, home movies, church programs, and activities of relatives.

When I visited my parents, Mom would talk about my sisters and their families; Dad would talk about problems at the church. Occasionally, I would find them looking at me with glistening eyes. Did they feel as if they were seeing me for my last holiday?

I had the feeling of floating, of being disconnected. Life went on around me undisturbed—not uncaring or insensitive, just undisturbed. My family, my people, had their lives to lead, their needs to be met, and their Christmas gifts to give and receive. I floated through their lives, their awareness, as I waited for the military machine to whisk me away to unknown places, hard places, where danger lurked and fear whispered in the night.

I had already separated from them all, all of them, even Karen. Sadness colored our time together. We were seldom alone, so we danced around our feelings. And if we had some time alone, she slept. She was suffering from the flu; she was lethargic, often nauseated. We did not make love because the "jiggling" was so uncomfortable for her. She felt awful. We both felt awful. I floated.

New Year's Eve arrived. Her parents, never given much to celebration, went to bed early, wishing us good night, Happy New Year, and reminding us to be sure to lock up. Around nine o'clock, Karen moved onto the sofa nearest to the television in the living room, and valiantly attempted to stay awake. "If I go to sleep," she'd said, "be sure to wake me at eleven o'clock so I can celebrate with you." I made popcorn; she thought that might settle her stomach. I ate the popcorn as she slept.

I ate, drank my Coke, and watched television. I tried to wake her at 11:00. She stretched, muttered incoherently, stumbled off to the bathroom, and then returned to the sofa, where she slept again. At 11:40, I tried again. She mumbled her apologies for being such a party pooper. She sat up, leaned her head back on the sofa, and fell asleep, her jaw falling open.

At midnight, I listened to Dick Clark counting down the seconds and watched as the ball of lights in Times Square descended. People screamed, kissed, danced, and proclaimed the arrival of 1970. From my chair across the room, I blew Karen a kiss and drank a Coke toast. *My last New Year's party,* I thought, *and not a soul to celebrate it with.*

My eyes clouded, and a wave of self-pity washed over me. I hated the feeling, but I couldn't shut it off. I knew in my bones that I would be dead, crippled, or somehow profoundly changed by the time the next New Year arrived.

I was right.

CHAPTER 8

▼

Over Hill, Over Dale, We Will Hit the Dusty Trail

January 2, 1970

A winter storm, oppressively dark, surrounded the house as the sounds of a howling north wind shook the windows and invaded our room. Our bedside clock tried to buzz us awake; I slapped it off and turned over.

Dreamlike, I felt Karen next to me, stroking my bare shoulder and kissing my neck, moving upward until her mouth pressed against mine. I moved my hands on her breasts and heard her breath coming in ever-quicker gasps. She pushed me onto my back and straddled me as she quickly pulled her gown over her head. She settled herself on me, and I realized that a part of my body was obviously a lot more awake than the rest of me. In seconds, she was moving forcefully, almost frantically. I heard the soft, high sounds that accompanied her climax.

I could feel her heart pounding when she stretched out on me. I rolled her onto her back and our bodies quickly fell into those ancient rhythms of giving and taking. We moved together until her soft sounds were matched by my own

Eventually my movements abated. I lifted myself off of her and rolled onto my back as she snuggled against me. Our breathing slowed. Feelings, words, and images swirled through my head as I pulled her tightly to me. I wiped the tears from her face and kissed her wet eyes as our whispers passed between us in the darkness of the room.

Our day began at 6:00 AM. Emily bustled around preparing breakfast, while Frank, Karen's father, kept peering out the kitchen windows, grumbling about having to shovel the sidewalk to remove a heavy overnight snow. There was talk of inconsequential things—of weather and items that I should take with me and items I wouldn't need. It was strange to consider that I soon would be so far away from familiar surroundings. Karen and I said little, as we each wandered off into our own thoughts. I kept thinking about a short poem I had written in one of my recent melancholy states. The last line was "… to live only as a memory is to die." The sentiment seemed more real with each passing moment.

I hauled my overstuffed duffel bag downstairs. It felt as if I had put bricks in it, and it looked like I was concealing a dead body. We put on our coats and gloves while Frank muttered on his way out to bring the car out of the garage. He helped with my duffel bag, and we thumped it into the trunk. We all climbed in, and Frank began his usual backing-out-of-the-driveway recitation as he drove ("… careful, not too close to the house. I hate this narrow damn driveway! Almost hit the damn rose bushes again. I keep telling you, Emily, you should move those damn bushes!"). I imagined he had given the same recitation every time he backed out of the driveway for all the forty-three years he had lived in that house. Karen and I smiled at the comfortable familiarity of his monologue.

We huddled together in the back seat. I felt her shivering through her heavy winter coat and asked if she was cold. "No," she said, putting her head on my shoulder, "I'm scared." She looked up at me, her eyes filled with tears. Emily and Frank had fallen silent in the front seat. Frank stared through the windshield as if he had never seen any of these familiar surroundings; Emily pulled a tissue from her purse and dabbed her eyes. I noticed him glance at her, and his features seemed to soften as he cleared his throat and reached for her hand.

"I'll be just fine," I said to Karen softly, trying to sound more confident than I felt. "The year will go quickly, and you'll be making this drive to the airport in no time." Inwardly, I sighed; I wanted to say something profound, something memorable that she could hang onto, but all that came out was trivial drivel.

We drove to my parents' house where my parents, a cousin and his wife, and some high school buddies had assembled to wish me farewell. All of them would accompany us to the airport, following along in their separate cars. Karen, her parents, and I had just stepped onto the porch and were exchanging greetings with everyone, when Dad, always impatient to get on with things, directed everyone to get into their cars and head for the airport.

Mom protested that there was plenty of time, that we should have some coffee and muffins. Besides, leaving right away would have us at the airport almost four hours before the plane was to leave.

Everyone laughed. Someone commented that with Dad's penchant for being early, he would be dead, buried, and walking the golden streets of heaven before Saint Peter knew he was there.

We all had some coffee, except for Dad who did not drink coffee because it made him fidgety, and then we decided to follow Dad's lead and go to the airport. Before the last person was out the door, we heard a car horn toot twice. Dad had backed his car out of the garage and was sitting in the driveway beside the house; two short beeps was Dad's signal to Mom to "hustle her bustle." At his funeral fourteen years later, we would cajole the funeral director into tooting the horn of the hearse in exactly the same way. Mom's reaction would be, "The man is dead, and he's still in a hurry."

The convoy headed to the airport. Dad's car was in the lead, and Karen and I were in the back seat again. I glanced back at the other four cars in our little caravan and was reminded that this was not unlike a funeral cortege.

I felt dazed and withdrawn by the time we arrived at Detroit Metropolitan Airport. I heard my voice and other voices, watched my arms embrace my family and friends, saw my mother's reddened eyes. Dad's face was flushed, something that always happened when he was feeling strong emotions and was trying to hide them. I heard and saw all of this, but felt insulated from everything that was happening around me, as if I was watching through a window.

We had been at the airport about an hour when Dad, who always had trouble making idle, non-religious chitchat, decided to have a prayer. I watched as he assembled his flock for the event. He shepherded Karen's parents and my friends, none of whom were church-going folk, into a semblance of a circle and asked us all to join hands. It didn't matter to him that we were at a boarding gate of a busy airport; he was going to pray for the safety of his son and, by heaven, he would assemble every person in the whole darned airport if that would help.

I had always felt uncomfortable with public displays of a religious nature, but for once I was not embarrassed. Instead, I felt a lump in my throat because this man—this impatient, restless man—loved me, and he was showing it in the only way he knew. I had never loved him more than I did at that moment.

Time passed quickly. The announcement was made that my flight was leaving in thirty minutes. It was time to start boarding. It was time to say good-bye.

I hugged my friends and relatives. Karen's father shook my hand and moved aside as her mother hugged me. Trying to cheer me up, she said quietly, "This, too, will pass."

"I know," I said, but I was afraid that I might pass with it.

Mom hugged me tightly and kissed me. She was remarkably dry-eyed for a woman who cried at the drop of a handkerchief. After I returned from the war, Dad mentioned that she had cried nonstop for the next three days.

Dad gave me the usual playful punch in the stomach and told me to take care of myself and to be sure to write my mother often, as she would be worried about me. My mother told me later that *Dad* cried for the next three days, and cried over every letter I wrote for the entire year.

Karen came into my arms. Everybody was suddenly looking for coins on the floor or developed a fascination for the plane schedules on the overhead monitors. I reached inside her unbuttoned coat, gathering her warmth to me. I would miss her desperately. She pulled back slightly from our kiss, and I opened my eyes to see a little smile: "If you go on the plane with a bulge in the front of your pants, you might give the stewardesses some bad ideas," she whispered.

"Maybe we could just excuse ourselves and find a dark corner," I said. "After all, the plane doesn't leave for another twenty minutes or so."

She became serious: "Ted, I want you to know that I love you so much; I love you more than I can say."

"I know you love me," I said.

She pulled back so there was a little space between us. "Please let me say this. I don't think I've acted like that lately. I've felt, I don't know, like I've had to keep my distance from you and I don't know why."

Her eyes fell to my nametag; she was looking at it without seeing it. "I think I'm afraid," she said.

"Afraid that I might be—"

She put her hand over my lips.

"Don't say it."

She kissed me. "I think ... I think I've been holding you at arm's length because it hurts too much to let you go." Her tears started. It felt like a fist was squeezing my heart when I saw her hurting like this. I pulled her to me, and she began crying.

Her tears passed. Her voice was muffled as she tried to speak again. "I wanted to make sure you know that I love you with all my heart, Ted. I've loved you since the tenth grade, when you sang in that Christmas concert." We sometimes bantered with each other about which of us fell in love first.

"I've loved you longer," I said. "I've loved you since I first saw you in ninth grade band."

She blew her nose again. "You weren't in love with me, you lusted after me," she said. "You told me that yourself." She tapped my chest playfully.

"True, but in the ninth grade, how could I know the difference?"

She raised her head and smiled, but the smile passed quickly. "Ted, *promise* me that you'll come back," she said. "I know it doesn't make much sense, but I want to hear you say it. Please."

I held her tighter. I could feel her body shaking as she fought back tears. "I love you with all my heart," I said. "And I promise I'll come back to you," I told her, knowing it was a promise I might not be able to keep.

She was shaking more.

"By the way," I said, "in the ninth grade? It was love."

She made a sound that was somewhere between a laugh and a sob. She threw her arms around my neck and pulled me into a long kiss. Then she let me go.

Reluctantly, I joined the short boarding line, presented my ticket to the attendant, and stepped into the corridor that led to the plane. Behind me, voices rang out: "Bye … be careful … we love you."

I found my assigned seat and strapped myself in. It was not long before the plane left the gate and taxied to the runway. As it trundled along, I remembered something Dad had said to me as I left home to attend college in Nashville, Tennessee.

The morning we were to leave for Nashville, Dad and I were closing the house while Mom waited in the car. Everything I was taking with me was in the truck of the car. I had said goodbye to Karen and all my friends, and now I was eager for us to be on our way. But as he and I were about to go out the back door, he put his hand on my shoulder and stopped me.

"I want to tell you something," he said. "When I left home and went away to seminary, I could hardly wait to go. Then when I went, I couldn't wait to go back home again. But the first time I went back home, I discovered that it wasn't home to me to in same way it had been before. It felt different. Do you understand?"

"I think so," I said.

"This will always be your home," he said, gesturing to the house. "And you will always be welcomed here, but as much as I hate to say it, you'll never really come home again."

He hugged me and said he loved me. Then told me to go to the car while he checked the house again. A few minutes later, as he backed the car out of the driveway, he turned to look over his right shoulder so he could look out the rear window. From the back seat where I sat, I noticed his eyes were red and puffy. He had been crying.

It wasn't until I went home for my first visit that I really understood what he meant. I was growing up, learning to be on my own, but they still saw me as the boy I had been and not the young adult I was becoming. He had been right: I had left home, never to return. As I sat on the plane filled with passengers bound for California, I wondered if the same was true for a soldier going to war. Would I ever really come home again?

I left Detroit in a snowstorm and landed in San Francisco in the rain. Following my written orders, I had traveled in my dress uniform, and by the time I exited the plane, it looked like I had slept in it, which I had done, in fact, for part of the flight.

An information booth sat in the main terminal. A large sign hung above it: MILITARY PERSONNEL INFORMATION. A tired-looking woman in civilian clothes sat in the booth, smoking. I approached the booth, my duffel over one shoulder and my orders in my other hand.

Before I reached her, the woman said, "Orders for 'Nam, honey?"

"Yes, ma'am."

"Ya go out these doors here," she said, pointing to the glass doors in the front of the terminal, "and turn right. You'll see a couple of military buses waiting to take you to Oakland."

I thanked her and went to find the buses. They were easy to spot: two ugly buses, shaped like school busses but painted olive drab, sat at the far end of the entrance, about twenty yards beyond the overhang that sheltered me from the rain.

I started to climb onto the nearest bus. The driver, wearing army fatigues, waved me off, telling me to go to the bus in front of him.

The door of the next bus was closed; the driver was asleep. The rain became more intense and started to soak me.

I banged on the doors. This roused the driver enough so that he looked around, stretched, yawned, and then pulled the lever that opened the doors.

I stumbled onto the bus. "Yer papers," he said. He wore the insignia of a Specialist Fourth Class, a "Spec 4," in army terms. All the chaplain's assistants had been promoted to Spec 3 upon graduation from Fort Hamilton. The rank meant little, other than a small increase in our measly paychecks. I had made more money driving a taxi in Ann Arbor part-time.

I handed him my rain-soaked orders. He rubbed one eye as he read. "Yeah, yer in the right place. Have a seat."

I was the only passenger, so I sat in the nearest seat.

"You'll have ta take yer bag off the bus so's I can throw it in the baggage compartment. I'll wait 'til it stops rainin'."

"Okay," I said.

The bus filled slowly over the next hour. When about three quarters of the seats had been taken and bags stowed, the driver left the bus, walked back to confer with the driver of the other bus, and then climbed back on the bus.

"Jes' double-checkin': Everybody here goin' to Oakland to be processed for 'Nam?" He pronounced it as if 'Nam rhymed with "spam."

There was no response, just glassy stares.

"All right," he said, jamming the bus into gear. The bus lurched into motion. Once we were on the highway, the driver picked up the microphone for a radio transmitter.

"Oakland, this is Bus Fifty-one. Over."

I heard static, then a male voice: "Fifty-one, this is Oakland, over."

"I'm underway. ETA about forty-five minutes. Haulin' fresh fuckin' meat for 'Nam."

Rain continued to fall as we lumbered off the bus. We had been delivered to the front of another of the large, nondescript buildings of which the army was so fond. A Spec 5, wearing his starched khaki uniform, escorted us into the building that revealed itself to be an enormous gymnasium. In normal usage, the floor of the arena housed six full-sized basketball courts. Bleachers lined the walls; we were told to sit in one section until we were called.

The large interior space had been partitioned off so that half the space was filled with bleachers, and the others half was further broken down into smaller processing cubicles, where weary army clerks checked our papers against pale green computer printouts.

So I waited, dressed in my olive drab dress uniform, my duffel bag beside me. I dug into it, looking for something to read. In addition to the clothes I had crammed into it, I found a note from Karen: "I am sorry I felt sick during your last few days home," it read, "but I will make it up to you. Please stay safe and come back to me. I love you."

The hours dragged by. Overhead, bare neon lights made buzzing sounds, like angry wasps, the unnatural light giving everyone a washed-out, slightly purplish appearance, as if we had all been drained of blood. The noise was incessant: mur-

muring voices, footsteps echoing off the wooden floors and concrete block walls, an unseen door slamming, rain from a winter storm beating on the metal roof.

Fatigue set in. I would doze off only to be jerked awake when a name was called, or the sharp edge of the seat I was leaning against cut through my improvised padding and embedded itself into my back. At irregular intervals throughout the day (afternoon? night? It was difficult to tell), a name would be called and that fellow would disappear behind the partitions, never to be seen again. This phase went on about five or six hours.

After my papers were processed, I was rushed, along with some other bleary-eyed enlisted men, into a long line that faced a set of closed double-doors; these doors swung open every half hour or so. When they did, thirty of us would be herded into the next room, where we were issued the jungle fatigues we would live or die in during the coming year. I waited in that line another three hours before my group was let in. We immediately stripped naked, jammed our dress uniforms, underwear, and shoes into our already-overstuffed duffels. Then we put on heavy, olive drab socks, boxer shorts and T-shirts that were thrown at us by a sergeant, who guessed our sizes without asking. Then we were lined up and passed by stalls, where we were asked shirt, pant, and boot sizes and issued those pieces of clothing. When we emerged from the final room, we were jungle-fatigue-clad soldiers, struggling with overstuffed duffels, clutching the files of papers that we had accumulated during the day.

We were ordered to assemble at a bus stop and wait for busses to take us to our assigned barracks. It was raining, windy, and cold as we stood outdoors in our thin new fatigues—clothing designed for tropical heat. We shivered, stomped our feet, and cursed the army as our teeth chattered during the two hours we waited. Pneumonia would probably kill us before the Viet Cong could.

Light from the weak winter sun had turned the black overcast sky to dark gray by the time the buses screeched to a halt in front of us. We were deposited in front of a barracks for transient soldiers, led inside, and told to take any bunk. Of course there were no sheets, pillows, or mattresses, and the bare springs of several bunks had become disconnected, but nobody complained. Wet, cold, and exhausted, I pulled the largest pieces of clothing out of my duffel to use as a mattress and covers and, shivering, I fell asleep. I had been awake for twenty-seven hours; I was too tired to feel wretched.

Ninety minutes later, a sergeant entered the room, turned on the lights, and yelled at us to get our worthless asses out of those goddamn bunks and out in front of the barracks in five minutes. I awoke in a stupor.

We were too exhausted to grumble as we filed out and were ordered to form into three lines. It was still cold and heavily overcast, but at least the rain had stopped. The sergeant gave us our temporary unit numbers and ordered us to police the area, dump the trash in bins on the next block, and then assemble to go to lunch.

Lunch? I guess that's right since the last meal I had was on the plane from Detroit, yesterday.

After cleaning up the area, we gathered our belongings and were loaded into buses again, driven far enough to reach the Mexican border, and deposited into another line to wait to get into a mess hall for lunch.

Ever try to hold a tray of food and a drink while dragging a thousand-pound duffel bag? I discovered that it could be done.

After lunch, my temporary unit assembled at the bus stop again. We were picked up and deposited at what appeared to be an aircraft hangar. The doors were pushed open and noise spilled out like water from a container, the noise of thousands of voices talking and yelling. The electronic drone of monotone male voices reading the names of individuals and units over loudspeakers was added to the sound of live male voices. The sounds merged and clashed—their dynamics neither rose nor fell but continued at the same noisy hum, the amplified buzzing of millions of hornets echoing in a mighty cavern. I felt as if my eardrums imploded, the aural pressure making my head feel like a paper bag from which the air was sucked out, its sides falling inward. Had Dante heard this cacophony, surely he would have given it its own special circle in hell.

The place looked like it once had housed a whole herd of B-52s: bunks, three high, and accompanying lockers, were crammed into about three-fourths of the space in long rows. The remaining space was partitioned off into temporary offices.

We were told to take whichever bunk was free. As I looked for a place to drop, I began counting the rows of bunks and estimating how many men might be in this one room; I stopped at twelve hundred.

This was home for the next thirty-six hours. At least, I think it was thirty-six hours, because I immediately lost track of time. The lights were always on, the live and electronic din never stopped, and even when my unit went outdoors to the nearest mess hall, I couldn't tell the time of day because the low gray clouds shut out any sunlight. We could only tell if we were eating breakfast or dinner by the food we were served. Even then, it was questionable.

I tried several times to call Karen or my parents, but the lines of men waiting to use the four phones never seemed to dwindle. I waited in one line for three hours and moved forward twice before I gave up, deciding to write instead.

Just when I had decided that I was to spend the rest of my tour of duty in that room, my name was called over the speakers. I reported to the appropriate office, where I was told to gather my possessions and report to a particular door. I did and, as usual, waited in that line for hours.

My final bus ride at Oakland Air Force Base left me outside a flat-roofed metal building next to an air control tower. My papers were checked, and once again I waited. This time, I was able to sit in a molded plastic seat—it was not pretty, but at least it was comfortable.

An airplane with a large orange palm tree painted on the tail appeared from out of the never-ending rain and mist. We hauled our duffel bags to a luggage cart, which was driven to the plane. We were told to walk across the wet tarmac and board the plane.

We were greeted by smiling stewardesses and told to fill the seats from the back of the plane to the front. I found an aisle seat on the left side of the plane, just behind the wings. Eventually, there would be one hundred forty military personnel on this flight.

The plane doors closed, the stewardesses began their litany of safety procedures, and we taxied through the mist to the end of the runway. The engines revved, the plane gained speed as it bumped and weaved down the runway. Then it lifted into the air. I had a brief glimpse of a city in the distance just as the plane entered the clouds, but the mist and fog quickly obscured the view.

We broke through the clouds into a brilliant, sunlit universe. The thick clouds below us seemed solid enough to walk on. The pilot's voice came over the intercom and told us, in the usual airline-pilot manner, to settle back and enjoy the flight. We would have a brief stop in Hawaii, another in Guam, and then arrive in our final destination, Binh Hoa Airport in Saigon. The trip would take sixteen hours. From the tone of his voice, he might have been taking us to an exotic, fun-filled vacation destination, where we could look forward to frolicking on the white sand beaches.

I looked around the plane at all the young faces. There were some older enlisted men and a few low-ranking officers, but most of my fellow travelers were teenagers, boys who looked like they were fresh from high school, boys who should have been finding jobs or going to college, or who should have been starting their lives instead of risking death in a faraway place for a dubious cause. I looked around and wondered how many of us would be on the return flight a year hence. Would I?

The plane climbed, lifting us heavenward, a giant bird carrying offerings to the gods of war. I laid my head on the back of my seat, looking out the window as we were borne to unknown dangers and uncertain destinies.

CHAPTER 9

▼

Up, Up and Away

3:00 AM, January 5, 1970

"This is your pilot, Captain Vaughn, speaking. We are approximately twenty-five minutes from landing at Binh Hoa Airfield. Unfortunately, Charlie's been active at the airfield tonight and they've been hit with some mortars and a rocket or two. Nothing serious though.

"We have a bright orange palm tree painted on our tail, so we make a damn good target. We'll want to spend as short a time on the ground as possible, so we would appreciate it if you would gather all your personal belongings now so you can disembark as quickly as possible when we land.

"As soon as we stop, an air force representative will come on board to give you a short orientation. As soon as he's finished, we would appreciate it if you would please exit immediately.

"That's about everything I have to say. We hope you've enjoyed your flight. Good luck, and God bless you all."

So much for public relations, I thought as I joined the melee of men opening the overhead bins, scrounging for their possessions. The long, long flight was almost over and our tour of duty in Vietnam was about to begin.

We had been in the plane for sixteen hours. We had played cards, read magazines, sung morbid songs ("Put a bright red ribbon on my plastic body bag …"), reminisced about our families, our wives, our girlfriends. For sixteen hours we had not dared to think of what might happen to us when we left this plane. Now, we were almost there. So we gathered our belongings, returned to our seats, and waited.

The plane had been descending for some time, but the tropical heat had suddenly become noticeable. Down … down….

The overhead aisle light went out. Down … down …

"Hey, I think they turned off the outside running lights."

"Really? I wonder why?"

"Because the pilot's afraid of snipers, asshole!"

"How high do you think we are now?"

"I dunno. Two, three thousand feet, maybe."

"The VC don't have anti-aircraft guns down here, do they?"

"Nah, at least, I don't think so."

Down … down….

Throughout the cabin, the men turned out their individual reading lights. Eventually, the only light came from the blood-red exit signs at the front and back of the plane. The landing gear ground down, and the plane banked for the final approach. There were few lights anywhere on the ground, so the runway lights—metal barrels filled with oil—stood out clearly. The only sound in the cabin was the screaming of the engines. The heat increased. The tension increased. The landing was rough.

The plane taxied for miles, it seemed, down darkened runways past concrete revetments. Jet fighters sat in the revetments, their noses shyly protruding from the shadows, as if sniffing the air for danger.

Our plane stopped. The noise of the engines died away and the noises of the ground crew began to filter through. Inside the plane, we sat still, listening, waiting.

There was a "bump" on the fuselage. I jumped, as did the man in the seat in front of me. A trickle of sweat rolled down the back of my head. A few seconds later, the front passageway opened. A man wearing fatigues, with a .45 swinging at his hip, moved quickly into the plane. He had our complete attention.

"I'm Staff Sergeant Smith, your air force representative. Everyone will leave this plane quickly: the men in the front half by the front exit, the men in the rear half by the rear exit. In case we come under attack by rockets or mortars, drop where you are and lie still until the 'all clear' is given. Go directly to the Processing Building. Okay. Move out!"

I felt a quiet, controlled panic as I stood waiting to move into the slowly moving line that clogged the main aisle. I wanted to get off—no, I *needed* to get off the large silver target that might be beckoning some guy in a rice paddy holding a mortar.

As I took my first shaky steps onto Vietnamese soil, I heard the dull thud of artillery in the distance. The sergeant's words spun through my mind: *"Lie still until the 'all-clear'"*

The Processing Building was just a tin roof supported by metal poles that were sunk into concrete—a roof that sheltered a concrete floor the size of half a football field. The lights that dangled from the iron beams overhead shared their space with electric fans that turned the torpid air as we straggled in from the plane.

The floor was filled with folding chairs, and in nearly half of them sat young men who appeared as weary as we were. Something about their weariness was different from ours, though; it seemed to be more than merely physical exhaustion. They stared at us with dull indifference.

After several minutes the sergeant in charge strode into the area and picked up a microphone. "Flight K3B4, for Oakland, California, now boarding."

A tremendous shout erupted from the men who had been so indifferent. Suddenly they were filled with life. Smiles and high fives were everywhere. They were going home.

Their excitement was contagious, and for a moment I shared it with them. But only for a moment. The men charged out of the building and mounted the steps of the plane.

A minute passed. The sergeant in charge looked in our direction and smirked. His voice boomed over the speaker: "Welcome to Vietnam."

Almost to a man, we slumped in our seats. So it began. *Welcome to Vietnam. Welcome to hell.*

CHAPTER 10

▼

I'm on My Way for to Stay a Little While

January 6

The heat and humidity was stifling as we endured another two hours of processing. I kept dozing off in the heat. Once, I even dozed off while standing in line.

At last, we were ushered out of the shed and into the darkness of the Vietnam night. Our leader, a Spec 4, told us, "You won't find no street lights here. Don't want to give Charlie any lit targets." I saw no point in mentioning that we had just spent several hours in a wall-less building that was lit up like a lighthouse.

Five ubiquitous, dark school buses, driving without lights, came growling out of the blackness and stopped in front of the group. As we filed on, I noticed the windows had heavy screens on the outside. "To keep hand grenades out," someone said.

We sat in sweaty silence as the bus lurched forward and passed through a gate guarded by armed MPs and drove toward Long Binh, wherever that was. As soon as we had left the post, two loud explosions, like shotguns, went off. Several men yelled; one sprang up from his seat as if to run. The rest of us, exhausted past being able to run, cringed in our seats.

The driver laughed. "We like to do that to you newbies. I can get this fucking bus to backfire like that anytime." No one else laughed. The bus, its headlights on now, careened through narrow streets. Thick clouds obscured the moon, so only outlines of buildings could be seen as we sped by.

We arrived at another guarded gate and were waved through. The sign over the gate read "Long Binh." The buses stopped in front of a tent; we retrieved our bags from a truck that had followed, then we carried our papers to tents where sweating clerks sat behind battered desks. We were then told to go to the next tent.

Newly typed and stamped papers in hand and dragging my duffel bag (since I no longer cared about protecting it), I lurched over the sand that passed for soil in that country, through the darkness between the tents, entered the tent where I had been directed, found a folding chair, and plopped myself down.

After the chairs were filled, a burly E-6 stepped to the front of the semi-conscious group. He was dressed in jungle fatigues, as we were. His belly stretched the shirt tightly around his waist, threatening to turn the buttons into deadly projectiles at any second. I was glad I was not in the front row.

He began speaking in a singsong voice, as if he had memorized the lecture from a book. "Men, my job is to tell you about all the health hazards you will encounter during your assignment to this country. You will stay awake for this lecture."

At that moment my eyes felt as if the lids were weighted; they would not stay open. Three sleepless days and the stupefying heat were making me feel like a zombie.

I remember very little about his lecture, but the high point for me came when he was explaining why we should not screw any women.

"The final thing: You are all men here and will naturally want to get some pus … will want to have sexual intercourse with women." All around the tent, the young men began sitting up in their chairs. A few nudged the guys sleeping in the chair next to them.

"The army officially does not encourage any such activities and advises you to see a chaplain or seek other forms of activity to keep your mind off fuc … women. However, the army recognizes that you will probably disregard this advice. Therefore, when you want to go fuc … have intercourse, be sure to always use a rubber." At this point, his voice dropped, and he stepped a little closer to the group. "Now listen up. I gotta tell you, it ain't safe to fuck around with no gook woman any time, because she might be a VC. I've heard that some of them put razor blades in their pussy, and then go get some stupid GI to fuck them. But as soon as he puts his dick in her—wham! Them razor blades slice it open like a hot wiener." This was greeted by shuffling and quiet exclamations ("Shit, man. No way!"). Some guys reacted by spitting in the sand.

The E-6's voice became "official" again. "Any questions?" Silence. "One more thing. All bunks are filled, so if you want to sleep, you'll have to find a place out-of-doors. You're dismissed."

Dragging our bags, we shuffled out of the tent into a slightly cooler breeze. As my eyes adjusted to the darkness, I saw the outlines of barracks. I kept hearing my drill sergeant's voice telling us to stay close to a bunker, but I realized I didn't know what a bunker looked like. *What if we are attacked tonight? What do I do? Where do I go? I don't know anybody in this whole country.* Surrounded by all those men, I felt completely alone.

I came to a barracks guarded by a five-foot-high wall of sand bags. About two feet of space separated the wall of sand and the wooden wall of the barracks. I dragged myself over to it, dropped my duffel bag, and climbed on top of the wall, having fuzzy thoughts that if we were attacked while I slept I would roll off into the space between the walls. I stretched out and realized that the sand bags were as hard as rocks and just as lumpy, but I didn't care. I was asleep in minutes.

I was awakened about two hours later by women's voices speaking a language I had never heard before—Vietnamese. Their voices rose and fell in strange rhythms and patterns as they both spoke at the same time. I opened my eyes just as they passed close to where I slept. They were very small, wore loose black pants, white blouses, and large, shoulder-width, cone-shaped straw hats. I decided to move off of my sleeping perch and tried to sit up. This was a mistake. My body had decided "if you can't fight 'em, join 'em" and had assumed the lumpy shape of the sand bags I slept on. My efforts to sit up caused me to half-fall, half-jump off the sand bags. I ended up face down in the sand.

I picked myself up and staggered off to find a latrine and a mess hall. After my first forgettable meal in-country, I made my way to the most logical place for a chaplain's assistant: the base chapel.

By the time I found it, the temperature had climbed from hot and humid to scorching and humid, even though it was only eight o'clock in the morning. The air-conditioned coolness was first thing I noticed upon entering the chapel; it felt like heaven. I looked for an assistant, but the office was closed, so I wandered through a set of swinging doors into the small sanctuary.

Unlike most of the other buildings on the base, the chapel had windows, so I was able to see several sets of uniformed knees sticking above the backs of several pews and an outstretched hand hanging over the end of one of them.

I set my duffel bag down on the concrete floor and breathed in the cool quietness; then I strolled down the aisle, looking at the prostrate forms sleeping in the pews. Most of the faces were unknown to me, but I recognized a couple from Fort Hamilton. This was the gathering place for migrating chaplain's assistants. I reached the front pew and found it empty. My body felt like it was moving through water, and my brain was still functioning at a snail's pace, so I decided to plop down and join the sleepers.

I was soon having a vivid erotic dream. I was back in Spoleto, Italy, in *The Italian Girl in Algiers*, the opera by Rossini in which I had performed. The orchestra was playing gaily along, and I heard singing all around me. The costumes for the opera had been white tie, tails, top hats, and white gloves for the men and harem outfits for the women. We were wearing those costumes in my dream.

In my dream, Karen emerged from the clusters of moving women, wearing the same harem costume, her dark hair flowing over her shoulders. A smile played on her face as she moved closer. I could smell the light scent of the perfume she wore as she embraced me. Suddenly, we were in the apartment in Ann Arbor, where we had spent all three years of our married life. We were naked in our brass bed, making love.

"Ted," she whispered. "Oh, Ted."

"Oh, Ted … Ted…. Hey, Ted, wake up."

I opened my eyes. Above me hovered the big-nosed, spectacled face of Rich Hindeman.

"Well, big boy. Is that a banana in your pocket, or are you just happy to see me?" he asked in his best Mae West voice. He had a big smile on his face as he looked down at my pants. I had an erection that was making the front of my loose-fitting fatigues look like a small volcano. "Jesus, Ted, it looks like you slipped a tent pole in there. Times are hard, eh?"

I was elated to see him again. Several of our classmates from Fort Hamilton had turned up at the chapel as well. Tom Spears—a guy from a small town in Wisconsin—was there. Tom was standing next to me when we first saw the lights of Times Square. We had both stopped dead in our tracks at the sight. Tom would be assigned to a base near the DMZ (so a DMZ *did* exist in Vietnam, in theory at least). He would die there three months later when a sapper set off an explosive charge at what he thought to be the heart of the military operations on the base—the chapel.

Pete Wilkowski passed through. "Saint Pete," we called him at Fort Hamilton because he was a fervent fundamentalist who believed that Jesus was the answer to whatever the question happened to be. He also devoutly believed all Communists should be sent to hell to teach them a lesson. He was assigned to Long Binh, the kind of comfortable in-country headquarters that most of us hoped we would get. Pete continued his fundamentalist ways, loudly, while also ministering to a number of hookers on the sly, one of whom gave him an incurable case of syphilis that led to an early medical discharge six months later.

Rich, ever the entrepreneur, had already met the local assistants and was getting a "feel for being in-country," as he put it. He had found a halfway clean latrine for showering, a little on-base restaurant run by Vietnamese that specialized in greasy cheese sandwiches with kosher pickles, and an EM (Enlisted Men) Club that was air-conditioned.

He was also trying to find out where the best and worst postings were in-country. "My admittedly unscientific poll of resident assistants indicates that (1) there is no good place to be sent in-country, and (2) the places to avoid, if at all possible, are anywhere near the DMZ or in the Mekong Delta. Of course, I've only talked to two assistants so far, both of whom work in this chapel, but it's a start."

Rich and I spent the next three days lingering around the chapel as we waited for our orders, trying not to get in the way as daily activities went on. The rest of the assistants had come and gone.

Once every morning, and then once in the afternoon, we made our way to the office where we had been told to report for assignment. The rest of the time we sat and read, played pool, or wandered around the base.

On the afternoon of the third day, just as we were beginning to think we might be in that limbo for our entire tour, our orders arrived. Rich was assigned to Long Binh, and I was going to the Mekong Delta.

CHAPTER 11

▼

Home Sweet Home

January 12

The cargo plane landed with a thump, followed by two smaller thumps. The blade pitch of the turboprops shifted, and we roared to a halt. I had arrived in the Mekong Delta near the town of Can Tho.

Approximately twenty-five of us, officers and men, had ridden as freight in the windowless belly of the air force plane, spending the trip strapped to seats that, in turn, had been strapped to the floor. The bay door opened and bright sunlight, accompanied by scorching heat, streamed in. Because we had landed at the air force base, we enlisted men who were destined for the Can Tho Army Base were ordered into the uncovered back of a truck for the final leg of our journey.

The truck bounced along a narrow, hard, dirt road on the way to the base. The road was lined with peasants' houses, the walls of which were constructed of cane held together with rope and covered by palm-leaf thatching. Small, naked children playing in the dirt around most of the houses stopped to watch the truck as it passed by. We passed a man who was squatting on the side of the road, defecating. His head turned as his eyes followed our passage, but otherwise he did not move.

Within a few minutes we arrived at the base where I would be stationed for the coming year, the base for the 164th Army Aviation Battalion of the 1st Brigade. The base covered thousands of acres, as it included a landing strip and support buildings for the choppers and housed five thousand men and a few women. It was completely surrounded by several layers of concertina wire—wire that had been designed to cut and tear at anyone who tried to pass through it. The wire was backed up every fifty yards by guard posts. Guard posts were actually little more than mounds of sand bags that had been arranged around a wooden frame to shelter the three or four men who stood guard. The base, like everything else in the Delta, was built on sand that had been deposited by the mighty Mekong River over thousands of years; dust from the sand covered everything in sight, including people.

January 12, 1970

Dear Karen:

Well, I'm settled in my new home for the year. I'm stationed near a city called Can Tho in the Mekong Delta at an army aviation base … this means they fly helicopters. This apparently is not like World War II, where troop movements were secret, so I don't think there is any harm in telling you where I am. However, if my next letter comes to you from the stockade, you'll know I'm wrong!

The barracks here are called "hooches"; I'm living in a hooch. The hooches have two stories and can house a whole company of men, about 120 or so. It is, as you can imagine, pretty drab.

By the way, I found out that none of us are here in the Delta–at least according to what the government is saying. While I was up in Long Binh, someone managed to find a real newspaper, and I discovered Tricky Dick has announced "all U.S. ground troops have been withdrawn from the Mekong Delta." Most people would think the headline said, "All U.S. *troops* have been withdrawn." He didn't mention the 50,000 *support* troops (of which your blonde husband is one) are still here. Ha!

I've met all the guys I'll be working with, except the head chaplain by the name of Riggles. He's off at another base for a couple of days. Wes Crawford, Riggles' assistant, is "short" (that's army talk for "I don't have much more time to serve in this godforsaken place"), so he will be training me for his job.

During my furlough, I didn't mention that I've been promoted. I guess I had other things on my mind. It seems that when we completed training at Fort Hamilton, they promoted all of us from E-1 (lowest scum on earth) to E-3 (higher level of scum), and I am now officially "Specialist 3rd Class Bertson." This means a substantial raise to … are you ready? Are you sitting down? $175 a month! Yea! So don't quit your job in Ann Arbor, because I can't support you in the upper-poverty style to which we have become accustomed.

I hope you're feeling better by now. Was it stomach flu, like I thought? I have to go; I've been chosen for guard duty tonight (my second day on base, and I'm not even sure where the perimeter is that I'm supposed to help guard), so I have to eat quickly and check out my gear.

My address is on the envelope. Say hello to everyone for me. I miss you.

Your distant husband,
Ted

How do you tell someone that you're lonely and frightened and feel like you're on the other side of the moon, but you don't want her to feel badly, too?

Wes Crawford, the senior assistant had met me at the incoming/processing building around three o'clock. He had helped me find my hooch, and then took me to the chapel to meet Ralph, an assistant who was leaving the next day. Wes was a tall, black-haired twenty-two-year-old from Ohio, who had just finished his undergraduate degree in business when he was drafted. He had volunteered to be a chaplain's assistant even though he had seldom attended church in civilian life, but he figured working for a chaplain was better than walking "point" in a squad in the bush—that is, until he began working for Major Riggles.

Major Riggles was a Southern Baptist minister and a professional military man—"regular army," as he liked to say, in order to distinguish between the real army and the "civilian" army, meaning guys like me. He also had a strong sense of duty, which meant going to where the men happened to be. Wes let me in on a little item that had somehow been overlooked in all of my training: By conventions of the Geneva Accords, chaplains never carried weapons in a war zone. This meant the chaplain's assistant served as the chaplain's bodyguard.

Because Riggles wanted to take the Gospel "to where the men were," he traveled a lot to interesting places, like artillery bases ("firebases") in the middle of rice paddies, with his assistant keeping guard of his person with any weapon at hand. I had a really bad feeling about my time in Vietnam.

Since Chaplain Riggles would not return for a couple of days, there was not much to do at the chapel, so Wes suggested I check in at Company headquarters and then snoop around the base to get acquainted with the layout. The little smile behind his thick black moustache should have alerted me that his suggestion was not completely innocent.

Headquarters for the company was a small frame building with the requisite flags—American, battalion, and company—waving outside. The inside was cooled by air conditioners that protruded from the windows. Master Sergeant Thompson, a big man about fifty years old, with a potbelly that strained against his fatigue shirt, was sitting behind his desk, smoking, when I entered. I wondered if having a large beer-belly was part of the job description for E-6s.

Thompson raised his head from the paperwork he was doing and revealed a face with heavy features and extra folds of skin that gave him the appearance of the English bulldog my parents owned. He took a deep drag on a cigarette while he looked me over. "What do you want, soldier?" he asked as I stepped into the coolness.

"Specialist Bertson reporting, Sergeant. I've just arrived on the base and thought I should check in."

"That's right considerate of you, soldier, since you would be declared AWOL within about twenty-four hours if I hadn't seen your ass in here. What's your MO, son?" Translation: military occupation (not modus operandi).

"Chaplain's assistant, Sergeant."

"Shi-it," he chuckled. "Are you another smart-assed college dickhead who figures he can fuck his way through this man's army?" He took another drag on his cigarette.

As I was trying to come up with a reply that was not also insubordinate, he pushed his chair back from the desk, stood up, and walked over to a wall where several sheets of paper hung. "By the way, Bertson, where is your insignia of rank?"

"My what, Top?"

"Insignia of rank. What the fuck rank are you? I don't see any stripes."

"Well, Top, I was just promoted to Specialist 3 and haven't had time to buy my stripes."

"You haul your ass over to the PX (Post Exchange) and buy some as soon as you leave this office, boy. Understand?"

"Yes, Sergeant."

He looked at one of the sheets on the wall. "I see we're shorthanded on guard duty tonight." He crossed a name off the list and wrote mine in. "Report in front of this building tonight at 1830 hours; you're goin' to be on guard duty all night. Don't that make you happy?"

I think my eyes glazed over. Guard duty? On my first night on base?

He turned and scowled at me. "I said, 'Don't that make you happy?' I don't hear you."

"Yes, Top Sergeant."

"Son, you better be in front of the building at eighteen thirty hours or your ass is grass. You understand?"

"Yes, Top Sergeant."

"That's all, Bertson."

I was anxious to leave, since I felt like I had walked into a hornet's nest. As I turned, Thompson stopped me.

"By the way, Bertson. Have you taken your malaria pills today?"

"No, Sergeant."

"Today's Tuesday. Pill day. Do you have them with you?"

"No, Sergeant."

"Well, I just happen to have some right here." He walked to his desk, opened a drawer, and pulled out a bottle. "Here. There's a water jug over there. Take them now so you don't forget them."

I was suspicious about his sudden concern for my health, but I also knew we were supposed to take the pills once a week because malaria was a problem in-country. So I took the pills, left the room, and headed for the PX to buy my stripes.

As I moved around a small section of the base, I had small insights into what it was like in a war zone. Saluting officers was an action that had been drilled into us in Basic Training, so my right hand automatically flew to my forehead at the sight of anything that smacked of "officer-hood." The first officer I saluted, a captain, was quick to let me know that officers were *not* to be saluted in-country and that I should stop standing at attention! When I explained I had just arrived, he pointed out that snipers could be lurking anywhere just waiting to identify an officer so he could be shot. Apparently the life of an enlisted man was of little concern to the enemy, an attitude that I found strangely comforting.

I had my first dinner in the mess hall that afternoon. It was smaller than the mess halls back in the States, but the smells were the same, redolent of mysterious, generic army food. I left the serving line and found a place to sit at a table with several other soldiers. Between bites, I watched Vietnamese scurry around bussing and cleaning the tables. They were civilians hired by the military for menial jobs on base. I wondered how they felt as they watched the large Americans sitting and stuffing themselves, while there was probably little food for their own families.

Whenever any of the other guys at my table left to get more water, they would say, "Watch my food." That seemed a bit strange to me since the food was hardly worth watching, but I soon found out why the custom had evolved. I eventually left the table for a few seconds to get more water, but I did not say, "Watch my food." When I returned my tray was gone along with half my meal, snatched away by one of the ubiquitous Vietnamese. The fellows sitting at the table seemed not to have noticed.

I left the mess hall and returned to my hooch. I didn't know how guard duty was handled in a war zone, but I'd had one experience as a guard at Fort Dix that was still vivid....

I had been assigned to a guard unit on a Saturday night. We were on duty from sundown to sunrise, standing guard in three-hour shifts (meaning three hours of sleep followed by three hours of standing guard). The assignment was to guard the offices of a company headquarters and other strategic buildings in the heart of Fort Dix.

It was October, but cold, winter weather had set in early. We had been issued helmet liners (without the metal helmet), fatigue jackets, and wool glove liners (without the gloves); otherwise, we wore our usual olive drab fatigues and black boots. The weapon we were issued to defend the building from our country's enemies was the old faithful M14 from Basic Training. It was unloaded, of course, so if filthy atheist Commies attacked us I guessed that I was supposed to use it as a club.

I was on the last shift from 4:00 AM to 7:00 AM. What sleep I'd had was sporadic. The guards were housed together in the same small barracks, and trying to sleep—fully dressed, under naked light bulbs, on bare mattresses, while other teams of guards came and went—had proven impossible. Radios blared, card games were played, and no one seemed interested in keeping his voice lowered. I was weary and half frozen as I trudged back and forth in front of the empty building on my last shift. I didn't care if the Commies came or not. In fact, I would probably have helped them sack the place just to have something to do.

The sun had risen clear and golden in the eastern sky. I was standing facing the sun and enjoying the warmth on my frozen face when the rifle was suddenly snatched out of my hands. I turned to face a captain in his dress blues and with a frown on his face.

I snapped to attention—at least, I think I did, as I had no feeling in my hands, arms, or legs due to the cold and fatigue. The captain began yelling....

I stand in front of the senior officers who are presiding over my court martial. "What do you have to say for yourself, Bertson, before this court has you shot, dismembered, burned at the stake, then dishonorably discharged from the army so you will never sing

again in this great nation of ours, which you so miserably betrayed because you were
trying to get warm, you wimp, pansy, Commie-loving puke?"

I came back from my reverie in time to hear the captain yelling. "... asking
you what did you do, you mother-loving dipshit, before you were allowed to be
in this man's army?"

"I'm a musician, sir."

"What kind of musician, you turdball scum?"

"A singer, sir."

"So you were a singer?"

"Yes, sir." *I thought I'd just said that. I wonder how many years I'll be in prison?*

"I want to hear you sing then, asshole."

"Now, sir?"

"Sing, asshole!"

"What shall I sing, sir?"

"You're going to sing the National Anthem, needle-dick. Now turn and face
that flagpole ..." There was no flag on it. "... and sing. I'll hold your rifle."

As I remember, it was not a very good performance, but considering the circumstances, it was passable. At least he hadn't shot me.

I appeared at headquarters at 6:30, as Sergeant Thompson had ordered. Fifteen of us had been given this opportunity to serve as guards for the company's
section of the perimeter. We were met by the Sergeant of the Guard. He checked
off our names, then walked us to the armory where we were issued M16s, magazines of bullets, flak jackets, and helmets. It was then that I really understood that
these guys were serious. This was the real thing: guard duty in a war zone. All that
training at Fort Knox, Fort Dix, and Fort Hamilton was about this: Being put in
harm's way and trying to survive. I was to defend—kill if necessary—and do
what I was ordered to do without question. Only five months earlier I was a
musician and a husband. All through basic training and AIT, I had felt like I was
pretending to be a soldier. But I shivered as I left the armory carrying the M16
and wearing a flak jacket and a metal helmet: no more pretending, no more feeling aloof from the fray. I was a soldier in a war zone where people wanted to kill
me.

We walked back to headquarters. The Sergeant of the Guard asked, "How
many of you guys have done this before? Raise your hands." Two guys out of fifteen raised their hands.

"Jesus-fucking-Christ! I'm going to have a bunch of newbies guarding my ass
tonight? All right, listen up. This ain't no game we're playing here. About three

months ago some people on this base got sloppy. Charlie hadn't hit us for about a year, so they forgot we're in a fucking war here. Some of the guys on guard duty thought it was a good way to catch up on sleep. Well, some sappers made it through the wire and cut the guards' throats, and then they managed to blow up a few choppers before they were killed. So I repeat: THIS AIN'T NO GAME. Understand?

"This company is responsible for five guard posts. There *will* be three of you at each post, one man sleeping and two on guard. You *will* call the Sergeant of the Guard for permission to leave your post for any reason. You *will* call the Sergeant of the Guard if you see any sign of enemy movement. You *will NOT* load or fire any weapon unless given permission by the Sergeant of the Guard. Is that clear?"

"Sergeant?" I said.

"Yeah?"

"Did I hear you correctly? We're not supposed to have our weapons loaded unless we receive permission?"

"Roger that."

"What if we're being shot at?"

"You sound like one of them college pukes. All right, I'll spell it out for you: YOU *WILL* CALL FOR PERMISSION TO LOAD AND RETURN FIRE. Now, you *will* all be relieved at 0700 hours tomorrow, and you *will* be off duty for the rest of the day."

With that, we were herded to the guard posts. My stomach gurgled several times as we were settling in for the night, but I thought little of it. Each post was equipped with a walkie-talkie, an M60 machine gun, and a grenade launcher that looked like a single-shot shotgun. None of the three of us had ever seen a grenade launcher before, let alone used one, so the sergeant explained how to load and fire it. All of us had fired an M60 at some point in our training but had never loaded one, so he showed us how to close the magazine and cock the weapon, then reopen the magazine and drape the ammo belt over it. My stomach gurgled again.

Our post faced a major road into Can Tho. As twilight fell, the road was filled with small motor scooters, bicycles, cyclos (a kind of pedi-cab), and people on foot, as they returned to their homes and Viet Cong units. Buses passed with men and women jammed inside them or sitting on the top or hanging from the sides. The people were all small by American standards, with the men averaging a height of five feet and the women even shorter. Older men tended to be thin and stooped, while older women tended to be rounder and rather squat. The younger men and women were generally slender and lithe. The young men affected American dress by wearing short-sleeved sports shirts and jeans, but most of the young women wore the traditional dark pajama pants with thin, light colored, long-sleeved blouses, topped by the wide, conical hats. Shop girls wore the dark or black silk pants with white *ao dai*—tight-fitting, long-sleeved blouses with cloth panels that fell in flowing lines to their ankles in the front and back. Their shining black hair fell to their waists, and they carried umbrellas to shield them from the sun. I would learn that fair-skinned women were considered most attractive because their paleness indicated wealthy families who did not work in the fields. Women whose skin was deeply tanned (the deep, beautiful, I-summered-in-Mexico tan envied by Americans) were shunned as peasants.

The air was filled with chattering, dust, and fumes from the poorly maintained motors; it surrounded the people as they surged past the base. We heard whistles and shouts from the other guard posts. The words were unintelligible, but the meaning was obvious because occasionally a girl would glance toward the post and then quickly move on.

By nightfall the flow of people on the road had been reduced to a trickle. The road was empty except for the occasional scooter or pedi-cab that buzzed from the darkness of the road into the lights that illuminated the perimeter of the base, and then back into the darkness on the other side. As the traffic died, the rats came out to play.

I thought I was looking at a small cat moving through the shadows, but something was wrong about the movement—it was too jerky. I eventually realized what it was. The largest rat I had ever seen was moving toward our post.

The story in the Stars and Stripes would read: "Soldier-Singer Devoured by Giant Rats. Ted Bertson, a tenor from Michigan, was eaten last night by giant rats while guarding his country from atheist Asian Communists."

I threw a rock at the rat and it scuttled into the night. My stomach gurgled again, but this time it was accompanied by a slight discomfort lower down. Then the mosquitoes came, accompanied by roaches and other creepy-crawly beasties.

Joe and Dan, my fellow guards, were eighteen or nineteen years old. *They ought to be cruising on some street in some town stateside, I thought, looking for girls, instead of sitting here in this guard post. All of us should be back in the States. I should be making love to Karen or going to a concert with her or singing or conducting a concert at the University of Dubuque, rather than sitting in this pit.*

I felt miserable; just that morning I had been at Long Binh, getting adjusted to that place, and by nightfall I was sitting in a guard post in Can Tho, with unloaded weapons, being eaten alive. And my intestines were not pleased with whatever was going on in them.

Around 10:00 PM, I called the Sergeant of the Guard to request permission to go to the latrine: My bowels were in a definite uproar. He granted permission, and I went looking for the nearest latrine. It seemed like everything I had put into my system in the previous two or three days exited quickly.

I went back to the post and drew lots with Joe and Dan on who would sleep first; we had decided we would sleep in two-hour shifts. Dan slept first but not for long because I had to be excused again to head for the latrine, and two men always had to be on duty. He had just dozed off when I woke him a second time for the same reason.

My next latrine visit was shortly after midnight. By now, the Sergeant of the Guard was growing annoyed with my calls requesting permission, and Dan and Joe were annoyed because I kept disturbing their sleep.

I put in my next call around 1:00 AM. The Sergeant of the Guard believed I was screwing around, so he personally escorted me to the latrine. By now I was eliminating all the food I had eaten over the past three years. The Sergeant of the Guard took one whiff, swore under his breath, and told me to get back to the post as soon as I could and to come back to the latrine without calling him, because he knew where to find me in case of trouble.

By sunrise I had visited the latrine so often that toilet seat bore the impression of my derriere. Getting to the latrine in time had become an exercise in sphincter control, and I had developed the ability to run in a duck-walk position for several yards at a time in between the paralysis brought on by severe cramps.

I was so weak that I was staggering when we were relieved of duty, and I immediately asked directions to the infirmary. I lurched into the air-conditioned comfort of the small building and stood in line, sort of, with the other guys who were checking in at the Sick Call window.

As I waited, stomach still gurgling over God-knew-what, I noticed grisly black-and-white pictures on the walls that showed male genitals in various stages of decay and putrefaction. A hand-lettered banner hung on one wall: ALL OF THESE PICTURES WERE TAKEN IN THIS CLINIC. USE THOSE RUBBERS!

I felt like I was about eighty years old, and I had the muscle tone of a jellyfish by the time I leaned on the ledge of the Sick Call window, giving my name, rank, and serial number. The clerk taking the information looked about sixteen years old; he had peach fuzz growing on his face. After asking my name, and so on, he glanced up and asked, "Have the clap?"

It took me several seconds to decipher the question, then several more seconds to get over the shock that this kid had asked me—Ted Bertson, married man, preacher's kid, all-round good clean boy—if I had venereal disease.

I slumped against the ledge. "No," I replied weakly, "I have dysentery."

He looked at me blankly.

"Diarrhea," I said.

"Oh." He filled in the form. "Sit over there, and someone will call you."

I took the form. In the space for "complaint," he had written, "Has the shits."

I began looking for the toilet.

I was coming out of the toilet when I heard my name called. I was taken to an examining room and told to take off everything above the waist. "My problem is *below* the waist," I said, but the orderly merely shrugged and didn't say anything.

Dr. Jim Prichard entered the room and closed the door. He looked to be about my age, so I thought he was an orderly or medical assistant until I saw his nametag.

"What's up?" he asked. "I see one of our learned clerks has written 'has the shits,' so maybe I should ask: Is everything coming out okay?" I was too weak to muster a chuckle.

I described my symptoms and when they began and said that I had just arrived on the base yesterday.

"What company are you with and what's your MO?" he asked. When I told him, he chuckled. "Did you meet a Sergeant Thompson yesterday?"

"Yes."

"By any chance, did he give you 'malaria pills'?" When I said yes, he chuckled again. "The pills gave you the trots. Here, have this prescription filled before you leave, have breakfast, then sleep as much as you can today. Also, don't take any more pills from Sergeant Thompson. The ones he gave you will give you diarrhea every time. We use another kind, the kind we give pilots who can't stop to take a shit at five thousand feet. You know, I never thought about this before … I wonder if they could hover at five thousand feet while someone hangs his ass out of the door of a combat-stripped Huey and craps all over this fucking country."

I left the infirmary, had breakfast—which I guarded jealously—and then decided I needed a shower. I had just stepped under one and was enjoying the lukewarm water (you couldn't get hot water on the base—unless, of course, what you actually wanted was cold water) when I heard women's voices. The showers didn't have curtains or doors, so I couldn't conceal myself; I wasn't particularly prudish, but I saw no point in displaying my white, soft-in-the-middle body to strange females, especially since diarrhea made my male ego weak. I thought maybe the women didn't know I was showering, so I began singing (quietly, of course, so I could avoid the usual ridicule from the other soldiers) to let them know I was there.

I didn't hear the women talking anymore, so, figuring they had reversed direction and left the building, I turned around to see if they had gone. There were four of them standing together in front of my stall with large grins on their faces as I looked back at them, wearing only soap suds.

They giggled with their hands covering their mouths, and then began chattering to each other as they wandered off. I knew then how monkeys feel in zoos.

I finished showering and trudged back to my bunk. The sun was hot and the humidity was rising, so even though I had dried myself after the shower, I was sweating again when I flopped onto my bunk. As I fell asleep, one thought came to me: *I've only been in Can Tho one day; I have 358 to go.*

I reported for duty at the chapel the next morning. Chaplain Riggles was still in the field and Wes said there was little to do, so he suggested we tour the chapel, a tour that took about two minutes.

The sanctuary of the chapel was a simple room with a cement floor, walls made of a layer of plywood—just enough to keep the rain out—covered by a tin roof that would cause an almost-deafening din when the rainy season came. A platform about four inches high that extended from wall to wall sat in the front of the chapel. This made a little stage on which the chaplains performed the mysteries of their faiths. Windows extended down from the top of the walls about eighteen inches and ran the length of the walls on both sides of the chapel. Someone had painted biblical symbols on the windowpanes in an effort to make them resemble stained glass. Here was a depiction of the stone tablets that bore the Ten Commandments; there was a Star of David, a cross, and a chalice. The painting was a little rough, but the effect was pleasant; rather like religious icons Grandma Moses might have painted had she been under the influence.

We walked down the center aisle past the wooded pews that an industrious chaplain had managed to procure. The chapel seated about a hundred people, if they didn't mind squeezing together a bit. As we faced the front of the chapel, an upright piano, the kind you might find in someone's living room, sat on the left with its back to the side wall. A small pulpit, made of light-colored wood, stood several feet from the piano, close to the edge of the platform. The altar stood in the middle of the platform. Its thick wooden top was three feet by six feet, and it was supported by cement slabs that raised it about waist-high.

To the right of the altar sat a small electronic organ. The keyboard that had fewer keys than a piano keyboard, one pedal that controlled the volume, four other pedals to use when the organist ran out of low notes on the abbreviated keyboard, and some levers above the keyboard that allowed the organist to vary the sounds, like a real organ. Of course, its sound was as close to the sound of a real organ as a nose flute is to a trumpet, but at least it was playable.

I went immediately to the piano and tried it out. It was badly out of tune due to lack of use and the high humidity. I had fooled around with tuning our family piano when I still lived at home because my father's salary didn't allow for a complete tuning more than once every five years. But the piano here in this chapel was beyond my skills.

I suggested to Wes that I might be able to do something with it if I had a crescent wrench, a handsaw, and a blowtorch. Wes fiddled with his moustache, a habit of his when he was a little nervous. He wasn't sure whether or not to take me seriously. Instead, he smiled and walked over to the pulpit and pulled out tools from a small shelf, the kind of tools that I had seen professional tuners use. I was elated. I had no idea how to use the stuff, but I was still elated. I felt as if I were an archaeologist who had stumbled across a small piece of ancient civilization: Here was an artifact of my profession. I didn't know if I would be able to tune the piano, but I was certainly willing to try.

Wes then explained the weekly schedule: Tuesday was usually our day off, a "comp" (for compensatory) day, as we had to work on Sunday, and the army tried to give most of the other soldiers Sundays off. I wondered if the Viet Cong had comp days.

On Mondays we filed reports with headquarters about how many men had attended services over Friday, Saturday, and Sunday. Later I learned that the numbers were arrived at rather casually; if the chaplains were around, we might ask them how many they thought had attended, but since the chaplains were usually not around when we had to file the reports, the assistants tended to guess. I discovered copies of some old reports that had been filed by an assistant who, rumor had it, had a drinking problem. According to his reports, on one Sunday, six services were held, and no one attended any of them. On another Sunday, three thousand personnel attended four services.

Our comp "day" on Tuesday was actually just the morning since we had to be on duty by Tuesday afternoon. In fact, most of the week the schedule was fairly fluid, which is what you might expect in a war zone.

Friday began the preparation for services for the weekend. If the Jewish personnel had a service on Friday night, any Christian symbols were removed and substituted with Jewish symbols. That meant storing the crosses, display Bibles, and liturgical draping, and displaying a menorah, the only Jewish religious icon we kept in the chapel.

Sometimes Jewish services were held on Saturday as well, so we had to wait until Saturday night or early Sunday morning to store the menorah and bring out the Christian artifacts.

Friday was also "bulletin day." This meant we typed and proofread the order of service for the Catholic, Protestant, and Lutheran services. (Lutherans were put in a separate category—a Lutheran chaplain once heatedly informed me that Lutherans were not Protestants. I wondered if Martin Luther knew that.) The typing was done on ditto masters, which I considered to be paper devices created by sadists for use by masochists. Dittos were what clerks swore at before they had copy machines to swear at.

Saturday was usually spent arranging the chapel for the various services—Jewish, Seventh Day Adventists, and any other group that decided to hold services. Sunday was the busiest day of the week. Early mass was held at 8:00 AM, if enough men requested it, but usually was not held until 10:00. The Protestant service was held at 11:00 AM. If a Lutheran minister strayed in, the Lutheran service was held at 1:00. However, there appeared to be only two devout Lutherans on the post, so the minister seldom visited.

I would find out soon enough that the quiet, orderly weeks, as Wes had described them, would also contain innervating boredom and teeth-chattering terror.

CHAPTER 12

▼

By the Beautiful Sea

January 25, Na Trang

Dear Karen:

I'm sitting in a whitewashed, concrete block chapel on the air force base in Na Trang, a beautiful tropical area of Vietnam, next to the South China Sea. I haven't been over here long, but I'm already getting the impression that the air force bases are more comfortable than army bases. The city and its surroundings remind me of Florida, with its white sand and palm trees. Why aren't you here to walk along the beach with me? Of course, no Americans are allowed to walk along the beach because snipers are hiding in every tree. So I guess we would have to find something else to do. Any suggestions?

I came up here with Chaplain Riggles for Chaplains' Conference. I wonder what they do in those meetings? We flew up on a small jet that Riggles managed to commandeer. I've never been on a plane so small that flew so fast. Nice trip.

Nothing exciting to report. I miss you.

My foreboding about Chaplain Riggles quickly evaporated when I met him. Imagine the pastor of a medium-sized church in a medium-sized town; a pleasant guy who doesn't want to make waves by being too conservative or too liberal in his theology. Imagine everything about his appearance as being neutral as well (mid-thirties, medium height, medium build, and short, sandy brown hair—cut to regulation length, of course). Put him in a baggy olive drab army uniform, and you have Chaplain Riggles. Everything about him was "medium."

He had a friendly, easy smile and worked hard to project an "I'm just one of the good ol' boys who happens to be a major" image. He did nothing in excess.

Riggles and I had flown to Na Trang for a chaplains' conference. Our morning had begun with a jeep ride to the air force base where we boarded a small, eight-passenger air force jet. Riggles sat in the copilot's seat—I would learn that this was something he would do whenever he could—and chatted with the pilot over the intercom mike.

I sat in one of the passenger seats and enjoyed the changing landscape as below us, the flat, sandy Mekong Delta, with flooded rice paddies reflecting the sun, gave way to the jagged mountain ranges as we flew to the coast of the emerald green South China Sea.

I was musing over the beauty of the land and the strangeness of the war when Riggles turned around and spoke to me. I had trouble hearing over the roar of the jets, but I made out the words "… down fast … base … attack."

The small jet began a steep descent, and my ears immediately began to block. We dropped from about fifteen thousand feet to ground level in about two minutes and then rolled to a stop.

I stepped out of the plane into what seemed to be total silence; it was as if someone had stuffed corks into my ears and pounded them in with a hammer. A chaplain's assistant was waiting for us in a jeep, and we were out of the plane, in the jeep, and on our way to the base chapel as soon as our feet hit the ground. My reduced hearing made me feel as if I were in a tunnel as we rode to the base chapel.

The resident assistants directed Riggles to his meeting, and then they suggested that I look around while I waited—they were busy making arrangements for the chaplains' comfort, so they had no time to give me a tour. I couldn't have heard much of what they said, anyway, so I wandered around until I found the chapel organ. It was a two-manual electronic job that no one knew how to play— none of the assistants was a musician.

I would learn the history of the organ from the senior assistant later, after my ears were unplugged. From his account, a former chaplain had ordered the organ, but he had then had been reassigned, leaving the organ to collect dust. Music for the services was either recorded (played over a reel-to-reel tape recorder), or played on a guitar by a former hippie who, knowing he was about to be drafted, joined the air force to avoid hazardous military service.

The chaplains had been pleased when he had volunteered to play the services, but they had trouble explaining to him that "If I Had a Hammer" was not an acceptable Protestant hymn. It turned out that the closest thing to a religious composition he knew was "Kumbaya," which he'd learned in his pre-military days, sitting around a fire on a beach in California, smoking pot, drinking wine, and being buzzed out of his head.

Around 2:00 PM, several hours after we had landed, my ears slowly unblocked. I was playing the organ when I heard a clap of thunder, as if lightning had struck very close to the chapel. Another peal of thunder followed, this time farther away from the chapel. The windows were still shaking when I looked out and saw a smudge of black smoke rising from a runway.

A siren started howling. As I stood in front of the chapel wondering what was happening, I saw the two assistants standing by a bunker gesturing wildly at me. I trotted over to them, wondering what was up. They grabbed me and shoved me inside, where I found Riggles and the other chaplains huddled together.

The "lightning" actually had been rockets exploding, fired by VC from the surrounding hills. Only two were fired before jets scrambled and began bombing the hills. By the time the all-clear siren sounded, black smoke from exploding bombs was rising from the green mountains. Men were dying on the mountains as we stood in the blazing sun, hands shielding our eyes, watching the jets attacking.

The chaplains returned to their conference and the assistants to their work. I had lost interest in playing the organ, so I went outside, leaned against the chapel wall, and looked at the mountains. I remembered the mountain I had stood on in Italy, only five months before, on a hot, humid, sunny day like this one. As I thought about how peaceful that valley had seemed, the shadows of clouds passed over the mountains that rose above the base, sending an unexpected chill of fear through me. I retreated into the chapel seeking shelter.

By the time I arrived back in Can Tho with Riggles, I was spooked. Riggles enjoyed telling the other chaplains, in my presence, about my sauntering out of the chapel door like I was going for a stroll in the park, and the look on my face when I realized we were under attack. I laughed along with everybody else, but I felt a little shaky. What if I hadn't walked out the door to investigate? Would anybody have known I was not in a bunker?

That night, back in the hooch, everything was normal. Most of the guys who were off-duty were drunk. Stereos that had been bought for a pittance at the PX were blasting away.

Every night, someone would play a stereo loud enough to be heard in the next hooch. This usually lasted for an hour or so, until the owner would pass out or go to sleep, whichever came first. On Saturday nights though, the air was filled with the Battle of the Stereos. Around 10:00 PM, soul music would start screaming forth from the vicinity of the hooch where most of the black soldiers lived. It usually began with one stereo system playing at a decibel level close to what is experienced when standing on the platform in a New York subway station as the train pulls in.

This was usually answered by a stereo in another hooch (a "white" one) playing rock music in retaliation. This, in turn, was answered by the soul music being played on two stereo systems, a matter of some coordination. At this point, some soldier would yell for the "motherfuckers" to turn off "the motherfuckin' music!" Of course, this was a signal for the volume to rise to the level of a twin-engine jet landing in your driveway.

Enter the military police! These brawny—and usually not overly bright—teenagers wearing helmets and carrying nightsticks, would arrive on the scene looking bewildered, until someone pointed out the hooches where the stereos were blasting away.

The MPs would enter the hooches; the music would stop. The MPs would climb into their jeep and pull away; the music would start again, this time with a vengeance. Then ad hoc committees would form in front of each hooch. The committees—composed mainly of guys who'd been smoking various types of illegal substances or drinking booze—would debate what to do. I never saw anyone from one committee actually talk to anyone from another committee, but eventually, the volume level of the music would start to drop until it reached a level that was agreeable to all—which was just loud.

On this night, the evening of my Na Trang excitement, the music had stopped around 2:00 AM, and I finally dozed off. I was jolted awake by a tremendous *wham*. In an instant, I had pulled back my mosquito netting, was out of my bunk, and had stumbled down the dark hallway of the hooch. I burst through the doorway expecting to see men scrambling for the bunkers. Instead, I ran into some guys enjoying the cooler evening air as they smoked cigarettes and reefers. They took one look at me in my olive drab boxer shorts and with a look of terror on my face, and started laughing.

"Hey, newbie, what's the matter?"

"Didn't you hear the explosion?" I asked.

"Yeah, man. That's Big Bertha over in the Special Forces compound."

"You mean we aren't under attack?"

"Fuck, no. Bertha is a deuce-and-a-half mortar that the Special Forces guys fire off now and then to keep Charlie honest. Go back to bed, man—and put on some dry shorts!"

A couple of nights later though, it happened again. I had sprayed a mist of bug killer over my bunk, quickly climbed in, and carefully tucked in the mosquito netting so I could sleep without mosquitoes. The music had stopped, and I had fallen, at last, into a sound sleep.

WHAM!

Jee-sus! Those Special Forces guys again. I'll probably never get back to sleep now.

WHAM!

"Incoming!" someone yelled. I didn't understand what it meant; I was too shocked to move.

WHAM!

I ran down the dark corridor, with guys yelling in front of me and behind me. Some wore shower thongs and were shuffle-running in the dark. I was pushed from behind and ran into someone in front of me. All the lights were out. We were in total darkness, running for the entrance in nightmare slowness.

WHAM!

God! What's happening? My body was moving, but I felt like I was watching from far away. We all piled through the entrance. We were on the ground floor of a two-story building; the guys on the second floor were scrambling down the stairs or jumping over the railing. I was pushed and shoved around the corner of the building and into the darkness of the bunker. "Get the fuck in!" someone shouted.

WHAM! WHAM! WHAM!

The mortars seemed to be getting closer. The musty air in the bunker made it feel like entering a swamp. The acrid smell of gunpowder began to fill the close air of the bunker. We were squeezed in tightly; I was hemmed in on all sides.

WHAM!

In the darkness of the bunker, everyone was tense, silent, hardly breathing as we listened to the mortars thudding in closer to us. Our black silhouettes flickered in the light from the explosions.

WHAM!

Another smell: vomit. Someone in the bunker had thrown-up. Someone else gagged as the smell filtered through the bunker. "Shi-it," a voice muttered. "I think I would rather die outside than in a pile of puke."

A high-pitched, slightly shaky voice asked, "Anyone know if this thing can stand up to a direct hit?"

"Fuckin' A. Those motherfucks could drop those fuckin' things on us all night an' this fuckin' thing'll take it."

"Hey, that you, Sarge?"

"Hey, Sarge. I think we got an injured man here."

That's when I heard someone gasping, struggling to breathe.

"Anyone bring a flashlight?" the sergeant asked.

"Yeah. Right here."

"Turn the fuckin' thing on, needledick, so I can see what's wrong with this man."

A beam of light appeared. The sergeant pushed his way to the injured man, who was slumped against a wall and looked like he was about fifteen years old.

The sergeant leaned over him and spoke in a low voice. The young soldier, still gasping, managed to say several words. The sergeant laughed. "He's okay. He was running under the stairs when one of you swinging-dicks jumped over the railing and landed on him. It's a wonder you didn't break his neck." There were several nervous chuckles.

"I think they've stopped," someone said. We all stood, straining to listen. Silence.

The sergeant spoke up. "No one goes out until the all-clear is sounded."

Someone spoke from a corner. "There wasn't no siren when the attack started. Maybe those fuckers at headquarters don't even know we been hit."

A siren began to howl as if in answer. Out over the perimeter, the lightships hovered, looking for our attackers. The lightships were Hueys that had large searchlights attached to the belly of the ship. Red tracers would occasionally appear like "dash marks" in the air from machine-gun fire.

Another sergeant appeared as we stepped out of the bunker and told us to stay put until roll was called. We waited for about an hour in the damp darkness, slapping mosquitoes and bitching about having to wait for whatever it was we were waiting for.

A Spec 4 came to call the roll. It quickly became apparent that most of the men whose names were called were not present, but I didn't think much about that; I was tired, hot, and mosquito-bitten. I just wanted to go to bed.

I was the first assistant to report for work at the chapel the next morning, and I had coffee brewing when Chaplain Riggles walked in. He sat on the edge of my desk, grim-faced. He had just attended the officers briefing that the CO had called.

The CO, he said, had been furious. VC had gotten through the concertina wire, found our guards asleep, and cut their throats. Then they set up their mortars within the base perimeter. Twelve men, including six sleeping guards, had been killed, and several more injured. Of the twelve who had been killed, the oldest was twenty; the rest were nineteen-year-olds.

The CO was also furious because many of the men were not on base, forty percent, to be exact. There were five thousand men and officers assigned to the base at Can Tho, so that meant about two thousand men were not where they were supposed to be. We were in a combat zone, and they were military personnel who were AWOL during a night when their base was attacked. If this were a *real* war, he had said, they would be called deserters.

Officially, no one knew the whereabouts of the missing forty percent, but unofficially, everyone knew—except the commanding officers, of course—that they were living "on the economy" in Can Tho. Many of them had arranged civilian marriages (not recognized by the U.S. government) and started families that they would abandon when they returned to the States.

A lieutenant colonel suggested (jokingly, Riggles hoped) a mass execution of everyone below the rank of E-5; that way, the army could make an example of the offenders but not kill off the noncoms. Eventually, the CO decided that the best way to handle the situation was to simply put the word out that muster would be called again tonight, and that every mother's son had *better* be where he was supposed to be.

The coffee was brewed by the time Riggles finished telling me about the meeting. Without another word, he walked over to the coffee pot and poured two cups, handing me one and taking the other with him as he headed for his office.

Riggles had almost reached his office when he noticed a military ambulance driving up to the Central Processing Morgue for the Mekong Delta that stood across the street from the chapel. He stepped into the chapel doorway, standing quietly for several minutes as he watched the black body bags being carried into the air-conditioned coolness of the morgue.

He turned and noticed I had been standing behind him. He shrugged his shoulders. "They were just kids. They're all just kids." Then he stepped into his office and shut the door.

The memorial service was held the next day at 2:00 PM. The sun, blazing in a cloudless sky, had turned the plywood-walled chapel into an oven. I walked to the front of the chapel, took my seat at the small electronic organ, and began elaborating on a selection from the hymnal.

I had seen my father perform many funerals during my growing-up years. In those Kentucky funerals, the body was always present, lying mannequin-like in an open coffin while the family and friends keened their sorrow. This, however, would be my first military memorial service.

I was playing "A Mighty Fortress is Our God" as the company came in. The soldiers, led by their officers, entered in two columns, shuffling wordlessly to their seats. The officers moved into the front pews, and the enlisted men filled the remaining rows. The only break in the silence of the chapel was the sound of the music and the men's shuffling feet. When everyone was in, a sergeant at the back of the chapel quietly said, "'Ten-*shun!*" as two flag bearers—one with the American flag, the other with the company colors—entered. Behind them came two more soldiers, each carrying a light-gray flight helmet. Chaplain Riggles followed them.

The flag bearers separated at the front of the chapel and placed their flags in stanchions at either side of the platform. Then they took their places at the outside ends of the front pews. The soldiers carrying the helmets placed them on a small table that sat in front of the pulpit. They then stepped to their places on the inside ends of the front pew. Chaplain Riggles took his place at the pulpit, and the sergeant said, "Be seated." I ended the music as the soldiers sat down.

Chaplain Riggles opened his Bible. "And they shall beat their swords into plowshares, and their spears into pruning hooks; nation shall not lift up sword against nation, neither shall they learn war anymore.... The Lord is my shepherd, I shall not want. He maketh me to lie down in green pastures. He leadeth me beside the still waters. He restoreth my soul.... Yea, though I walk through the valley of the shadow of death, I will fear no evil, for thou art with me; thy rod and thy staff, they comfort me.... Surely goodness and mercy shall follow me all the days of my life, and I will dwell in the house of the Lord forever."

Silence filled the stifling chapel. The rows of sweating men sat, barely moving, as the commanding officer of the company, a major, moved to the front of the chapel. He was a compact, muscular man, used to giving orders; clearly, he was ill at ease in a situation where emotions were so close to the surface.

He did not step up to the pulpit; rather, he moved to the side of the table that held the helmets. He glanced at the men under his command who were seated in front of him, and then raised the sheet of paper on which he had typed his speech. "We have come to honor the memory and sacrifice of our comrades who gave their lives in the service of their country." He paused, cleared his throat, and began reading their names: "Private Michael Peters; Corporal John Masters...." On and on he went, intoning the names of the twelve dead soldiers. "These men lived among us and worked with us, some for only a short time, but they leave many friends who will miss them. The Department of the Army has authorized the following citations to be awarded them: for Private Michael Peters, the Vietnam Campaign Medal, the Good Conduct Medal, and the Purple Heart. For Corporal John Masters, the Vietnam Campaign Medal...."

I wondered how many of the men here actually had known the soldiers. Would they, in fact, be missed? And the medals: What would they mean to the families whose sons would never wear them?

The major finished his reading. Chaplain Riggles stepped to the pulpit again and began his address. From my vantage point, I was able to see most of the young, blank-faced soldiers as they stared at the chaplain or gazed at the floor. Like their CO, they were stiff and ill at ease in this setting, looking as if they would rather be anywhere else but here, listening to words about honor, duty, death, and everlasting life. What did they know, or care, about everlasting life? God, eternity, heaven—these were abstract ideas. What was real was drinking, doing their job, and screwing.

What could Riggles say that meant anything to them? How could he use words to break through the shell each had built to shield himself from facing his own mortality? And why should a nineteen-year-old *need* to face his own mortality?

Riggles ended his address and nodded to the CO sitting in the front. The major stood, and the rest of the company followed. The sergeant in the back of the chapel softly commanded, "Ten-HUT!" I stood and came to attention, as a bugler outside the chapel began playing "Taps." As I listened, a boyhood memory arose in my mind—Cub Scouts sitting around a campfire, singing "Taps":

Go to sleep.
Go to sleep.
Day is done, night has come, go to sleep.
Angels watch over thee.
Go to sleep.

The last long note of the bugle faded into silence. Quietness settled over us, holding each of us suspended. For a moment, our separate lives melded together and formed into one being who peered into the blackness.

Someone moved, and the spell was broken. Riggles glanced at me and nodded. I sat down at the organ and began playing the recessional. The solders rose from the pews and stood at attention as the flag bearers, followed by the soldiers carrying the helmets, moved along the aisle toward the door. Riggles completed the recession. When the solemn parade had left the chapel, the sergeant said, "Dis-MISSED." Wordlessly, the soldiers left their seats and shuffled out of the chapel into the bright sunlight.

I stopped playing as the last soldier passed through the door. The music seemed weak somehow, as if it were removed from me. It had been formed for a world other than this dusty, banal, death-ridden hell; it sounded trite, out of place.

I leaned back against the wall, thinking that the sudden swiftness of death could strike us, even behind our armed barriers. Those twelve soldiers would never grow older; they were frozen in eternal youth. Their lives, their dreams, had ended in the damp blackness of a bunker. And for what?

Beneath these thoughts, soft, distant voices, like a radio with its volume turned low, kept repeating over and over in my head:

Go to sleep ...
"They were just kids."
Night has come ...
"And I will dwell in the house of the Lord forever."
Go to sleep.

C H A P T E R   1 3

▼

Far from the Home
I Love

February

"Have any coffee for a wandering Jew?"

Seated at my desk, I looked toward the source of that question. Rich Hindeman stood in the doorway, smiling from ear to ear. I yelled his name and met him as he came through the doorway. Riggles, stepping out of his office, found us hugging and slapping each other's back as if we were long-lost brothers. In a way, we were; to me, Rich meant civilization, the States, home.

I introduced Rich to Riggles, who suggested I take time off to show Rich around. At that moment, another man appeared at the door of the chapel. He was about my height and age but seemed older and quieter. Rich introduced Riggles and me to his "boss," Chaplain Ira Mosher. Ira was one of two rabbis serving in Vietnam and the only Orthodox rabbi in Vietnam.

The two chaplains headed into Riggles' office, and Rich and I left for a tour of the base. The tour lasted until we arrived at the EM Club.

I had a Coke while Rich had a beer, and we caught up on what had happened since we had last seen each other. He teased me about having a Coke, but I explained that I was still trying to follow the tenets of my Southern Baptist upbringing.

He shook his head and chuckled. "Ain't we a pair? Remember all those discussions we had back at Fort Hamilton about our liberal education and our religions? You were trying to hang on to your beliefs, and I had spent most of my life trying to forget mine."

I nodded, smiling.

"Well, prepare yourself: I have discovered that I enjoy being a Jew." He began singing, using the tune to the popular song "I Enjoy Being a Girl" but singing "Jew" instead of "girl."

"So, when did this happen?" I asked. "You have a revelation or something? A Saul of Tarsus experience, in reverse?"

He suddenly became serious. "No. You remember that my field—at least, what I hope will be my field, assuming I get out of this war alive—is Renaissance history? I was interested in the role of Jews in Western culture; stuff like that. I was raised in the Jewish culture, but my parents never talked about their religious views much, so I never had much sense of what a Jew was. I would tell my friends I was Jewish, if the topic ever came up—which it didn't, much—but I said that because my *grandparents* were Jewish. I didn't know what the hell being Jewish meant.

"Then Ira comes along. I had never been around an Orthodox Jew before; I had heard about Hasidic Jews—those guys really are weird—but didn't know about my Orthodox cousins. There's something about Ira. I don't know really, it's just that he really lives what he believes. I've never been around anybody who really did that. You know that Orthodox Jews eat strictly kosher. Well, the army sure as shit isn't going to keep a kosher kitchen, you know."

"Yeah," I said. "I guess I never thought about it."

"Well, me neither, until I get assigned to Ira. The guy lived in-country for six months without setting foot in a mess hall except to get something to drink. He was living strictly on Jewish Care Packages."

"What's that?" I asked.

"There's a Jewish Welfare Society that sends these kosher packages to nice Jew-boys in the service—matzo, gefilte fish, stuff like that. It tastes terrible. Until now, Ira had a goy assistant who couldn't have cared less about what, or when, Ira ate. But *now* he has me.

"Do you know that certain types of liquor is considered kosher? I did some research and found out that some scotch and brandies are kosher. You should have seen Ira and me last week. We had flown north of Saigon to visit any Jewish personnel we could find, and we got back to the chapel after being out about sixteen hours. The mess hall was closed; Ira's care package hadn't come yet, so there we were, with nothing but scotch to drink.

"You know what happens if you drink on an empty stomach? No, I keep forgetting you don't drink … yet. You wait—this war will sure-as-shit get to you someday. Anyway, after one swig apiece, we were zonked. But we didn't stop with one drink 'cause we were as thirsty as fish after being out all day.

"We went through the whole damn bottle. I don't remember much about it, but I have a vague recollection of Ira doing some folk dance in the front of the chapel, and the two of us crawling under the pews in a race from the front of the chapel to the back. I think I remember sprawling on a pew, with Ira on another one, singing something in Hebrew, but I don't remember what.

"The next day, Ira stayed in his hooch, and I got the priest's assistant to cover for me. I wanted to die. You know what it's like to be throwing your guts up in a latrine, with hooch maids trying to clean around you? No, you wouldn't, but I don't recommend it.

"Talking about food; you found any good places in town?"

I suddenly realized that I had not spent much time in Can Tho. I had driven through it several times, always on the lookout for anything that struck me as dangerous, but I had never gotten out of the jeep to explore on foot. When I told Rich, he suggested that we find someone who might know. I immediately thought of Wes.

Wes had the day off, so Rich and I walked over to his hooch. He was lying out in the sun, working on his "short-time" tan, the kind of deep tan the guys would try to get just before they were sent back to the States. The tans made them stand out next to the paler civilians and stateside troops they would encounter, so they wore them like badges of honor.

Wes mentioned a good Chinese place he liked, Olga's. The owner was a Vietnamese doctor who had the reputation for keeping the kitchen very clean and the cooks healthy; he also ran the cleanest whorehouse in Can Tho. Wes said he could recommend both establishments.

On the way back to the chapel, Rich asked, "Are you getting any?"

"Any what?" I asked.

"Laid. You know, sexual intercourse, doing the dirty deed, hiding the sausage, stuping. Are you just being coy, or are all Southern Baptists naïve?"

"Well, no, it's just that, well, I try not to think about it," I said. "Do you know how many strains of venereal disease they have over here? Even kissing is dangerous because so many Vietnamese have TB. So, I figured I should get a lot of exercise and take cold showers."

"Yeah, me too," he said. "That, and the hairy palm. I was just wondering. Bobbie—remember, I told you about my wife, Bobbie?—she and I talked about it before I came over, and even though I kind of have her permission, I figure the risk isn't worth it.

"Tell you what," he said, grabbing my arm. "Let's you and me promise to keep each other safe. You know—if we're out somewhere, and it looks like I'm going to go off and bang some sweet young thing, you stop me. I'll do the same for you, okay?"

"It's a deal," I said. I borrowed Chaplain Riggles' jeep and Rich and I drove into town.

With Rich along, I paid more attention to the town but still kept an eye out for anything that might appear sinister. Most of the people lived in clusters of connected apartment-like rooms on the outskirts of the town. Imagine the older, one-story motels that are found in the States; then picture each room as being made of different material and slightly different dimensions. Complete the picture by having the building stretch for several blocks, with other buildings of similar construction on either side, separated by narrow alleys, just wide enough for two or three people to walk abreast. This is what the "suburbs" of Can Tho looked like. The living quarters were made of anything from metal sheets, to canvas, to plywood. Many families had only one room in which they worked, ate, and slept.

On the other hand, the commercial buildings in Can Tho bore the influence of the French. They were no more than three stories high, with the exterior stucco walls painted in white or pale pastel colors. Inside, the rooms had high ceilings and often had large windows, without glass, that let in the brilliant tropical sunlight and any breezes; the windows had shutters that were closed during the monsoon season. Some of the better-kept buildings reminded me of the old Hollywood movies from the '40s that were set in French Algiers, with overhead fans slowly turning in the sultry air of high-ceilinged rooms. However, most of the buildings had been subdivided several times until they were more like a series of little cells under one roof. Small family businesses inhabited these cells.

The major roads leading into the town were mixtures of stones and dirt that had been excavated and raised to form a roadway. They were very functional during the dry season, as long as no one objected to the clouds of dust that the vehicles left in their wake. I would discover that they became quagmires in the rainy season.

The streets in the downtown district were wide boulevards lined with buildings. In front of the buildings, on what passed for sidewalks, were vendors selling fish, produce, and the basic foodstuffs.

Smaller streets, leading to more businesses and dwellings, branched off the wider boulevards. We found Olga's on one of these. It was as clean as Wes had said it would be, and the food was excellent.

Rich and I gorged ourselves, and then staggered out into the hot, sun-drenched street. It was approaching midday, when the heat would be at its maximum, so the townspeople were heading indoors. The Vietnamese did not take siestas like Europeans and South Americans who lived in hot climates, but their normal pace did slow somewhat. Only the invading Americans seemed determined to lumber about, sweltering in the afternoon heat.

Compared to the Vietnamese, Rich and I seemed tall and ungainly as we maneuvered along the sidewalks, peering into the small shops, inspecting the produce on the open-air stands, and basically acting like tourists. We forgot for a short time that we were in a war zone.

The only people who seemed impervious to the heat were the children. The younger children, whose ages looked to range from about four years old to eight or nine, moved quickly as they played games. The older children, those in their pre-teenage years, had already developed the blank-faced stares so common in the adults. Some of the more aggressive ones would accost us, speaking pidgin English, asking for money or selling their sisters or mothers. "Hey, GI! Mother number-one boom-boom. Cherry girl," they would say, pointing to a tired-looking woman, often surrounded by several small children, sitting at the end of one of the narrow alleys.

Rich had already been accosted on the streets of Saigon, so he was neither surprised nor shocked, but the first time a young boy approached me with his sales pitch, I must have looked bewildered. I stood speechless, looking at this small pimp as he tried to convince me that his mother was a virgin. Rich grabbed my arm and pulled me away.

"They practice immaculate conception over here," he chuckled. "You'll get used to it."

"How can you get used to something like that?" I asked. "The kid was trying to sell his mother."

He shook his head. "Offends your sensibilities, huh? Well, on one hand, mine are offended too. But, as a historian, I can tell you that this has gone on from time immemorial. Anywhere poverty or war exists, prostitution exists as well."

"But it's wrong!" I said. "I mean, this shouldn't be happening, and I hate it when you get that academic tone."

He shrugged. We were walking on the sidewalk that ran along a wide boulevard lined with palm trees. Can Tho had, perhaps, been a beautiful city before the endless wars. The heat was becoming oppressive, but I was having a good time. It seemed like years since Rich and I had talked like this, but according to the calendar it was not even two months since he and I had one of our strolling debates. I really missed him.

"We've talked about this before," I said. "I still believe that the government has good reasons for our being here, and something good will come out of this war."

He shook his head wearily. "I don't think so. I think this war is a crock, but I figured that serving in the army was better than being on the run as a draft dodger, so here I am." He offered me a weak grin. "Look, we're both over here, and neither one of us wants to be here, so I figure we'll have to make the best of the situation." He stopped walking. "Jesus, listen to me! I sound like a Jew. I sound like something from *Fiddler on the Roof*."

"You *are* a Jew," I laughed. "All you need is a violin and a roof to sit on. You're a Tevia in olive drab."

Rich struck a pose with both hands in the air, elbows bent, and began singing one of Tevia's songs from *Fiddler* in a nasal voice, as he moved in a slow folk dance. I tapped my foot and played an imaginary fiddle.

This had been one of the routines that we had slipped into at Fort Hamilton. And now, Vietnamese children watched as two soldiers stood on a sidewalk in a city in the Mekong Delta, singing and dancing to an imaginary orchestra, dreaming of a life that existed far away across the ocean—a life neither of them could be certain of ever sharing again.

CHAPTER 14

▼

Consider Yourself
at Home

February

"Ted, this is Skip Lauton, another Michi*gander*, like you," said Bob Perkins, a short, wiry warrant officer and helicopter pilot. "I don't know if I'll be able to stand having two Michi*ganders* on the same base." He laughed because he knew I disliked the term "Michigander" because it sounded like some kind of bird.

I had met Bob when he joined Sunday night Bible study that met at the chapel. Looking back, I realize that I had started the group as part of my effort to hold on to the last shreds of my religious beliefs. I was becoming a closet convert of the Age of Aquarius.

Still, the conservative voices in me were strong. I had suggested the idea to other soldiers who had appeared at services and wanted to get together to talk about the Bible and "spiritual things" on a regular basis. I needed a group to shore up my fundamentalist wall before it collapsed completely. Bob had been a member of the group for the four Sundays it had lasted.

He was, for the most part, quiet and reserved. He stood about five foot six, just barely making the height requirement for flight training. He sported a jaunty mustache, trimmed to military specifications, that was as black as his thick head of hair; it gave him the look of a World War I pilot. All he needed was the scarf to complete the picture. Like most Huey pilots, he had a mixture of quiet courage and bravado—flying into a "hot" landing zone, known affectionately as an "LZ," was not for the timid. Also like most Huey pilots, he had been shot down and wounded. Fortunately, he had been rescued and patched up enough to travel to Tokyo, where he had spent six weeks recovering. As soon as he was pronounced fit, he was sent back to the war.

He was also quietly religious and had a deep faith that God would, somehow, make things turn out right. Before enlisting, which he had done to avoid the draft, he had studied commercial design. After arriving at Can Tho, he had used his artistic ability to create stained-glass windows in the chapel out of clear glass and heavy layers of paint. When the sun shone through them in the early mornings and late afternoons, they created lovely patterns in the drab chapel, even though I still thought the drawing was akin to Grandma Moses.

Skip Lauton was the physical opposite of Bob: He was over six feet tall, clean-shaven, and had sandy blonde hair, slightly darker than my own. He was already slightly rounded in the middle and would be rotund in middle age.

He had been in law school at Michigan State University and had seen the inevitability of being drafted, so, like Bob, he had enlisted and been accepted at flight school. Guys would do anything to avoid the draft. He flew an attack helicopter called the Cobra.

The Cobra was a sleek, slender craft, in which the pilot and gunner sat in tandem. It carried automatic cannons, called miniguns, which fired six thousand rounds a minute and had several clusters of rockets as well. The Cobra was literally a flying weapon and was used in support of troops in ground fights.

Skip and I immediately established an easy rapport. Since I had attended the University of Michigan, the archrival of his alma mater, we quickly started bantering about the rivalry between schools. I saw both Skip and Bob several times over the next few weeks, usually together, and I realized that besides being physically different, their attitudes about life were quite different as well. For one, Skip was as irreligious as Bob was devout. Every third word out of Skip's mouth had to do with sexual penetration of animate or inanimate objects, while the vilest language Bob ever used was "Darn!" and that was only when he was very upset. Somehow, though, this didn't matter to either of them.

Once, Bob and I were walking around the base, taking in the late-afternoon breeze that seemed to just stir the humidity. We both wore fatigues, but somehow he managed to look dashing, while my clothes wrinkled as soon as I put them on, and they hung loosely on me so that I always felt as if I were wearing a tent. Bob, on the other hand, managed to make his fatigues look freshly starched and more fitted. He usually wore a bandana around his neck as well, and he completed "the look" (as he called it) by wearing aviator sunglasses. I once told him that if he added a corncob pipe, he would look just like General Macarthur. A smile appeared at the edges of his neatly trimmed mustache as he contemplated the resemblance; he said he might take up smoking.

During our stroll, we talked about trivial things until, as usual, our conversations turned to Skip's latest exploit in the air or some *bon mot* he had uttered about the degradations of religion and clean living. One night at the Officers Club, Bob had become annoyed by Skip's using "fuck" several times in every sentence.

"You know, I don't appreciate that kind of talk, particularly from an officer," Bob had said.

Skip just smiled. "Actually, I never used to talk this way, but there's something about your tight-assed approach to living that seems to bring it out. It's like waving a red flag in front of a bull. And you know, your ass has gotten tighter since Ted appeared on the scene."

Skip concluded that Bob and I had a *beaucoup* serious case of anal-optic infection. When Bob asked what that was, Skip replied, "That's a disease that occurs when the anus and optic nerve somehow get mixed up together. It gives you a shitty view of the world."

We laughed and said that maybe Skip was right; maybe our view of the world was shitty, but at least our beliefs gave us something to hang on to.

Later, walking back to the chapel, I asked Bob how he and Skip had gotten together, since they were so different. A strange look passed over Bob's face; he asked me if I knew that he had been shot down and wounded. I had heard a little about it; now, Bob said that Skip was the reason he was alive.

"What happened?" I asked.

"First, you have to have a little background. Do you realize that helicopters are about the dumbest kind of attack aircraft you can use?"

Since I was part of an army aviation (read "helicopter") unit, that didn't make any sense to me. "No," I said, "I thought choppers were God's gift to warfare."

Bob shook his head and looked as if he were about to explain quantum theory to a child. "Well, look … if you fly three or four thousand feet above the ground, then you're fairly safe from small-arms fire, because bullets lose most of their force before they hit you. So the underside of the ship needs only minimal armor, which means you can fly faster.

"But if you're flying very high, your machine guns and other armament won't be very accurate or particularly useful, so you have to fly closer to the ground to provide fire support for any ground troops. The closer you are to the ground, the more armor you need to protect the crew, and the ship flies slower because of the weight. A really well armored ship couldn't even get off the ground.

"So the military tries to have it both ways—as much crew protection as possible, with as little armor as possible. The problem is that when it's fired upon, the ship needs to move fast and keep up a lot of air speed in order to protect itself. But we're not supposed to protect ourselves; we're supposed to protect the ground forces, and to do that, you have to come almost to a standstill. And when you do *that*, a little old lady with a BB rifle can bring you down. I almost bought the farm because of that."

About ten months earlier, on the day he was wounded, Bob had flown as support for a group of three choppers picking up American troops from a landing zone. The pickup had gone okay, and the last of the soldiers had just boarded when Viet Cong snipers had opened fire. The VC had learned to wait until the ships were loaded before firing—more Americans could be killed that way when the chopper was brought down.

Bob, in his support role, had flown in over the trees, while his door gunner opened fire. The other ships carrying the troops had managed to leave unharmed, and Bob was disengaging when his gunner was hit and slumped to the floor of the chopper. Without the fire from Bob's ship to keep the snipers pinned down, his Huey was an easy target.

Bob was trying to move his ship out of firing range, but the engine was hit, oil lines were punctured, and about two miles from the LZ, a pilot's nightmare happened: The overhead blades froze. Even with a dead engine, as long as the main blades are turning, a pilot has a chance of gliding to a landing. If the blades stop turning, the ship falls like a rock. Bob's ship fell.

Bob remembered the ground rising toward him and the copilot radioing a Mayday as Bob struggled to control the ship. Then there was nothing.

He regained consciousness and, in a haze, realized that the Huey had landed on its right side. He called his copilot's name. No answer. His seat belts had saved his life, but now they were cutting into his flight suit, and one was stretched tightly across his chest, making it hard to breathe. When he moved his right arm to release the belts, pain shot through his shoulder, almost causing him to pass out again. He had been shot.

He managed to free himself and half-slid, half-fell on his copilot who, because of the tilt of the ship, was beneath him. Most of his copilot's chest had been blown away; he probably had died instantly.

Struggling against nausea and pain, Bob managed to climb back into the midsection of the ship, looking for the gunner. Since gunners had to stand to move the machine gun, they wore harnesses that were bolted to the floor. He saw his gunner's harness strap leading over the edge of the ship. At first, he thought it had been severed, but when he pulled it, it wouldn't give. It was still attached to the gunner, whose body lay crushed under the helicopter.

He managed to climb up to the left side of the ship, pull himself out of it, and jump to the ground. The impact made his shoulder feel like his arm had been torn from the socket, and black holes opened up in front of his eyes, but he managed to stagger a few yards from the downed ship. The chopper had plowed a furrow into the ground when it hit, clearing a space in a field of cane that rose over his head, blocking his view in all directions.

He was trying to decide what to do when he heard voices in the distance: the VC were looking for him. They had seen the smoke from his ship and had followed it, waiting for it to crash. Now, they were coming through the cane, and he could hear the dry rustle of the leaves as they used machetes to hack their way through. They knew—and *he* knew—that he was trapped; it was simply a matter of time before they found him. They were deliberately noisy, speaking mostly Vietnamese to each other but occasionally calling to him in broken English. They couldn't be sure anyone had survived the crash, but they were acting as if someone had. They taunted him, asking, "How many VC you kill, GI? How you feel now, GI?"

He had heard that the VC in that region took no prisoners. He had heard stories of GIs who had been staked to the ground, skinned alive, and left to die in excruciating pain.

He was wearing the .45 automatic. He managed to dig it from the holster with his left hand, and then hold it with his right hand as he operated the mechanism to chamber a round. The voices were moving closer and seemed to come from all around him, mixed with the dry rustle of the cane stalks.

"You know," he said as we strolled along, "I realized I was going to die, but I felt real calm, like it was happening to somebody else, and I was just watching." He stopped walking and picked up a clod of dirt. "I remember realizing that what I was about to do was suicide, but it seemed okay. In fact, it didn't matter at that point whether it was right or wrong, I guess. I just wanted to die quick. I had a lot of feelings, all at once, but mostly, I felt this calmness." He shook his head. "Funny thing. I can still hear those stalks rustling as Charlie came toward me. Now, when I hear palm leaves blowing in the wind, I break out in a cold sweat." He threw the dirt clod and turned to smile at me. "I remember thinking, 'I wonder what God looks like?'"

Four Hueys passed over us at about two hundred feet, and we stopped to watch. I was still fascinated that such awkward-looking craft could even become airborne, but Bob was trying to read the markings, wondering who was flying that day. They entered their landing pattern, their blades making the characteristic *whup-whup-whup* as they banked into their final turn. We could see the helmeted door gunners breaking down the M60s and stowing the ammo belts.

The lead Huey had a large number six painted on its belly—this was the brigade commander's ship. I asked why the commander didn't have a number one on his ship to show his rank. Bob said that VC snipers would shoot at the ships as they flew overhead, and they had learned to look for the number one, because for several years, that had designated the ships flown by command officers. The army had caught on and stopped using the number one on any of its choppers. Of course, choppers with the number six were being shot at a lot.

We started walking again as he continued his story. He told me that he'd had the gun barrel in his mouth when he heard Skip's Cobra (although at the time he didn't know Skip). There was a strange stillness in his voice as he talked about coming so close to blowing off the back of his head; it was like he was describing a scene from a movie or book. I couldn't see his eyes behind the sunglasses, but I imagined they had a thousand-yard stare.

He shook his head as if he were waking up. His voice regained its normal pitch as he explained that Skip had been returning from a mission when he had picked up the Mayday and started looking for the wreckage. "Man, that Cobra coming over the trees was the most beautiful thing I had ever seen. The VC opened fire as soon as they saw him, but he opened up with his miniguns. Didn't kill all of them, though, because I could hear some of them moaning and crying as their comrades carried them away to safety."

He stopped and turned to me. "You know, I believe we're all made in God's image and all that, but I was glad some of those bastards were dead, and I laughed when I heard them moaning. I was cheering and yelling and waving my good arm like I had personally won a battle." He turned toward me. "That's not right, is it? Gloating over someone else's death? I mean, what kind of Christian does that make me? Shouldn't I feel some remorse? But I didn't then, and I don't now." The day was headed toward dusk, and the rays of the sun seemed to ignite the airborne dust all around us, bathing us and everything around us in a strange rosy light. Bob glanced over at me. "That's what bothers me the most, I think."

"What?"

"That, well, that I don't feel anything anymore. You know? I mean, I don't want to sound neurotic, but it's like I've lost all feeling inside me. Like I've had to turn it off to get through this stuff, this war."

I didn't know what to say. I just shrugged and put my hand on his shoulder. We kept walking through the rose-colored dusk.

Bob was quiet for several yards but then said, "Anyway, Skip couldn't pick me up, but he kept moving around the area, shooting anything that moved. He had radioed my location and stuck around until the Evac chopper came. I asked the Evac pilot to get the Cobra pilot's name 'cause I wanted to thank him personally when I got out of the hospital." He chuckled. "So that's the story of how I got to know that foul-mouthed s.o.b. You think there's any chance we'll convert that guy?"

I smiled. "Don't know, but we'll keep trying, unless he *un*-converts us first." We walked for a few more minutes as the sun set. Bob went to his hooch and I went back to the chapel to write some letters. Wes met me at the chapel door; he was smiling broadly under his thick, black mustache.

"You look like the canary-eating cat," I said.

"I got orders late this afternoon. I'm going home a month early. I leave in two fucking days!"

"Great!" I yelled, and we both started jumping up and down, beating on each other's backs and shoulders.

Wes said, "Look. I've got some friends meeting me at the EM Club, and I came back to get you. Come on; I'll buy you all the Cokes you want. Man, am I going to get plastered! I figure you're the only one who will be sober in a few hours, so you have to stay and guide me back to my hooch, or I'll stagger into the fucking perimeter and get shot. All right?"

He was as bubbly as a schoolgirl as we partly walked and partly jogged over to the EM Club. He had never talked much in the few weeks we had worked together; now, he babbled like the proverbial brook about his car, his dog, his wife—in that order—and the great times he would have with them all.

We walked into the club and were greeted by seven or eight of his friends. They had pushed a couple of tables together, and the popcorn and beer were already flowing. I was still the newbie in the group, so I had little to add as they laughed, swore, and generally carried on about various things they had done during their tour. Most of them, like Wes, were "short," so they were looking forward to receiving their orders soon.

As the evening wore on, I tried to get into the spirit of the festivities, but my insides felt like they were turning into lead as I thought about all the days, weeks, and months that stretched before me. I looked around the club; like most buildings on the base, it was a large wooden structure with a tin roof, built over a concrete slab that served as a floor.

The overhead lights—high-wattage bulbs screwed into metal bowls and suspended by their electrical cords at intervals throughout the high-ceilinged room—cast sharp shadows throughout the room that was filled with smoke. Soldiers sat at the surrounding tables, drinking and smoking. Some were talking in a quiet, desultory way, hardly looking at each other as they spoke, almost as if their drinking partners were not there, and they were speaking to no one in particular. Others sat at tables and stared, glassy-eyed, at nothing and nobody, their trance-like eyes glazed over and lifeless. "It don't mean nothin'" was the commonly used phrase. They had made it their catechism, and it was etched on their faces.

I saw that look and heard that phrase often as I walked around the base. While on duty, the men moved slowly, shuffling their feet though the omnipresent dust, lethargic in the intense heat. Off duty, they moved a little quicker as they went to chow or to find something to drink. But as soon as they sat, they seemed to shut down some part of their brains, and their faces and bodies sagged into a stupor. They turned into nearly inanimate lumps of flesh, covered by olive drab.

As the days and months passed, I would see moments when those same inanimate bodies would suddenly flare up in anger, as if the inertia were a way of keeping a lid on a burning rage. A rage over what? "It don't mean nothin'," they would scream in unison as groups of them lurched out of the EM Club into the bleary night.

But here, tonight, with Wes and his friends celebrating his luck and their own "shortness," I could only partly share in the excitement, as my own tour had hardly begun.

I thought about Bob and his unending tour. The army needed every chopper pilot, so most of them spent their entire enlistment period, three years, in Vietnam. If pilots were injured, and many were, they were allowed time to recuperate then they returned to duty. For them, the only way out of Vietnam was to finish their enlistment, be so disabled that they could no longer fly, or be sent home in body bags. Far too many returned home in caskets.

CHAPTER 15

▼

There Ain't Nothin' Like a Dame

March

The attack in January was only the first of several. I could never get used to the unearthly wail of the attack siren as it started its ascending howl, or coming awake in my bunk in the early morning darkness, heart pounding and legs shaking as I groped my way through the darkness of the hooch, pushing and being pushed into the damp night, running for the bunker.

By late February, we were getting hit every third or fourth night. Men were injured in the attacks, and Chaplain Riggles and I began to make regular visits to the Field Surgical Unit that was located on the U.S. Air Force base about five miles from Can Tho.

Hospital visits were not new to me. My father had often taken me with him to visit sick and dying members of his congregation from the time I was twelve years old. (It never occurred to me that such visits were, well, unusual for a child.) Riggles had asked me about visiting injured men with him and seemed pleased when I told him about my background. He said he needed an assistant to accompany him on the visits and to take over when he was out of town, but none of his assistants had been willing to do more than drive him to the hospital—well, except one, he said. And that assistant assumed that hospital visits in a war zone were like visiting a sick aunt.

Once, in the ward for the seriously injured, Riggles leaned over a bed to talk to the badly injured man who occupied it—that was when he heard a soft sigh, followed by a thud. He looked around for his assistant but didn't see him. He asked a nurse, who happened to be passing by, if she had seen him. In a matter-of-fact voice, the nurse said, "I think that's him, lying on the floor." Riggles said that from that time on, that particular assistant would drive Riggles to the hospital and then head for the EM Club.

As a child accompanying my father, I had seen people in the last stages of terminal cancer, as well as victims of car accidents. I thought I knew what suffering looked like, so I felt undaunted by the prospects of accompanying Riggles.

The afternoon of my first visit, Riggles told me to alert Company Headquarters that we were leaving the base. Of course Company Headquarters was where Sergeant Thompson worked—when he was sober enough to report for duty. After my first, memorable encounter with Sergeant Thompson, I had usually managed to avoid him and deal with the company clerk, who was a Spec 3, like me.

I called Headquarters and, of course, Thompson answered the phone. I identified myself and told him what the chaplain and I were doing. Thompson said that I would have to have a weapon because we were going to be so far from the base, and that I would have to bring my young ass over to Headquarters to get it from him.

I hung up and told Riggles what Thompson had said and that it might take me a while to get the form from him to check out the weapon. Riggles understood; he said that Thompson had a strong dislike for anyone with a college degree—I had two—and particularly for chaplain's assistants with college degrees. Thompson figured a chaplain's assistant with a degree was a draft-dodging hippie who had one of the cushiest jobs in the army.

We were in the dry season, and the sun was very hot and the air was filled with dust as I walked the unpaved road to Headquarters. The building was one of the few on the base with air-conditioning, so it felt good to walk into the refreshing chill. Thompson glanced up at me when I entered, then returned to his work, stamping the date and time on various forms that were received in his office.

"I have a shitload of work here that I have to get through, so you're just going to have to wait," he said, stamping with extra force.

Chuk, thump.

"I understand that, Top Sergeant, but I think Major Riggles wants to go fairly soon," I said in my most pleasant voice.

Chuk, thump.

"You just stand there and shut your trap. I'll get to your stuff when I fuckin' get there." He glared at me.

Chuk, thump. Chuk, thump.

The phone rang. *Chuk, thump.* Thompson answered. He listened, and his face got redder. "Yessir," he said, and he hung up. *Chuk, thump.* He opened a desk drawer, pulled out a sheet of paper, scratched something on it, and then, in a very deliberate manner stamped it—*Chuk, thump*—while looking at me. In a very controlled voice, he said, "Here's the fucking form you need to check out your weapon."

"Thanks, Top Sergeant," I said, and turned to go. "By the way, where is the Weapons Room?"

Thompson didn't say a word but pointed out the window. *Chuk, thump.*

I checked out an M16 from the Weapons Room and the jeep from the Motor Pool. MPs saluted as Riggles and I drove through the gate and turned south toward the air force base. The military had paved the road with gravel because it was used as a major link between the bases, but successive rainy seasons had left it pitted and difficult to travel. "Driving" meant traveling at about twenty miles an hour while constantly swerving to avoid the worst of the potholes; it was the kind of road where driving under the influence probably would have been helpful.

Clusters of shacks lined the road. They were made from bamboo mixed with pieces of metal scrap, and roofed over with palm fronds. Several of the clusters of houses had sprung up around the areas where the American bases dumped their garbage; entire communities of people who had been driven from their farms and villages would be reduced to picking through the garbage for food.

We came up behind a garbage truck from the base. I noticed several Vietnamese nuns, wearing the black and white garb of one of the Catholic orders, riding in the back of the truck.

"What are they doing?" I asked.

"They work in one of the orphanages in town and have permission to ride our trucks to the dump. They salvage what they can and sell it on the black market to feed and clothe the children."

Being raised a Southern Baptist, it had been ingrained in me that the Catholic Church was the Enemy, but I doubted that many Baptist ministers would be willing to ride on a garbage truck for their parishes.

As we swerved along the shack-lined road, adults and older children would stop whatever they were doing and watch us with expressionless faces; the younger children continued playing. I wondered how old they would be before life wiped the play from their hearts as well?

We arrived at the air force base and were waved through the gate. We stopped by the MP post to check in the M16, and then drove to the hospital.

I had thought the army base was large, but the air force base seemed immense. There was a large PX that made the army PX look like a mom-and-pop store. Riggles pointed out the EM Club, barracks, and several other buildings, all made from cinder block, not wooden buildings like on the army base. Almost all the air force buildings, including the barracks, were air-conditioned. Air-conditioned! I almost regretted my decision not to join the air force; obviously, the air force was more civilized than the army.

The Field Surgical Hospital was a whitewashed, one-story, cinder block building that sat in the center of the base; it basically was a long hallway with different wings branching off to the left and right. A helipad sat near the receiving doors on one end of the building, allowing rescue helicopters to land very close to the hospital.

We arrived mid-afternoon, and Riggles and I both were sweating from riding in the open jeep under the blazing sun. I parked the jeep in the shade of the hospital and we walked the few yards across the hard, dusty ground to the white-painted metal doors.

We entered an air-conditioned world of long hallways with concrete floors, pale green walls, and white ceilings with fluorescent lights. But most of all—best of all—it was a world inhabited by American nurses.

I had been concerned about the soldiers I would see and had forgotten that hospitals had nurses—and that nurses were usually female, and American military hospitals would probably have American female nurses. I must have looked astonished, because Riggles clapped me on the shoulder.

"These are the first round-eyes you've seen for a while, aren't they?" he chuckled.

"Round-eyes?"

"That's what the soldiers call any woman who is not Vietnamese. I remember that I was kind of taken aback when I first walked in here. The nurses are one reason I enjoy visiting this place; makes my duties as a chaplain almost enjoyable." He sighed, suddenly shifting gears. "Also makes me miss my wife, so I don't allow myself to come unless I have wounded to see: helps keep me out of trouble."

We walked down the hallway and were passed by nurses dressed in fatigues, going about their duties. Some looked haggard; others looked fresh. I imagine they looked like the nurses you could find anywhere in the United States—all shapes, sizes and ages—and they all looked beautiful to me. I had grown used to the small, boyish shapes of the Vietnamese women who worked as hooch maids and bussed the tables in the mess hall, and I had forgotten how big and curvaceous American women were; even the small ones seemed larger than their Vietnamese sisters. Vive la différence!

Riggles found the head nurse, Major Marjorie Crawford, and introduced me to her. She looked like she was in her thirties. She was about my height, had a broad face topped by light brown hair (cut to regulation length), and had a no-nonsense look to her. She smiled and shook my hand, then got to work, telling Riggles that six men had been injured in fire fights in our region the night before; they were all army. Corpsmen had managed to keep all of them alive until they reached the hospital, but two had died on the operating tables. Two of the remaining four had less serious injuries and were stable, so they had been sent to Saigon; the other two were unstable and were in Ward A. I would eventually come to understand that Ward A was where the most seriously wounded were cared for, and that an injured soldier came out of Ward A in one of only two ways: on a stretcher bound for a hospital in Saigon, or in a body bag headed for Can Tho.

Riggles and I began the visit in Ward C. This was, he explained, for the men who had no injuries but who needed treatment for other illnesses that could not be handled by an infirmary. We walked through the swinging doors into the ward, and I saw what looked like a typical hospital scene in a open ward back in the States, except the patients—about fifteen in all—were young men. They all looked miserable. Several were asleep, while others read, talked to their neighbors, played solitaire, or just looked bored. Five or six had IVs attached to their arms.

Riggles began his rounds, introducing himself and me. He then began what I came to recognize as a standard list of questions: What's your name? Is there anything you need—toiletries, someone to write a letter home for you, reading material? Do you go to church? Would you like to talk to a minister, priest, or rabbi?

Most of the men had nothing in particular to say, so Riggles continued his rounds, making lighthearted banter. Eventually, he came to a young man who asked to talk to him, even before Riggles could begin his introduction. I continued making my way around the ward talking to the other soldiers, as Riggles spoke privately with the soldier.

Riggles and the soldier were still talking in quiet voices when I finished, so I stepped outside the ward to wait for him. Several minutes later, Riggles pushed through the swinging doors. "Poor kid," he said, shaking his head.

We went into Ward B, the ward for the men who had been injured and were stabilized. Some were waiting for transportation to other hospitals in Saigon or stateside for surgery, while others would recover enough to be sent to in-country areas for recuperation and relaxation—"R&R." I felt queasy for the first time as I looked at heavily bandaged arms and legs held suspended in the air by cables attached to stainless steel poles. The layers of white bandages made the appendages look immensely swollen and misshapened; some soldiers' heads and faces were wrapped with the bandages, giving them a mummy-like appearance.

I followed Riggles as he moved from bed to bed, going through his greeting ritual in a cheerful and quiet voice: He had a good bedside manner. But I was torn between staring at the grotesque shapes lying in the beds and averting my eyes. I realized I felt uneasy partly because I was afraid that I could be lying there someday, looking through bandages, wondering if my wounds would heal, wondering how badly scarred I would be.

I was pulled from those thoughts by a hoarse voice whispering, "Chaplain. Hey, Chaplain!" I had been called by a black man with both bandaged arms suspended in the air. His face remained expressionless as I approached his bed.

"Did you call me?" I looked at the medical chart at the foot of his bed. "Private Rollins?"

"Yeah. I have a favor, sir."

"Well, I'm not a chaplain; I'm just a chaplain's assistant."

"That's all right, man. I don't care if you're the chaplain or sweet Jesus hisself, I just want you to scratch my damn nose. It's about to drive me crazy." He moved his head, and I saw the short breathing tube sticking from his neck. A small rubber stopper sealed it, enabling him to talk.

"Sure," I said, grabbing a facial tissue from a box next to the bed. "I'll rub with this, and you tell me if I got it." I moved the tissue over his nose as he moved his head.

He sighed. "That's it. That's it. That's better than fuckin' a two-dollar whore. Sorry Reverend." As he let his head fall back on the pillow, he apparently noticed that I was glancing at his arms and the bandages on his chest.

"Mortar," he said. "Got me yesterday when Charlie hit us."

"Where are you stationed?"

"Can Tho."

"That's where we're from," I said.

He was having a problem swallowing. "Damn throat keeps closing up. They put this tube in my neck, said I was chokin' or somethin'."

"Is there something I can get you? Do you need a nurse?"

He moved his head and grimaced. "No. I knew better."

"You knew better?"

"Not to run. You know ..." He looked at me with bloodshot eyes. "They told me, 'We get hit and you're in the open, fuck the bunkers, roll in a ditch or somethin', but don't run.' 'You run,' they said, 'you get killed.'"

Riggles stepped to the other side of the bed, glanced over at me, and then turned his attention to Rollins. "This is Chaplain Riggles," I said.

Riggles smiled. "How're you coming, son?"

Rollins closed his eyes and tried to take a deep breath: "Not so good, sir."

"Is there anything we can do for you?" Riggles asked.

"The assistant chaplain here wiped my nose already. There ain't nothin' more you can do for me, 'cept maybe pray."

"I'll do that," Riggles said. "Would you like me to pray with you now?"

Rollins struggled to swallow again. "No. What you could do for me is get a nurse. I need a bedpan."

Riggles looked over at me and smiled. "Ted, please get a nurse for him."

I walked out into the corridor and found an orderly sitting at a nurses station. By the time I got back to the ward, Riggles was coming out the door. He had been told there was no one in Ward A, so we left the hospital and went to the EM Club for a soft drink before the dusty trip back.

Walking out of the bright sunlight and into the club was like walking into a cool, dark cave. We were sitting at a table, drinking sodas, when Riggles told me that I did okay, and he thought we would make a good team.

"You know that kid I talked to in Ward C?" he asked. "The one who wanted to speak to me privately? Seems he picked up a strain of syphilis that the doctors can't cure. They've told him drugs can control it, but he'll have it the rest of his life."

"Too bad," I said. "Is he contagious?"

"Yep. That's part of what makes it so bad; any woman he has sex with is liable to catch it, so he either has to tell her—and no woman will touch him—or keep quiet about it and spread it around. He said he's engaged to a girl back in the States, but...." He shrugged and turned his glass in his hands. "I feel real bad for the kid. He's just nineteen, just starting his life." He took a drink, then sighed and seemed to shrug off the mood. I finished my drink and we headed to the jeep for the bumpy ride home.

Back on base, I heard a rumor that the GIs had decided to boycott the cathouses until the girls told their VC boyfriends that the attacks were hurting business. It worked. The attacks stopped for a week.

CHAPTER 16

▼

Just Molly and Me

A Sunday in March, 7:00 AM

The sunshine was white hot, and the humidity made my clothing stick to me as I trudged into the air-conditioned Quonset hut that housed the MARS (Military Amateur Radio System) station. I was calling Karen on her birthday.

MARS allowed servicemen to make a personal phone call, free of charge, back to the States in case of a family emergency. If there was no emergency, you could put your name on a waiting list and, when your name came up, could make a free ten-minute call. I had waited three weeks for my turn, and it had arrived at long last.

The Spec 3 explained the system to me. The radio from our end sent out a beam to the United States, which was, hopefully, picked up by an amateur ham. If the "ham" felt so inclined, he (or she) would signal a response, and then would dial the long distance telephone number given by the military operator. Once the telephone was answered, assuming the other party was home, the telephone would be patched into the radio system, and the caller would be allowed to talk for ten minutes. Because several sets of dials had to be switched from "send" to "receive," whenever I finished saying what I had to say, I ended the sentence with "over"; Karen had to do the same

I waited anxiously as the Spec 3 went into the control room, closed the door, and began whatever arcane ceremony he had to perform for this magic to occur. I could hear him calling, "This is Roger Charlie Peter four-six-niner-five." He repeated the chant several times before the static crackle was broken by the sound of a man's voice responding in his version of the chant.

More minutes passed as the telephone number was given, then repeated, and dialed. The Spec 3 signaled me to go into the room that contained a chair and a specially equipped telephone. I sat down and waited. My heart was beating like it did on my first date; sweat beaded my forehead and began to run into my eyebrows. I had the telephone receiver pressed against my ear. The line was dead.

The Spec 3 had said he would not activate it until the call had been completed, but I kept wanting to yell, "The line is dead!" Instead, I waited. I watched a fly land on the wall in front of me. I noticed the swiss-cheese effect of the holes in the wallboard. Someone had drawn lines connecting the holes into crude dot-to-dot drawings of a penis aiming for a vagina. *Poor thing,* I thought aimlessly. *Always aiming in the right direction, ready for action, but can't move. Talk about frustration.*

Suddenly, Karen's voice was in my ear. "Ted? Hello, Ted? Oh, right. Over."

What I thought was: *I miss you so much! I couldn't wait to hear your voice. God, you sound wonderful. I'm about to go crazy. Is that really you?*

What I said was, "Hi. Yeah, it's Ted. Happy birthday. Uh, what time is it there? Uh, over."

"Oh, Ted. It's, uh, it's eight o'clock at night. I miss you so much. I keep reading about attacks in the Mekong Delta. Are you all right?" She started crying. Another silence. Then, in a shaky voice, "Over."

"I'm fine. I'm great now that I hear your voice. Don't cry. I'm okay." I started to choke up. "Over."

She blew her nose near her mouthpiece and almost deafened me. "I'm sorry I'm crying," she said.

"That's all right," I said, but she couldn't hear me.

She continued, "I'm okay now. Just a few showers there. Honey, I have something important to tell you. Over."

"Okay. Over."

"Honey, you know how we both thought I had the flu right before you went to Vietnam? Over."

"Yeah." *Holy smoke! What is she leading up to?* "Over."

"Well, that was actually morning sickness that lasted all day. Over."

"What? Over."

"Well, we're going to have a baby. Over."

My God! A baby? I might be killed any time, and she's having a baby? How could this happen? She'll be a widow with nothing to live on and a baby to raise. The "send" light was on for me. Between us, connecting us, sat God-knew-how-many people, listening to one of the most intimate and important moments a man and woman could share. Twelve thousand miles away, the woman I loved was waiting for my response to news that I was to be a father, and I sat in a small, hot room, stunned and speechless. The fly sat motionless: He was waiting, too. I said the first word that came into my mind.

"Congratulations. Over." *That was real romantic. The least you could say is, "I hope you'll both be very happy."*

"Ted, I guess this is real sudden for you. I've tried to hint at it in my letters, but I guess I'm not very good at hinting, huh? Over."

"I'm sorry. It … I'm just surprised. I had no idea. Are you feeling all right now? Are you going to a doctor? When did the doctor think the baby will come? I think I have military medical insurance. That ought to help with the bills. Have you checked on that? Hello? Karen, are you there?"

The voice of the Spec3 came over a small speaker attached to the ceiling of the room. "Hey, Bertson, you've got to say 'over.' Slow down, man."

"Right. Over."

The sound of Karen's laughter filled my ear. She sounded so good, so warm and alive. "Oh, Ted, for a minute there, I was afraid you were mad at me. The doctor thinks the baby will come in August. I'm fine. Mom and Dad are taking good care of me, and your folks are thrilled. Over."

The father is always the last to know. "I, well, uh, I'm just, uh …"

The Spec3 spoke again. "Sorry, man. Your time is up."

"Has it been ten minutes already? Karen, honey, I've got to hang up, or whatever it is you do with this thing. I love you and miss you. I want to hold you right now. You seem so far away. Over."

"I love you, too, Ted. And I miss you." I could hear the catch in her voice as she fought back the tears. "Remember what you told me once, 'I'm only a dream away.' I think about you all the time. I love you. Bye. Over."

"Bye. Over."

Just as I set down the receiver, I heard a woman's voice. I picked up the receiver again and said, "What?"

"I said, 'Godspeed, Ted.'"

"Thanks." Who was the woman who spoke to me? I never knew. I laid the receiver down, pushed the chair back, and stood up. My legs felt shaky. I had considered myself as good as dead when I had arrived in the war zone, and I had found some strange comfort—a kind of freedom—in that thought. Now I had a child on the way and a wife who depended on me to somehow emerge from this quagmire alive and reasonably intact. I couldn't let them down. *Tell that to the VC.*

CHAPTER 17

▼

Bombs Bursting in Air

March/April

As February drew to a close, the weekly routine of the chapel was well established. Wes had shown me the ropes and was spending most of each day lying in the sun getting his Depart En Route Over Seas (DEROS) tan. The "shorter" he got, the more nervous he became about being injured or killed. This kind of nervousness was so common that it was known as "short nerves." When guys started grumbling about leaving base or taking any kind of risk, even though they previously might have taken the same risks often, their buddies would nod their heads and say, "Just short nerves. It don't mean nothin'."

I had become familiar with Chaplain Riggles' easygoing ways and had grown friendly with Father Rooker, the Jesuit priest who was the Catholic chaplain. I had been raised in a strict Southern Baptist home and had learned that Southern Baptists intensely disliked Catholics. So I was surprised to discover that the Catholic "Enemy" I had been raised to fear turned out to be a nice guy.

I had been taught that priests, as representatives of the Church, were to be treated with suspicion, because they liked to skulk away with decent Southern Baptist children and turn them into Catholics. The only thing Father Rooker was interested in skulking away with was his nightly scotch-and-water on the rocks and a decent book. He was a thin, gangly man, with a gray fringe of hair that surrounded his bald pate. His face was long, and his army-issue glasses enlarged his kind gray eyes. He had a soft voice and a gentle smile, and was a vicious card shark.

I had lived a sheltered life, not having been allowed to play card games with standard playing cards, so Rooker and Riggles decided that they would teach me the way of the world. They began with some of the easiest poker games, but I was a complete incompetent and couldn't remember which combinations of cards were higher than any other.

They eventually realized that the only game I seemed able to learn was Hearts. I became a Hearts fanatic and probably played fifty thousand games during the year I was in 'Nam, but I could never beat Father Rooker. I once accused him of sprinkling our playing table with holy water before a game so he would have an advantage, but he denied the charge and said that God made priests good card players to compensate for denying them the pleasures of women.

The VC stepped up their attacks in March. U.S. forces had moved into Cambodia to try to interrupt the VC supply lines. Officially, of course, we were *not* engaged in military operations in Cambodia, but lo and behold, there we were.

News correspondents kept reporting otherwise, and, of course, Tricky Dick's guys were saying such reports were lies fabricated by a leftist-leaning press. But the VC knew we were there and had decided to wipe out the army base at Can Tho that provided air support for the invasion.

The enemy only used mortars in their attacks on the base because mortars were easy to smuggle into the area and set up. It was usually between two and four in the morning when the VC, wearing black pajamas, would walk into the rice paddies that surrounded the base and set up shop. They would site the first couple of rounds on some target in the base, and then fire the rest as fast as they could load them, because the lightships would take off and circle the perimeter looking for them. The VC never had to run because they were never fired upon. This was because each lightship, in addition to its regular crew, had a Vietnamese government official or military officer on board who was playing both sides of the fence. If the Huey pilot found VC in the field, he had to request permission from the Vietnamese official to open fire. The obvious intention of the policy was to prevent U.S. forces from shooting innocent civilians, but like all the other well-intentioned policies, it backfired.

The Vietnamese advisor would never give permission to fire, because, according to the advisor, the men running the field in the middle of the night were innocent farmers, checking their rice paddies. We speculated that the only time an advisor would give permission to fire was when the local VC were late with their bribe money.

The fellow I had met on my first hospital visit, Private Rollins, had been right after all. All the men I talked to who had been injured in mortar attacks had, indeed, been hit as they were running to the bunkers. Mortars were deadly if you were caught moving in the open, so the best defense was to fall where you were and lie flat, unless you were very near a bunker.

I discovered that it took a powerful mixture of courage and fear to force yourself to lie still as the mortars came toward you. The VC usually hit us in the wee hours of the morning when everyone who was not on guard duty would be sleeping. One night, maybe because the VC had decided to get a full night's sleep, they hit us early, around 11:00 PM.

I had been in a vicious game of Hearts with the chaplains at the chapel, and I was walking back to my hooch when the first round landed with a hollow "thump." I had already learned that the sound used in Hollywood war scenes— sharp explosions with cracking reverberations—was nothing like the real thing. The real sound was not a sharp crack, but a dull *thump,* like a large balloon exploding.

I froze for a moment, not knowing what to do. The second mortar hit close enough for me to see the flash. I hit the ground and tried to make myself paper thin. Images of the Plastic Man character in the comic books I read as a kid flashed through my mind; he could *really* make himself flat. My heart was thumping and every nerve in my body kept trying to get me up and running. Talk about a brain/body split! There I was on the ground, with my brain yelling, "Down! Stay down!" while adrenaline shot through my muscles and tried to get me to run. Meanwhile, there was another part of me trying to keep from wetting my pants.

The attack siren eventually went off, sending its high, nasal-metallic wail up and down the scale. We heard that sound often while our forces were in Cambodia. I hated that sound.

The following year, 1971, I would be back in the States, sleeping with my wife in a warm room while a January storm blew around our house. The wind, finding an opening in the old storm window of our room, would begin to howl up the scale like that damn siren, and I would be on the floor of our bedroom, trying to crawl under our bed, or yelling "Incoming!" and thrashing around until she could wake me.

But here in Can Tho, in 1970, I couldn't stop the shelling by simply waking up. Every light on the base went out. I lay in primordial darkness that was broken only by the flash of exploding mortars. The slightly cool breeze carried the acrid smell of gunpowder. Absolute silence filled the darkness between the exploding shells.

It was during one of these dark pauses that I felt something brush against my left leg—something warm and furry. *Hellfire! I'm about to be attacked by a giant rat!*

I heard a whimpering as the creature nuzzled under my arm, and I realized that it was a dog. Underfed strays were sometimes seen on the base. These were the dogs lucky enough to have escaped becoming served as the main course at a family meal while they were pups. One of these survivors now was trying to plaster itself to me for protection.

I circled the dog with my left arm and pulled him to me. It was comforting having this animal next to me.

The mortars started "walking" toward us, each explosion growing brighter and louder; the smell of gunpowder stronger. The dog was shivering, and I turned my head to talk to it, to tell it everything would be okay, but fear had a stranglehold on my throat, and all that came out was a constricted grunt. The dog licked my face, its soft, wet tongue leaving a trail of moisture that was cool in the breeze.

The shells moved closer. *Where are the lightships? Why isn't anyone firing from the perimeter? Somebody do something!*

Terror and anger took over; my brain stopped sending out messages that could be put into words. Blind rage tightened every muscle in my body, and I squeezed the dog to me as I willed myself to stay down. *Stay down!*

I would do anything to stop that shelling. If I could reach the enemy, I would shoot, slash, choke. I would do anything to survive. Survival was not a thought; it was a gut-wrenching emotion.

The shelling stopped as abruptly as it began. I heard the "whup, whup, whup" of the lightships as they arrived to scan the fields surrounding the perimeter; the VC had heard them, too.

It was still pitch black. The dog sensed the danger had passed and wriggled free of my arm. My arm felt like the muscles had cramped in that encircling position, and I wondered if they gave Purple Hearts for muscle spasms suffered during an attack.

The dog scurried into the night as the siren sounded again, howling the all-clear up and down the scale. I stood up and looked around in the darkness, listening for ... I didn't know what. Later, whenever I saw a stray in the compound, I wondered if it knew me. I wondered if it had any memory of the danger that we had shared.

I made it to my hooch and was glad I had been assigned to a ground floor—that meant the roof and the floor of the second story would protect me in an attack. I dragged my flak jacket and helmet from my locker and placed them under my bunk. That night, and every night I slept in that bunk, I recited a litany: *If we're hit, on the floor, under the bunk, helmet on, flak jacket on. Don't move!*

I would recite this over and over as I drifted off to sleep. From that time on, whenever we were hit in the middle of the night and I was sleeping in the hooch, I would be on the floor under the bunk, protected by my helmet and flak jacket, before I even woke up. It was a lullaby litany that would become so automatic that I would continue it several months after returning to the States.

As I surrendered to sleep on this night, I kept thinking about the dog. Two creatures had endured that night huddled together in the exploding darkness. Then we had gone our separate ways. One had learned he could turn to a human for comfort; the other had learned he could kill.

CHAPTER 18

▼

A Pretty Girl is Like a Melody

The attacks intensified over the next weeks. As the casualties mounted, so did our visits to the field hospital. Wes had departed weeks before for stateside, leaving me as the senior assistant. I even received another promotion to become an E-4.

Promotions were not complicated in those days. The enlisted man—me—was called before a board of two or three officers, often a captain and a lieutenant or two. My record was reviewed for recommendations from my supervisor—in this case, Major Riggles—and I was asked the question that I had been asked several times before: With a graduate degree from the University of Michigan, why hadn't I gone to Officer Candidate School (OCS)? The real answer was that I hated the military—the army, in particular—and did not want to stay one day longer than necessary, which would be necessary if I were an officer. But what I said was, "Sir, I was accepted into OCS, but I want to pursue a career as a musician and university professor, and I want to return to civilian life as soon as possible." The answer was both truthful and diplomatic and worked every time. I always got the promotion.

I was once told that I could be treated well as an officer or like scum as an enlisted man. What I did not say was that two years of being a scum was still better than three or four years as a low-grade officer.

Riggles would sometimes be called away on other duties, so he would ask me to go to the hospital in his place. By then, I had the drill pretty well down: Ask what I could do for the patient; get word to the rabbi or priest, if needed; and forward any requests to Riggles if there was something I could not handle.

Riggles had been watching my reactions on Wards B and C. I knew I had passed some kind of silent test when he told me we would visit Ward A together. He said he had debated whether to ask an assistant to go there, but he needed someone he could rely on to visit the men if he could not. I appreciated his trust but was apprehensive about going there; I was not sure how I might react.

We were in the jeep on our way to the hospital when he said, "Ted, I got word that a forward firebase to the west of Can Tho almost got overrun last night. They took a lot of casualties; at least six men were killed. The Evac choppers went in this morning under heavy fire and managed to get the injured out and over to the field hospital." He stopped, as if considering his next words. "I think you're ready for Ward A; at least, as ready as you'll ever be."

I looked at the shacks where children played, naked from the waist down, in the sandy mud. The sun was so brilliant that we were both squinting behind our dark sunglasses.

"I think I can handle it," I said with the optimism of youth.

I regretted those words as soon as the strong smell of the antiseptics assaulted my nose as we pushed through the swinging doors into Ward A. I stopped just inside the doors as I tried to orient myself. Wards B and C were large rooms, with vertical plywood walls that supported an inverted V-shaped metal roof. They could accommodate up to three parallel rows of beds, which were seldom curtained off, unless some procedure was being performed that might upset the men in the adjacent beds.

Ward A was housed inside the curved metal walls of a Quonset hut. White paint coated the walls, reflecting and diffusing the florescent lights so that the room had a soft glow. The ward was also narrower, with room for only two parallel rows of beds. Curtains on both sides of every bed concealed the wounded one from the other.

The head nurse had given Riggles a list of the men who were conscious and who had asked for a Protestant chaplain. He started down the walkway, looking at the ID cards pinned to the outside of the curtains.

The ward was quiet, except for an occasional comment exchanged among the staff. The curtains at the foot of the beds were partially open, making it easier for the nurses to look in on the patients. As I passed by one bed, I saw a movement—

a young soldier lay naked on the bed, propped up by pillows. His face was ashen, and his eyes were glassy as he stared at something he held in both his hands. At first I could not make out what he was holding because a doctor and an orderly, both wearing masks, hovered over his lower torso. The doctor was pouring a clear liquid over the injured man's hands, and the orderly sponged up the overflow.

Without thinking, I stepped forward for a closer look. The doctor stood up to wipe his forehead, and in that instant I saw what was the center of their attention. In his cupped hands, the injured man held a portion of his intestines. They were a grayish brown and smooth, and the clear antiseptic made them glisten in the light.

I turned away in disbelief and caught up with Riggles, who had found the man he had come to visit. My legs felt heavy, and the lights seemed to dim. I needed to grab something, to hold onto something, or I might fall over. I noticed a chair beside the man's bed, and I dumped myself into it.

Riggles whispered his introductions as I sat down. When he said my name, I tried to smile, but I was afraid to open my mouth. I told myself that I was *not* going to pass out. I took a deep breath, stood up on shaky legs, and looked at the soldier, named Wilson. A hoist-like contraption attached to the bed frame suspended Wilson's right arm. It was swathed from fingers to shoulder in gauze so thick and lumpy that it barely resembled an arm.

Wilson's head was bound like his arm, with loops of gauze covering a thick bandage over his right eye. The visible portions of his face were streaked with the remnants of pale yellow antiseptic, so his skin looked as if it was one large bruise.

Against my better judgment, I forced myself to move toward the head of his bed to stand opposite Riggles. I tried to listen as I focused on my breathing, and in a minute or so I felt recovered.

Wilson had been told his injuries, while serious, were not life-threatening. He was being evacuated to Saigon later in the day and wanted to let his wife and family know where he would be hospitalized. He was concerned that his wife might only be told he was wounded, and he didn't want to cause her undue concern.

"She's havin' our baby," he said, "and she's been havin' problems, physical problems, ya know?"

"I'll contact the Red Cross and get this to her right away," Riggles said. "You just concentrate on getting better." He patted Wilson's shoulder.

Wilson did not respond. His chin began to tremble, and a tear trickled from his left eye. He took a shuddering breath. "I thought I was goin' to die," he sobbed.

Riggles pulled out a couple of tissues from a bedside container. Gently, he wiped the tears from the soldier's face and then wiped his nose.

We stood silent as his emotions passed. Riggles occasionally wiped away Wilson's tears, and I fought back my own. I thought about Karen and the new life she carried. The loneliness I had managed to keep at bay swept back into me, reminding me of how much I had to live for, how much I loved her, and how easily all of that could be lost.

Eventually, Wilson sniffed loudly and took a deep breath. "I think I'll be all right now. Thanks, Pastor." Wilson turned his head toward Riggles, "Sorry, sir. I guess I forgot myself there for a second."

"That's okay, son. The reason for this," Riggles said, fingering his uniform, "is to get me right here." He patted the bed. "Besides, I've been called worse things than 'pastor.'"

Wilson tried to smile, but he winced in pain.

"I think we should go now. Would you like to have a prayer before we leave?"

"Yes, please."

Riggles said a short prayer, patted Wilson's shoulder one last time, and told him not to worry, that this wife would be contacted right away.

On the way out of the ward, I glanced toward the bed where I had seen the sight that had unnerved me. The bed was empty.

"Had a bad spell in there for a time, didn't you?" Riggles said as we stepped into the bright sunlight.

"Yeah. Sorry if I let you down. I—"

"Ted, no apologies are necessary," Riggles broke in. "The first time I went onto a ward like that was in Korea. I walked in, expecting to carry the word of the Lord to the dying, and the next thing I knew I was sniffing ammonia and looking up at a very pretty nurse. She was so pretty, it was almost worth the embarrassment and the bump on the head I suffered when I fainted." He smiled. "There was no way I could prepare you for what you might see. I still get squeamish, sometimes. You did just fine." He looked me over. "You think you'll be able to keep your breakfast down long enough to ride back to the base?"

"Sure. But you might try a little less weaving around the potholes, just in case."

The base kept getting hit, so Riggles and I were making lots of runs to the hospital. I never got used to the sights and smells that greeted me in Ward A, but with repeated visits, my reactions were dampened—although maybe "pushed underground" is more appropriate than "dampened." Seeing mangled soldiers dulled my sensitivity to some degree, but the sights would never be forgotten.

The first time I set eyes on Josie O'Malley was when I was coming out of Ward B. I ran into her, literally. She stormed out of the surgical wing across from Ward B, just as I pushed through the swinging doors. I had turned to say good-bye to one of the nurses and did not see O'Malley until we collided.

She fell back a step or two, and I turned to see who I had run into. Her eyes were filled with tears.

"Are you okay?" I asked, afraid I might have hurt her.

She shook her head and bit her lower lip. Time seemed to stop for an instant. I noticed the way her coal black hair, pulled flat against her head, reflected the lights in the corridor. Her almond-shaped eyes were dark, and the brows above them were as thick and black as her hair. She was almost my height, and in that instant, as we looked into each other's eyes, my heart stopped. I had never seen such a beautiful woman.

She muttered something about being all right and ran down the corridor.

At that moment, two other nurses came out of the surgical wing, their faces gray with fatigue. "She took that pretty hard," one said to the other, nodding in the direction that the almond-eyed nurse had taken.

The second nurse sighed and shrugged. "I'll never get used to it, either. Those children were so tiny. I thought we had a chance to save the last one."

They continued walking away from me, but as they turned the corner, I heard one of them say, "I hate this goddamn war."

I sat down on a wooden bench in the corridor. I had been feeling sorry for myself—I was missing Karen, trekking back and forth between bases, visiting the wounded, and seeing their suffering—but I would never see the horrors that the nurses and doctors saw every day in the surgical room. I wondered how they were able to withstand it, how they themselves would survive.

This had been my first visit alone. Riggles had been called to Saigon for the day, and had received word about wounded just before he left, so he sent me. There was no reason to hurry back, so I wandered over to the EM Club to have a Coke before the hot drive back to the army base. Stepping into the EM Club on the air force base was like entering a refrigerator. The army concept of ambiance stood out in stark contrast to the air force as well. Whereas the air force provided soft, indirect lighting to make the Club more inviting, the army's idea of indirect lighting was a naked bulb dangling from a single cord that swung in the hot breeze of an oversized electric fan.

It took my eyes a few seconds to adjust to the absence of glare as I entered the EM Club. I noticed a couple of air force medics I'd come to know on my frequent visits. I was on my way to join them at their table when a movement from a dark corner caught my eye. The almond-eyed nurse sat there, alone, a mug of beer resting between her hands.

I greeted the medics, Joe Wilson and Bill Avery, and was invited to join them at their table. After we exchanged gripes about the military, a form of pleasantry, it seemed, among enlisted men in every branch of the service, I asked about the nurse in the corner.

"Oh, her," Joe said, looking toward her table. "Easy on the eyes, isn't she?"

"Name's O'Malley. Lieutenant O'Malley. Haven't been introduced, so's I can't say I know her first name."

"Hear she's a pretty good nurse," Bill chimed in. "'Course, they're all pretty good nurses."

"She's been here a year or so," Joe continued. "Coulda DEROS'd outta here but keeps hangin' around. Maybe she likes the action. I think every swinging dick on base has wanted to fuck her, but she keeps turnin' everyone down, far as I know. Maybe she's a lesbo—who knows? She sure puts wood in my pecker. She's an officer, but I think she comes here cuz she's tired of fighting off the officers at the OC. Probably figures no enlisted puke would try hitting on her. Wouldn't stop me, though, if she even breathed in my direction."

"Joe, here, has trouble thinking beyond the three inches of his dick," Bill heckled. Joe nudged him with his elbow. "What Joe would like to say, if he could only get his mind to rise above his pubic hair, is—"

"Bill, here, is an educated man, like you, Ted," Joe interrupted, grinning, "so he can talk dirty and make it sound like he's saying something important."

"Since we're in the company of an assistant chaplain, asshole," Bill countered, "I thought we should try to clean up our act a little bit."

"I'm not an assistant chaplain," I said. "I'm a chaplain's assistant."

"Same difference," Bill said, taking a sip of his beer.

"Anyway, I couldn't help but notice her," I said.

"You and eight thousand other guys," Joe said. "Too bad she's such an iceberg." He glanced over at her. "Hard to believe."

I stayed for a few more minutes, just long enough to finish my soda. I had a hard time not staring at the lovely nurse who seemed so forlorn. I tried, without success, to follow the bantering of my companions, but I gave up after a few minutes.

Throwing my tab onto the table, I excused myself and strolled toward the door, hoping to catch O'Malley's eye so I could at least nod to her. No luck; she seemed mesmerized by the liquid in her glass.

Three days later, Riggles received word that a chopper had been shot down near the Cambodian border and a couple of seriously injured men were being taken to the hospital. He had another meeting, so he sent me on another solo visit. Father Rooker was off at another base but would be back in the early afternoon. I was to call him if I needed help.

Another chaplain's assistant, Henry Fuller, recently had been assigned to the base. I left Henry in charge of the office (a duty that, at mid-week, consisted of sticking around the office in case someone came to see the chaplain, drinking Cokes, and chatting with Ba Lin, the middle-aged Vietnamese woman who cleaned the chapel every day). I picked up a jeep, checked out a weapon, and drove to the main gate to find a convoy that might be headed toward the air force base. Except for the nighttime shelling, the region was quiet, but soldiers were discouraged from traveling alone.

I checked in with the MP on duty and gave my destination. I was, as usual, told to stay with the jeep, and they would wave me in to the next departing convoy.

As I waited, I was surprised to feel my pulse rise at the thought of seeing O'Malley again. *Horny as a bullfrog in heat,* I thought. I tried to picture Karen— to see her hair, her eyes—but the image of O'Malley kept intruding.

The drive over to the hospital was dry, hot, and very dusty. I was toward the end of the convoy of supply trucks. By the time I pulled into the air force entrance, I was covered with a fine layer of dust mixed with sweat.

I cleaned up as best I could in the latrine of the EM Club, and then made my way to the hospital. Keeping my mind on my business was difficult. I kept looking around, hoping to see O'Malley—but also hoping I wouldn't. What would I say to her?

I'll just get back in the jeep, go to the MARS station, and call Karen.

The head nurse, Captain Hauchsted, spotting me from the end of the corridor. "Specialist Bertson."

"Yes, ma'am."

"Is the chaplain here today?"

"No, ma'am. He was called away, so he sent me. Father Rooker is at the base, though."

"No time, Specialist." She looked at me carefully. "There is a young man in there," she said, pointing to Ward A, "who is dying. He insists on a chaplain, a Protestant chaplain."

"Ma'am, I'm not an assistant chaplain, I'm—"

"I know, I know, but you've had the training. You know the gobbledygook to say. You'll have to do."

"But—"

"You *will* give this boy comfort. He will *not* die alone. He wants a Protestant chaplain, and goddammit, he's going to get a Protestant chaplain. Do you understand me, Specialist Bertson?" Her jaw was set, and her eyes blazed; a mother protecting her young.

I swallowed hard. She didn't have the authority to order me to do what she wanted, as it definitely called for a chaplain. But she was a woman who would not be denied.

"I'll do what I can," I said.

Her face softened, and she put her hand on my shoulder. "You'll do just fine, Specialist."

She led me inside Ward A and said softly, "We've done everything we can. He survived the crash of his chopper, and then stepped on a mine on his way to the rescue bird. Lost both legs, lots of damage. We did everything we could. Everything...." She pointed toward the last bed on the right. "He's there. A nurse will be standing by."

My legs felt heavy as I walked to his bed. I steeled myself for what I might see as I pulled back the curtain at the foot of the bed.

A nurse with short blonde hair was adjusting the IV tubes and was quietly talking to him. She nodded to me.

"The chaplain's here now," she said. "I'll wait outside." She slipped past me and said quietly, "His name is Ryan White." She pulled the curtain closed as she stepped away. The little cubicle seemed to shrink. The light over the head of the bed was off, and the space was bathed in a soft, white light that filtered through the curtains.

Several blankets had been spread over the bed, and I shivered inwardly at the sight of the flattened covers where his legs should have been. His abdominal area was wrapped in bandages, and I could only imagine the appearance of his lower body. Yet from his upper chest and upward, he appeared to be a healthy, young, sleeping black man.

His eyes opened drowsily as I moved to the head of the bed. A radiant smile broke over his face, and his white teeth glistened as he smiled.

"Hi, there, Reveren'," he said slowly. He seemed to be having trouble forming words.

"Hi, there, Ryan." En route from the doors of the ward to his bed, I had decided that I was going to be whatever or whoever he needed me to be.

"Is my mother here?"

"No, not yet. She's on her way," I lied. I wondered if the chaplains lied to dying men. At that moment, his mother might have been doing anything, been anywhere, unaware that her son was near death. Would she torture herself with wondering about what she had been doing at the moment he died? Would irrational grief drive her to wonder if maybe, just maybe, she had been doing something else, perhaps he might have lived? Would she lie awake, trying to remember her last words to him?

"Is there anything I can do for you, Ryan?"

He raised his right hand slowly. "Would you mind holdin' my hand, Reveren'?"

I took his hand in both of mine and then began to softly rub his forearm.

"Momma used … tuh … do that. Feels … good."

We were quiet, and he seemed to doze.

"I have … things … to say."

"I'll listen," I said.

"I'm a Christian. B'lieve in Jesus. Be with Jesus soon."

"Yes, you will," I said.

His lips trembled and tears ran from his eyes. Then his eyes flew wide open. "I'm goin' to die. I don' wan' tuh die. Please, don' let me die. Please, please!"

I bent over him, trying to calm him. He threw his arms around my neck, pulling me down over him. Out of the corner of my eye, I saw an IV stand almost topple over.

His arms had been strong, but they shook now as he held me close. I moved so I was half-sitting on the bed and slipped my arms around him, under his shoulders. He lay his head against my shoulder and wept. His strength, like his life, was ebbing away. I cried, too.

It was not long before his breathing calmed and his hold on me loosened as he slumped back onto his pillow. I sat next to him, holding his hand. His eyes were closed.

"Ryan, can you hear me?" I asked.

"Yeah," he said in a whispery voice.

"Is there anything you want me to tell anybody? Your mother?"

He was still for a moment. "Singin'. Mamma sings."

"Would you like me to sing to you? Is that what you want?"

More stillness. "'mazin' Grace ...'mazin' Grace."

I bent near him and quietly sang, "Amazing grace, how sweet the sound that saved a wretch like me."

I heard a soft noise and stopped singing. He was trying to hum along. His face was peaceful, placid, as he lay there, humming tunelessly, his weak, breathy sounds breaking the silence. He was drifting off, drifting far away into his dream of peace, his dream of grace.

I kept humming that old hymn as I watched a man die. Did I believe the words of the song? It didn't matter. This man was dying, and I wanted him to leave this life with his ears filled with sounds of comfort and hope.

Minutes passed. He took a long shuddering breath, inhaling the antiseptic scents of the ward, filling his body as if grasping for one last moment of life before sinking into darkness. His face changed. Was it a grimace of pain or a smile of surrender? I will never know, for as the air left his body, he seemed to sink into the bed, to grow smaller before my eyes. His face went slack.

I heard the curtains part at the foot of the bed and felt a touch on my shoulder. I stood up in a daze with tears running down my face. Hands guided me through the curtains and onto a wooden chair against the whitewashed wall. My legs felt like lead. Far away, in the distance, I heard the quiet rustle of activity around Ryan's bed and the soft murmur of voices.

I felt someone standing next to me, and a woman's voice said, "He's gone." She paused. "You'll have to go now, Specialist."

"Okay. Sure," I replied, wiping my nose. She left to join the doctor and nurses working around Ryan's bed, and I stood to leave.

The ward seemed to have become much longer since I had first entered. I stepped into the busy corridor that I had traversed so often in the past weeks, but it felt strange, alien. The cinderblock walls closed in around me, so I looked for the nearest exit—anything that would lead me back into the bright sunlight.

Within moments, I was standing outside, hundreds of yards from the hospital, watching a warplane take off. A drainage ditch, bone dry, ran parallel with the runway. I plopped down on its edge.

The fighter roared away into the sky, its afterburners flinging the ship off the shimmering surface of the tarmac. Leaning back onto the sand and feeling the sun's heat pressing on me, I imagined Ryan's spirit slipping out of his body, sliding off into the void of eternity. Did he feel fear, sorrow, hope? Anything?

The fighter ascended, its roar diminishing to silence as the plane became a dark speck against the bright clouds. "God bless you and keep you, Ryan," I said to the empty blue sky. "May his face shine upon you and give you peace."

CHAPTER 19

▼

It Never Entered
My Mind

The feeling of floating, of disconnectedness, had returned. Fatigue hovered over me like a cloud as I drove back to the army base. I wanted to sleep, to fade out, and to be somewhere else. A voice inside me said I had better shape up; I had been in-country less than three months. The months ahead seemed to expand outward toward infinity, and I was already exhausted. I drifted through the rest of the afternoon with little to do.

After dark, Harry and I had been sitting on the low stone walls that flanked the dirt walkway into the chapel taking in a slightly cooler evening breeze that was passing through. The walls we sat on had been the idea of an enterprising lieutenant who—hoping to get on the Lord's good side—had rounded up some idle enlisted men and ordered them to build the walls. They used the same combination of cement and head-sized rocks that had been used as the base of the altar in the chapel. While the walls added some sense of permanence, they always struck me as a little incongruous, because the path between them was unpaved and the rest of the chapel was built of plywood and tin.

Harry and I talked about nothing in particular as we sat and smoked. Harry was from Chicago and had been drafted out of a small college in Illinois, where he had been enrolled for two years in a vain effort to avoid the long arm of the Selective Service. He had majored, he said, in Fucking Anything in a Skirt, while minoring in Alcohol Abuse, so his grades had not been high enough to warrant the prized S-1 exemption. He had somehow managed to get through Basic Training without winding up in the brig and had decided that, if nothing else, being in the army got his Republican parents off his back. So two years of military semi-captivity did have some reward. He had volunteered to be a chaplain's assistant on a hunch that anything to do with God and churches would probably not be too strenuous or dangerous.

The light from the inside the chapel spilled through the front doors and fell on the dust of the road as Harry was introducing me to the art of smoking cigars without inducing nausea. He was well into his third cigar and second can of beer—beer that was illegal outside of the EM Club—and I was struggling to keep my first cigar lit. A convoy of trucks clattered around the corner, interrupting the quiet.

There were four of them, military ambulances about the size of UPS trucks, moving with headlights off. We heard the low rumble of their engines before they appeared, moving in tandem down our street, an olive drab cortege. They came to a stop at the morgue across the street. Harry noticed them first, in mid-draw on his cigar.

"Shit," he muttered, spitting in the dirt.

"What?"

"Meat wagons." He spat again, and then took a swig of his beer.

The driver of the first vehicle walked into the morgue and re-emerged moments later, followed by several men. The drivers and passengers from the other trucks had dismounted and were opening the back doors of the trucks. Stretcher after stretcher was pulled from their innards, each stretcher bearing a formless mass covered by a shiny, black plastic bag.

"Looks like they're bringing in a goddamn squad," Harry muttered.

The men were silent and efficient, and in no time the trucks were emptied and their doors shut. Then they rumbled off into the night. The large crosses on the trucks' sides, which were bright red in daylight, looked like ugly, black plus-signs in the semi-darkness as they passed us.

"Wonder where they're from?" I said.

"I heard we've gone into Cambodia," Harry said, his words muffled by the cigar clenched between his teeth. "Heard it at the EM Club."

"Oh."

We fell silent as we watched the rank cigar smoke curl into the humid night air. After a few more drags on his cigar, Harry swigged down the remainder of his beer and then threw down his cigar butt.

"I'm turning in," he called over his shoulder as he sauntered off toward his hooch.

I finished my Coke, crushed the rest of my cigar into the sand, and then sat alone in the semi-darkness for several minutes, contemplating the lives lost in the past few hours. Just that morning, those men had been healthy and whole; now, all that remained of them was shrouded in black plastic in the coolness of the morgue.

Having given up on sleeping much in my hooch because of incessant noise, I had started using the assistants' office as my sleeping quarters. I had not cleared this with Riggles, figuring it was easier to apologize later than to ask permission beforehand and open unforeseen cans of worms. Nor did I mention it to Harry or the other chaplains. Bed checks were only made after an attack, and I could make my way to the hooch in plenty of time, as it was only a five-minute shuffle from the chapel.

My nighttime routine was simple: Set up a cot, close the windows, fill the air with an aerosol to kill the mosquitoes, and then close the door for a few minutes to allow the spray to do its work. I would head for the nearest latrine (the one in the Infirmary, next to the chapel) while the spray settled. Once back to the chapel, I would turn out the lights, enter the office, close the door again, strip down to my shorts, turn on a table fan that would blow across my sweating body, and fall into bed. It didn't occur to me to question the healthfulness of inhaling the fumes that still filled the room; if an autopsy had been performed on me, the examiner might have found my lungs encrusted with Raid.

I had trouble getting to sleep that night as I thought about all those bodies that had been carried into the morgue.

I wonder if we'll get a call from the Air Force Hospital tomorrow? I thought as I drifted off. We did.

Riggles was still away, and Rooker had flown to another outpost, so he was gone for the day. So when the message reached the chapel that more injured men were in the hospital, it fell to me to go back.

Ryan's death was on my mind as I entered the hospital. I shook it off, promising myself to mull it over later. By the time I arrived, the most grievously injured had already been sent to Long Binh. Those men who remained were mostly unconscious—from drugs, fatigue, or shock—and of those who were conscious, few were awake enough to talk.

I wandered over to the EM Club. *Too bad I don't drink*, I thought. *I bet a beer would taste good right now.*

The Club was cool, dim, and quiet, as usual. I ordered a Coke and took the bottle and glass over to a corner table to be alone. My time with Ryan was gnawing on me. Maybe someday I would find a way to come to grips with what had happened; maybe I could come to accept my own mortality. Or maybe not.

I was called from the recesses of my emotional turmoil by a woman's voice. "Mind if I join you?"

O'Malley stood next to my table, holding a beer. I started to stand, but she waved me off as she pulled a chair away from the table and sat down. "I heard you had a rough time in there yesterday." She nodded in the direction of the hospital.

"Yes, ma'am, I did." I took a sip of my Coke. "I felt helpless."

She nodded again, this time in understanding. "I feel like that a lot of times." She took a sip of beer.

We both stared at the table for a moment.

She cleared her throat. "I hear you're a chaplain's assistant. Is that true?"

"Yes, ma'am," I replied. "It sounds like you know the difference between a chaplain's assistant and an assistant chaplain."

"Mm-hm," she responded. "Do people mix it up a lot?"

"Most of the time," I answered.

The silence between us was awkward.

She peered across the table, reading the nametag sewn on my fatigue shirt. "Well, Specialist Bertson," she said, "I just wanted to let you know that the nurse on duty thought you did a good job in a tough situation."

I lowered my eyes. "Thank you, ma'am. I didn't feel very helpful at the time. But I appreciate your saying so."

She leaned forward. "Look, Specialist, the real reason I wanted to talk to you was to apologize for running into you the other day and then walking off without saying anything. You probably don't even remember that, do you?"

Is she kidding? I would like to do it again, just to get that close to her.

"Yes, ma'am, I kind of remember it. That's all right, though. You looked like you had a lot on your mind."

"I did. I usually hold up pretty well, but I let it get to me that day." She gazed into her glass.

I saw her starting to sink into the pit she had been in that day. "Could I ask what happened? It's none of my business, but sometimes talking about things can help, ma'am."

She was quiet for a time. Then, after taking a drink, she said, "We get a lot of children in here—kids caught in the crossfire or who stepped on a mine. Things like that. That day—the day I ran into you—we had six brought in. One of our gunners had opened up on them in a rice paddy. The pilot went in to confirm the body count and when he saw the mistake, he called it in. At least he had the guts to admit what had happened. Lot of pilots don't." She gazed at the door. "An Evac chopper brought them here."

She took another drink, holding the glass with both hands. Setting it on the table, she looked at it intently; I guessed it was to avoid making eye contact. Her voice was calm, and her face was placid as she said, "We worked on them for five hours; lost them all. Never knew their names, their ages, nothing. Just six little bodies." She took a drink. "But hey, we're the good guys. We did our best. Mistakes happen. When those kids died, we put them in body bags and sent them back. Someone called the ARVNs to come and haul them back to their village."

When she said "ARVNs" I was reminded of what a strange term that was. The acronym stood for "Army of the Republic of Vietnam," but when I first heard it shortly after I had arrived in-country, I thought it sounded like something I might have heard on *Star Trek*.

She pulled me back from my short excursion when she took another sip of her drink and then said, "They call that 'collateral damage.'"

"What?" I asked. "What does that mean?"

"Civilians. Civilians are called 'collateral,' like money you have in the bank. You kill civilians; you've damaged your 'collateral.' Nice term, huh?"

I looked around to see if anybody had overheard her, but the only other patrons were three guys talking at a table on the other side of the room. They had eyed us a few times, as very few officers—female officers, in particular—ever visited the EM Club, but they were ignoring us now. None of the officers I knew ever criticized the military in the presence of enlisted men. She was treading on thin ice. I had the hunch she might have had more than alcohol before she showed up at the Club.

"Maybe we should go, ma'am," I said. "Maybe take a walk."

We walked together into the humid, late morning heat. Once outside, she seemed to change, as if a wall had dropped between us. "Well, Bertson," she said, glancing again at my nametag, "nice talking to you. Maybe I'll run into you on some of your other visits."

"Yes, ma'am. I'll look forward to that."

She walked toward the hospital, and I headed for the jeep. I left with jumbled feelings: Ryan's death, O'Malley's sudden appearance, and the peculiar course of our conversation, had left me feeling strange. I wanted to get back to the place I knew. I fell in behind a convoy heading toward Can Tho, and for the first time I felt as if I were going home.

CHAPTER 20

▼

Let Us Break Matzo
Together on Our Knees

I was sitting in the chapel office, working on the final pages of the chapel inventory, when Rich and Chaplain Mosher pulled up in their jeep. I was grinning as I met them at the door—Rich always had an air of unexpected surprise around him, like the scent of good cologne. This trip was no exception.

Ira settled into the vacant office in the chapel, and Rich and I went off to get haircuts—Rich decided that since he needed one, I should have one, too.

We went to a Vietnamese barber who had set up a small shop on the base. I had discovered the shop in January and found that the barber did as good a job of giving the short "white wall" cuts as any military barber. It cost a few *piaster* (which GIs referred to as "p") at the Vietnamese place, and the military barbers were for free, but the kind of doting attention we received was worth the small fee.

Rich took one look at the place and decided to ask for "the works." I had seen the term on the hand-printed cardboard sign, but my timid streak had been greater than my curiosity, and I had been hesitant to ask about it.

"Exactly what are 'the works'?" I muttered to Rich as we sat waiting for our turns.

"Hell if I know," he said with a shrug. "It just sounded like something I'd like to try." He leaned toward me. "Did I tell you about the bath and massage I had in Long Binh?"

"Nope."

"I checked it out with some of my informants before I went, and they said it was worth the experience. So I went over there about a week ago. Ira and I had been out on the road, and I was pretty tired and dirty and needed a bath anyway.

"So I go in, and this beautiful Eurasian girl wearing a kimono meets me at the door, takes me to the back, and points to a kind of a large bathtub filled with water. God knows how many GIs had been in it, so I say no way. She gives me this smile, unties the kimono, and drops it on the floor. Then, naked, she steps into the tub and stands there, waiting for me to get in. I don't care how many GIs have been in the water. Hell, I wouldn't have cared if piranhas were in the tub; I was on my way.

"So I get in, facing her, and she turns me around and sits me down."

"Was the water hot?" I asked.

"I didn't notice, nor did I care," he said. "I was too busy doing research."

"Research? What kind of research?"

"For my newest get-rich-quick idea," he said.

"What's that?"

"You realize that by telling you this, you and I become partners, and you can't share this secret with anybody?" He raised his dark eyebrows, waiting for my confirmation.

"Okay," I said, offering my hand. "Deal." We shook hands. "So, what were you researching that's going to make us rich?"

"Porno. You and I are going to write porno novels, like Harold Robbins, and make millions," he said. "Look, you like to write; you told me so at Fort Hamilton."

"Yeah."

"But you've led a sheltered kind of life, being a PK and all," he continued. "Plus, you tend to live in your head—you know, thinking great thoughts and hearing great music. Stuff like that."

"Well, kind of, I suppose," I said. Rich and I had engaged in several long, philosophical talks back in Brooklyn, about our lives and plans for careers and what we wanted to do after we got out of the army. We had decided, at one point, that had we lived in the Middle Ages, I would have made a good ascetic and he, a good rollicking monk. He had been quite taken with the concept of a free-living monastery for Jewish monks.

"Aw, come on. You know that when we talk about physical awareness, you're only aware of feeling from your shoulders up and a small area to your south. Everything in between is a void for you," he said.

"What do you mean 'small area'?" I asked.

He ignored my question and continued. "Me, on the other hand, I like everything from the middle on down."

The barber gestured for him to come to the chair. It was not necessary to give military barbers your tonsorial preferences because all cuts were short, with almost no hair left on the sides—the look known as a "white wall." Civilian barbers working on military bases were no exceptions.

Rich plopped himself into the chair and pointed to the sign that read "the works." The barber smiled and nodded vigorously.

Rich talked as the barber worked. "So there I am, sitting in this dirty water, and this beautiful, naked woman starts washing me. She starts from the top of my head and works down. She gets down to my man-center—"

"Your 'man-center'?" I snickered.

"Yeah. You ought to remember that term for our book," he continued unabashed. "So, she gets to my man-center and doesn't even slow down. She gets out of the tub, comes around in front of me, and just grabs me, like she's going to suspend me from the ceiling by my dick. I fall back into the tub as she yanks me up and starts cleaning that thing with a vengeance. Felt like she's using Boraxo—no, worse: felt like I was being circumcised again."

I cringed.

"She lets go, and I'm trying to stand up to see if my woman thriller is still there—"

"Woman thriller?"

"I hope you're writing this stuff down. I mean, who wants to read something like, *She looked at his erection and gasped,* when they could read, *His woman thriller was standing tall*?"

I laughed. "You know, if we're going to make our stuff semi-legitimate, like Henry Miller tried to do, maybe you had best leave the writing to me."

"Hmm. Legitimate pornography—now there's a thought," Rich said.

The barber whisked away the cloth he had draped over Rich to catch the hair clippings, walked behind him, and grabbed Rich's head between his hands. He gave a quick twist.

Rich yelped but then moved his head gingerly. "Hey, that feels better."

The barber smiled and nodded. Then he reclined the chair until Rich was semi-prone and proceeded to crack joints, starting from the shoulder and moving to the elbow, to the fingers, and then to the knees and ankles. Rich jumped at most of them but declared that he felt better afterward. His session ended with the barber's slapping fragrant cologne on his face.

Rich stumbled out of the chair, declaring that "the works" was worth the extra few p's. I decided to forego the joint-popping pleasure and stick to a haircut.

"So, tell me what happened with your massage," I said as the barber began snipping.

"Oh, that," Rich said, his mind elsewhere. "She washed me until she was satisfied that my love wand didn't look diseased, and then she threw me a towel, wrapped one around herself, and started working me over.

"She kind of put her fingers together, like this," he said, entwining his fingers, "and worked up and down my back and shoulders. Felt pretty good, too." He moved his meaty shoulders around. "Then came the pièce de résistance—she walked up and down my back, barefoot."

"How was it?"

He leaned back against the wall. "It was great. There's something about an almost naked, barefoot woman walking up and down your body that defies description." He sighed. "I would have come all over the table, except I was so relaxed that my loins refused to cooperate."

"Your 'loins'? I haven't heard that term for a while," I said.

"Back a couple thousand years ago, we Jews thought about our loins a lot. Then the *goyim* started following a minor rabbi who had up and got himself crucified, and voilà—we had lots of other things to think about, like staying alive."

"Are you back on the Crusades again?" I asked.

"Yeah. I told you—I'm going to prove that the Jews won the Crusades." He crossed his arms over his ever-increasing girth.

"As I remember, the Jews didn't fight in the Crusades. I told you that," I said.

Rich nodded his head. "I know you said that, but that's my point: They got the *goyim* to do each other in. Then they could take over their land again. Of course, it took a few centuries for that to happen."

The barber whisked the cloth away. "Woks?" he asked, a big smile on his face.

"Woks?" I repeated.

"Woks," he said, pointing to the sign above the door.

"No. No, thanks," I said as I paid him.

Ira was waiting in the doorway of the chapel when we strolled up. "Did you ask him?" he asked Rich.

Rich slapped his head. "Nah. I was too busy defending my thesis about the Crusades. Ted," he said, putting his hand on my shoulder, "we've come to ask if you would like to attend Passover services in Saigon."

It was a completely unexpected invitation. For a moment I was speechless as I looked at both of them.

"I've already talked to Riggles," Ira said. "He's okay with it, if you are."

"Well, sure. I'd be honored."

Two days later, I was in Saigon. Rich had reserved a room for me in the American Hotel, a place built by the French that might have once been quite lovely. By 1970, though, it was a five-story, pastel colored building that had not been cared for during the several decades of fighting. Paint was flaked off most of the outside walls, and the building, which housed Americans and other non-Vietnamese nationals, had been the target of random rifle fire on several occasions. Large sections of stucco had fallen off the outer walls as well.

An eight-foot wall of dark green sandbags, topped by concertina wire, surrounded the building. Armed guards flanked the entrance, rifles at the ready. It was depressing.

I arrived in the afternoon—I'd had a chopper flight from Can Tho, followed by a dusty bus ride from Long Binh to the hotel. I was sweaty and covered with a layer of grit, a state I was quite used to by now, so the first place I headed to in my room was the shower. The plumbing looked like it had been manufactured during the Ming dynasty, and from the high-pitched squeaks it made as I struggled to turn it on, it had not been used since. After great gurgling and banging, rusty water dribbled from the spigot into the cracked porcelain tub. The tub, which once had been white, had turned a gritty gray that I didn't want to look at too closely. As long as nothing seemed to move of its own volition, I figured the space was clean. Besides, at least the water had a semi-steady trickle. Back at the base in Can Tho, we had already had the first of several water shortages, so I had gotten used to sponge baths, using one-pound coffee cans half-filled with water.

My room had chartreuse walls and a high ceiling. Chunks of plaster had fallen from the ceiling, revealing the lath beneath. A fan hung in the center of the room, its blades turning slowing in the sluggish air. Back in the States it would have been a miserable room, but it was better than my space in the hooch in Can Tho, so I had no complaints.

After my quick sponge bath, I pulled on my olive drab boxers and flopped down on the sagging bed. Flopping was not the best way to enter the bed, though, because large clouds of dust (and, I assumed, microscopic dust-lovers) erupted from the bedding. I watched the minute debris floating in the rays of the late afternoon sun and felt it settle, at last, on me. I was in the throes of sneezing and coughing when someone began banging on my door and shouting, "Military police! Open up!"

Although I was pretty sure it was Rich, I was unnerved—until I opened the door and saw his goofy grin. A voice several doors down the hallway shouted, "Shit! Muthafucka," and slammed the door.

Rich scooted past me into the room. "Looks like someone was a little concerned about the MPs showing up," he chortled.

"It's stuff like that that's going to get you shot someday," I said, shaking my head.

"So, how's my favorite goy?" Rich said in his best Yiddish accent.

"Hot and tired but rarin' to check out this burg. Is this going to be like New York?" I asked, harkening back to our many explorations of that city.

"No," Rich said with a tinge of nostalgia. "Nothing can compare to that metropolis of the senses. We'll probably get some offers for various kinds of services here, but you'll just have to ignore them." He looked around my room. "This is bigger than the room I'm sharing with Jason."

"Who's Jason?"

"He's another assistant at Long Binh. I wasn't sure you'd be able to make it, so he and I reserved a room several weeks ago. Pretty cheap." He walked over to the window that overlooked the street. Sunlight poured in the window, casting him in silhouette. His baggy fatigues and untucked shirt with rolled sleeves made the lines of his long, dark shadow appear lumpy and indistinct. After glancing out for a few seconds, he leaned out and pulled the slatted wooden shutters closed. "You have to be careful, being in a lighted room after sunset. Snipers, you know."

"So," Rich said, rubbing his hands together, "here's the plan for the evening: a four-course dinner in a charming French café, followed by appropriate dessert crêpes, cognac, and exquisite Cuban cigars. Scantily clad round-eyed dancing girls are extra."

"There's really a place like that left in Saigon?" I asked, feeling skeptical.

"Sure. Follow me," he said as he headed out the door.

Mess Hall No. 3, at the 64th Battalion Headquarters, Long Binh, was just like all the others in South Vietnam. Rich drove us over in his borrowed jeep and feigned surprise as he parked near the mess hall. "I could have sworn La Chez Français was here last week. Somebody has moved it," he said in dismay.

After the filling and almost tasteless meal, we got back into the jeep and drove to what had once been an elegant hotel district. Four five-story hotels rose above the low-slung homes that surrounded them. After years of war, the stucco walls of the four hotels had long ago shed their colorful paint, and the façades of the homes were pockmarked from bullets and the pounding by the seasonal rains.

Garish neon signs, some missing letters, flashed such names as "—otel Tropic—l" and "Sai—o—Hot—l." Rich led the way to the Hotel Tropical as I gawked at the sights. Up and down the block, lights were turned on as the sun set. While the lighting was a far cry from anything that could be found in a small American town, it looked like Las Vegas when compared with the relative darkness of the base at Can Tho. Civilians riding bicycles and motor scooters moved around and between military vehicles of all sizes and descriptions. There were military personnel in fatigues mixed with civilians in native attire. Military police in white helmets, both U.S. and Vietnamese, strolled along both sides of the street. I had forgotten what it felt like to be in a city without barbed wire and guard posts, and having so much activity all around me. My nerves were on edge. I took a few deep breaths, and the feeling went away.

We went through the wooden doors of the hotel. What had once been a reception area with a registration desk had been abandoned and was now used for storing bicycles and motor scooters. There was no carpeting; the cement floor was exposed. For unknown reasons, sections of the cement had been removed, revealing the dirt beneath and leaving holes that made walking treacherous.

Rich was huffing as we climbed the broad flights of stairs. He pointed out that some of the rooms had been turned into living quarters for families who had come to Saigon from the surrounding countryside. A row of rooms on the top floor had been preserved as bedrooms. I noticed several couples—American soldiers and miniskirted Vietnamese girls—coming and going to the rooms.

"These are the 'ten-minute' rooms," Rich observed.

"Ten-minute rooms?"

"Yeah." He pointed up the last flight of stairs. "The girls bring the guys down here from the rooftop bar, where we're going. The guys fork over the 'p' and get to fuck the girls for ten minutes or until they come, whichever occurs first." He started climbing the last flight of stairs. "Of course, most of these guys have been out in the bush, so it takes about thirty seconds for them to go from arousal, to a twenty-one-gun salute, to collapse of the Empire." He stopped suddenly and grabbed my arm. "Listen, is our deal still on?"

"Which deal?"

"We look out for each other? No one surrenders to the siren call of the flesh?"

I pictured the soldiers in the hospital beds, suffering from incurable VD. "Yep. The deal's still on."

The stairwell peaked above the floor of the roof; otherwise, rainwater would pour down it in monsoon season. We stepped down into another world.

The roof of the hotel, as was the custom in that balmy part of the globe, served as an open-air bar. A section had been covered over with a brightly covered material to keep the rain off the patrons, but at least half the roof was open to the sky. A few scraggly potted plants dotted the edges of the area.

The breeze—hot, humid, and laden with dust at the street level—seemed cooler and cleaner at this higher elevation. On one side, a rock band, all Vietnamese men, performed a pretty good imitation of various rock pieces that were popular in the States. Although their instruments were amplified, the noise was kept at a tolerable level.

Strings of colored lights were hung around the periphery and crisscrossed over the roof, casting a soft, multi-hued glow over the milling patrons. Indirect lighting bathed the bar and the mirror-lined wall behind it, giving a soft glow to the area. About a dozen young Vietnamese women moved within the confines of the waist-high wall that surrounded the roof. They worked the soldiers who sat sullenly at the rusting tables, attempting to lure them to the hot, dirty rooms on the lower floor.

Two "tea" girls—the appellation soon becoming apparent—approached us as soon as we arrived, touching our arms and shoulders, urging us to buy them drinks.

"The idea is that for every drink we buy," Rich explained, talking over the tops of their heads as they hustled us to an empty table, "—which, by the way, will be overpriced, so watch yourself—we buy them the same. Of course, theirs will just be tea."

The tiny girls had almost pushed us into empty chairs by the time Rich ended his short discourse on the workings of this particular bordello. The girls never used their Vietnamese names; the one who considered herself my date was called "Kim."

"You t'irsty, GI, need drink," she said. "You buy me drink? Yes?"

I looked over at Rich for guidance, but he was involved in a similar negotiation with his girl.

"Dear Mrs. Bertson," the letter from the Pentagon began. "We regret to inform you that your husband, Specialist 4th Class Ted Bertson, has been killed in Saigon. His

body was found in a seedy hotel beside Miss Kim, a notorious prostitute, with whom he was about to engage in sexual activity."

"I, uh," I stammered.

Rich spoke up, "Jesus, Ted. It's okay to buy them drinks. We have to, if we want to even talk to them. That doesn't mean we're going to fuck them."

Kim looked back at me. "Yes?"

I nodded.

"Wha' you wan' drink?" she asked. The strangeness of the situation seemed to slow my brain as I tried to understand her pidgin English.

"Coca-Cola," I replied.

"Get it in a bottle with the cap still on," Rich instructed. "Have them bring it to the table with an opener."

"Sure, sure," Kim said to Rich's suggestion. She said something to her colleague, who was sitting beside Rich. They both giggled, and then Kim ordered for all of us.

Kim moved closer, and I fought the urge to back away; I had never been around a woman who was so sexually aggressive. She then said something to the barmaid, who brought us our drinks. The barmaid looked a little younger than either of our girls; she wore little makeup, and the effect was that she seemed less hardened.

I tried to pay for our drinks as discreetly as I could, without flashing a wad of piasters that I had bought in Can Tho in preparation for my trip. Buying "p" at black-market rates, which were almost double what the army was giving for exchanging military scrip, had given me a twinge of guilty pleasure; I had broken the law and gotten away with it. Following Rich's advice, most of my illegal loot was in a corner of my suitcase in my room, wrapped in a pair of underwear.

Rich's date, Karen (which she pronounced "Kalen"), and Kim had a brief exchange that gave me time to look closer at Kim. When she had first approached us, I had noticed her long black hair and her red dress. The dress was very short and hugged her slender body, and its scooped neck revealed the tops of her small breasts. With her reddened lips and false eyelashes, she fit my image of what a prostitute would look like. It was an image she had cultivated for her GI clients; without the makeup, she might have been an attractive young woman.

Kim and Karen didn't stay with us very long when they realized that we just wanted to talk. They moved on, looking for better possibilities. Rich saw a couple of acquaintances and sauntered off to talk to them. Carrying my bottle of Coke, I wandered over to the edge of the roof.

The hotel provided a good vantage point to see a large section of the city. This was Saigon at night, the Paris of the Orient. The full moon was up, and its soft light washed over the city, making it seem almost beautiful. In the distance, the moonlight sparkled off the river that snaked its way through and around the town. The river looked inviting, until I remembered that it was the main sewage system for several million people. I had seen children playing in that water as Rich drove us over a bridge en route to this hotel, and I wondered how many would die from the diseases borne in its inviting coolness.

The party on the roof was picking up. Rich was dancing with one of the girls as the band performed a Beatles tune. Leave it to Rich to be the only GI on the dance floor. He was holding the scantily clad girl close to him, and I wondered how much he had paid her to dance with him.

The other soldiers moved around the area. Some had their brimmed "boonies" hats hanging down their backs by a cord around their necks; others, like Rich and me, had baseball caps stuffed under our belts. Shirts were untucked with sleeves rolled up; it was time to relax. Some of the GIs stood at the bar, talking to the girls, bargaining for their services. Others, who already had struck their bargains, were heading to the rooms downstairs with their arms around their girls. It was the free enterprise system in action.

A girl approached me. She wore a very short, very tight pair of black hot pants, a looser-fitting print blouse, and black, open-toed stacked heels. She smiled, revealing uneven, yellowed teeth behind dark red lips. Her path ended right in front of me, close enough that I could smell the scent of cloves on her breath.

"Hello, GI. Me number-one girl. You like me? No?"

"Sure, yes, I think you're very pretty," I stammered.

"You, me, go boom-boom. Yes?" Before I could respond, she continued, "Me cherry-girl. Clean. No give you Mr. Drip."

The strangeness of the situation, my discomfort, the girl's pidgen English—all of it conspired to make me feel almost giddy. And "Mr. Drip"? I tossed down some Coke, hoping to stifle the laugh. It didn't help; instead, it made me choke.

I went into a coughing spasm and began beating on my chest. The girl said something in Vietnamese and walked away in a huff as I struggled to regain my breath.

I was still trying to steady my breathing when a commotion broke out at the entrance. Several of the girls had surrounded a newcomer—a somewhat taller girl—and were making angry, high-pitched sounds. A man, wearing a white shirt and black pants, appeared from around the corner, speaking in a loud, angry voice. The girls fell silent and walked away. The girl they had surrounded stepped into the multicolored light and a hush descended over the patrons. The band in the corner was playing a piece with a slow tempo, good for dancing. The newcomer wore a short, tight dress similar to others in the establishment, but she carried herself differently, more erect. Everything about her carriage spoke of elegance, even though she wore the same cheap clothes.

"Officer pussy," a soldier on my right muttered to another. The woman walked to an empty table, without looking around, and sat down. The white-shirted man stepped to her table and said something. She nodded without meeting his eyes.

The sound rose to its former level. Several soldiers eyed the lone woman and made comments to each other. Guttural laughter followed, but no one approached the table. She looked even more out of place than I felt as I strolled over to her table.

"Can I buy you a drink?" I asked. She didn't respond. I decided to adopt the pidgin English of the other girls "You want drink?" She seemed to consider my offer and then nodded. The barmaid appeared with an unopened bottle of Coke for me and a shot of "whisky" for her. I sat in a chair next to her.

I'd never had the occasion to talk to a prostitute before, so I was at a complete loss for words. I asked the first dumb question that popped into my head: "Do you live in Saigon?"

She threw me a puzzled look, and in that moment, I understood why the other women had not wanted her there. She was stunningly, naturally beautiful. It was obvious that she came from mixed parentage because her features showed the best of both cultures. Her nose and lips looked Caucasian; her black eyes and hair, high cheekbones, and slanted eyes spoke of her Asian heritage.

The puzzled expression faded, and her face became a frozen mask. I was groping for something to say to this stunning creature, but it was usual for me, when I was with a beautiful woman, to either babble like an idiot or lurch into bumbling silence. This time was no different.

"I wish I spoke your language," I said.

"I speak yours," she said in accented English.

I put my bottle down. "You speak English?"

"You Americans do not think a 'gook' can speak your language," she said flatly. Her voice was lower and mellower than other Vietnamese women I had heard.

"That wasn't what I meant," I replied. My Midwestern liberalism was a bit offended. "I mean, most of the girls here speak pidgin English, but you're fluent."

She sighed. "Yes." She took a drink of tea and put the glass down decisively. "Seven dollars," she said.

"Seven dollars?"

"Seven dollars for fifteen minutes—after I wash you. I will give you head, or you can come in me. No rough stuff. Okay?" she said.

Having no experience in these matters, my brain was about four sentences behind her.

"No, wait," I sputtered. "I don't want to have sex with you." That was a lie, of course. At that moment, having sex with her was what I wanted more than anything. Her presence and the lightly scented perfume she wore was enough to get my testosterone flowing. I tried to clear my mind. "I just want to talk to you, that's all."

"Sure, GI. Just talk, no sex," she said cynically. She studied me for a moment. "Seven dollars, fifteen minutes of talk."

I pulled out my piaster.

"The piaster are for here, GI," she said, indicating the bar behind us. "For sex or talk, it is seven dollars, military scrip."

I told her to wait, and I looked for Rich. He was having a one-sided discussion with a girl who sat looking at the milling solders, as if she was wanting to escape the incoherent babble coming from Rich.

"You think you would consider walking up and down my back for a fee?" he was asking as I approached.

"Rich. Sorry to interrupt. I need seven dollars." I was embarrassed to be asking for money.

He looked around me to where the Eurasian girl sat. "Ted, maybe we should be going." The concern was clear on his face.

"It's not that way," I said, more embarrassed now. "She won't even talk unless I pay her in scrip."

"So, what is it you're so hot to talk about?"

"I don't know, exactly. I guess she's aroused my curiosity."

"You sure that's all she's aroused?"

I saw a soldier at the bar eyeing her, checking her out. "Look, it's okay. I just want to talk. Do you have it or not?" This was feeling stranger all the time. Why was I so set on spending time with her? My hands felt clammy.

"Just like all *goys*," he said, pulling out his wallet. "You only think of us rich Jews when you need our money."

"Here," I said moments later, back at our table. My hand shook a little as I took a swig from my Coke bottle.

She picked the money up and tucked it between the swell of her breasts. I had never envied military scrip until that moment. She started to stand up.

"Where are you going?" I asked.

"Downstairs. That's what you want, isn't it?"

"No. I said I just wanted to talk to you."

"Why?" she asked, sitting down hard.

I looked at the Coke bottle and shrugged. "I don't know, really."

"Do you think you are in love with me? That you can take me away from this life?" Her voice was tinged with anger.

"No. I just want to talk, to try to understand—"

"Why a beautiful girl like me is a whore? Is that what you want to know, GI?"

"Why are you so angry at me?"

Seconds passed as she looked at me, as if she were trying to see inside my head. Then her shoulders slumped, and she sagged back into the chair.

The man in the white shirt was glancing at her from his position behind the bar. I waved to the barmaid and ordered more drinks.

"How old are you?" she asked.

"Twenty-four." Suddenly, that sounded ancient.

She looked at me again, a softer look. "I am twenty. If I live to be twenty-four, I shall look like an old woman. He will drive me from here." She looked around, settling her gaze on the white-shirted man. "This place that I have fallen to. I will be useless to him; no man will want me." She sipped her tea. "And if the war is over and all the GIs have gone home, then the VC will send me to the country-side to work as a slave on a farm."

"Why would they do that?"

"Because I have consorted with the enemy, and because I come from the wealthy, ruling class, like the leaders who destroyed this country." Her matter-of-fact voice pricked me like small darts being pushed into my skin. Until this moment, I had never met a person who had no hope, no future. I was peering into a void, a bottomless black hole, and if it scared me, what must she be feeling?

"What? How?" I asked.

Her eyes softened a little as she looked at me again. "You are different, aren't you, GI? Why do you want to know?"

"I come from a sheltered life. Do you know what I mean by that?"

"Not exactly."

"I mean that I have been spared many bad experiences. My parents are not rich, but they have made sure that I have been taken care of. But I know that if life had taken a couple of other turns, I could be—"

She leaned forward on her elbows. "Fucking me right now?"

"No, that's not what I was going to say, exactly." I leaned forward, reaching for her hand, but I stopped myself. I could feel myself being seduced into her wretchedness.

She gazed into the distance, and the hard lines on her young face softened some. "It has not always been so with me. My mother comes from a wealthy family; she was very beautiful, more beautiful than I could ever hope to be." She touched her face. I realized at that moment that her accent was French. And she confirmed it for me. "My father is, was, a Frenchman, an officer in the army. When the French were driven from my country, he would not go because he loved my mother, and she would not leave her family. Also, they had married. I had been born, and Maman was expecting again. He had many contacts with the government. They protected him, and he made them rich as his business grew."

"What did he do?" I asked.

"As women, we did not ask too many questions, but I think he was in the business of importing and exporting. We were very wealthy. I had French tutors and went to school for a year in Paris." She looked around the setting on the rooftop. I could imagine her comparing this to her time in Paris. She looked into her glass, and I glanced over to the white-shirted man. He was becoming concerned that we were just talking. His money came from drinks and his girls, and I was taking time with one of his hot, new moneymakers. To mollify him, I ordered another drink, even though I had not finished my Coke. This conversation was getting expensive.

Her voice was soft and hard to detect as she continued her monologue. "In the dry season of 1965, four men came to our villa. They cut the throats of our guards and burst in as we were having dinner. Maman screamed, but Papa told her to be quiet, to not show fear. He kissed me, my brother, and my sister, and he embraced Maman, telling her to contact a friend in the government.

"The men ordered us outside. Papa begged them to leave us alone, but the soldiers were indifferent. I recognized one of them—Xuan, a boy I had known at the catechism classes. I asked him to tell me what was happening. He would not look at me." Her voice took on a sense of urgency. "We had a beautiful palm tree in front of our villa. It had been there many years and was very tall and very round. They tied Papa to the tree. Xuan … he held Papa's head so he could not move it. The other three men pushed Maman to where Papa could see her. Then, two of them held her arms as the other cut off her hair." She looked at me. "Do you know why Vietnamese women have long hair?"

I shook my head.

"It is, as you Americans say, our 'crowning glory.' No man of taste or wealth will look at a girl who does not have long hair. Girls with short hair live in the country and work on farms. Their skin is dark and hard from the sun, not soft and pale like a girl from the city. Maman's hair was very beautiful," she said, almost wistfully. She swallowed hard as her eyes welled with tears. "After they cut off her hair," she said, her voice flat, almost dreamlike, "they tore off her *ao dai*— her dress—and pushed her to the ground. Then each man raped her. One man would hold her arms so she could not fight, but she did not struggle." A tear fell onto her arm. She looked at it blankly.

"Papa begged them leave her alone, to do what they wanted with him. But they did not listen. When the three men were finished with her, the leader spoke to Xuan. He glanced at me. The leader called his name. He let go of Papa and went to where Maman lay looking at up the sky; then he raped her, too.

"When Xuan was done, the leader spoke to him and handed him a pistol. Xuan said something, and the leader struck him. Xuan then walked to my father and shot him in the head."

She was so spiritless that I shivered. She continued, as if she were describing those horrors from a great distance. "The leader came for me. I was holding my sister and brother, trying to shield them. I wanted to run away, but I knew they would shoot me if I tried. Xuan called to the leader to stop, and fired the pistol when the leader did not stop. The leader stood for a long time, looking at Xuan, and then he signaled the men to go."

She shrugged again, as if the story she had just told meant little to her. Had it been an elaborate lie, a way to win my sympathy, or was she so used to trauma that it was just one of many horrors she had endured?

"The rest of my story is nothing. I found employment with the Americans because I could speak Vietnamese, French, and English, but they would not pay enough for me to care for my mother and sister and brother. I did not want to use the black market, but I had to. I sold our possessions, and we moved to a small cottage on the land Papa owned.

"Your fine American officers who worked at the Embassy offered me *beaucoup* money to sleep with them. I knew my beauty was much admired, and my family needed the money. I consented. I was of seventeen years when your Texas president visited—"

"President Johnson slept with you?" My naiveté was showing.

She looked at me as one looks at a child and then continued. "After him, I became the bedroom companion for visiting generals and ambassadors, until last year, when a general who had used me became ill with syphilis. The Americans' own doctor checked me regular to make sure I was clean, but the general was sure he had caught it from me. I was fired from my job. Then I became the property of a junior American officer."

"Hold on. What do you mean by 'property'?"

"My father owed much to a Vietnamese merchant. When I lost my job at the Embassy and no longer was given gifts by the important American men, I could no longer pay my father's debt. So he sold me to an American officer who wanted a girl."

"Jeee-sus," I muttered.

"About a month ago, the American officer came home with two friends, also officers. They were drunk." As she took a sip of tea, her hand shook. It was the first sign I had seen that she was able to feel any emotion. She took a breath. "My officer, my owner—"

"You don't have to talk anymore if you don't want," I said. She looked like she was starting to crumble.

She grabbed my hand, hard. An angry glint was in her eyes. "I will tell you this because you said you wanted to know, GI." She released my hand. "Don't you want to know that your officers raped me again and again, until I was bleeding? That my owner threw me into the street? That he said he was through with me because he was going home to the States?"

Her voice had risen with anger. The soldiers and their girls were looking at us. The white-shirted man stepped from behind the bar and was heading in our direction.

He came to our table. "She give you problem, GI? I make her go with you." He grabbed her wrist.

"No! Leave her alone!" I was surprised at my vehemence.

He released her and said something to her in Vietnamese. He sounded angry. She lowered her head in submission as she answered him. He turned to me. "You pay her only talk, GI? Why you not go fuck? You no like girl?" He waved his hands in disgust. "You talking done. No more talk. You pay, you fuck her, or go 'way."

I felt an arm reach across my shoulders, pulling me away. Rich, to the rescue. He dragged me to the edge of the roof, next to the wall.

"I can't take you anyplace," he said. "Here you are, an assistant chaplain, consorting with whores and pimps." I didn't appreciate his attempt at humor just then and told him so. He backed away. "Come on, Ted, I'm just doing my job, following our agreement. You have to admit that it was looking rather tense there for a minute—you and the pimp arguing over a girl."

"We weren't arguing. We were—oh, I don't know what we were doing." I kicked the wall.

I looked over to where she had been sitting. Another soldier had moved in. Rich was talking to me, but I couldn't hear him. She was leaving with the soldier. He had his arm around her, propelling her toward the steps. Before passing through the door, she turned and looked at Rich and me; her face was beautiful and blank. I shivered in the heat of the night.

Later, as I fell asleep in my room, I thought of all she had been through and wondered at her strength. She was like her nation: beautiful and devastated. As I dropped off, I whispered, "God, what have we done?"

Passover in Saigon. The sound of those two words and the cultures they represented made a strange combination: Passover in Saigon. The service was held at the American USO, a haven of Americana for soldiers like me. The building was a large, three-story building that rambled away from the busy street that it sat facing. It also had an unaccustomed airiness about it since a Viet Cong had seen fit to blow a massive hole in the roof with a mortar round.

The hole allowed the large room where the service was to be held to be completely open to the broiling sun. It would have made it very uncomfortable to sit and partake of the various traditional dishes that accompanied the ceremony, had not some clever person found a parachute to drape over the opening. The parachute happened to be yellow, so it cast a bright yellow glow over all the surfaces and personnel beneath it.

Chairs surrounded the long tables in the room. In front of each chair, plastic plates, bowls, and metal utensils were in readiness for the hungry hoard of Jewish men—and a couple of women—who were to partake of the feast.

I told Rich that I felt like a gentile spy and had no idea of what to expect.

"So, you've come to see if we really do eat the Holy Host after we've pricked them to make them bleed," he said gleefully.

"I'm a Southern Baptist, remember?" I replied. "We don't have no truck with them thar Catholic superstitions."

Rich hitched up his pants. "Just watch me, kid, and I'll show you what to do. Nobody messes with no friend o' mine," he said as he swaggered into the room.

More than two hundred people had filed into the yellow light-filled room and had taken their places. We stood as Rabbi Mosher and another rabbi led in the prayers of thanksgiving, and then the congregation sang and sat down.

The meal began with—what else?—chicken soup. Rich and Ira had overseen the preparation of the soup to ensure it was kosher, and Ira had offered the appropriate blessings while ignoring the looks of the Vietnamese cooks. After the soup, I had my introduction to gefilte fish and matzo.

"Ira and I got this straight from the Jewish Care Packages that he requested. Gefilte fish and matzo: What else could an Orthodox Jew wish for? Even Ira, though, has said that he's not sure he will ever be able to eat either one much longer. Some days, that's all he has to eat." He grinned at me. "Did I tell you that water buffalo, correctly slaughtered and prepared, is kosher?"

I swallowed some fish. "Yes, you have, a couple of times."

"You just have to be sure to cut its throat just so," he said, slicing the air, "and then hang the carcass upside down."

"Rich, you've told me this already. I'm having enough trouble getting this fish down."

He looked at me more carefully. "You're looking slightly jaundiced. You feel okay?"

"Of course I look jaundiced. You look jaundiced; everyone under this parachute looks jaundiced!" I said.

"Yeah, so they do." He gazed around the room and wiped his hand across his face. "I'm pretty tired, I guess."

"How come? Did you go out again after you got me back to my room unscathed?"

"Nah. I went to the room Jason and I are sharing. I thought I should write to Bobbie."

"How's she doing?"

"Okay, I guess. You know, we had less than a year of married bliss before Uncle Sam yanked my butt over here. Great guy, Uncle Sam. Anyway, I was in the middle of a letter to Bobbie when Jason shows up. He has a hooker with him. She was kind of pretty but not anything like the girl you met.

"This pissed me off. Here I am in Saigon, and my best friend is back in his room, licking his wounds from a close encounter with Susie Wong."

I cringed at the memory.

"So I'm looking at either wandering the city alone, where I'll probably get killed by a ten-year-old sniper, or telling this asshole to go somewhere else where *he'll* probably get killed by a ten-year-old sniper, so I'll have *that* on my conscience."

"Is this what they mean by Jewish guilt?" I asked.

Rich frowned. "My friend, the goy, makes jokes now. Just eat your matzo and listen. So Jason says, 'I don't mind if you stay. Hell, you can even watch if that gets your rocks off.'" Rich shook his head. "That Jason, he's such a *schlemiel.*"

I couldn't stop myself. "Did you know your East-coast Jewish accent gets more pronounced the longer you're with Mosher?"

Rich threw up his hands. "He's a linguist now!"

"I'm sorry; I keep interrupting. I'll be quiet and eat my yucky Jewish food." I stuffed some matzo into my mouth.

"So, ask me what I did," he said.

I shook my head.

"Ask me, already," he commanded.

With my mouth still full of food, I muttered, "I said I wouldn't interrupt."

"You aren't interrupting; you're asking me a question that I asked you to ask me," he said with exasperation.

"Okay," I said. "I'll ask. What did you do?"

"I took notes," he said.

"Took notes?"

"For our best-selling porno book, remember?"

It was about then that Ira tapped on his glass to get people's attention. He then began reading, in Hebrew of course. I enjoyed being a part of an ancient celebration that was being celebrated all over the world, even if I couldn't understand anything that was being said.

After the celebration, Rich and I wandered back into the large entranceway that led into the reception area. I had a few hours before I had to return to Long Binh to catch a flight, so we debated about how to spend the time. Rich was describing what transpired between Jason and the prostitute the night before when Ira emerged from the crowd. He had an attractive, dark-haired woman with him, and he had been looking for us.

Her name was Ellen Lake, and she worked as a correspondent for the *Christian Science Monitor*. She was Jewish—which is why she attended the celebration—and had wanted to meet some other Jews. "There aren't a whole lot of us in Vietnam, you know," she said.

After introductions, Ira excused himself and Ellen, Rich, and I went to the lounge area for drinks. We went to the bar and ordered our drinks, then found a table. Although the lounge was on the same floor as the large room where we had the celebration, its roof was intact. It was nice to be back in a room where the lighting was normal.

I mentioned this, and Ellen said she had been in Saigon when the USO was attacked. "A lot of journalists hang out here when we're in town. We're not the most popular people with the military, as you can imagine," she said.

"The first reports said the entire USO was destroyed. One of my friends said that he knew that the military wanted to make our lives miserable in Saigon, but destroying our watering hole crossed the line," she said with a smile. "We were relieved when we realized that the roof of the dining hall was all that was destroyed. When they hung the yellow parachute, we dubbed it the "Jaundice Room."

She took a drink, then said, "What the military forgets is that the Monitor has the policy of trying to find positive information about whatever is going on. By "positive," we mean what *really* is happening. What pisses the government and the military off is that they prefer to *tell* the public what is happening, and there are times when reality contradicts what they say."

"In other words, you catch the military telling lies and they don't appreciate that," Rich said.

She nodded. "That makes being a woman and a journalist in a war zone pretty intense at times, especially since it is a testosterone-driven, hierarchical military system I have to deal with," she said.

She looked at me and smiled. "Ted, besides being a reporter, I'm a Jewish woman which means I ask a lot of questions. So, are you Jewish? You don't look Jewish."

We all laughed. Rich jumped in. "No, he's not Jewish yet, but we're working on him," he said. He proceeded to tell her that he was a Renaissance historian and I was a classically trained singer. He told me later that he did this because he didn't want such an attractive, smart, worldly woman to think she was dealing with run-of-the-mill, eighteen-year-old dolts.

"A real musician?" she said. "I was a music major before I switched to journalism. I studied the piano until I realized that there were a lot of starving pianists out there, and I wanted something where I could make some money."

That led to us talking about our favorite music and favorite composers. She accompanied singers when she was piano major, so she knew some of the vocal repertoire as well.

Rich, looking bored, excused himself to talk to someone he had noticed in the lobby. After he left she said that we might have been boring him. I agreed. "But you're the first musician I've talked to in a couple of years, so I couldn't help myself. It's lonely here for many reasons, but sometimes I miss being around classical music and musicians most of all. Its like my soul dries up without music," she said. I told her that I felt the same.

We talked almost non-stop for the next hour about music, writing, her experiences in the field, and what we wanted to be doing several years in the future. I mentioned Karen and our unborn child, and she talked about the lonely life of a globetrotting journalist.

She was visiting Can Tho, she said, in about a month, and asked if she could look me up when she was on the base. I told her to just ask for directions to the chapel; it was the only one on the base.

We said our good-byes, and as I watched her leave the building, I thought about how nice it would be to see her again in Can Tho. Then I went looking for Rich, and found him having an animated conversation with a middle-aged woman. They were in the "Jaundice Room." The parachute that covered the room was slowly rippling in the breezes, causing darker shades of yellow to mix with the brighter yellow. The darker shades moved randomly, making it seem that the room itself moving. Rich and the woman looked like they were underwater on a sunny day.

Rich noticed me, made a few more gestures with his hands, and then shook hands with the woman. She went through a doorway that led to the kitchen and Rich met me at the entrance of the room.

"That was Irene. She runs the kitchen here," he said. "She wanted my recipe for chicken noodle soup. Actually, I think she wants my body, but I thought we would start with the recipe and see where it progresses."

I knew that Rich viewed all talk between a man and a woman as being about two things: food or sex—in his case, sometimes both. So when he looked closely at me and said, "You and Ellen seemed to hit if off very well," I knew what he was implying

"She's a smart and very interesting woman," I said, ignoring his implication. We started walking toward the front of the building. There was a check-in counter there, and a storage room where I had checked my duffle. I had brought it with me from the hotel when I checked out.

"Ha!" he said, clapping his hands together. "I knew it. So have you two arranged a rendezvous?

"Rich, not everything is about sex," I said. "But I might see her again if, *if* she comes to Can Tho."

A big grin spread over his face. "You dog, you!" he said and patted me on the back. I shrugged. There was no way I would convince him that our intentions were perfectly innocent.

I retrieved my bag and he took me to the airport where I would hitch a ride back to Can Tho. On the ride, he finished telling me about his study of Vietnamese foreplay—there was not much beyond cleaning the man's genitals, it seemed—and how we needed to incorporate it into our best-selling porno novel.

It felt like a long ride. What none of us could possibly know was that Ellen's life would soon change forever, and I would never see her again.

During our conversation, she had said in passing that she was visiting a base near the Cambodian border the next day. She had heard rumors that we had invaded that country, but the government was covering it up, so she wanted to get closer to see for herself. The next afternoon, she and a photographer were traveling by themselves in a jeep near the Cambodian border, and they were captured by VC.

Six weeks later, long after the date of her proposed visit to Can Tho had come and gone, I was sitting in the chapel reading an old copy of *Time* magazine when I came across the story that related the capture of Ellen and a photographer who accompanied her. I felt sick at the thought of what might have happened to her, of the atrocities she might have experienced before she died.

From then on, I read all the magazines I could find, looking for any word of her fate. Late in the summer, news came that she and the photographer had been released unharmed. When the VC had discovered that they were journalists, they had been handled with care and taken up and down the border of Cambodia and Vietnam to see the Vietnamese side of the war.

Upon their release, Ellen and the photographer met with other journalists in Saigon and declared that the United States was wrong to stay in the war and should leave Vietnam to the Vietnamese. The story was printed in newspapers and magazines around the United States, and the government in Washington had the military ship her and the photographer out of Vietnam as soon as possible. The story the military put out was that she was taking a well-deserved holiday to recuperate from her horrible ordeal.

But on this day, as I flew back to Can Tho in a military transport, I was in a reflective mood. I thought about the conversation with Ellen, and looked forward to seeing her again in Can Tho. I remembered the sights and sounds of the ancient Jewish celebration and the strangeness of the setting.

I also thought of the beautiful prostitute I'd met and the tragedy of her life. At one point in our brief conversation, I had asked her why she continued to do what she hated. She had looked at me impassively and said, "So my sister will not have to."

As I sat rocking in the bowels of the plane on the flight to Can Tho, a verse of scripture came to mind: "Greater love hath no man, but that he was willing to lay down his life for his friend." Sometimes, dying is the easy way out.

CHAPTER 21

▼

Safe in the Arms of Jesus

I had not seen much of Skip or Bob for several weeks. I pulled guard duty with certain regularity, and when I saw a Cobra's scarlet tongue streaming death from the sky to VC on the ground, I would wonder if it was Skip. Cobras, according to local gossip, were the helicopters that the enemy feared the most. They would come diving out of the sky, their miniguns throwing out their six thousand rounds a minute.

Bob, the Huey pilot, would wave as he drove his jeep to the airfield on the rare occasions I saw him on base, but he didn't have time to stop. Something big had been going on for several weeks, but although I had heard some rumors about action in Cambodia, I assumed they were just the usual scuttlebutt.

Early on a Saturday morning, Chaplain Riggles walked briskly into the chapel. "Ted, get over to Armory and pick up your gear. Be sure to take lots of extra ammo. We're leaving from the airfield at zero-nine-thirty."

As I drove to the Armory, I wondered what was up. I was used to picking up an M16 and flak jacket, but why the need for extra ammunition? My recently eaten breakfast turned to lead in my stomach as I reminded myself that, in spite of all my efforts to forget, I was still in the army in a war zone. I had gotten used to guard duty, with the dampness, mosquitoes, elephantine rats, and various creepy-crawly critters. Even the occasional tracer coming from the ARVN camp next to us seemed almost commonplace. I had become complacent, and I knew that complacency could get me killed.

I arrived back at the chapel with a bandolier of loaded magazines, and a Colt .45, a weapon only officers were supposed to be issued. The corporal was a devout man and when I mentioned the chaplain had told me to bring extra ammo, he had offered the .45 as additional protection. "Sounds like you might be heading into a tight situation," he said.

"You ever fire one of these things?" he asked.

"No. I've heard they kick some."

"You'd have more accuracy if you threw a rock, so don't use it until the enemy is on top of you."

An hour later, I was strapped into my seat in a doorless Huey, sitting on my flak jacket, a box of hymnals wedged between my legs, my M16—unloaded, of course—jammed into an upright position between the seats, the bandolier heavy across my chest, and the illegal .45 flopping from my right side. The engine was turning over, its jet starting to howl, when I leaned over to Riggles, who was strapped in next to me.

"Where are we going?" I yelled over the noise.

His voice was almost drowned out by the engine. He cupped his hand around his mouth to direct the sound: "Cambodia!"

We were heading into the rainy season, and the temperature would continue to climb as we entered the summer, but this particular day felt cool by comparison. The sky was almost cloudless, and the water that covered the rice paddies below us shimmered in blinding light.

The rumors had been true: We were in Cambodia. That's what had kept Bob, Skip, and the other pilots hopping like water in a hot skillet. That also explained why there were two gunners on this flight. Usually, we flew over pacified country so we didn't have a gunner. Someone, however, was expecting hostilities on this trip. My heart rate started climbing.

About forty minutes into the flight, I had fallen into an almost trancelike state, lulled by the noise and wind and the shaking of the chopper. I was thinking about what I could tell Karen about this trip, other than that I missed her terribly.

I was jolted back to reality by several "thumps" on the floor between my feet. I leaned over to see if something had fallen, and at that moment, the chopper went into a dive. My stomach rose to meet my ears, and I felt my body strain against my harness. We were heading for a grove of trees at about 150 miles an hour. I would have yelled, but my lungs felt as if all the air had been squeezed out of them.

We leveled out about thirty feet above the treetops. Riggles leaned over and tapped me on the shoulder. I lifted the thick black ear protector away from my ear. "Snipers!" he yelled. "We took some hits!" He pointed to an area between my feet. "Treetop level. Makes us harder to hit."

I nodded that I understood and glanced down at the floor. I fought the urge to pull my legs under me and sit on them, but to do that I would have to undo my harness, which was definitely not a good idea at the moment.

The trees flew by us, some of them looking like they could almost graze the skids. Dizziness set in if I looked straight down at the green blur beneath us, so I kept looking ahead. Low-altitude flying is very dangerous because even a small downdraft can hurl you toward the ground without time or room to maneuver. But my fear turned to exhilaration—it was also one of the most exciting moments I would have in the war.

The machine we were in throbbed with power that seemed barely tamed, challenging the forces of nature to dare stop it from its mission. In my mind, Wagner's "Flight of the Valkyrie" began playing. This was what his mythical warrior-maidens would have seen as they soared over the battlefields looking for the bravest fighters. The ancient bards imagined it, but I was seeing it, feeling the hot winds against my face, feeling the breath being blown out of me. I gripped the door opening, and it seemed that the machine was alive, pulsing with energy. For an instant, all of us in the belly of the mechanical beast seemed invincible, invulnerable.

A few years later, I would see the movie *Apocalypse Now* and feel a small tingle during the scene when a sky full of choppers approach a beach with the "Flight of the Valkyrie" thundering on the soundtrack. The thrill of awesome power was as close to the real thing as a movie could make it, but for a few minutes in 1970, I had felt the real thing. I had lived it.

We swooped and climbed, dancing the shape of the earth that threatened to rise up and crush us. All of a sudden I saw a small, dark, ugly canker sitting on the plain becoming visible as we topped a smooth landform. It was our destination, a firebase.

We were soon on top of it. The trail of dust that had been following us, churned up by our prop wash, now enveloped us as the pilot slowed by pulling the nose up, like a cowboy making his horse rear up.

Crossing the layers of concertina wire that surrounded the base, we sat down on a leveled-out area so gently that I hardly knew we had landed. The gunners jumped off, and then Riggles and I exited on either side of the chopper. I jumped into Cambodia.

Armed Forces Radio, ever the voice of truth and justice, had been running stories of how the North Vietnamese, lying scum that they were, were accusing the United States of invading Cambodia. President Nixon's administration had labeled these accusations as lies, saying that the United States would only go into Cambodia to interdict (good word, that) the godless, slimy Viet Cong if and when the Cambodian government would ask them to. And because the world knew that the Cambodians were sympathizers of the Viet Cong, that was unlikely to happen.

But here I was, standing on a dusty, barren plain in Cambodia, looking for a place to take a leak, and trying not to drop the hymnbooks or accidentally shoot someone—or be shot by some trigger-happy kid who was short on sleep.

Riggles was directed to the officer-in-charge, a captain who looked to be my age. He commanded a battery of Howitzers, the workhorse of the field artillery. As cannon went, Howitzers were light, very mobile, and deadly over several miles. While the captain explained the way the troops were deployed, I recalled the time when I had considered applying for the Army Officers Candidacy program.

I had been an undergraduate and knew there was a strong possibility that I could be drafted, so I had gone with a buddy to take the qualifying tests. Several weeks later, I met with the recruiter to evaluate the results. He told me that my eyes were too weak for flight school (no news to me) but that my math scores were strong enough—news to me, as math and I had never gotten along too well—that I qualified for all other schools. I was in luck, he said. The army was running a special program that, for someone with my test scores, would guarantee that I could enter the Officers Training School (OTS) of my choice. At this point, he lowered his voice, and I couldn't understand what he said. I asked him to repeat the last part.

"*If* that school has openings," he muttered again.

Even in my undergraduate naiveté, I felt that something was not quite right. "What schools are open?" I asked, as if I could tell the difference.

He folded his brawny arms across his brawny chest and with great seriousness said, "Artillery and Infantry. These are the two schools that career officers really try to get into, 'cause that's where you can shoot up the command ladder." He smiled. I noticed he had stripes on his sleeves, so he was an enlisted man, not an officer. He sure seemed to know what he was talking about.

I demurred giving him an answer, saying I had to think about it. I looked up my good friend Gus, who was finishing his undergraduate degree in music after having been an officer in the army. Gus had been a lieutenant in a tank corps during his three-year hitch. When I told him what the sergeant had said, Gus shook his head.

"You know why there are openings in Infantry and Artillery? Because all those lieutenants go to Vietnam and get killed. Look, if you're a 'looey' in an infantry unit, you'll be slogging through the rice paddies, leading a squad on patrol. If you're in an artillery unit, you'll be slogging through the rice paddies leading an observation squad, and calling it back to some first lieutenant or captain who was lucky enough not to get his dick blown off doing what you'll be doing. So pick either OTS and you're ass is grass. Get into grad school, have four kids, tell'em you're a queer, or go to Canada, but *don't* sign up for OTS."

Riggles motioned to me to go with him. As I passed the captain, I said, "I bet this is a pretty hairy spot for you and the men. Right, sir?"

He nodded. "Yeah, but not as bad as it is for my second lieutenant right now. He's out there about three clicks." He pointed to a distant swatch of greenery. "He's leadin' a squad lookin' for Charlie."

As I joined Riggles, I quietly said, "Thank you, Gus!"

We held the service under a green mesh tarp that, theoretically, helped us blend in with the vegetation. The bright, hot sun was high overhead, its rays casting wavering shadows on us all, shadows that shifted in the light breeze.

Six men attended, all white guys, all very young and from their stone-faced looks, very scared. I led them in a couple of hymns, but in fact I sang alone except for an occasional drone from the minuscule congregation.

As Riggles read some scripture, I stood to one side where I looked at the small congregation. These men were living in constant, unremitting terror. They were far from any help, waiting for the enemy to appear, and dreading the approaching night. Their job was to tend to the guns, like a colony of ants tend their queen. They were to be as selfless, emotionless, and stupid as ants. But the ant-queen bore life; the queens these men tended bore destruction, and the enemy would have their lives for it.

For the first time, I wondered what the chaplain meant to them. Was it a sense of comfort? A touch of normalcy in the midst of insanity? Hope? I didn't ask them, knowing that my questions would have no meaning.

Men in suits, sitting in comfortable rooms in a faraway city, had moved some numbers around and played with lines on maps. They had decided to send some troops to "deploy" cannon and "interdict" supply lines. Those men had made their decisions and then had slept in elegant rooms, as nineteen-year-olds, half a world away, strained their eyes and ears in the night, waiting for the static of the radio to tell them where and when to make their steel queens spit out death.

These boys knew that. They knew they were both destroyers and targets. Whatever happened during the hot night, no help would arrive until the dawn. Somehow, they had survived for a week already. Several of their comrades had either been killed or wounded and replacements had been brought in, but these men had survived.

The service ended and Riggles said he would stay under the mesh to talk to anyone who wanted to talk to him. I packed up the hymnals and my weapons and waited with the pilot and copilot by the chopper. Minutes passed while Riggles waited alone. Finally, a tall, thin kid, ill at ease, made his way under the mesh. I used the time to look around the firebase.

The compound was a model of crude efficiency. It was in the form of a circle with a diameter of about fifty yards. There were four guns and a combination of trenches. Bunkers of olive green sandbags were arranged into three-sided sheds to provide storage for the shells. The command bunker was of the same construction but with a fourth side to provide better protection against snipers for the officers. A wooden frame that fit between sandbags served as a window. Concertina wire surrounded the compound in a circle, the ends of which didn't meet but overlapped instead, forming a small opening that required anyone passing through to zigzag around the posts that anchored the ends of the wire. I pointed this out to the pilot, and he told me that the patrol would enter there, if they could make it back.

They were spotters for the artillery and would do everything they could to not draw attention to themselves. They were relieved every two days, during the night, if there was no contact with the enemy.

Three days earlier, a patrol had found the enemy and the compound had sprung into action. Of course, by firing on the enemy, it had announced its presence and had immediately become a target. The firebase had been attacked with mortars the following two nights. The cannon had been untouched, but three of the soldiers had been injured and one had been killed. The officers expected a full-out assault at any time. The men were on edge and showing signs of strain. Which is why the captain had requested that the chaplain come.

The soldier with Riggles appeared at the edge of the mesh that covered them. He wiped his eyes, put on his cap, and shuffled away. Riggles followed a couple of minutes later.

He shrugged as he reached the chopper. "I guess no one else is interested in talking right now. I'll check out with Captain Wilson and then we can go."

The pilot waved to the gunners, who were off smoking with some of the troops, then got into the chopper and started his checklist. The blades were just starting to pick up speed as Riggles jogged over and climbed in. There was something different about his face as he put on his helmet.

"You okay?" I shouted over the noise.

"I was just wondering," he shouted back, "how many of those kids will be alive tomorrow." His face looked different because his jaw was set; he was holding back tears. He slipped his sunglasses on and strapped himself in.

As the chopper passed over the concertina wire and circled the compound I saw the thin young soldier below stand up and wave. It was a sign of thanks to Riggles. The muscles along Riggle's jaw flexed as he gritted his teeth.

As the firebase shrank in the distance I could only imagine what the kid felt like as he watched our chopper disappear. I wondered if he or anybody else there would live to see the sun rise tomorrow.

CHAPTER 22

▼

Onward, Christian Soldiers

The rainy season arrived in late April. I had heard about the rainy season and had read about it in books, but I still was not prepared for the endless outpouring of moisture from the sky and the earth. When rain was not falling in buckets, the heat turned the humidity into steam until I felt as if I was in a natural sauna. There was a series of movies in the forties and fifties called *Life with Father*, a television series devoted to the rainy season in Vietnam would be called *Life with Mildew*.

Everything became coated with a fine layer of mold. Uniforms, freshly laundered, starched, and pressed by hardworking hooch maids, seemed to attract moisture like sponges—they became damp and sticky as soon as I put them on. Father Rooker seemed not to mind the discomfort.

He enjoyed stripping down to his boxer shorts, slipping on shower thongs, and washing his jeep in the pouring rain. Washing his jeep became his regular pastime. I guessed his age to be about mid-fifties, and he had a thin body topped by a bald head. I accused him of flaunting his body to any female who might pass by. He retorted that any poor woman who was attracted to his bony carcass was welcome to it.

Since my arrival at the chapel, after Wes had shown me some tools for tuning pianos, I had tinkered around with the little upright. During my music studies at the university, I had engaged in several conversations with the piano technician about tuning systems and how he went about that ancient art. What I had learned from our conversations, however, was that I knew nothing about how to tune pianos. I set out to demonstrate my ignorance by becoming the *de facto* chief piano tuner for the Mekong Delta.

Over several months time, I learned what "mean tempering" meant. I had read that this was the system in use before the time of Bach; with it, certain scales would sound okay while others would sound out of tune. During Bach's lifetime (1685–1750), "well tempering" was developed, in which all keys sounded in tune.

It was quite a leap forward in the history of Western music, but I seemed destined to return all the pianos I touched to the tuning of the more primitive age, before any kind of tempering was invented. Call it a gift.

Riggles came into the chapel one day as I struggled to get the lower notes on the keyboard to vaguely approximate the pitches of the notes at the upper end. Besides working in a hot, humid building, the additional exertion of tuning the piano without breaking any of the irreplaceable strings had me in a sweat.

"You look like you're working up a lather there, Ted," he said.

"Blood, sweat, and tears are the price of great music," I replied, wiping my face with an olive drab handkerchief. "That's what one of my professors told me at Michigan, but I don't think this is what he had in mind, exactly."

"After you're done here, I'd like you to go with me to meet the Adkersons. They're a couple of Southern Baptist missionaries who live in town. They have a piano that needs tuning, and I told them you could do it for them."

"I really don't know anything about tuning a piano. I've told you that I'm working by instinct here, and my instincts limit me to C major and a couple of related keys. Playing in any other keys makes it sound like a honky-tonk piano being played by a guy who's had too much Ripple."

Riggles chuckled. "That's the musician in you talking. The rest of us can't tell that much difference."

"Lord help us all," I muttered.

"So I told them we would show up at their place late this afternoon, that you could tune their piano in their air-conditioned house, and they could make us dinner. Sound like a deal?"

"You mean I would miss having dinner in the mess hall?"

He nodded.

"Okay, I'll go, but only under protest."

He smiled and patted my shoulder. "We'll leave at sixteen hundred."

The Adkersons' sat in a wealthier district of Can Tho, in a residential area that I had never seen. The French had built the district; the streets were wider than most streets in an American city, and lined with palm trees that swayed gently in the breeze. I had found another world within the poor, crowded surroundings of the rest of the city.

The nine-foot wall of pinkish plaster that surrounded the house gave it a cool, Mediterranean look. We walked through a painted wooden gate and into a well-kept flower garden, where we followed a stone path up to the house. The house continued the Mediterranean motif, with light pink walls and a red slate roof that peaked in the center, the peak running from the front of the house to the back.

The Vietnamese housekeeper greeted us at the front door, ushered us into the airy front room, and then went scurrying off to fetch her mistress. Lucille Adkerson appeared, looking very cool in a white blouse and light blue skirt.

She was a tall, slender woman, just under six feet, with shoulder-length dark brown hair. Her face was elongated and rather plain; she wore no makeup, as befitted her missionary image I supposed.

Lucille ("Lucille, not Lucy, please," she had said when I inquired about how I should address her) shook hands with Riggles and then extended a warm, soft hand to me. She said Robert, her husband, would not be back for a while, and she asked if we'd like some hot tea while we waited. We accepted. She stepped to an entrance that led deeper into the house and rattled off something in Vietnamese to someone.

Lucille and Robert had been in Vietnam for fourteen years, she told us as we all sat down, and had lived in Can Tho for ten.

"What brought you to Vietnam?" I asked. I didn't understand why a Western civilian would choose to come to a country that seemed to be fighting an endless war.

"Why, the Lord, of course," she responded. "I had always wanted to be a missionary, to serve God in a foreign land. Robert and I met in college, where he was studying for the ministry. We married while we were still in school and we dedicated ourselves and our marriage to the Lord, to do with us as he chose." She looked around the bright room. "He sent us here to work with these poor people, to bring them the gift of salvation." The housekeeper appeared, carrying our tea and some cookies. Tea was served in delicate china cups perched on thin china saucers.

As Lucille and Riggles chatted, I flashed back to the rare church services where the missionary, back on vacation from some exotic, hellish country, would tell of the great need of the poor wretches to whom they'd ministered. I wondered if all of the missionaries suffered in conditions like these.

Robert appeared. He was wearing white pants and a flowery short-sleeved shirt. Like Lucille, he had dark hair and was tall and slender. They both looked middle-aged, but since I was just twenty-five, "middle age" was a hazy concept.

Robert greeted us cordially and joined us for tea. It was not long before the inevitable questions began; having lived in a fundamentalist minister's home, I came to expect them as a regular topic of conversation when meeting new people.

"Chaplain Riggles tells us your father is a Southern Baptist minister. Wonderful. Of course, you've had a personal experience with Jesus, haven't you?" Robert began.

Lucille eyed me over the top of her teacup. Even as a child, I had never been comfortable in such conversations. Of course, as good evangelical Christians, Robert and Lucille felt compelled to find out if I had found the Truth, and what I had done with it.

I had tried to explain this evangelical obsession to my non-evangelical friends over the years. According to evangelical reasoning, if you have truly "found Jesus," then you will want to share that new discovery with others. The theory is that the fervent Christian (that is, the one who has gone through the proper steps in order to be "saved") witnesses to others because of love for the Savior and for the "unsaved," the unsaved being those poor wretches who have not yet been "born again."

I answered the Adkersons' question with what they wanted to hear: I had been saved when I was eight years old. They assumed that the person before them was a sanctified, purified, born-again believer. Amen and amen.

What I didn't tell them was that I had started questioning the faith as a university student, but I kept my concerns to myself, mostly for financial reasons—I supported myself as a minister of music in various Southern Baptist churches. Intellectually, I wanted very much to believe the kind of cant that I heard twice on Sunday and every Wednesday, but in my heart of hearts I knew I had serious reservations. Those reservations had not only grown in Vietnam, they had sprung into full bloom in the face of what I experienced. I had no one to discuss my doubts with, not even Rich, since he had already assigned all the Christian doctrines to the same category as belief in fairies and various cannibalistic rites.

Sitting in the Adkersons' cool living room, hearing myself talk about a religious experience that I was supposed to have had as a child, I experienced an epiphany—the religious beliefs that had been drummed into me since I was a child, and that I had always accepted, were slipping away and I was not mourning their loss.

We chatted for a few minutes, then I got to work tuning their piano after having told them that I didn't know what I was doing. They insisted that I still knew more than they did and that the piano had not been tuned for at least ten years. It was a challenge.

Afterwards, we had a light supper of vegetables and rice—Vietnamese fare, or so I guessed. It was very tasty but not very filling, and I thought I would go to the EM Club and have a dessert of a grilled cheese sandwich with chips. I must have passed muster with Lucille and Robert because they invited Riggles and me to come back for dinner later in the week. We immediately accepted their offer.

On the drive back to the base, Riggles told how they had looked him up when he had first arrived on-base the previous year. They had been eager to be around another Southern Baptist, and he was glad for their company even though he had moved away from the rigid stance that denomination represented. As a non-denominational chaplain, he was careful not to espouse one particular set of beliefs more than another. It was a position he was comfortable with, and he said he might leave the ministry after his retirement from the army, rather than try to find a church to pastor.

He looked around at the city and then the countryside as we drove. After a few minutes he said, "You know, after living this kind of life—following my profession in military posts around the world—settling down in one place for a long time seems pretty dull."

"I don't mean that I want to keep dragging my family from place to place. Jenny is almost done with high school, and Josh will be starting next year, and it would be nice to be there for them. My wife would love for us to be together in a regular house in a regular town." He looked over at me. "You're too young to appreciate what it's like to be on the move every two to three years, changing posts, being separated for long periods of time."

"I'm learning pretty quickly," I said. "It was not my idea to have an extended visit to this Oriental paradise."

He smiled. "You have a point, Ted." He gazed out at the landscape. "Still, you'll have to admit that this could be a very beautiful country." We passed two young women, walking along the side of the road, their white *ao dais* swaying in the humid breeze. Riggles sighed. "They certainly are a lovely people."

CHAPTER 23

▼

Beyond the Sunset

As the Cambodian invasion continued, memorial services became more frequent. So did the trips to the field hospital at the air force base. Our base at Can Tho was attacked more often because we provided the main air support for the ARVNs. The VC were pissed and wanted to make sure we knew they were.

Bob Perkins showed up every now and again, looking tired and a little frayed at the edges. He was pulling a lot of missions.

After one of the few Sunday services he had been able to attend, Bob and I had gone for a short walk. He had complained about being cooped up in his chopper and needed to stretch his muscles.

We didn't say much for a time, just preferring to enjoy the cooler morning air. We were into the hot season, and it was in the low 80s, with maybe 70 percent humidity, so it felt almost cool.

"Did I tell you that I killed twenty-one VC yesterday?" he asked.

"I don't think so."

He twiddled with his mustache. "And I injured four others, all with one rocket."

"Holy cow! You going to get a medal or something?"

He smiled. "Probably not; just in a day's work for a courageous chopper pilot."

We walked in silence; I knew something was bothering him. We came to a deserted part of the dirt road. Guard posts squatted on the perimeter about fifty yards to our right, and the interlocking metal grids that comprised the runway were about one hundred yards to our left. No vehicles or other soldiers on foot were near us. Bob glanced around, as if to confirm that we were alone.

"You want to know the truth? I don't know that I can claim any kills at all this week. We fired at suspected VC a few times, maybe wounded some, but I don't think I killed any."

"But you just sai—"

"What I told you is what I reported. Darn! I hate this." He slapped his hand against his leg.

"What?"

"The lying. We go on a mission, see some farmers working their rice paddies, maybe see someone where he shouldn't be, fire some rounds, and come back to base. I file a report: Fired on three possibles; one confirm kill, two injured. I turn it in to the XO (executive officer); he sends it back, saying we're below this week's quota and that I should re-evaluate. So I send it again: Spotted five possibles; three confirmed kills, one injured, one unknown." He kicked sand into the air. "I give the real numbers; my XO sends them back and more or less tells me to lie. So I lie, then he lies to the CO, and those numbers go all the way to the top. Nobody up there knows what the heck is happening, so they keep sending us out to make up more numbers.

"How can I call myself a Christian and lie like that? How can I call myself a Christian and participate …?" He stopped walking and looked me in the eye. His face was pale. He glanced at my insignia of rank. "Ted, I've said too much."

"What? No, you haven't. I won't tell anyone."

"Maybe not, but I've broken regulations. I mean, I'm talking to an enlisted man, telling him—"

"Wait a minute. I thought we were just friends out for a walk, shooting the bull."

His stood, arms akimbo, and began lecturing me. "This isn't the University of Michigan, Ted. We aren't just two students in a bullshit session. We're in the middle of a freaking war. I'm an officer; you're enlisted. I'm not supposed to talk to an enlisted man about classified matters."

I stiffened. "I'm cleared to Secret, if that's what's bothering you."

His face was tight. "It's just better for both of us if you forget I ever said anything about numbers. All right?"

"Sure. Okay … *sir*." He missed the acerbic edge in my tone. I was hurt and puzzled by this sudden change. What had happened to him?

We walked back in silence, two strangers who just happened to be walking together. We passed a barracks, and Bob peeled off, departing with a short, "See you around." It was a strange ending to a casual Sunday walk.

Years after the war, historians would compile the numbers of killed and injured reported by the U.S. military during the Vietnam Conflict. They would discover that according to the numbers that made their way to the Pentagon, every man, woman, and child in both North and South Vietnam had been either killed or wounded. Twice.

The processions of flags, the helmets sitting on white cloths, the monotone voices of the officers naming the dead, all of this began blurring together as the number of memorial services mounted. We heard of one chaplain on another base who thought the services should be more personalized, in the hopes of raising morale on the base. He had his assistant place the names of those who were to be memorialized on a sandwich board outside the chapel for all to see. That effort died when the list of names grew too long for the board to hold, and the CO told the chaplain to cease and desist.

Harry and I shared the duty of getting the bulletin prepared for each memorial service. The format of the service remained the same, only the names changed, so the duty soon became routine. Riggles or Father Rooker or Captain Collins (a Methodist chaplain who moved into the third office of the chapel in May) would receive word of a death (or deaths) and convey the relevant information to Harry or me so a service could be scheduled.

All too often the cause of death was not war-related but due to stupidity, bad luck, or a combination of the two—like the eighteen-year-old who was driving a jeep while drunk and flipped over into a drainage ditch, drowning in three inches of water; or the men who died when a small mortar round exploded after their buddy, who had found it and was keeping it as a souvenir, dropped it. There was the drunken mechanic who was wandering on the runway when the Cobra landed, impaling him on one of its skids, and the corporal on a firebase in Cambodia who stepped on a land mine while looking for a spot to relieve himself. I asked Riggles how the army reported such deaths, and he replied that they were all listed as KIA (killed in action). After all, he said, they *were* in a war zone. No one wanted to tell a bereaved family that their son got drunk and drowned in his own vomit while lying on the barracks floor. All the dead died bravely—heroes, giving their lives in the service of their country. That was the way it had always been done and would always be done. Amen.

Captain Collins came in one day and told us to prepare for a service for a couple of Cobra fliers who'd been killed in a crash. Collins explained that they had been called in to support a firebase that was under attack. The Cobra was taking fire, too, so it couldn't hover and fire. Instead, it circled to gain altitude, and then came in firing while diving. The Cobra was underpowered for the heavy armament it carried, Collins said, which was a problem with all the Cobras. When it came in at 250 knots in a dive, it was hard to judge when to pull out. Pulling out too early meant it would overshoot the target, but pulling out too late meant it would crash.

"The worst part," Collins said, "is that the main prop—the one overhead—comes down and shears the canopy on impart, and the pilots are cut in half. These poor guys were decapitated."

"No shit," Harry exclaimed, as if he had heard a funny story that he could amuse his buddies with at the EM Club.

I thought of Skip but figured that he had been flying missions for almost a year, so he knew the dangers. I'd have to ask him about the Cobra problem the next time I saw him.

There were two services the next day, both in the afternoon. Collins was performing the first service and Riggles the second. I had been playing the same music for the last three or four services, and Riggles had joked that he had heard it so often that he could almost play it himself. It was time for a change. While Harry worked on the programs, I scoured the hymnbook for new pieces I could improvise on, given my limited skills. The organ's one virtue was that it stayed in tune because it was electronic. It was not affected by the weather or by my clumsy efforts at reinventing mean temperament.

I was still picking out possible melodies to play when Riggles arrived in his vestments, which consisted of a purple cloth stole on which a gold cross was embroidered. He told me the company was lining up outside and would come in as soon as I started the music.

The eerie ceremony began again—the officers leading two lines of soldiers down the middle aisle, the call to attention, the flags and helmets, Riggles reading from Psalms, the terse, awkward words of the company commander, "Taps" played by a bugler outside the chapel. I was only half-listening to the service, as my mind was distracted by my not having chosen the piece for the recessional. When the time came, I fell back on one I had played often, and I played it until the last man had left the chapel. The hot, stuffy, humid chapel was almost unbearable by the end of the service, and sweat was rolling off of me. I went to the small refrigerator in the office, opened a can of Coke, and stood in front of the fan with my shirt unbuttoned.

Riggles stuck his head in. "Don't get too comfortable. We only have twenty minutes before the next one. I'll be back soon as I check with the CO. He's coming to this one."

"You mean the colonel? Has he been to any of these before?"

"No. I guess he knew the pilot and wants to say something about him. I'll be right back. Start the music in twenty. Got that?"

"Okay."

Exactly twenty minutes later, I began the processional. I had worked out what I would do for the recessional and felt prepared. Riggles always made a big deal over the colonel's coming for anything, so I wanted to the service to go well. Sure enough, the colonel led one line of men, and the XO, a lieutenant colonel, led the other.

Riggles read a Psalm, a prayer was said, the names of the dead were read—all according to plan. I was not paying much attention.

The colonel stood up. He was a stocky, muscular man of medium height. His black hair was graying around the edges. The pilots and enlisted men on the post held the colonel in high regard, and stories of his exploits were, it seemed, based on reality. I was curious as to what he would say.

He stood ramrod straight, shoulders back: a commanding presence. He cleared his throat and began.

"We've come here today to honor the lives and the sacrifices of First Lieutenant Richard York and First Lieutenant Charles Lauton. I knew Charles because I served with his father in Korea. Charles, or "Skip," as many of you called him...."

The breath was knocked out of me. I grabbed the bulletin I had set on the organ, unread until now. There it was in print: Charles "Skip" Lauton. Charles "Skip" Lauton. Charles "Skip" Lauton. My mind was stuck like a needle on a record, playing the same notes over and over: Charles "Skip" Lauton.

Skip was the Cobra pilot Chaplain Collins had described. Decapitated. Cut to pieces. Dear God, it was Skip.

Warm, salt-laden saliva backed up in my throat. I was going to be sick. My heart raced, and I was panting for breath. Skip. I gripped the bench I sat on, gripped it hard. The nausea passed.

I thought of Skip's wife—what was her name? We had shown our wives' pictures to each other. "She wants four kids—four! Two is as many fucking kids as I ever wanted," he had said, smiling. "Shit, we'll have six or eight, as long as she doesn't get fat, ya know?"

He had looked at her picture again before putting it away. His voice changed. It grew gentle and rather sad. "Man, I really miss her, ya know? I really miss her." It was the only time he had ever let his lively, vulgar guard down with me, even for an instant.

Every word we had exchanged replayed in my head. We were going to get together to chew the fat, we'd said. But we hadn't. Now we never would.

The colonel sat down. Riggles said a final prayer and "Taps" began. I thought my heart would break. Tears streamed down my face, and I bit my lip to keep from breaking down. The last note of the bugle died, and silence filled the chapel.

From somewhere, I heard my name. "Ted?" Riggles called to me, quietly, from the rostrum. I looked at him in a fog. "The recessional?" he said again.

I nodded and stared at the keyboard; the hymnal was open. I began playing the first hymn I saw, oblivious to its title or melody. I played slowly because I was having trouble seeing the page. I didn't know what hymn I had chosen; I just played. I didn't care.

The last man left the chapel. I stopped, turned off the organ, put my head on my arms on the keys, and cried. Later, as I shambled back to the office, Riggles asked if I was okay.

"No, not at this moment. I knew … I knew … Skip," I said, breaking down again.

Riggles put his arm around my shoulder and patted me with his other hand. "Take the rest of the afternoon off. I'll close the organ and straighten up the chapel. Go on."

"Thanks," I sniffled. I wandered around the base for a while, and then found myself in the EM Club. It was almost deserted at this time of the afternoon.

I sat down at a corner table.

"Hey, buddy. Ya got to come to the bar. No table service," the bartender said.

I went to the bar.

"Whaddya want?" he asked.

I started to ask for a Coke but stopped. *This is a wake*, I thought. *My private wake for Skip, a friend I might have had. Ol' foul-mouthed Skip.*

"Give me a beer," I said. "Give me a fucking glass of beer."

CHAPTER 24

▼

I Believe

April 29

It was about nine o'clock in the evening. Humidity made the air thick and unbearable indoors, so Harry and I had retreated to our "smoking posts" in front of the chapel. I had bought a pipe at the PX that morning and was anxious to learn how to smoke it. Pipe smoking had always struck me as a desirable activity when pondering life's Great Questions, and I wanted to know if I would like it.

Harry had come back to the office, looking for a personal letter he had started writing and wanted to finish. When he saw me struggling with my pipe, he decided to join me with a cigar, and we sat on the ends of the walls, smoking, or, in my case, attempting to smoke.

An acquaintance of mine walked by and was moving pretty fast, considering the heat and humidity.

"Joe, what's up?" I called. "You look like you're off to the races."

"Hey, there, Ted. I can't talk now," he said. "I'm on my way to find a radio. Our beloved commander in chief is about to make some kind of announcement."

"Westmoreland?" Harry asked.

"No, the head honcho, our esteemed president, God's gift to the deodorant industry. Richard Nixon," Joe called over his shoulder. "I'll see you later."

Harry shook his head. "Maybe he's fired Westmoreland," he speculated.

"Maybe he's found Jesus," I added.

"Does Jesus know he's lost?" Harry asked as he flicked his cigar away. I called out to Joe that we had a radio, and he went into the chapel with us.

We turned on the radio in our office, grabbed a couple of soft drinks, and settled down to listen to the important announcement. Harry adjusted the antenna for the clearest reception, and we heard the Armed Forces Radio announcer introduce Nixon.

Nixon would give his address on both radio and television. I could imagine his thinning, dark hair, slicked tight to his head, his jowls shaking with sincerity as beads of sweat appeared on his forehead. He would look directly into the camera, striving to give the appearance of honesty and trustworthiness as he addressed his countrymen.

What would he say? I had been in-country only four months, but I had come to believe that the protesters were right—this was a futile war. A part of me also was desperate to believe that someone in our government was honest and sincere in his efforts to end it, to stop the killing.

Nixon began his address. "My fellow Americans." I remember how I had cringed at LBJ's pronunciation of those words: "My fellow 'muracans." At least Nixon's diction couldn't be faulted.

"Today, I am sending our armed forces into Cambodia."

I was stunned. Harry, who had propped his feet on his desk, almost fell over backwards.

"Fuck! Motherfucker! Do you hear that motherfucker?" he was yelling.

"Harry, shut up! I can't hear the radio."

Nixon's voice popped up between the words of Harry's tirade. "Viet Cong ... necessary interdiction ... brave soldiers at risk ... end the war ... pray...."

Harry stomped outside, and I tried to concentrate on what our president was saying. It was prattle—pabulum for a credulous public.

I flashed back to movies about World War I: The men wait in the trenches, smoking, writing letters to sweethearts, singing sad songs to harmonica accompaniment. The runner makes his way through the mud, dodging sleeping men, throwing a scrap of food to the cur. He approaches the hard-boiled but softhearted sergeant, salutes, hands him the message, turns, and scuttles off.

The sergeant reads the message with a stony face, takes out his pocket watch, flips the cover open, checks it, and then slowly closes the cover. Cut to close-up of face: Sergeant's eyes move. Cut to view of trench, showing what the sergeant sees: sleeping men, singing men, etc.

Back to the sergeant, who now looks like Nixon. He sends the corporal to rouse the men. Next scene: Sergeant addresses the men. "Viet Cong ... brave soldiers at risk ... etc." Dawn comes; the soldiers stand poised, bayonets fixed, ready to climb over the dirt embankment. Sergeant Nixon blows the whistle. The mottled-uniformed soldiers, M16s blazing, laugh as they charge into the jaws of death.

As I imagined these scenes in the collective mind of the American public, I began to giggle. Harry came in, wondering what was going on. I told him about my vision. He didn't see the humor and stalked off into the night, saying he was going to get fucking loaded.

My giggles turned into laughter. I made my way into the empty, dark chapel and laid down on a pew, giving my imagination full rein to replay the absurdity of Nixon's announcement—the lies he'd told, the looks and sounds of practiced sincerity. Years later, I would remember this night with sadness, for in the darkness of that makeshift building died not only the last of my innocence but also my trust.

CHAPTER 25

▼

Rock Around the Clock

May, June, July

Greg Ripley walked into the chapel early on a Monday morning, just as I was finishing the Morning Report. I had inherited the job from Wes, who, as the departing highest-ranking assistant, gave it to me, the next highest-ranking chump. I, in turn, would pass it to whoever was unlucky enough to follow me as the Protestant assistant when I rotated stateside.

Ancient armies might have traveled on their stomachs, but the modern army floats on a sea of paper. I became convinced that far over the ocean, within the bowels of the Pentagon, sat a gnome-like figure hunched over a typewriter, searching for new ways to create paper forms that could create the maximum amount of madness among army clerks.

To complete the Monday Morning Report/Base Chapel, I had to list the number of Services/Religious/Protestant and the number of Personnel/Military who attended said services. This was followed by the number of Bulletins/Religious/Protestant that were printed and used by Personnel/Military, and the number of Bulletins/Religious/Protestant that were unused by whomever. I was fortunate to be the assistant of the Chaplain/Military/Protestant and not the Chaplain/Military/Catholic, as that assistant was to provide figures for not only Bulletins/Religious/Catholic and attendance by Personnel/Military but even the number of wafers (Wafers/Catholic) that melted in the Personnel/Military mouths.

It was fortunate that Conversions/Religious/Protestant (or/Catholic) were not listed as a method of determining the efficacy of the chaplains' work. The chaplains made it clear that they were not interested in converting the masses to their particular dogmas but rather were there to give spiritual non-answers to the questions that troubled the Personnel/Military.

I was making up some numbers when Ripley appeared and introduced himself: Specialist 3, Greg Ripley. He asked if we had any good books that we could donate to the library.

"Library?"

"Yeah. I'm putting together a library for the base."

"How come? I'm surprised anyone would want one."

"I'm bored with my job over at headquarters, so I thought this would be a good way to keep my brain from drying up."

I offered him a seat and a Coke. He was about my height but stockier, and had reddish blonde hair that was wavy and about two inches long.

He had a master's degree in geology, he told me, with a specialty in historical geology. When I confessed I had never heard of a specialty like that, he explained that his real love was fossil evidence of ancient sea life; that's what historical geology was.

Asking him to explain what that meant was like pushing a button. He talked for several minutes on how oceans were formed and dissipated, how the remains of creatures that had lived at the bottom of the early oceans could be found in the highest mountains—mountains that had been pushed up with the movement of landmasses.

He explained a new theory that was quite popular—that the earth, as we knew it, was floating on the molten core of the planet. That there had once been one large landmass that had broken apart to form continents, and that the "plates," as he called them, were running into each other, and their collisions were creating the mountains.

I was fascinated by a theory I had never heard. He said it was called "tectonics," and it was the center of a lot of controversy in his field.

"My major thesis advisor at the University of Washington, Dr. Bascom, said he thought the theory was a lot of crap, and he would stop teaching if it was ever proven," he said at the end of his oration. "Sorry, I got carried away for a while. I guess I've not met anybody who's interested in this stuff." He grinned. "That's why I'm here. I could feel my brain getting moldy, you know, from lack of use. Felt like I needed to do something constructive."

I said that I didn't have any books, other than the ones I'd brought from home.

He seemed surprised. "Don't you know that all the publishers of paperbacks send copies of their newest books to the overseas military?"

"No. Never heard of that."

"Yeah, they send them to all the headquarters companies to hand out. They're free."

"No one ever told me about that," I said.

"I bet they have a ton of them over at your captain's office. The sergeants don't know what they are since they can't eat 'em, shoot 'em, or fuck 'em."

"You sound like someone else I know," I laughed, remembering that Rich held the "Lifers" in disdain. Rich often said that he was glad the Lifers had found a home in the army; otherwise, they might be living next door to us civilians.

Greg and I left the chapel together; he returned to his clerk's job, and I headed for the company commander's office. I avoided the place whenever possible, but we had a new first sergeant—that much I had heard. Still, the less I was seen around there, the better.

I walked into the air-conditioned office, removed my hat ("head gear" in army terms), and spoke to the corporal in charge. The sergeant and captain were out to lunch, he said. I thought that was descriptive of the normal state of affairs but decided not to fire from the lip. I noticed that it was only nine-thirty in the morning but decided not to mention that either.

He ushered me into a small adjoining room. There were shelves filled with new, bright-colored paperback books of all types. I thought I was in heaven. There were books on philosophy, the social sciences, history, and fiction of all genres. It was the most beautiful thing I had seen on that dismal post.

The corporal, unimpressed, had gone back to his desk to write a letter. I stood for a minute, motionless, letting my eyes jump from title to title. Then I carefully, reverently, took several. The corporal stopped me.

"Only two per customer, Specialist. Gotta make them last."

"Does anybody else come for them?" I asked as I decided which to take.

"Fuck, yeah. Anything that has tits on the cover disappears like that." He snapped his fingers. "What you have there is what no one else wants. Far as I'm concerned, if it ain't got fuckin', then it ain't worth readin'."

"Thanks. I'll remember that when I write my first commercial novel."

He caught the sarcastic inflection in my voice. "Motherfuckin' college asshole," he said, shaking his head. I left the building hugging my newfound treasures and knowing in my heart that the corporal, if he survived the war, would return to the States and sire a large brood of children, to whom he would pass his ignorance.

That afternoon, I wandered over to Greg's office. He had pointed it out to me before he left the chapel, telling me that I should meet some of his fellow conspirators. There were four others, all college grads: Frank, who had been drafted out of law school and was trying to get into the judge advocate's office; Ron, a biologist by training; Steve, who studied American literature; and Carl, who had been drafted out of business school. The five of us made an interesting group, coming from such diverse backgrounds, but what we had in common was the desire to not allow our brains to atrophy, like so many of our compatriots.

The Gang of Five, as we dubbed ourselves, set up a lecture series at the USO on the base. As an incentive to keep learning, we would each give a lecture in a subject in which we had not specialized but wanted to know more about. As the painter Jackson Pollock said when he was caught pissing into his host's fireplace, "It seemed like a good idea at the time."

I was interested in a subject that surely every red-blooded American guy wanted to know about—the history of philosophy. Since I came from a performance background, the Gang chose me to start off the lecture series.

Greg had been scouring the base for some time and had already assembled a considerable number of books. His library at that time consisted of one shelf and a dozen cardboard boxes in a storage room at his office. Each box was labeled with the genre of book it contained. Since he had gotten the boxes from the trash at his mess hall, they each had various stains and slight odors, but they served their purpose. So I rummaged in boxes that bore words like "Produce—lettuce, history," or "Meat—frozen, philosophy: beef—DO NOT ALLOW TO THAW." I should have taken it as an omen.

Two weeks later, the Gang of Five walked into the meeting room at the base USO. Metal chairs, about fifty of them, had been arranged into rows. I looked around the empty room, and my heart started racing. What had I agreed to do? I was a singer, not a lecturer. True, I had studied several hours every day, pouring over every philosophy book I could find in Greg's boxes, trying to understand the turgid texts so I could boil the ideas down to small, manageable, and understandable portions. I had written an outline of my lecture and practiced in the privacy of my office/bedroom at the chapel. I was ready, but I felt as nervous as if I were making my Metropolitan Opera debut.

We were ten minutes early. Greg went out into the open reception room of the USO, muttering something about flyers. Two minutes before the appointed starting time, three soldiers shuffled into the room, followed by Greg. He pointed in their direction as they made their way to the front, as if to say he had done what he could.

He came to the front and stood next to me. He introduced himself as the director of the lecture series (a few snorts erupted from the back row), made a few comments on the rationale of the series ("… important to keep our minds occupied … mental calisthenics …"), introduced me, and sat down.

I had prepared, if I might be forgiven for saying so, a brilliant lecture. The crux of the lecture was the need for a well-thought-out philosophy, because without one we would have no more direction to our lives than a lowly slug. I planned to begin with a catchy example of the individual's responsibility and how little happened in life, aside from accidents or major illness, which was completely, well, accidental. The example had to get the audience's attention, to make the listener think about what was said. Personal responsibility, that was the key.

So, with a dry mouth, I uttered my first statement: "We're all here in this room tonight, in Vietnam, because we chose to be here." The short silence that followed was broken by the three soldiers saying, in almost perfect unison, "Fuck you!" They stood up and shuffled past me on their way out of the room.

My performance background, while preparing me for many eventualities, had not given me any idea of what to do if my audience simply walked out. So there I stood, clasping my three-by-five cards in my sweaty hand, speechless.

My partners in crime, the other four, looked at each other, their eyebrows twitching as they tried to hold back their laughter. They urged me to go on, and I did, but the wind had been taken out of my sails. My career as a lecturer on the history of philosophy was in ruins.

As it turned out, mine was the first and last of the lecture series. The Gang of Five dwindled away. Greg persevered, though.

One day in November I saw a hand-made sign leaning against a small trailer: Base Library. I went in, and there was Greg working his way through boxes of books, all paperback, that had been donated by the publishers. The library had been open for several days, and he was still cataloguing and shelving books. I stayed for a couple of hours to help.

He filled me in on his latest exploits, such as looking for fossils on the mountain peaks that thrust through the detritus that the Mekong River had deposited over eons. He would twist an off-duty chopper pilot's arm into conveying him to the various peaks; I never knew what he promised the pilot in return, but I had the feeling the pilots would have said yes to just be left in peace. Greg could be very persuasive.

CHAPTER 26

▼

Mazel Tov

Somewhere in the middle of June, Father Rooker returned to the States. The other chaplains and Harry and I wanted to throw a little going-away-wish-we-were-going-too party, but Rooker declined the offer, saying he hated good-byes. We were able to have one last hot game of Hearts. If it had been a game of Strip Hearts, Rooker would have had all of us not only naked but also giving him dibs on our clothing allowances for the next year. He was in excellent form. When it was remarked that he seemed to be playing in a particularly savage manner, he gave us his most beatific smile and said, "Grief sharpens my senses."

The next morning, Riggles and I saw Rooker off on his Huey flight to Tan San Hut with hugs, handshakes, and back patting. Two days later, I greeted Father George O'Brian as Rooker's replacement.

O'Brian and Rooker had two things in common: They were both Catholic, and they were both captains. Other than that, they were very different. Where Rooker had been easygoing and willing to improvise when necessary, O'Brian expected everything to be on time, in place, and in order.

Once, Rooker was holding a service on a base in another sector of Vietnam. The resident assistant set up everything, he thought, and then left to run other errands. It was, of course, a "no-no" for an assistant to do something like that, but Rooker had become so accustomed to the professional efficiency of the Can Tho staff that he assumed everything would be in order.

"I arrived a minute before the service," Rooker had said, "with only enough time to don the vestments that the assistant had set out for me. I threw them on, processed down the aisle, and began the service. I noticed the chalice and wafers were in place, but the chalice was empty. I reached under the altar for the silver wine container, but it was not there. There was no wine in sight. This, as you can imagine, was a problem. The service came to a halt while the priest looked for wine.

"I went back through the chapel to get the wine from the office. It was locked, and the assistant had the key. The men in the chapel were beginning to fidget and kept looking around to see what was going on; there were sounds of coughing and shuffling feet.

"I walked back to the altar to see if I could find a spare key. No such luck. I did, however, find a bread knife. I had no idea why a bread knife would be under the altar, but there it was. I grabbed the knife and strode back to the locked door, as the congregation sat wondering what the hell a priest was doing with a bread knife.

"I jimmied the lock on the door, found a bottle of wine, and processed to the altar once again, carrying the bottle of wine and a bread knife. Such is the life of a priest in a war zone. You work with what you've got."

Rooker later told the errant assistant to never again leave during a service; O'Brian would have crucified him on the spot. Or at least shot him, just as he once threatened to shoot me.

O'Brian was a stickler for beginning the service at the stated time. That meant that if the service was scheduled to begin at 11:00, then he should be processing down the aisle exactly at 11:00—not standing in the back of the chapel listening to some damn theme and variation but moving down the aisle with the congregation on its feet.

Two weeks after O'Brian was in his new position, Rich and Rabbi Mosher arrived for Jewish services. They came on Friday and would depart Monday, so Rich decided to sit in on the Catholic service that I was playing for.

Harry, who had been assigned to O'Brian, told me that O'Brian was a hard son-of-a-bitch and was making his life miserable. Having seen how Riggles trusted me with the operation of the chapel and helping out with the work, Harry had hoped his new boss would be as accommodating. O'Brian was anything but, insisting that Harry clear everything with him and was always picking at Harry's work. Harry could be inattentive to detail, so O'Brian's concern was justified, but Harry was chaffing under his scrutiny.

Where Rooker had been able to accommodate beliefs different from his, O'Brian was as militant as a chaplain was allowed to be. He also believed that the Church held the Keys of Truth, and all others were in error. He was, in short, like most of the Southern Baptists I had known, Riggles being the one exception.

When Harry told me to be sure to start the processional exactly on time, I took it seriously—but not seriously enough. With Rich in the congregation, I wanted to make the prelude interesting. I chose "A Mighty Fortress Is Our God," knowing that Rich would be the only one there who would understand that I was playing a hymn written by the Great Heretic himself, Martin Luther, for a Catholic service conducted by a very conservative priest.

Rich loved it. I went through a couple of variations before I saw O'Brian running in; he had held an earlier service at the air force base. I glanced at my watch: 10:59—enough time for another witty variation. I had modulated a couple of times and was trying to return to the original key when I glanced at my watch again: 11:01. I looked toward the rear of the chapel to see if O'Brian was ready and almost fell off the bench. O'Brian, wearing his vestments, stood in the back of the chapel with an M16 pointed right at me.

Years of training in musical theory and correct harmonic resolution went out the window. I jumped to the first major chord I could find, threw the Catholic hymnbook open to the processional, and started to play. My ending to the prelude was so abrupt that even Rich jumped in surprise.

After the service, I asked O'Brian if the rifle had been loaded. He smiled and said, "You'll never know. Just don't ever keep me waiting again." I made a mental note to buy Harry a drink some time and offer my condolences.

That night, Rich and I went to the EM Club for a drink. He was surprised that I ordered a beer, and I explained that I had reconsidered my religious views about drinking—and a lot of other things as well.

Rich loved mysteries. "So," he said in his I'm-not-letting-you-off-the-hook voice, "what brought about this transformation?" He leaned forward, peering into my eyes. "Might it be a woman, perhaps?"

I shook my head. "Nope. Nothing like that."

Rich smiled. "Those blue *goyishe* eyes tell me this is not completely so. Come on; you can't fib to your Uncle Rich."

"This," I said, holding up the mug, "is not about any woman, exactly."

He slapped his hand on the table. "I knew it!"

"It's not that," I said. "Look, a friend, an acquaintance, was killed. He … it's hard to explain."

Rich grew quiet and fiddled with his glass. "Oh. Sorry." We sat quietly for a minute, but Rich couldn't resist pushing on. "So, you said something about a woman?"

I chuckled. "No, *you* said something about a woman. But yeah, I've actually talked to a round-eyed woman."

"Have you done the dirty deed?" he asked, leering hopefully.

"Hell, no. Nothing like that. I've only talked to her once. Actually, she did most of the talking. She's an officer, so—"

"Ah, yes. Fraternization raises its ugly head," he said.

I put my hand on his shoulder. "Slow down. You're getting way ahead here. I'm married, remember? We're supposed to help each other *not* fool around."

He took a drink. "So, things are not so well between you and Karen?"

I frowned. "I didn't say that. We're both lonely, you know?"

He nodded. "She must be pretty far gone by now, right?"

"What do you mean?"

"You know, hanging out to here with your soon-to-be first born," he said, folding his hands in front of his imaginary natal protrusions.

I put my chin on my hands. "Yeah. Did I show you the latest picture?" I reached for my wallet, fished around through the military scrip, and brought out a black-and-white photograph. Karen was posed in front of some shrubs that ran beside her parents' house. She was wearing a "tent dress," as she called it, and her hands were resting on the shelf of her growing abdomen. Sunglasses covered her eyes as she looked up toward the bright sun; her dark hair was pulled back into a ponytail. I hardly recognized her in her strange and alien form.

She had found a new position at the university and commuted to Ann Arbor every day. Karen had always been good with math and had worked her way up from a secretarial pool to working with researchers on computers. Computers were still in their infancy, and she was having a good time learning about them, along with everybody else. One "everybody" was named Louis, her supervisor. His name had begun appearing in her letters on a regular basis. He was single, in his thirties, and very complimentary about her work. He had even taken her to dinner a couple of times to talk to her about her natural abilities in programming and the various career possibilities that could open up for her.

As much as I tried to feel otherwise, jealously tickled my nerves as I read her letters. *I am not the jealous type*, I told myself, but "myself" wasn't listening. The distance between us seemed to grow wider with every letter. I wrote about innocuous things I did, never mentioning the attacks. If I mentioned helicopter rides, it was in the context of noticing how beautiful the land was, or the time we were cruising at a slow speed and a large hawk flew beside us, as if challenging us to a race. Or how Riggles had invited me to play tennis with him at the air force base, and how we had begun playing any time we could. Of course, I wrote that I missed her, but the more I wrote about it, the worse I felt. If I described how I wanted to touch her, caress her, her reply would be slightly scolding, reminding me that sometimes censors would read military letters and that we should keep things like that to ourselves. She once wrote that she didn't miss the physical side of "things" if she didn't think about it. Then Louis crept into her letters.

Rich listened to my litany as he looked at her picture. I lapsed into silence. He handed the picture back to me and then went to the bar for another round of beer. Depression settled over me like a fine mist.

He came back, sat down, and then proceeded to tell me that he was having the same feelings about his wife, Bobbie. "I'm not swimming in jealously, like you," he said, "but—"

"Wait a minute. I'm not jealous. I don't get jealous ..." Rich's face radiated disbelief.

"... much," I finished. "Well, maybe a little."

Rich wrinkled his nose, as if sensing an unpleasant odor. I began sniffing, too. "What do you smell?" I asked.

"Bullshit," he said. "My nose is my second biggest asset, and it detects the subtle fragrance of bull dung wafting on the breeze."

I couldn't help but chuckle. "All right, Rabbi Hindeman. I get your drift. I'm jealous of anyone who gets to spend time with Karen, who hears her laugh and sees the way she runs her hand through her hair when she's thinking, and—"

"Enough, already," he said. "If you start talking about her skin, her lips, her breasts, or any other part of the female anatomy, I'll have to deliver the Jewish Death Blow to put us both out of your misery."

I started laughing. It was contagious, and soon Rich was laughing just as hard. We talked late into the night. As we walked back to the chapel from the EM Club, we didn't say much; we just savored the cooler night air and the clear sky. On such nights, I remembered that we were in a tropical country, full of lush jungles, glistening beaches, and a handsome people. None of that, however, was near Can Tho. Can Tho was a flat land surrounded by rice paddies.

"Nice, eh?" Rich said, as if sensing my thoughts. I nodded. "Nights like these help me to remember I'm a historian by training and disposition," he said, "and that I want to spend a few years in Italy with Bobbie, shuffling through ancient documents, surrounded by the remnants of the glories of the Renaissance. We will, of course, spend most of our time on the coast of the Mediterranean, being tended by nubile, sensual, Italian girls—"

"Does Bobbie know this? What if she takes exception to all those nubile girls?"

"She, of course, will have me to tend to her every fleshly desire, so how could she be jealous of me sharing my riches?" he said.

"Just checking," I replied. "By the way, what is a Jewish Death Blow?"

He put his arm around my shoulders, pulling me close to his side as he growled, "Pray that you'll never find out."

The next day, Monday, Rich, Rabbi Mosher, and I went to the Air Force Field Hospital. Both Rich and I were armed, as usual; Mosher said he felt safe and very honored to be protected by two of the army's finest chaplain's assistants-slash-bodyguards. He waved a hand in blessing as he said, "The Holy Ark of the Covenant should have been so well guarded."

"Keep it up, Ira, and I might have to use this on you," Rich said from the back seat, patting his M16. He and the rabbi were on a first-name basis whenever they were alone or with me. I had noticed it in their earlier visits. It never occurred to me to call Riggles by his first name; he was so thoroughly "military," I thought, that even his wife probably called him "Major, honey."

At the hospital, Rich went to scout out any Jewish personnel in Ward B, while I accompanied Ira on Ward A. Ira greeted the nurse as we walked in, asking if she knew of any Jewish personnel on the ward.

"I don't know, sir," she said, eyeing his collar insignia. At first she seemed a bit puzzled; he was a captain, but what did that funny looking star on his collar mean?

Ira began his rounds. He would check the name at the end of the patient's bed, and then, if the patient was awake and responsive, he would move to the patient's side.

"Hello. I'm Ira Mosher. I'm a chaplain," he would say in a soft voice.

Often, the man lying in the bed would nod or speak, if he could.

Ira would lean in. "Are you Jewish? You look Jewish. Stein—that's usually a Jewish name."

"I'm Catholic, Father" or "I don't go to church" were the typical replies from the young men, most of whom had seldom, if ever, darkened the portals of a church. Some, noticing Ira's yarmulke, stared at the strange skullcap on this chaplain. I wondered how many of them had ever seen an Orthodox Jew, much less a rabbi. Few, I suspected.

As we left the ward, I mentioned to Ira that I had been taught, in my liberal education, that it was a faux pas for a gentile to ask whether a person was Jewish or not. It would be bad form to walk up to a stranger and say that he looked Jewish.

He smiled and shrugged his shoulders. "What can I say?" he asked rhetorically. "I have to get the job done, and I don't have much time, so *humph* to social niceties."

As we started into the next ward, he stopped at the door. "Tell you what: You go ahead of me and identify the goyim, and I'll concentrate on the rest."

I declined the offer, saying that I was not sure that men would know what I meant if I asked, "Are you a gentile?"

"No, go on. It could get interesting," he insisted.

So I walked up to the first men who looked awake and able to talk. "Hi. I'm a chaplain's assistant, and this is Rabbi Mosher. I was just wondering—"

"What's a rabbi?" the young man interrupted.

"He's a, a kind of a Jewish minister," I said. "Anyway, I was just wondering—"

"What is that thing you're wearing on your head, Reverend?"

"It's a yarmulke," Ira answered, as if addressing a child. "It's a sign of our faith." "Yeah, but what's it for?"

Ira considered for a moment. "It's very cold where we live, so we wear it to keep our heads warm."

"Cool."

"Well, we should see some more men here," Ira said. "Nice to chat with you."

"Yeah, good to talk with you, too, Reverend."

Ira leaned close to me: "Since when does the army draft idiots?"

"You, an officer, are asking me, an enlisted man, this question?" I replied.

Ira stepped back and looked at me closely. "Are you Jewish? You sound Jewish."

Rich met us as we exited the ward. He told Ira that he had not found any Jewish personnel where he was, and Ira went to talk to the head nurse to be sure he had not missed anyone. As he walked away from us, he turned and pointed at me and said to Rich, "Him. I found him. I think he is a closet Jew." He chuckled.

Rich maneuvered me to the nearest bench. "I saw her."

"Her, who?"

"Your nurse, Josie. Man, oh, man, she is a doll."

"Josie? You mean Lieutenant O'Malley?"

"You didn't do her justice, the way you described her."

"Wait a minute. What's with this 'Josie'?"

"I asked Lucy."

"Who is Lucy?"

"Lucy is a Spec 4 who works here. I met her last time I was here."

I sat back and folded my arms. "Rich, how do you do it? You'd make a great spy, the way you gather information. You're like an information sponge."

A big smile covered his face. "I *am* pretty good at this, aren't I? Of course, how else can I keep Rumor Central up and running?" He leaned toward me. "I can see why you're smitten with her. That black hair, those dark eyes, those luscious lips—"

I put my head in my hands. "Oh, please. Stop. I've only talked to her once. I'm not *smitten*, for Pete's sake."

"Me thinks thou doest protest too much," he said, wagging his finger. "I know you, and last night you sounded smitten."

O'Malley appeared at the other end of the corridor. Rich saw me look in her direction and stopped his teasing.

O'Malley was talking to another nurse, who was wiping her eyes with an olive drab handkerchief. They stopped and faced each other; O'Malley said something else, and the nurse nodded. O'Malley hugged the woman and patted her on the back. The nurse walked to the swinging doors at the other end of the corridor, looked over her shoulder at O'Malley, raised her hand in a farewell gesture, and walked away.

O'Malley's shoulders sagged. She stood looking at the doors until they stopped swinging, wiped her face with her hands, and then turned and walked in our direction.

Rich and I made ourselves busy, looking at the duty roster on the bulletin board behind us. We were embarrassed, knowing that we had intruded on a private moment.

O'Malley, heading out the doors, glanced over at us.

I said, "Hello there, ma'am."

She stopped. "Specialist, um, Bertson," she said, reading my nametag. "Here for more assistant chaplain stuff?" A little smile played at the corners of her mouth.

"Actually, ma'am, we're not assistant chaplains, but—" Rich began.

I nudged him. "She knows the difference."

"I do, indeed, Specialist Hindeman," she said with a smile. "Are you one of those strange people yourself?"

Rich offered a slight bow. "Yes, ma'am. And I might add that you will find few chaplains' assistants stranger than either Specialist Bertson or myself." She giggled in a way that was charming and infectious. Ira stepped into the corridor near us. Rich nodded in Ira's direction. "However, our strangeness is eclipsed only by the chaplains we serve. Here's one now." Rich seemed to be serving as master of ceremonies for this impromptu occasion, as he said, "Chaplain Mosher, this is Lieutenant O'Malley, a wonderful nurse in this facility."

Ira spoke first. "Nice to meet you, Lieutenant."

"And you, sir," she replied.

"I was just going to invite my splendid bodyguards to the Officers Club for refreshments. Would you care to join us?" Ira asked.

O'Malley nodded. "Sure. I haven't had such a charming invitation in years. I can't stay long, though."

As we walked through the bright, hot sunlight to the Officers Club, she asked what Ira had meant when he called us "bodyguards." I explained that chaplains could not bear arms, so it was up to us to protect them. Rich chimed in that nobody had thought it necessary to tell us this when we volunteered to be assistants. Ira suggested that had we been told this, we might have opted to be real soldiers and could be slogging through the rice paddies in Vietnam, even as we spoke.

Rich rose to the bait. "Nixon has already pulled all U.S. ground troops from the Delta, so we wouldn't be in the Delta today. Instead, I would be on the survey team."

"The survey team?" O'Malley said. "What survey team?"

I had a feeling that Rich was heading into dangerous territory. O'Malley might be an upright, conservative, professional military person who might not be amused by some of our mutual fantasies.

"The one laying out the parking lot," Rich answered, as if to say that he thought everyone knew this.

O'Malley lunged ahead. "The parking lot for what?"

Rich brought our little group to a halt as he took the stage. "Ted and I have created the solution for ending the war. Nixon declares that he's won and then has B-52s drop millions of tons of asphalt on North and South Vietnam, turning the entire country into a parking lot for China." Rich beamed while I eyed O'Malley for her reaction. She was smiling; then she began to chuckle.

Ira waved his hands at Rich as he said to O'Malley, "You know, I've tried and tried to help him understand that Nixon can't do that. No. The unions would be all over him for unfair labor practices. Besides, people in New Jersey would be too afraid that they were seeing the handwriting on the wall, especially if they lived in Newark. I can see the picket signs now: First Vietnam, then Newark. No, it would simply never work."

We reached the Club, kibitzing the entire way. I had not felt so lighthearted for some time. It felt good to smile and laugh again. There seemed to be something about Rich that brought levity to any situation.

Cokes in hand, the four of us sat in the coolness, making small talk and getting to know each other. After a few minutes, Ira, irrepressible as always, asked, "So, what brings a beautiful nurse like you to a place like this?" He raised his eyebrows in imitation of Groucho Marx. I looked at Rich, knowing that Ira's behavior was caused by Rich's bad influence on him. Rich shrugged.

O'Malley looked at each of us in turn and sighed. "If I can't talk to a rabbi and his faithful guardians, who can I talk to?" She fell quiet for a few seconds and then said, "Let's just say that I'm on a mission."

"That sounds intriguing," I said.

She looked at me. "Yes? Well, I'm not comfortable saying much more."

Rich, sensing that we were in delicate territory, changed the subject. We talked about little of importance as we finished our drinks. O'Malley reacted with interest only when Rich mentioned that I was a classical singer.

"I love singing," she said. "My mother's parents came to the States from Ireland, and my father's parents were Mexican—those cultures love singing, you know."

"I know," I replied. I couldn't resist making the secret wish that she liked singers, as well as singing.

She asked the usual kind of questions that non-musicians ask: What kind of music did I sing? When did I start singing? Did I study singing in college? Had I performed any operas?

I loved the attention. Then she and I noticed that Ira and Rich were not talking. They were sitting back in their chairs, observing our conversation.

O'Malley stood up, excusing herself, saying that she had to get back to work. When she reached the door, she turned. "Specialist Bertson, maybe you could sing for us sometime, here, at the hospital?"

"Yes, ma'am," I answered, "I'd be happy to sing for you, for the hospital, sometime."

"Maybe we could arrange something. I would like to hear you," she said with a smile. Then she was gone.

Neither Rich nor Ira said anything for several moments. I had finished my drink before I noticed the funny look on Rich's face—a smirk. I was a little annoyed. "What?"

Rich folded his arms. "Oh, nothing," he answered. He sensed my irritation. "Well, actually, I think we have ourselves a little situation here." He sounded a little like the prison captain in the movie *Cool Hand Luke.*

"There is no situation here," I said.

Ira stood up. "I think we should toddle along. You two are getting testy."

On the return to Can Tho, Ira sat in the back seat so Rich and I could sit in front, allowing us to argue. "Jews love arguments," Ira said once. "Arguments help keep the blood circulating in our Hebrew veins. A Jew without an argument is like a day without sunshine."

"Isn't that what is said about wine?" I had asked.

"Perhaps, but whoever said that got it from us!"

Rich began his rundown of the conversation as soon as we stepped into the jeep. "You should have seen the sparks between you two. Like lightning, it was. Lightning!"

"Have I told you that your Yiddish accent seems to come and go?" I asked. I was not eager to talk about this.

"And," he continued, oblivious to my attempted diversion, "you two are treading on dangerous ground, fraternization and all that."

"Rich, there is no 'you two'. You and Ira—sorry; you and Chaplain Mosher—"

"That's all right, Ted," Ira called out from the back seat. "My mother calls me Ira, too, just like Rich does."

"You and Ira," I started again, "were present for the second time Lieutenant O'Malley and I have ever spoken. There is nothing, nor will there ever be anything, going on here!" I hoped my tone carried more conviction than I felt. "Also," I went on, "you forget that I'm a happily married man."

"As am I," Rich said. "If I remember correctly, we have an agreement that when one of us feels the other is slipping, he is to be reminded that he is married, and all that."

I thought about it. "True. Okay, I know I'm attracted to her. Who wouldn't be?"

"And, I swear, she is attracted to you," Rich insisted, "even though she is an officer and a gentleman."

"And such a gentleman!" Ira added.

"Chaplain Mosher!" I said. "I'm surprised that you should take such notice of a woman. A nice Orthodox guy like you."

"Ah, but remember," Ira said, "I'm the one who is not married! True, she is of the *goyim*, but maybe she will consider conversion."

I laughed. "Okay, both of you, there can't be anything going on between Lieutenant O'Malley—"

"Josie," Rich interjected.

"Between *Lieutenant O'Malley* and me. Period. Bottom line. End of story."

CHAPTER 27

▼

Jesus Loves the
Little Children

Chaplain Riggles made every effort to keep Harry and me as happy as two disgruntled draftees could be, so he gave us a full day off as a comp day. We could have either Monday or Tuesday. I chose Tuesday.

It was on one of my Tuesdays off that I drove into Can Tho to visit the U.S. Information Center. I had passed the Center a couple of times and was curious what function it served in a war zone. The Center was situated in a part of the city that was dominated by houses that had been built by the French. So it had the graceful, Mediterranean look to it that resembled the buildings around it. Unlike the other buildings, however, it was very well maintained.

On walking through the wrought-iron double-doors, I was greeted by a pretty Vietnamese girl wearing a white *ao dai* with black silk pants. She stepped from behind a wooden desk, introduced herself as the receptionist, and asked if she could be of assistance. I caught a scent of a delicate perfume that was very appealing in my current celibate state. I tried to get my mind off of that scent as I told her that I was just interested in looking around and would like to know more about the Center.

She held up her hand, indicating I should wait. She disappeared through a door into an adjoining office. The stucco walls of the room where I waited were painted a flat white and on them were various posters of American scenery. I heard the clicking of the girl's high heels on the tile floor as she re-entered the room, followed by a tall American man, who looked to be in his thirties. He had on cream colored linen slacks and a pale green, open-collared short-sleeved shirt. White soft-soled canvas shoes completed his wardrobe, giving him the cool, comfortable appearance of a young professional in a tropical country. After months of OD uniforms and *ao dai*-and pajama-clad Vietnamese, his appearance came as a shock: Civilians still wore real clothes!

His name was Chad Jeffrey Williams. I imagined that a person named Chad was more at home in Ivy League circles, bantering about the stock market with others of a similar station in life, but here he was, out in the wilds of Can Tho, Mekong Delta, good ol' Vietnam.

Chad pointed out that few soldiers came into the Center, but that I was most welcome to have a look around. He would give me a personal tour.

The Center consisted of two public rooms: a reception area (where I had entered) and a small library. Beyond the reception area, there were private rooms used for political meetings and various other confidential undertakings. His living quarters were on the second floor of the building, set back on the first floor to allow space for a railed balcony.

The library, another whitewashed room like the reception room, had three walls lined with shelves; the fourth was lined with portraits of Nixon, General Abrams, and various other official-looking people. I asked several questions about the purpose of the Center as I looked over the books. He had all the answers on the tip of his tongue, as if he had rehearsed them.

He asked about my background and, when he discovered that I was a singer, asked if I had studied other languages. When I replied that I had studied Italian, French, and German, he clapped his hands together and smiled.

"Have you ever taught a language?" he asked.

"No, I just studied them."

"The reason I ask," he said as he escorted me back to the reception room, "is that I need an English teacher for some Vietnamese students. Would you be interested?"

"I've never thought about it."

"I have two teachers," he explained, "soldiers like you, who volunteer to teach English. One of them is on R&R and will be DEROS'd within a week or so after he returns. I'm looking for a replacement."

I shrugged noncommittally. "I don't think I'm a good choice. I've never taught English, and my schedule is always changing."

"How about tonight? Are you free?

When I left the Center, I carried a list of students, a map to the building where the classes met, and a much-used paperback book that the students used as a text. I had agreed to teach the next four classes, as long as Riggles could get my guard duty reassigned to a different night. As I drove back to the base, a tune from *Oklahoma!* kept going through my head, with a slight change in text: "I'm just a boy who cain't say no."

The text for the class was a dreary collection of stories with language that was not much above the "See Dick run" level. The perspective of American life was one in which every family, all pleasant Caucasian folk, had their cozy house, and the children led safe, trouble-free lives. The major activity of these families, according to the text, was shopping. To the Vietnamese students, it must have been tantamount to reading about life on Mars.

I was working with another disadvantage: I had no idea what the class, which had been meeting twice weekly for two months, had been studying. Did they have assignments? Were there supposed to be tests? Chad had not been able to tell me much about what went on in the classes, even though he was ostensibly in charge of the entire operation. He was also in the dark about the American teachers' quality of work, but felt that because he had recruited them as volunteers, there was no way to monitor them. Even I, who had never taught, knew these were not the best educational circumstances for the students. But I agreed to teach anyway.

The classes were held in a guarded compound in the city. All Vietnamese who wished to enter the compound were stopped, their identification verified, and their personal belongings checked for weapons. The sixteen students who entered the classroom were eager to practice their English.

Incompetence has never been a state I have enjoyed, even though I have visited there often. I was unnerved. I introduced myself, writing my name on the blackboard, all the while realizing that Western script, particularly my wobbly Western script, was quite strange to them. They used a combination of Chinese symbols with lots of extra dots, dashes, and other markings that were created for them by a French priest, a Jesuit missionary who had lived in the country in the 1700s. He had, in effect, given them a written language at a time when most Asians who were not of the ruling classes were illiterate. Where was he when I needed him?

After introducing myself, I explained, in the simplest terms I knew without lapsing into pidgin English, that I would be their teacher for the next two weeks. I told them, as a way of further introducing myself, that I was a chaplain's assistant, which for most of them had as much meaning as saying that I could perform fioratura in Baroque music.

However, Mr. Nguyen (as he introduced himself) understood the term "chaplain." He raised his hand, and when I recognized him, he stood and asked, "Teacha, chaplain is ..." He waved both hands in the air, looking for the right term "... *c'est un frère?*"

French! Of course! Many older Vietnamese would know some French. I replied, in my college French, that a chaplain could be a Catholic priest or Protestant minister. Mr. Nguyen turned to the class and said something in Vietnamese, to which they murmured and nodded their understanding.

The class introduced themselves, struggling with English as they stated how old they were—their ages ranged from sixteen to sixty-four (Mr. Nguyen's age)—and said something about what they did. There were four men in the class: Mr. Nguyen and three boys who were sixteen. Women of various ages made up the rest of the class.

We proceeded with mixtures of three languages: Mr. Nguyen's French mixed with English, my English mixed with French, and the students' Vietnamese mixed with French and English. We were a class of linguistic mongrels.

Later, when class was over, I asked Mr. Nguyen if there were other students in the class who had not attended because there were more names on the class list. I showed him the list, and he studied it for a time. He looked up at me through his glasses and nodded his gray head. Yes, he said, there had been others, but they were young men who were now in the military. He explained that they had been removed from their homes two weeks earlier and forcibly enlisted. Mr. Nguyen had brought the three sixteen-year-olds to our class in the hopes that when the boys went into the service, they would be safer if they spoke enough English to be assigned to work with Americans.

As I drove back to the base, I mused over the fact that Americans still lived in the "Land of the Free." Our "greetings" from Uncle Sam still came in the mail. In Vietnam, it sometimes arrived in the middle of the night, armed, and barging through the front door.

The next class was smoother. I sat on the desk with my feet dangling, like the young professors at Michigan did, as I tried to get the students to simply talk, using all the English they could. The topic for the evening was "work." "What do you do to make money?" I asked. Mr. Nguyen worked for the Catholic Relief Agency. The French had still ruled when he was a young boy, so it had been easy to learn their language. "Now," he said with a shrug, "I learn English. I older, and it much harder."

The boys were vague about what they did, just as most sixteen-year-olds would be. Not speaking English only complicated the problem. The women all worked with Americans in various jobs; several were office workers and a couple of them were maids.

"My lady, she say she pay much money for me study English," one said. That was the first I had heard about tuition. Where did the money go?

We worked on asking directions and on basic questions and statements: Where is a bathroom? I am hungry. I am thirsty. I am sleepy. How much does that cost?

We counted things, named common objects (those that were in the room), wrote the names of the common objects (nose, ear, pencil, desk), and gave simple commands: Stand up, sit down, go there, and come here. I gained a great appreciation for the opportunity to learn a language, any language, as a child.

By the third class, we were becoming much friendlier. There was more laughing (from the men) and behind-the-hand giggling (from the women), as they struggled to learn. I also realized that I was recognizing each of them more easily; they were becoming individuals to me.

Prejudice is an insidious mind-set. Looking around the class as they worked in pairs, practicing their English on each other, I became aware that I fell into the "they all look alike" attitude whenever I was in the company of several Vietnamese. Those words would never have passed my liberal lips, but I knew that was what I had thought. The Vietnamese had become an indistinguishable mass of Orientals to me, a formless "them." But the class, these students, had awakened me to my casual racism.

My fourth class arrived all too soon. As I stepped into the room, I had a small regret that I had not signed up to teach longer since I had come to look forward to our time together.

I called the class to order and began the lesson. I had the students carry on short conversations that included polite greetings, saying good-bye, and expressing simple feelings. What I felt was sadness that I would not be their "teacha" anymore. I ended the class by saying good-bye, and that I hoped they would continue with their studies.

Mr. Nguyen hung back from leaving with the others after class. He asked if I had noticed the three boys were absent. I said yes. He said they had been taken by the military the night before. They could be anywhere, in some training camp or on their way to one. His eyes filled with tears as he said that their families would probably never see them again. He wiped his eyes. He said he also wanted me to know about the children.

"What children?" I asked.

There were children of soldiers in an orphanage run by Catholic nuns. Could I do something to help them? I told him I didn't know what I could do, but I would go to see the children, if he would go with me. I had to receive permission from Riggles, but I was pretty sure he would allow me to go. I wasn't sure if I really wanted to go myself, but I didn't want to let Mr. Nguyen down.

Three days later, I picked Mr. Nguyen up at the Catholic Relief Center and drove with him to the orphanage. The sisters had settled the orphanage into what had once been a school. The thick walls—textured plaster painted with a chalky whitewash—served as barrier to the heat, keeping the cool, moist air inside the shadowed rooms.

Children were everywhere, and the nuns seemed to be right behind them, gently herding them from one part of the facility to the other. Many of the children were so small that their heads hardly reached past my knees.

Mr. Nguyen spoke with Mother Superior; at least, I dubbed her that since she seemed to be the oldest and in charge. The average Vietnamese woman was like a lovely flower, whose youthful bloom faded quickly. By the time she reached thirty, her face was lined, weathered, and aged. I had never developed the knack of guessing ages among Caucasians, so for all I knew Mother Superior might have been between thirty and seventy. Her energy level, though, as she bustled after the children and their nun-attendants, was admirable. Even as she spoke with us, her eyes tracked the comings and goings of her charges and their attendants.

Mr. Nuyen explained to her, in a combination of Vietnamese and French— the French being for my benefit—that I worked for military chaplains and that I might be able to find a way to contact people over in the United States for some help.

Mother Marie, as she called herself, smiled and bowed. She spoke to me in excellent French, explaining that she had spent several years in France during her studies to become a nun. Her speech was better than my understanding, so I was often asking her to speak *plus lent* (slower).

The children needed everything, she said—medicine, clothing, food—but at that moment, medicine and clothing were highest on the list. I wondered where their food came from, as the memories of nuns riding in the back of dump trucks flickered in my head.

Mother Marie said that anything I could do would be appreciated. Then she hurried off, saying that she was late to her class. Mr. Nguyen explained that the sisters taught school for the older children, as well as tending to the smaller ones. This was the only formal schooling the children would receive because few public schools remained open anywhere in the country, and regrettably, most of these children would not be welcome in the schools or any part of the Vietnamese society.

After dropping Mr. Nguyen off at the Agency, I drove back to the base, feeling disgusted. These children were another American legacy in Vietnam that would survive for decades, as easily forgotten by the nation that had sent their fathers to war as they were forgotten by the fathers who sired them. I felt ashamed to be an American and a soldier.

Back at the base, I talked to Riggles about what could be done. He had received his DEROS orders two days earlier, and, as I would discover, it was difficult to keep focused on the day-to-day activities, let alone any long-term planning.

"The army doesn't really have any channels for distributing food, clothing, and medicine to orphans," he said.

"These children aren't orphans," I pointed out. "They've been abandoned by their mothers after their American fathers abandoned them."

"I understand," Riggles said, "but the army isn't in the welfare business." He sighed. "I know this sounds harsh, but I tried to do something similar with an orphanage in Korea when I was stationed there some years ago.

"I learned real fast that the people who run orphanages can become dependent on handouts from Americans." I started to protest, but he stopped me. "The military's mission is to carry out the orders of the civilian leaders, and the mission of the chaplaincy is to sustain the soldiers in the field."

He came around from behind his desk and leaned against it. "I was reminded of that by my supervising chaplain when I was spending a lot of time and energy in channeling supplies to a nearby orphanage. He told me that I was neglecting some of my duties on base, and I had even missed a couple of briefings given by the base CO. Well, the CO found out that I was engaged in non-military activities when I should have been listening to him yammer about his arranging for that year's beauty queen's visit to the men. He called my supervisor, who then called me." He returned to his chair behind the desk, shaking his head. "Besides, it takes a lot of planning and a sustained effort to arrange for any long-term support. You might not be here long enough to do much."

"What do you mean?"

"Since I'm leaving, I though you might want to move up. There's a Spec 5 slot that's going to open up at Battalion Headquarters in Saigon, and I thought I might put you up for that," he said with a smile.

"But I'm only a Spec 4," I reminded him.

His smiled broadened. "I've also recommended you for promotion. The Board meets next week."

I was both surprised and frustrated. After thanking him for his recommendation, I stepped across the hallway to my office to catch up on some paperwork and think about my changed circumstances. A promotion meant more money, something Karen and I could use, especially since our baby was due soon. Saigon sounded, well, I was not sure how Saigon sounded. It was the biggest city in South Vietnam, but having been there, I knew it was another version of Can Tho, only dirtier and more congested. Hundreds of thousands of people from the countryside had crowded into the city over the course of the war, hoping to find employment and safe homes for their families. Instead, they had found no homes and no work, poverty, crime, and the threat of guerilla attacks that seemed unstoppable. The more I thought about it, the safer Can Tho seemed.

I thought about it for several days and then talked to Riggles. I explained that I really wanted the promotion but would prefer to stay where I was. He thought that would be okay.

Meanwhile, I had not forgotten about my promise to help the orphanage. I had driven into Can Tho and talked to Chad at the Center. He listened somewhat distractedly to my story of the orphanage and my desire to find some way to provide them with what they needed. He was wearing white tennis shoes, white shorts, and an aqua shirt. He kept glancing at his watch as we talked.

"Your intentions were very fine—admirable, even," he began. I felt like I had just been patted on the head and told I was a good boy. "But although I'd like to provide assistance, that is, alas, not my mission in-country. I'm charged to act as a source of information about the U.S. to the local politicos. And I have my hands full with that. Besides," he said dismissively, "these people don't use what we give them; they just sell it on the black market."

The pretty receptionist I had met on my first visit was working at her desk next to us as Chad and I talked. She seemed oblivious to his references to her and her countrymen.

These children were a Vietnamese problem, Chad said, and the Vietnamese would deal with them in their customary way. The United States had no right to impose its society's norms on an ally. He looked again at his watch. "Well, I have to dash. I'm late for a tennis game. Sorry we can't be of assistance."

I watched him climb into his chauffeured car and leave. I turned to say good-bye to the receptionist and found her looking at me, an act that seemed unusual for a Vietnamese woman. She smiled and returned to her work.

I passed by the Adkersons' home and decided to stop. I had not seen them for some time because they had removed my name from their Good Person list. During a dinner at their home where Riggles and I were guests, I had the temerity to disagree with them about their belief that God would send a person to Hell simply because the person happened to be a Communist. They thought "yes," and I thought "no." I had also suggested that God was not in favor of any particular economic system (for example, capitalism) over other economic systems. I don't know which belief offended them the most, but I had not "broken bread" with them since. However, I was hoping that they might be able to overlook my particular shortcomings and see that the children needed help.

Mrs. Adkerson was at home, the maid said as she hurried off to get her. Mrs. Adkerson clearly was not thrilled to see me, but she invited me in anyway. After a few awkward moments, I told her why I had come. Yes, she knew of the school and the work of the nuns and she wished them well. But it was a Catholic operation, and as Southern Baptist missionaries, she didn't think they would be able to help.

"You see," she explained, "the nuns are indoctrinating those dear children into the Church, and we can't condone that. So if we give the nuns assistance, we would be helping them find more children to bring into the Church. The churches that support us would never stand for providing support to the Catholics, even though on the surface, it seems like a humanitarian thing to do. You see what I mean, don't you?"

I gritted my teeth. I understood that close-minded attitude very well; I had grown up in it. Hearing it coming from a missionary helped me to see how small and asinine an attitude it was.

I didn't say what I thought. It seemed futile to argue. My grandfather once told me, "Never argue with a drunk or a fool." She seemed stone cold sober to me.

My last chance, it seemed, was my dad's church. Later that day, I wrote a long letter to my parents about the plight of the children. Could their church organize some sort of food or clothing drive? "The Lord will bless you and the church if you could help out," I wrote. I was not above pulling a few spiritual strings if it would help the children.

CHAPTER 28

▼

Heartbreak Hotel

I mailed the letter on my way to pick up my gear for another exciting evening of guarding our perimeter, not expecting to hear from my folks for a couple of weeks. This particular night, rather than going to our usual post, the Sergeant of the Guard told four of us to wait for the truck.

After he left, I asked my comrades what truck he had referred to.

"The one that'll take us to the villa," a short, stocky Southern boy answered. I dubbed him "Billy Bob" in my mind.

"What villa is that?" I asked, still in the dark. The other two soldiers spit then sat down on the ground to wait for the truck.

"The officers' villa," Billy Bob answered, his tone being one that questioned what planet I had been visiting.

One of the seated soldiers answered my next question before I asked it. "A bunch of the officers pool their money and rent this big fucking villa in town. A rich Frenchman built it and lived in it before Charlie fertilized the front yard with his guts. Officers took it over several years ago, so now it's passed along to other officers when they draw this post."

"Army don't know nothin' 'bout it," the third volunteered. He sounded like a Midwesterner, so I dubbed him "Detroit." The three of them laughed at my ignorance.

Billy Bob was warming to the topic. "Army don't know nothin' 'bout nothin'. 'Course that means the motherfuckin' Sergeant of the Guard is about to send our sorry asses out to guard somethin' that technically ain't there. Somebody high up knows about this little set-up, but nobody talks about it."

"Know what fries my balls?" Detroit asked, even though no one seemed interested in the state of his testicles. "Those cocksucking officers live like kings already, and they get the best pussy in town, just by makin' a couple of calls. No cathouse for them; they get pussy on the hoof."

The truck arrived and we piled in with our M16s and extra ammo. No machine guns or grenade launchers for the villa guards. No sir. We were goin' to guard officers and gentlemen, warriors all. We were driven to a crowded neighborhood that surrounded the villa. In its prime, it might have been a lovely, elegant house, but what greeted us as night fell was a large stucco house of indeterminate color, protected by a high fence of barbed wire topped by concertina.

The house was well lit on the inside but almost entirely dark on the outside, save for swatches of incandescent light that passed through the windows. The light drove the moths, millers and their ken, crazy as they battered the windows, trying to enter so they could immolate themselves in the radiant heat.

They, in turn, drew their predators—spiders and lizards—to the flying feast. These hunters attracted *their* stalkers until it seemed that insects, reptiles, and rats from far and near were gathered beneath the windows. The rat-tat-tat of exoskeletons on glass, followed by grassy slithering, would make for interesting background noise against the stillness of the alley. Several window air conditioners clattered away, bathing the inhabitants in dry coolness, while we slathered insect repellant over our sweat, hoping to deter the flying man-eaters for as long as possible.

Two of us went to guard the front entrance, while Billy Bob and I settled into the small bunker next to the rear gate that faced an alley. I pulled the two-hour first watch, while Billy Bob tried to catch some early shut-eye.

Having the alley so close felt uncomfortable—threatening. An occasional scooter would buzz by, setting my nerves on edge; it would be quite easy to drop a satchel charge or get a little small-arms practice by shooting at the sitting-duck GI guard while driving past. I would scrunch into the small bunker without rousing the sleeping Billy Bob every time a scooter passed.

The sky still held some light when the first call girl arrived. I had been patrolling the fence, which meant that I walked six yards in one direction, turned, and retraced my steps. I was trying to find a way to stay awake.

I heard footsteps coming down the alley. A girl in a tight dress was walking down the middle of the alley, a slower walk than most Vietnamese and with a little hesitancy in her step. The shadows hid her features until she was close to the gate. She nodded.

"Enter, please," she said.

Her accent was so strong that I didn't understand her at first.

"GI, you open gate; I go in," she said in a stronger voice, pointing toward the villa.

"Sure," I said. "Okay." It felt very awkward as I unbarred the gate and swung one side open. As she stepped through, I noticed the thin straps that held the high heels on her feet and caught the fragrance of a delicate perfume. Her jet-black hair was wound around her head, held in place by a comb-like ornament. The rustle of her dress made an almost imperceptible fluttering sound as she walked toward the villa. She *was* lovely. I sighed as my feelings alternated between disgust and desire.

The face of the prostitute in Saigon rose before me. Was this young woman like the one in Saigon, trapped into this life, or was it something she wanted to do for her own reasons?

I decided that it would be safer to concentrate on my assignment: guarding the damned officers. My imagination took off. As far as I knew, the officers might be in danger. She might be VC. She had opened her little clutch purse for me to check, but I hadn't held it or poked through the contents. She could be armed. I didn't think so, considering the tightness of her clothes, but I hadn't searched her, hadn't "patted her down."

Jesus, Ted. One whiff of perfume and you go bonkers. Get back to work. Hormones, I reminded myself, have a way of getting out of hand.

By the time the third girl had passed through the gate, I was feeling like a butler in a bordello. They were all pretty, all made up for their "Johns." I had just roused Billy Bob when the next girl arrived.

"How many officers are in there?" I asked, not really expecting an answer.

"'Bout tin or twelve," he said as he stretched. "Me and mah buddies tried to git a fuckin' head count last time I wuz here. That's whut we figured."

Another girl stepped up to the gate and spoke, but her voice was so light and small that it was unintelligible. I walked over, raised the bar, and glanced at her. She was the receptionist from the U.S. Information Center.

She passed through the gate, then she held out her purse for me to examine it, but I didn't even look. I gestured for her to go on. She looked up at me, and for a second she hesitated, her eyes narrowing slightly. Then she smiled and nodded and walked quickly to the villa.

Had she recognized me? I doubted it. Americans all looked alike to Vietnamese, or so one of my language students had once told me. I didn't know why I was surprised and saddened to see her, but I was. My surprise was short-lived, however. It was a good thing my watch was over so I could rest for a couple of hours, for I was suddenly very tired.

I had the last shift of the night, so I watched the sky brighten at dawn. The hookers had left sometime during Billy Bob's watch, or so he had muttered as he had dragged himself into the bunker after his last watch. I was glad that I had not seen her—or any of the others—leave. I felt soiled just by being there, like I had somehow participated in the girls' degradation.

The guard truck announced its arrival by the roar of its engine as it turned into the quiet alley. Billy Bob staggered out of the bunker as I opened the gate for the truck to enter the compound. Our replacements jumped out of the back of the truck. The two guards from the front of the compound came shuffling around the corner of the house, and the four of us dragged ourselves onto the truck. We sat on the wooden benches on both sides of the truck, and we swayed and bounced our way out of the alley and onto the main thoroughfare.

Morning traffic, in the form of mopeds, scooters, bicycles, pedi-cabs, and carts of produce pulled by vendors, flowed into Can Tho with the sunrise. The truck stopped, lurched forward, and stopped again, as the driver tried to edge through the traffic. None of us paid any attention; we were trying to keep from falling off the benches as the truck jostled us back to the base.

It stopped again; this time for a little longer, it seemed. As I leaned back against the truck, I noticed that the sky was a cloudless blue, just like I had seen so often back in Michigan. I was trying to calculate what time it was there when I noticed a movement out of the corner of my eye. Before I was able to react, fingers reached under my watch, pulled it away from my wrist with a twisting motion, and snapped the band. Looking up, I saw a boy's face disappear over the edge of the truck; he was grinning.

I jumped up, looking over the top of the truck. "Shoot the fucker!" one of the other guards said. I grabbed a clip from my webbing and shoved it into the M16. Everywhere I looked, people moved briskly, as they went about their business in the early morning before the day's heat took its toll. I though the boy had run into the narrow, twisting alley that led off of the main road, but he was nowhere in sight. The truck's engine revved just then, and I grabbed the edge of the truck to avoid being thrown off.

The watch had cost twenty dollars. I'd been ready to kill a kid for stealing a cheap watch. What was happening to me? What was I becoming?

Back at the base, I trudged to my hooch feeling like I would sleep the day away. At that moment, I wanted only to shower and sleep. First, another coffee-can bath; then, after falling into my seldom-used bunk, I began sweating in the stifling air of the hooch.

Just as I felt myself falling asleep, a tear rolled down the side of my face. I wiped it away, wondering at it. I felt like I was losing something I couldn't describe, something that I could never recover. Deep inside me something was changing, and I mourned its loss.

CHAPTER 29

▼

Unto Us a Son Is Born

August

By the end of July, Riggles had returned to the States—DEROS, good-bye Charlie, gone home. Early one morning, I had driven him to the chopper that was to carry him to Saigon. He was excited about returning to his wife and children in Texas. He had a month or more of leave coming, he said, and would love to spend at least half of that in bed with his wife and the other half playing golf.

"Of course, I suppose I should spend some time with Jenny and Josh as well, so I'll have to work them in," he said, chuckling.

"I don't talk about them much 'cause," his voice caught. He cleared his throat, but his voice quavered as he tried to continue. "'Cause I miss them so darn much." He wiped at a stray tear. My eyes teared as well. He cleared his throat and changed the subject. "Did I tell you that I was considering resigning my commission?"

I was surprised. "No. I had no idea."

"A couple of weeks ago I had just about had it. Being away from Helen and the kids had become more than I could stand, or so it seemed at the time."

"You never let on that anything was bothering you," I said.

"Of course not. I'm a professional—a minister and an officer. We're not supposed to have to lean on other people for support; they're supposed to lean on us. That's probably one reason why so many officers are alcoholics. Can't trust anyone, can't let your hair down." He looked over at me. "You might find that out if you stay in the army."

"No way would I ever want to stay in this man's army!" I said. He smiled.

Riggles' chopper was warming up when we pulled up. We jumped out of the jeep and threw his bags into the ship. I wanted to salute him, to show him in some small way that I respected him as an officer and as a man; to tell him that he had made my stay in this hellhole more worthwhile and that I had valued the trust he placed in me. Instead, he nudged my shoulder with his fist, and then, after a quick handshake, he scrambled into the ship, strapped himself in, and gave me a thumbs-up as a broad grin wreathed his face. He was going home.

I backed away from the downdraft of the rotors, shielding my eyes with my hand against the blown sand. The Huey lifted, moved forward as it picked up air-speed, and rose quickly into the pale blue sky.

I arrived back at an empty chapel. Harry and Father O'Brian had flown to another base earlier in the day. Chaplain Collins had gone to Saigon for meetings for a couple of days. The only sounds inside were those made by the electric fans that stirred the hot air.

All the paperwork had been done for the day, and no services were sched-uled—there was nothing to do. I tried to read for a while, but my eyes kept clos-ing, so I eventually gave up even trying to look awake. I moved one of the fans to the end of a pew and lay down to sleep for awhile.

As I closed my eyes, scenes from my childhood summers crowded before me—the late-summer sounds of crickets, chirping birds, splashing water. The long shadows of twilight as the golden sun set in the sky played in my memory. The sweaty excitement of boyhood games that had us running across miles—it seemed—of fenceless lawns in Sarasota, and the touch football games with high school buddies that ended when it grew so dark we would lose the football. Memories of summers moved before me as I sank into sleep in the hot breeze from the fan, memories stirred by Riggles' departure.

His leaving ended another episode of my life that would not be repeated. I understood then that he had been a kind of anchor for me in the military sea, and now my anchor was gone. We had received word that a new chaplain would arrive in a couple of days but I knew nothing else about him. For now, it was enough to regret Riggles' leaving, look forward to my own homeward return in the distant future, and doze in the humid fan-stirred breeze.

According to an ancient Chinese saying, time is like a river. If that is true, then I was sure the army had found a way to reduce the flow to a slow drip. At least that was how August 1970 felt to me. Captain Evert, the new chaplain, arrived two days after Riggles' departure. He had been in the army for five years, but this was his first overseas assignment, and for the first few days he was overwhelmed.

He was around forty and he had trouble with the change in time zones, so he was mentally and physically sluggish for a while.

My work had become routine, so it only took a couple of hours in the early morning to complete. There were fewer casualties, it seemed, so hospital visits and memorial services became more infrequent. The deaths that did occur were often not combat-related; drunkenness, youthful high spirits, or simple, everyday stupidity.

I was almost a victim of an act of stupidity. I had been in the EM Club when several young soldiers made a noisy entrance. They grabbed some pitchers of beer, carried them to the table, and then started their evening's drinking. As I passed the table on my way out, one of them said, "Look what I found." I kept walking, thinking that whatever it was would probably not interest me. I was outside the Club, about twenty yards from the entrance, when the explosion occurred.

I hit the ground, thinking it might be incoming. The attack siren was silent. After a few seconds, I got up and brushed myself off, feeling a little foolish for diving to the ground at every loud noise.

A minute later, I heard sirens heading in my direction. There was yelling the in EM Club. I ran back inside. The stench of cordite and coppery smell of blood hit my nostrils. The table near the door, where the group of soldiers had sat, was gone. The soldiers at the table and several surrounding tables had been blasted off their seats. Several of them were little more than crumpled lumps of meat, their fatigues dark with blood.

Other soldiers who had not been injured or had been injured only slightly knelt beside the wounded, using their hands or hats or torn fatigues as pressure bandages. A soldier was screaming in pain, waving a stump of an arm as two other soldiers struggled frantically to hold it down and apply a tourniquet.

Behind the counter, a sergeant—one of the bartenders—was shouting into a phone, calling for medics—anyone who could help. He started waving the phone around, talking to the room.

"The motherfucking son-of-a-bitch had a grenade! A fucking M30 grenade! I saw it when he pulled it out of his pocket. I yelled at him to set it down easy. Fucker laughed. Tossed it to the guy across the table; he missed. Next thing I know, I'm lying on the floor behind the bar, can't hear 'cause my ears are ringin'. Motherfuck almost killed me!" he screamed, as he started beating the phone on the bar.

There was nothing I could do there, so I ran toward the chaplain's quarters, hoping to find Chaplain Evert. I wasn't sure what I thought he might be able to do, but on I ran.

The officers' quarters were about a mile from the Club, but I had no idea where Evert's quarters were. My breathing was ragged and I was drenched in sweat when I reached the area where the officers lived, but I didn't slow down.

I had forgotten my original goal as my feet pounded the ground, carrying me through the night. I tripped, recovered my balance, stumbled a few yards more, and tripped again, falling, scraping the heels of my hands along the coarse sand and gravel. I got up. I felt exhausted and sharp pains were running up both sides of my body.

I was disoriented as I looked around trying to get my bearings: I was on Main Street, the section of dirt road that ran past the PX and the little shops that the Vietnamese had built. There was the barbershop and the movie theater across the road. Company Headquarters was farther ahead, and the Infirmary sat at the other end. There were a few lights on there.

I shambled toward the chapel that lay just south of the Infirmary. My heart was racing, even though my breathing had slowed, and I felt like I was coming down with a chill. The chapel was dark and quiet. I went to the assistants' office, threw the bunk together, and fell onto it. Sleep came, eventually.

I dreamed that night: I was in the Club, passing the table as the soldier pulled the grenade from his pocket. I knew what was going to happen. I tried to run but felt like I was swimming in molasses. The projectile was flying through the air, about to hit the table. I was screaming, throwing myself to the ground, but I couldn't fall. My hand, waving in the air, hit something hard, something loud. I awoke as I fell out of the bunk. My hand had hit a metal filing cabinet, and I would have a welt on it the next day.

Scrambling to my feet in the dark, I scraped my back against a handle on a drawer. I gritted my teeth against the pain that radiated from the abraded skin and jerked forward, stumbling across the bunk. I fell across it, my shoulder whacking the metal filing cabinets. I sat down hard on the bunk.

Tears started running down my face. I had received my share of knocks and scrapes while growing up but had not cried over them since I was a child. Yet something came welling up in me from deep inside, pushing the tears ahead of it.

"You dumb shit! You almost killed me!" I shouted into the darkness. Now I knew why the bartender had screamed at the dead soldier as he slammed the phone against the bar.

Chaplain Evert found me sprawled in a pew the next morning. From the way he addressed me, I must have looked like death warmed over.

"Are you okay, Ted?" he asked as he gently shook me awake.

I tried to move, but my body felt like it had been grafted to the bench. "Yes, sir," I said with a groan as I tried to stand. "Sorry you found me like this, Chaplain. I had a bad night."

He wrinkled his nose. "You smell like you had a bad night. At least I don't smell booze on you. I would bust you to private if I thought you were coming to work drunk."

I was mortified. It would be a long time before he would trust me the way Riggles had, if ever.

He walked to the door of his office. "Get yourself cleaned up, son. There was an explosion in the EM Club last night, and I need you to drive me to the Air Force Field Hospital to visit the survivors."

"I know. I had just left the Club when the grenade exploded."

He moved back in my direction but kept his distance—the fan was blowing toward me, and he was downwind. "You were? Why didn't you come to get me? I should have been there right away." He shook his head in frustration.

"I was coming to get you, but—"

"I lost some points with the CO because I didn't know about this until this morning's briefing," he said.

"I apologize, but—"

"Being sorry doesn't get the job done," he said, waggling a finger at me.

I felt like I was six years old, being scolded by my teacher. "This has never happened before, and it won't happen again, sir," I said.

He dropped his hands and took a deep breath. "Sorry, Bertson. I'm uptight about a lot of things, and I shouldn't take it out on you. This living in a combat zone is still pretty new to me. I'll, uh, you go get cleaned up, and we'll go," he said as he walked into his office and closed the door.

Riggles never closed the door unless he was counseling someone, I thought.

Evert was tense as he drove to the hospital. I was his guide as well as his bodyguard since this was his first time going to the hospital. The dirt road had grown more pitted during the rainy season, and the jeep bucked and jerked as he stepped on and off the gas pedal, swerving as he tried to avoid the worst holes. Eventually, he stopped dead in the road. He turned to me and said that I should drive and he would hold the M16. Just holding a weapon is not the same as using it, he said. If someone asked about it, that's what he would say, he declared. I began to wonder how he would hold up at the hospital.

Almost as if he read my mind, he said that I was probably wondering how he would respond to the wounded. He confessed that he had a great dislike of hospitals and avoided them as much as he could. His last stateside postings had been at training centers, so he seldom had to visit anyone who was seriously wounded.

"I didn't like it either," I said, "and I know I'll never get used to it. But I've been to this hospital a lot, and had gotten to know the doctors and nurses a little. They knew how to keep an eye on me and not let me screw up too badly."

He smiled. "Maybe you should keep an eye on me since you're an old hand at it."

"That's part of the MO for the well-trained chaplain's assistant, sir," I said. "'Keeping the Chaplain from Screwing Up' was the first thing we studied at Fort Hamilton."

"I hope you've been reviewing of that part of the manual, Ted," he said.

I introduced Evert to some of the doctors and nurses, and he seemed to relax a bit with them. As he chatted with the head nurse, Captain Robertson, I kept looking around, hoping to spot O'Malley. It had been some time since I had been to the hospital, and I couldn't be sure that she was still there.

There was a commotion down the corridor. Robertson smiled and said that it was Lieutenant O'Malley's birthday. The other nurses had thrown a surprise party for her.

"You know Lieutenant O'Malley, don't you, Bertson?" Robertson asked.

"Yes, ma'am. We've spoken a couple of times."

"Why don't you and Chaplain Evert join us?"

"Always ready for a party," Evert said immediately. I liked him more all the time.

Captain Robertson ushered us into the staff lounge, which was festooned with balloons and colorful crepe-paper streamers. O'Malley, wearing a pointed party hat, was the center of attention. For me, being in a room with so many "round-eyes" was the stuff of fantasy.

"Specialist Bertson," O'Malley said as we walked in. "What a nice surprise."

"Happy birthday, Lieutenant," I said. "This is Chaplain Evert. He's here to visit some injured, and Captain Robertson invited us in."

"Thanks, Marge," O'Malley said.

"You're welcome, Josie. Actually, I had an ulterior motive. Didn't you mention that Bertson is a singer?"

Josie beamed. "That's what I've been told."

"He's my present to you." Robertson said. The other nurses let out a long "Ooooooo." Robertson laughed. "Not that kind of present, ladies." Everyone laughed. "Bertson, would you sing 'Happy Birthday' to Josie for us? This group of females sound like cats fighting when they try to sing."

There were calls of "Hey, Marge, speak for yourself," and "What a thing to say!" As their calls died out, another female voice said, "Yeah, but it's true." This was followed by more laughter.

I started to decline since I hadn't sung for months, but when I saw the expectant look on Josie's face, I decided to try it.

My vocal cords felt like I was rubbing two rusty nails together as I sang, but I felt courageous enough to interpolate a high note at the end. The nurses applauded, and a couple of them hugged Josie.

There was a momentary lull, the kind that happens when a group is deciding what to do next.

"Specialist Bertson," Josie asked, "do you know 'My Wild Irish Rose'?" All the faces turned toward me.

"Yes, ma'am," I answered.

"Would you sing that for me?" she asked. The room grew quiet.

Looking at her lovely face, I wanted to say something poetic, but all I said was, "Of course, if I can remember it."

I had learned that song from my high school choral director, Mr. Rudd. He used it often in choral warm-ups, and his eyes often grew misty as we sang. He was the reason I went into music as a profession. So the song already had strong, warm memories for me as I stood singing for the nurses, for Josie.

The song ended, and the room was silent. Tears ran down Josie's face, and a couple of the other nurses wiped their eyes.

"My papa used to sing that to my mom," Josie said. Her chin quivered. Then she laughed. "Of course, he sang with a Mexican accent—'da sweetest flowa dat blows.'"

She came over to me and, without pausing, put her arms around my neck and hugged me. For a moment, I didn't know what to do. Was it illegal to hug an officer? Throwing reservations aside, I hugged her back.

She pulled back and looked into my eyes. "Thank you, Ted. You've made this a very special day for me." Then she turned and joined the other nurses, who were pushing candles into a small cake.

Ted! She'd called me Ted! She knew my name! I was trying to remember whether or not I had ever told her my name was Ted when Evert put his hand on my shoulder.

"That was beautiful, Ted, really lovely. I didn't know you were a singer."

"I think I had forgotten, too," I said truthfully. "That was a nice way to be reminded."

August passed by, one sultry day following another. Evert settled into his job and had us on the go visiting various bases in the Delta that were without chaplains, as well as firebases on the border of Vietnam and Cambodia. We flew whenever we could, but occasionally we would convoy with jeeps and trucks on the supply runs to other bases.

On the afternoon of August 21st, we had returned to base after several hours of eating dust behind a convoy of engineers that we had stumbled onto earlier that afternoon. I was sitting in a sweaty, grimy stupor as we drove through the base gate. Any energy I'd had at the start of the day with had been drained out of me by the blazing sun.

I turned the jeep back to the Motor Pool and dragged myself to my hooch for a shower and a snooze. There was enough water for me to stand under a shower and use its weak spray to remove the layer of grit that covered me from head to toe. It felt wonderful.

I was making my way back to the hooch, wearing only a towel, when I heard my name called from a distance. Rich Hindeman came running toward me, waving a piece of paper.

"Rich!" I shouted as he got closer. "When did you get here?"

"We'll talk about that later," he said. "Here! This came for you at the chapel. It looked important."

It was a telegram from the Red Cross. My heart skipped a beat, and my mouth dried up as I took it from him. Something was wrong back home.

The words had been printed on a strip of paper that had then been cut up and pasted onto a sheet: IT'S A BOY. STOP. BORN AUGUST 21. STOP. MOTHER AND SON FINE. STOP.

I looked at Rich, and then read the message again. I was having trouble comprehending what it meant.

The expression on Rich's face alternated between concern and curiosity. "Well?" he asked, trying hard not to snatch the paper from me. "*Well?*"

I opened my mouth, but nothing came out. From a distance, I watched my hand extend the paper to Rich.

He read it silently, looked at me, and then threw his head back and shouted, "It's a boy!" He grabbed me in a bear hug, lifted me off the ground, and spun me around. "You've got a son! A manchild!"

I snapped out of my shock. "I'm a father?" I asked.

"Yep! Says so right here!" he said, slapping the telegram with his finger.

"I'm a father! I've got a son! Is Karen all right?"

"Yep! This says she's all right, too!" My towel had fallen off. I was naked, except for my black, military-issue glasses. "You might want to put this around you. You're scaring the hooch maids, Papa," he grinned.

I threw the towel over my shoulder. At that moment I didn't care if I was standing naked; I was a father—I could do anything!

"Look," Rich said, laying a hand on my bare shoulder, "you go get dressed. I'm going to the PX to get some cigars and champagne. I'll meet you back at the chapel."

"Don't tell anybody, okay?" I asked. "I'd like to tell them myself."

"Sure," he said, "my lips are sealed." He made a gesture of zipping his lips together and then hurried away as I went into the hooch.

I sat down on the lower bunk—my bunk, officially—and read the telegram several times as I tried to make its meaning seem real. I was a father.

Karen had gone through everything alone. I knew she had her parents and family there, helping, but it felt like she was all alone. *She's not alone. You are,* said a little voice in my head. My throat tightened and tears started.

This was supposed to be the happiest moment in a man's life, the birth of his first child, and here I sat, bawling into my towel. I missed her, and I needed to hold her, to hold our son, to feel them near me. I needed to hear the sounds of our families as they welcomed the new arrival, to be with friends as they lied about how much the baby looked like me or her, to see my parents' joy over their newest grandchild. I felt miserable.

I wiped my face, opened my locker, and pulled out my "civvies." I was taking the rest of the day off, with or without military permission. On the way over to the chapel, I decided to keep up a good front. There was no use in moping around and depressing everybody just because I was twelve thousand miles from where I wanted to be.

As I walked up the dusty road to the chapel, I saw them all standing outside: Harry, Father O'Brian, Evert, Collins, Rich, and Ira. When I was a few yards away, they all reached into their pockets and pulled out cigars. I started laughing.

"Congratulations! Way to go, Dad!" "Good work, Ted!" and a "Mazel Tov!" or two greeted my arrival.

As they were lighting up, I looked at Rich: "What happened to your sealed lips?"

"The seal broke," he shrugged as he went into the chapel. He appeared a few seconds later. He passed out paper cups as he said, "I couldn't find champagne in that barbarous PX, so I had to get the next-best thing." With that, he poured some Lancers Rosé into each cup. Ira waved him off, went into the chapel, and reappeared with a bottle of Mogan David wine, the same as he used in his services.

"A good Orthodox guy like me can't be too careful, you know," he said as he poured a liberal amount into his cup.

They raised their cups in a toast. "To a long and happy life for you, your wife, and your new son," Evert said.

Ira chimed in with, "May your name be blessed unto the seventh generation."

"Speaking of names, what are you calling him?" Rich asked.

"Robert, I think."

"You don't know for sure what you're naming your son?"

"Well, we had agreed on Robert Arnold, for his grandfather, if it was a boy, and, and I forgot what we decided for a girl ... Ellen, I think," I said to the crew.

"To Robert Arnold," Evert proclaimed.

O'Brian cleared his throat. "Bottoms up!"

"That's what started all of this in the first place," Harry said. We all laughed and drank.

Within a few minutes the Lancers was gone, and the wretched cigars were put out. The group dissolved. Rich had informed me that that he had commandeered Ira's jeep and that we were going to Olga's for dinner—his treat. As he ran to get the jeep key from Ira, I sat on one of the concrete pillars in front of the chapel.

My head was full of conflicting thoughts and feelings. It had been a strange afternoon. I had gone from elation to despair to, what? Comfort? Peace? Acceptance? I didn't know. I missed what my life had been before I had been yanked into this war. I felt like the character in the *Li'l Abner* comic strip—the Dick Tracy look-alike who, after being riddled with bullets, walked around with holes in his body so it was possible to see completely through him. I felt like I had holes in me, in my heart. They just couldn't be seen.

The image of the chaplains and assistants greeting me with their cigars crossed my mind. As much as I hated this place—this war—these men made it bearable. I needed them to get me through this. I stood up, walked across the street, and looked back at the chapel. It was, all in all, a crummy structure, its impermanence stamped on it as clearly as the white paint on its plywood walls. But for me, it was home.

CHAPTER 30

▼

The Days Grow Short
When You Reach
September

September dragged by. The routine of military life continued on its monotonous way as the days blurred into one another. We were hit with mortar attacks, but they seemed to be less frequent as the weeks passed. Not that I withstood the attacks any better than before Robbie was born. If anything, I was more nervous than ever because I wanted to go home whole and unscarred. No place was completely safe, a lesson that was brought home to me again in October.

I was sleeping in my assigned bunk in the hooch on the first night of October, something I had not done often since discovering that I could easily convert the assistants' office into a bedroom of sorts. There were disturbing racial overtones to the battle of rock 'n' roll vs. soul. The black troops had managed to segregate themselves by unofficially reassigning themselves to two hooches. Any white soldiers who had not taken the hints that they should look elsewhere for housing would find their personal effects trashed; offhand suggestions were made that they would be able to sleep safer in other quarters. It was not long before the company clerks got the word: Soldiers were to be assigned to certain hooches, based on their race. This was done unofficially, and company officers winked at the practice.

On the night of October 1, the musical combatants were quiet for a change, so I decided to try sleeping in my bunk again. My bunkmates changed frequently, so I was not surprised to find a new name on the locker next to mine. He was nowhere around when I arrived in the small, three-sided area that contained the two lockers and double bunks.

It was around eleven o'clock, and I was tired. It didn't take long to sponge off, brush my teeth, exchange pleasantries with a couple of guys, and ensconce myself in my bunk under the protection of mosquito netting. I kept a small can of Raid under the netting with me for the couple of beasties that inevitably made it through. My bunkmate arrived after I was asleep, but his shuffling and locker-banging served to drag me up from a sound sleep. He left for the latrine, I supposed, and I drifted off again, only to be shaken awake as he climbed into the upper bunk.

Sleep returned for a time, until I felt the bunk shaking. It didn't take long to figure out that my bunkmate was vigorously jerking off, masturbating with great enthusiasm and no rhythm. I started to chuckle but then decided that silence was the better part of valor in such an indelicate situation. Three sharp lurches were followed by several small tremors, and he was done, or so I hoped. Again, I drifted off. Then the snoring started.

I was tossing and turning in irritation when the mortar hit. It exploded on impact when it hit the tin roof of my hooch, turning the metal into hot, razor-like shards. The soldier sleeping on the top bunk, just under the impact area, was sliced to shreds. A few smoldering fragments made it through his mattress and imbedded themselves in his bunkmate, sleeping below him. Hundreds of fragments penetrated the wooden floor, standing upright like blades of steel grass.

The lights all over the base were shut off as the attack siren worked its way into a shriek. Lying under my bunk in the darkness, covered by my helmet and flak jacket, I waited for more incoming. Above me, the soldiers who had been sleeping near the now-dead soldier stumbled out of their bunks and headed for the bunker. Most of them were barefoot.

Chaos erupted in the darkness. The first men to step on the upright shards screamed in pain as their feet were pinioned to the floor. Other soldiers, barely awake and groping their way to the exits, ran into their hooch mates, knocking them over and then falling onto the sharp fragments themselves.

I was cringing on the floor below them, hearing their cries and screams but not knowing what was causing them. Two sergeants, carrying flashlights and checking for casualties, arrived minutes later, and what they saw must have looked like a scene from Dante's *Inferno*. The narrow beams of the lights revealed a writhing mass of men, drenched in blood as they pushed, shoved, and screamed in pain.

The sergeants yelled for medics as they tried to untangle the injured men. I heard the sergeants' calls but was too afraid to move. There had been no all-clear; more mortars could be flying toward us. A voice in my head shouted for me to get up, to go help, but I kept seeing the maimed soldiers in the Field Hospital, the ones who had been running when the mortars had downed them. I wasn't a medic, for God's sake; I was a fucking *chaplain's assistant!* What could I do? I lay in the darkness, afraid and ashamed, cursing the enemy, God, and myself.

The all-clear sounded, and the lights came on. I scrambled into my fatigues and boots and ran outside and up the stairs. Help had materialized already—there were four or five soldiers, fully dressed and wearing flak jackets, lifting the injured off the steel pins and onto stretchers and applying dressings to their wounds. Sirens announced the arrival of the MPs and ambulances. There was cursing and pushing as the men who lived on the second floor were pushed out, along with me, and told to keep out of the way so the wounded could be helped.

I wandered away from the milling soldiers, going no place in particular. Sleep would be impossible for the rest of that night. It was not long before I stood in front of the chapel. Two ambulances were still sitting at the side door of the infirmary. For the first time I realized that the mess hall, chapel, infirmary, and morgue sat clustered together: food, faith, sickness, and death, represented by four shabby, temporary structures. There was probably some meaning, some profound message that could be drawn from such a juxtaposition, but it was beyond my reckoning.

The chapel doors were open, as usual, and the darkness was inviting. I sat on a pew in the darkness for a time, letting my thoughts and feelings run after each other. The air in the chapel was still and dusty, and the darkness grew heavy. I turned on a light, then turned on all the lights, wanting to push the night outside. I opened the door on the side of the chapel, near the front, and set up a portable fan in the doorway in an attempt to draw in and circulate the cooler night air.

My collection of J. S. Bach's *Preludes and Fugues* sat on the upright piano. I had gotten into the habit of practicing them at night when the chapel was empty, hoping to keep some of my musical skills intact.

I felt disoriented, jumbled up, my thoughts and feelings disorganized and confused. *I couldn't have done any more for the boys who were injured tonight,* I thought to myself. *Was I a coward because I didn't run to help immediately? Or did*

I do the right thing by trying to protect myself, like the guys hunkering down in the bunker?

It don't mean nothin', the typical enlisted man's retort, whizzed through my head. *It don't mean nothin'.* I sat down at the piano and tried to play.

The walls shook.

CHAPTER 31

▼

Bewitched, Bothered, and Bewildered

November

As the new year approached there was more and more talk of troop pullouts. On one of my visits to the Field Hospital, Lieutenant O'Malley asked me if I had heard any rumors about U.S. forces leaving Vietnam. We were outside, enjoying an unseasonably cool day and watching a squadron of fighters lining up to take off.

"Gee, I thought commissioned officers had an elaborate network that kept them up on the latest rumors," I said.

She squinted at the bright sun. "Most officers, maybe. But not nurses—at least, not this nurse." She looked around to see who else might be able to overhear us. We were alone.

We never talked about fraternization, which is a serious issue for career officers, but I thought about it a lot. I rationalized that she would know more about the rules and regulations than I would, so I was content to follow her lead in deciding when, where, or if we would spend any time together alone. I suppose I decided that ignorance could be bliss, at least sometimes.

"I've heard a couple of rumors. Chaplain Evert has said something about the possibility, but it's nothing definite."

She looked around again. "Bertson ... Ted ... I have something I want to talk over with you, but you have to promise to keep it to yourself."

"Sure," I said. "I have a top-secret security clearance; I'm safe." She didn't smile. *So much for lightheartedness,* I thought.

She looked away, as if gathering her thoughts. "I'm married. I've been married for two and a half years."

I was surprised. No one I'd talked to had any idea that she was married. Why hadn't she told anyone? Why the secret? I was surprised that I also felt a twinge of disappointment.

"Why is this a secret?" I asked, trying to get past my own mixed feelings. "Aren't a lot of the doctors and nurses married?"

"Most of the doctors are," she said edgily. "Although you can't tell the single ones from the married ones, the way they all hit on us. I have my reasons for keeping my marriage a secret."

"Your reasons are none of my business," I said. "I'll keep this to myself."

She took off her sunglasses, too, and looked at me closely, as if measuring my trustworthiness. "I know it's my business—but I need someone to talk to, and I feel like I can talk to you, that you'll listen."

"Huh? Did you say something?" I teased.

She chuckled and playfully hit my arm. "You know what I mean."

"Yes, I do." I smiled at her. "Of course, if you tell me that you're a VC infiltrator, I'll have to turn you over to Military Intelligence for torture."

She smiled. "You make me laugh and I like that," she said. "I don't laugh, or even smile much these days, I guess."

"You see things every day that make me wonder how you keep your sanity, let alone your sense of humor."

"I'm afraid I'm losing mine," she said.

"Your sanity or sense of humor?"

She shrugged. "Sometimes, I think both."

A fighter roared down the runway. We covered our ears as the second and then third screamed their ways into the cloudless sky. We stood watching until they became small dots. She seemed mesmerized by the sight and sound.

"My problem is not just that I'm married but that I'm married to a pilot, another career military officer. The military doesn't smile on marriages between career officers."

"Sounds a trifle complicated," I said.

She smiled wanly. "It's a trifle complicated for sure. I don't want to leave the service, and he sure as hell doesn't, didn't...." Her voice trailed off.

"Didn't?" I asked.

Tension crept into her face. Several moments passed in silence as she stared intently across the runway, seeing nothing. "Doesn't," she murmured.

"Did something happen?"

She glanced at me, took a deep breath, and exhaled loudly. "His name is Carl. He's a captain in the air force. We met three years ago in Japan. He had been injured during a rocket attack in Na Trang and sent to the hospital in Tokyo, where I was stationed."

The cork was out of the bottle, and the pressure of her self-imposed silence propelled the words from her. She spoke of how they met, how Carl had struggled through physical therapy to regain his flight status.

"Lots of guys get crushes on their nurses, and lots of nurses can feel real close to patients they care about. We both knew this, but it happened. It was like we couldn't stop ourselves. Pretty melodramatic, huh?"

"It does sound like something from an old movie," I said.

"I know. But it was our old movie, Carl's and mine. He was so different from the other arrogant, tail-chasing jet jockeys. He loved music, poetry, art." A smile played at the corner of her mouth. "He made me laugh, too. I was so happy … *we* were so happy." She was silent for a moment. Then, with a sigh, she continued. "The short version is, we married; we wanted to be together for the rest of our lives, somehow. And we wanted to do it so neither of us had to give up our dream. We kept it a secret from our superior officers, we found a way to be stationed here together. We knew we would have to deal with it sooner or later, to fight to stay in the service together, but we figured we could make it work if we only had enough time. Time—that's all we wanted. Enough time."

Her voice shuddered, and a sob rose in her throat. She took several breaths before she spoke again. "Carl returned to flight status and was immediately sent back. He was sent here, to this base." She flung her arms outward. "I pulled all the strings I could and was transferred here two months later." She shook her head, as if she couldn't quite comprehend what she was telling me. "That last month, I didn't hear from him. He had been writing every day, something. Sometimes not much more than 'Hi, I love you,' but it was something, you know?"

I nodded.

"Then the letters stopped, but I assumed he was busy. I was worried, but, hey, I would see him soon. We had to be kind of discreet, so I couldn't just call his superior officer, you know?" Tears welled up in her eyes. "When I arrived…." She swiped at her face with the back of her hand. "When I arrived, I found out he wasn't here."

"Had he been transferred again?" I asked quietly.

"No. He had been the lead plane on a routine mission. He had been shot down."

My impulse was to hug her, but I didn't, I couldn't, not here were anyone could see us. Instead, I said, "I'm sorry."

She wiped her face again and kicked some sand into the air. "Me, too."

"Was he ... had he been...." I stumbled.

"MIA: missing in action," she said bitterly. "That means nobody knows what the fuck happened. He might be a POW, or his body might be lying—" She broke off again. Tears ran down her cheeks, and she wiped her eyes. Her face was tired and filled with sadness, and her shoulders slumped. When she looked up at me, I felt an urge to hold her, to comfort her. She seemed to sense it too. We stood motionless, not touching, isolated.

Sounds of an approaching helicopter broke the moment. She put on her sunglasses and looked in the direction of the sound.

"I have to go back," she said with a sigh. She squared her shoulders abruptly, transforming herself from Josie to Lieutenant O'Malley. We were once again an officer and an enlisted man, walking back to the hospital.

She slowed. "Ted, thank you," she said.

"You're welcome ..." I hesitated, suddenly uncertain which one of her I was addressing.

"Josie," she said, sensing my thoughts.

"Yes, ma'am. Josie ... ma'am."

From beneath her cap, she smiled. As we approached the door, another nurse pushed through on her way outside. "Maybe I'll see you on your next visit, Bertson," Lieutenant O'Malley said as she walked inside the hospital.

"Yes, ma'am," I said, as the door closed.

As I drove back to my base, I thought about what she had said about Carl writing her everyday. I was pushed to write Karen once a week. It seemed like every week was like the other weeks, so there was little news. I could at least write "I love you" more than once a week.

Rich had been right; I had been smitten with Josie, a feeling I put in the category of an adolescent crush. But she'd trusted me with her secret, and the landscape had changed, if subtly, but I couldn't put my finger on exactly what had been altered.

I tried to picture Karen, but the mental image kept changing. A memory would start with her, but she would become Josie.

Josie. I wanted to know her, to know more about her—and this scared me. *I love Karen*, I told myself. *Karen loves me. I won't hurt her.* But another voice asked, *So why are you working so hard to remind yourself that you love her?*

C H A P T E R   32

▼

Bless This House

Thanksgiving loomed on the horizon. Karen and I had been together in New York City, seeing the sights and creating our son, during the previous Thanksgiving. Because I'd been certain that I would be sent to Vietnam to die, the future had looked as dreary as the chilly, dank, gray weather that had settled over the city then. But a year had passed, I was in the war, our son was born, and I was alive—so far.

Soldiers in Vietnam tended to become superstitious as their tours wound down. When they were really "short," I had seen even the most energetic of them become lazy bums who just wanted to sit in the sun to work on their DEROS tans. Engaging in any activity that might result in injury became terrifying. As my tour was winding down, I wanted to stay busy, to keep a normal schedule, and to try not to get into a superstitious snit.

The loneliness of the Thanksgiving season was bearable because two days later, I would leave for seven days of R&R—even the sound was pleasant as it rolled off the tongue. However, my R&R would not be as pleasant than I had hoped because I would not be with Karen.

Early in the summer, we had agreed to meet in Hawaii. Our plans, however, did not take the baby into account as well as we might have. We had purposely delayed the time that I would take the R&R until late in my tour. That way, if Karen delivered in August, the baby would be old enough to be left with Karen's parents in November or December, so she could meet me in Hawaii. Her mother had suggested this solution—I always liked that woman. But it was not to be.

Although Robbie had been born without complications, he apparently was not happy that he'd left his fetal home. He made everyone's lives as miserable as he could by having colic and crying incessantly. Karen wrote that she and her mother, bless her, had been up most of the night, every night, carrying him and rocking him into fitful sleep. She decided that she couldn't leave him to join me in Hawaii, and bringing him along would not allow us any time together.

I was so disappointed that I toyed with the idea of skipping R&R and applying for an early DEROS. Evert, who had to approve of leave requests, advised against it. He was hearing rumors of a drawdown, that troops might be rotated out several weeks short of their full tour. Besides, he asked, if I wanted to go to Australia or Hong Kong—the two most popular destinations—when would I ever have the chance again to fly there for free? He was right; Karen and I "discussed" it via the mail, and ultimately, I opted for Sydney.

With the passing of the monsoon season the sun had returned, so Thanksgiving Day was bright and warm. Chaplain Evert decided to hold a special Thanksgiving service that morning as a way to celebrate the season. About eight men showed up for the service, which included my singing "Bless this House" as I accompanied myself on the organ. It was not a memorable performance.

I made my way to the mess hall around noon. A rumor had been circulating that morning at breakfast that some beauty queens were going to join us for lunch. For once, a rumor was true. Miss America and her court were touring several military bases and ours was on the circuit.

The mess hall was buzzing with talk of the impending visit. A couple of guys expressed the hope that the girls would wear their bathing suits, like they had in the pageant. Their wishful thinking caused some laughter and crude remarks about the guys having shit for brains, since "no beauty queens don't go 'round wearin' nothin' but bathin' suits all the time."

The girls, five of them, arrived looking fresh and barely wilted in their white dresses. Each had her state name "Miss _____" printed in large letters on the sash that she wore, which ran from her shoulder to the opposite hip.

"They're gonna be eatin' with guys from their states," someone said.

"Me? I don't wanna eat *with* Miss Louisiana. I wanna *eat* Miss Louisiana," another countered.

"You ain't from Louisiana."

"I know that, but *she* don't know that."

There was scattered applause as the girls entered. Each wore a big, beauty pageant smile and waved beauty contestant waves, the kind where the elbow is bent, the forearm raised, and the hand waggles back and forth at the wrist. (This was to ensure that the loose skin under the upper arm didn't flop around in an unbecoming manner, I supposed.)

They also were wearing enough makeup, collectively, to paint one side of the mess hall. As they quickly passed by me and a hundred other guys to go to the front of the serving line, it was easy to see that their flesh-colored powder bases had begun caking in the heat.

If this is the epitome of feminine American beauty, Lord help us if the powder mines run out and mascara wells dry up, I thought as they passed.

Five tables had been set aside for the girls and their escorts. Each table had a state name printed on a card placed in the middle. Alas, the tables were in the officers' section, the portion of the mess hall that was partitioned off from the plebian section by Japanese screens. Someone, undoubtedly an officer and a gentleman, had decided that such feminine grace should remain unsullied by contact with enlisted rabble.

In honor of the occasion, six large turkeys, beautifully cooked, sat beckoning on top of the stainless steel platform that sheltered the food that was served to us. It became obvious that these turkeys were not being carved for us; the enlisted men were served the usual pressed turkey loaves, the same rubbery, multi-hued concoction that we ate on a regular basis. The real turkeys were reserved for the officers and distinguished visitors. We enlisted types did, however, have stuffing and cranberry sauce, two gustatory requirements for Thanksgiving. Such was the army's idea of a holiday treat.

To say the food was undistinguished would be to elevate it several gastronomical levels higher than it deserved. However, the effect of the visiting feminine pulchritude on the unwashed enlisted masses made the experience stand out. The language was a little less colorful than usual, fewer sons were accused of having sex with their mothers, and there were more smiling faces as many young men fantasized about the living, breathing round-eyed lasses under the same roof with them. I wondered how many would tell their children about the Thanksgiving dinner they shared with Miss America.

R&R dominated my thoughts, eclipsing the loneliness of the holiday. I would soon be on my way to Sydney, Australia—and I might see Josie there.

We were not going to Sydney together, and we had not made definite plans to see each other there, but we both knew the other would be there at the same time.

Josie had been in-country for fourteen months, so her R &R was long over-due. She had delayed leaving her post because she felt she should be there in case information arrived about Carl. In order to get information, she made friends with some Intelligence officers who had agreed to pass along anything they learned about him. She had told them she'd nursed Carl back to health in Japan and was concerned about him. She never disclosed any more about their relation-ship, preferring to let the Intelligence people think that she and Carl had been lovers, if that was what they wanted to assume.

"Odd, isn't it, that the air force—the Keeper of Marital Morality—will wink at an affair but would send my butt home and kick me out of the service if they thought I was a concerned wife," she once said.

So for fourteen months she had tried to carry out her duties, tending to the wounded and dying, dousing the unwanted attentions of various males in her vicinity, and holding her secret marriage in painful loneliness.

Since the day she told me that she was married, our relationship changed. We were very circumspect, considering our ranks, but we still found ways to talk when I visited the hospital. I asked her once why she felt she could trust me. She answered that she felt drawn to me on the day that I sang for her birthday, that she had the strong feeling that she could trust me. "Besides," she added, "you've not hit on me even once. That's got to count for something. Your wife is a lucky woman." I had blushed at this, considering the less-than-innocent fantasies that had flashed through my mind about her.

Visiting Australia—and maybe running into Josie. Good times lay ahead.

C H A P T E R   3 3

▼

Waltzing Matilda

I visited the hospital the day after Thanksgiving and had found Josie in a stew; she was having second thoughts about leaving. Her traveling companion, Lieutenant Cindy Howard, had changed her mind, Josie said, because a handsome new doctor had arrived. Howard had instantly fallen in lust with him and couldn't even think of leaving until she "had" him, just as she'd "had" so many other doctors. Besides, Josie said, Cindy would rather go to Australia with a man.

"So Lieutenant Howard is the nurse who sleeps around." I said.

"How come when a male doctor sleeps around he is 'sowing his wild oats,' but when a nurse, a woman, sleeps around, she's promiscuous?" Josie fired back.

"I, uh, I don't know," I stammered. "I guess I never thought about it that way."

"Well, maybe it's about time you and the rest of the members of your sex start thinking about it!"

"Yes, ma'am!" I said, saluting.

She sighed, her shoulders dropping. "I'm sorry," she said. "I just get so tired of these damn double standards."

When I was a graduate student in music, the antiwar movement had been on the periphery of my consciousness, but the women's movement had been only a distant rumble of thunder. I had heard enough to feel uncomfortable with some of the ideas the women were shouting about, but I had not taken time to consider the validity of any of their arguments. I had the feeling that I would be challenged to do just that by the woman standing in front of me. I wondered if the army issued leather jock straps.

"Anyway, Cindy won't be going with me. Maybe I shouldn't go."

"I think you could probably find someone to go with you, to be kind of a, uh …"

She grinned, her dark eyes twinkling over a cup of coffee. We were sitting in a small break room in the hospital. No one else was there. She leaned forward: "You're going, right?"

"Yes, ma'am. The day after tomorrow."

"Well, why don't we meet up after we get there. We wouldn't have to spend all our time together. Just maybe have dinner together, once or twice. Being in a strange country can be very lonely, you know," she said with mock seriousness.

What I wanted to say was, "Are you kidding? I'd love to see Sydney with you." But what I said was, "Yes, I know."

She knew her presence made me uncomfortable, and she seemed to delight in my awkwardness. She smiled. "Good. What hotel are you booked at? I'll need to know where to call you."

I told her I didn't remember but that I would get the information to her the next day.

That day, however, found me occupied with a last-minute memorial service and other duties around the chapel. Then Chaplain Evert absconded with the jeep (assistants tended to consider the chaplains' jeeps as personal property), and one thing led to another, so I didn't make it over to the hospital. I was so busy getting ready to leave for Australia that it was not until late that night that I realized I had forgotten to get the name of the hotel to Josie. Ambiguity was my sleeping companion that night—disappointment that I would probably not see her, but relief that my fidelity to Karen would not be put to the test.

The next morning, five enlisted personnel from Can Tho Army Base were shuttled to Tan San Hut Air Force Base via helicopter. We rode in silence as the hot wind blew against our bodies and the engines vibrated around us.

I looked around at the other four men. Two of them, who looked like they were fifteen years old, knew each other and were discussing their plans as we buckled in.

"Shit, I can almost taste that Australian pussy right now!"

"Man, I'm not goin' to taste no pussy; I'm gonna fuck it. I'm gonna fuck 'til my dick starts waving a fuckin' white flag, and then I'm gonna fuck some more!"

"Lissen, you muthafucka, I'm gonna be fuckin' after your dick has shribbled down to the size of the fuckin' pencil lead."

They both guffawed at their clever repartee as they looked at their three traveling companions: a black sergeant, a white corporal, and me. The sergeant glanced in my direction and smiling, shook his head, as if to say, "Boys will be boys." I was thinking that I would probably see them in the hospital, IVs dripping penicillin into their syphilis-invaded veins.

"Everyone strapped in?" the pilot asked. We all nodded, and the chopper lurched off the runway.

From Tan San Hut, we were herded into hot buses along with other men going on R&R, and driven to another gathering point. I gazed through the mesh wire covering the bus window as we passed through the various slums that surrounded Saigon, remembering the ride in a similar bus on my first night in-country. It seemed like years had passed since that night.

At the holding area, we were met by a Spec 4 and told to go a particular building where our orders would be checked. Our duffel bags over our shoulders, we walked to the building where we stood in line. After an hour or so, a clerk appeared and told us to go to another building across the compound where we would be given meal passes.

Someone in the front of the line asked, "What about our orders?"

The clerk shrugged. "We're shutting down for the night. You'll have to have those checked in the morning."

"What are we supposed to do tonight? Some of use are supposed to leave in a few hours. Where do we sleep? Where do we eat?"

The clerk was sweating, as were we all, and was becoming exasperated with us because we didn't know what to do or where to go. My flight was supposed to leave in six hours; a lot of the other men standing in line were probably on that flight. My temper started to rise, as did the tempers of several other men. We each had ten days of R&R coming, but the army didn't care if we were a couple of days late in starting it. There were about fifty of us standing in that damn line in the hot sun, and it appeared that every one of us was about to blow his top.

The clerk held up his hands. "Wait. Give me a minute. I think I can work something out." He disappeared back into the building.

Ten minutes later, he reappeared. "Okay, there are about 120 of you (I was never good at estimating crowd size). What we're going to do is this: Get your orders out. Have your military IDs ready, and don't ask any questions. Okay? Everyone got that?"

One hundred twenty heads nodded in unison. One hour later, we were wandering into another building where we were ordered to put on our civvies and check in our uniforms. Our trek ended in yet another building where we turned in our military scrip for "real" money, American money. It looked strange compared to the military scrip.

Time passed as we milled around waiting for the next shoe to drop. Some of us were trying to find some shade alongside the buildings, while others simply sat on the sandy soil, leaning against their duffels. Buses arrived and began taking us to the airport. I began to think that I might make it after all.

The buses disgorged us at a very large building that was recognizably an airport terminal. It was late afternoon; I had missed lunch and was tired and sweaty, but I felt exhilarated as I walked into the building.

The only uniformed personnel in sight were the MPs who were strolling around. Airport duty was probably the easiest they had, particularly where men were *leaving* the country.

There were clumps of men gathered here and there; by all appearances, officers. Even in so large a space, the officers didn't mingle with the troops.

I found a snack bar and, after waiting in line for thirty minutes, ordered a grilled cheese sandwich, a soda, and a small bag of potato chips. It tasted wonderful. I sat on my duffel eating and watching the milling crowd.

About an hour before my flight, I began looking for Josie. I had not seen any women, other than some Vietnamese women behind the counter at the snack bar and cleaning the latrines. I had reconciled myself to not seeing Josie in Sydney since I had not gotten my hotel address to her, but still, it would have been nice.

I meandered toward the departure gate and noticed a distinguished-looking man with a corncob pipe. He was maybe five foot six or so, and stocky, with a short "flat top" haircut that made his gray hair appear as stiff as a wire brush.

Shyness has seldom been noted as one of my virtues, so I walked over to the gentleman as he was struggling to keep his pipe lit.

"Excuse me, sir. I'm with 164th Aviation Group, 1st Aviation Brigade, and I've heard about a colonel who smokes a corncob pipe. His call sign is 'Corncob 6.' Is that you, sir?"

He smiled as the tobacco lit. "Yep, that's me, son. Joe Williams. I know the 164th pretty well." He extended his hand.

"Specialist 5 Bertson, sir. Ted Bertson. Happy to make your acquaintance. I've heard about you from some of the officers I work for."

"Just remember, son," he replied in a smooth baritone, "half of what you hear is a lie."

"How do you know the 164th, sir, if you don't mind my asking?"

"'Cause I'm the commanding officer of the 1st Aviation Brigade," he said, sucking on his pipe.

Open mouth; insert foot. While I felt a little foolish, I remembered that I'd heard about a courageous officer who never asked his men to do something he had not already done himself. Whether it was sliding down a rope from a rescue helicopter in a hot zone or simply standing in a chow line, waiting his turn like any other soldier, he was a favorite of the average enlisted schmoe. One story had him jerking a line-jumping officer out of line and sending him to the rear to wait, much to the silent glee of the enlisted men.

He asked what I did in civilian life, and I mentioned I was a musician—or at least studying to become one.

"What do you do? Sing? Play?"

"My degrees are in singing, sir".

"*Singen sie Lieder?*"

"I've almost forgotten what language that is," I said. "Yes, I do sing Lieder, lots of it. I'm surprised you know what it is."

"When you're an officer in Germany, during your off-duty hours you play Bridge, drink, fornicate, or pick up some culture. I chose culture—it causes fewer problems with home life." He sucked on his pipe, then took it out of his mouth and squinted at it.

"Damn thing's gone out again," he said, digging into his civilian pants for his lighter. "Actually," he said between puffs as he relit the pipe, "I was studying music myself when I was drafted. Pianist. Studied at Juilliard. Was going to light up the musical world."

"You were drafted out of Juilliard?"

"Yep. Uncle Sam needed me more than the musical world, I guess."

"Was that the Korean War, sir?"

"Korea was not a war, son, it was an International Police Action that had never been ended by the United Nations. That's your history lesson for today. Now, to answer your question: I was drafted into the army in WWII, toward the end of the war. I was mustered out as a captain."

"Did you go to OCS?"

"No. I went in a private and received several field commissions; that happens when the ranking officers keep getting killed or wounded, you know."

"You said you were mustered out."

"Well, it's a long, sad story, Ted. But the short version is that I was just getting my feet wet as a pianist when Korea came along. Rather than train a new officer corps, they just called former officers back to active duty."

I shuddered at the thought of finishing this active duty, only to be called back.

"Those things happen, you know." He shrugged, tamping the tobacco in his pipe. "I figured that the writing was on the wall, that I was going to have a career in the military, so I decided to plunge in and make the most of it. From time to time, I think I've made a difference." He paused and looked at a small cluster of butch-cut young men, officers by their bearing. "But then I run into some of these new hotshot junior officers and wonder what the hell I was thinking. It's the same old 'brown shoe' army that it always was."

Giving up on keeping his pipe lit, he walked over to a knee-high, sand-filled shell casing that served as an ash tray and emptied it. The casing was a reminder that although it looked like a civilian airport, we were still in a war zone.

My flight was called. When I mentioned this to the Colonel, he said it was his flight too. We were both going to Sydney.

"Traveling with anybody?" he asked.

"No, sir." A fleeting image of Josie passed through my mind.

"Why don't you travel with me?" he asked. "It's nice to find a classical musician. It's been a long time since I've talked with a real musician."

"I'll be glad to join you, sir. Although you might remember that singers are not considered musicians by some people, particularly musicians."

He chuckled as he stuck his pipe into his pocket. "Seems like I've heard that about singers," he said. "I've also heard something similar about real soldiers and generals, but I can't recall the details, offhand."

He put his hand on my shoulder. "Tell you what, Ted. We're both in civvies, and we're both heading out of a war zone. You can drop the "sir." Seems a bit formal since we're going to be traveling companions for a few hours."

"Yes, sir," I said. He smiled, patted me on the back, and we walked to the boarding line together.

I remembered hearing that Corn Cob 6 was up for his first star. It was reassuring to think we would soon have a general who was down-to-earth and remembered the enlisted men.

The flight, like most long-distance flights, was tiring. The large jet was jammed with soldiers eager to leave 'Nam and spend time in other places, preferably in the company of round-eyed women. Colonel Johnson was a wonderful traveling partner. We chatted when we felt like it and read or slept the rest of the time. He was a very cultured, well-read man who had a love of history, as did I.

We flew through a sunset and sunrise, landing in Sydney in mid-morning. I stepped out of the plane onto the portable stairway and shivered. November was springtime in Australia; we had left a hot, humid, tropical Asian country for the dry, cool spring in Sydney.

It was a beautiful, sunny day, with white fluffy clouds filling the sky. As we walked into the terminal and toward the baggage claim, I stopped in my tracks several times. The place was filled with young men, like me, all of us gawking in wonder. Young Australian women were all around us, strolling casually through the terminal. They all seemed to be wearing miniskirts that revealed long, shapely legs, and most of them had hair that flowed over their shoulders and fell down their backs or cascaded over voluptuous bosoms that pressed against tight blouses. Compared to the small Vietnamese women, these girls were giants. Amazons.

I said good-bye to the Colonel and wished him a pleasant time in Sydney. Then I strolled slowly through the terminal toward the baggage claim, enjoying the lovely women.

"Please, God," I whispered, "let one of these Amazons club me over the head and drag me off to take her pleasure with me. Please!"

I collected my duffel from the luggage area, dug the name of the hotel out of it, then trudged out to the front of the terminal and began looking for a taxi. One pulled up to the curb. The driver jumped out of the passenger side, threw open the trunk, and opened the back door for me. I hopped in and settled back in the seat. He got in on the passenger side, and we pulled away from the curb.

I almost yelled, "Hey, who's driving this thing?" when I remembered that drivers in Australia sat on the right-hand side of the car. Still, I cringed as he steered to the left side of the road and into what seemed like oncoming traffic.

A few minutes into the ride, the taxi was in a tight turn around a traffic circle, and I began to feel sick. My stomach was in a knot, I could feel sweat on my forehead, and I was having trouble breathing. I felt as if the taxi was closing in on me.

The doors! There were doors on the damn car! I hadn't ridden in an enclosed vehicle for almost a year. I rolled the window down.

"You look like you're coming from a right hot place there, mate. You might find it a might nippy," the driver volunteered.

"That's all right. I'd rather be cold than sick," I replied. "I haven't been inside a car with doors for some time, and I was feeling a little nervous."

"American, aren't you?" the cabby asked.

"Yes. I'm sure my accent gives it away."

"Coming from 'Nam?" He pronounced it as if it rhymed with ma'am. "Soldier, right?"

"Yes. Right about that, too."

He chuckled. "I get a lot of you blokes. I'm a vet myself," he said, shifting more upright in the seat. "The Pacific War, World War II, and all that. Damn fine war, that was. Lot o' women willing ta spread their legs for men in uniform, ya know what I mean?" He glanced over the seat at me, man to man.

"I just hope to make it home in one piece to my wife and child," I said self-righteously.

"Well, hotel's right up there. Have a bloody good time 'ere in the 'down under,'" he said heartily, ignoring my moral tone. "Don't use it if it's not wrapped," he said with a wink, his hand near his crotch encircling an imaginary penis.

I thanked him for his advice, paid the fare, and looked at the hotel. It was the Sydney Hilton, a towering edifice of concrete and glass. Compared to the buildings in Vietnam, it was a skyscraper. I had vague memories of the buildings in New York City being taller and more impressive, but they came from another life, another time. For me, this was a new city in a new land, and I had eight full days to enjoy it.

Having been in the army, I adopted the attitude that snafus were normal. Even the term "snafu" had its origin in the military: situation normal, all fucked up. So I was pleasantly surprised to discover that the hotel did, indeed, have my reservation. I was in room 1216.

I was both tired and elated as I rode the elevator up to my room. I was in a real city and, for a short time, free of officers and other nincompoops who could tell me how to dress, where to go, and when to be there. Eight days of freedom.

I stepped off the elevator, noted the exit sign, and began looking for a bunker in case we were hit. Perplexed because I couldn't find it, I wandered all the way to the opposite end of the hallway and arrived at a window. The city of Sydney lay below me. Other tall buildings, many topped by cranes, were visible in the distance.

I'm in a city. There is no war here, I told myself. *There are no bunkers on the twelfth floor. There are probably no bunkers anywhere in the whole damn hotel.* It was a strange feeling, not having a bunker close by, but I quickly became accustomed to it.

Once I was in my room, I opened the drapes, unpacked my duffel, and laid down for a nap. According to my internal clock it was very early in the morning, and I had been awake all night. I thought a short nap would feel good.

Four hours later, I awoke. I didn't know where I was. Sunshine poured in the sole window, and distant traffic noises passed through the glass. I fell back on the bed. Sydney. Sydney, Australia.

I found a pair of jeans and a long-sleeved shirt—the only long-sleeved shirt I had with me—and wandered out of the hotel. The concierge at the front desk had provided me with a small map and directions to a nearby district where there were restaurants and clothing stores.

I bought a cheap, lightweight jacket to keep the chill off. I had my Nikkormat camera with me—one that a friend had bought for me in Hong Kong—plenty of film, and a few dollars that I would spend carefully. I had learned to bury the loneliness I felt at being separated from Karen, so I was adept at getting through the day with only an occasional twinge of sadness. I was young, healthy, and out of Vietnam. For the moment, life was good.

The morning of my first full day was as sunny and cool as the previous day. My alarm went off at 8:00, not very early according to the local time, but still early on my body time. I showered, dressed in my warmest clothes, and then set out for the hotel dining room. I needed coffee.

After a light breakfast, I stopped by the concierge desk, picked up another map—this one of the city—and headed out for my first adventure. At the Festival of Two Worlds in Spoleto, I had sung with a baritone from Sydney, Rodney Miller. Rodney had mentioned his studies at the Royal Conservatory of Music. I needed to hear some music, live music, and the Conservatory seemed a good place to visit for information about the various performances in the city.

It was a great day to be in Sydney. The air grew warmer as I walked, enough so that I took my jacket off and tied it around my waist. Everywhere I looked, new skyscrapers were being erected. The streets were filled with shoppers and business people bustling along on their endeavors. Buds on the trees looked ready to explode, and the perennials were already in full bloom. Compared to the hot, dusty atmosphere I had lived in for eleven months, it was like a trip to the mountains.

I was in no hurry and was easily distracted by the storefront displays. It had not taken long to forget the endless variety of clothes people wore in the West. The shapes and sizes of the round-eyed women also intrigued me. Their bodies looked so different from the boyish shapes of the Vietnamese women. I had forgotten how many delightful curves the female figure had. I decided I shouldn't spend too much time eyeing the women, or I might be arrested for voyeurism. I could imagine my trying to explain that to Karen when I called her from my jail cell.

The building that housed the Royal Conservatory had originally been built to stable the horses of a garrison of the Royal Guards. It was a beautiful white building, with gables and leaded-glass windows, three stories tall and almost as long as a city block.

Entering through the thick wooden double-doors, I entered a large room that was the reception area. Students passed by, chatting about things that music students tend to talk about—boyfriends/girlfriends, a big date for the weekend, a hot new recording, auditions. Sounds of practicing greeted me as well—a tenor struggling with a passage from an aria, a cellist sawing away, a piano thundering a Chopin etude—sounds muffled by the closed doors of the practice rooms in which the students labored. It was wonderful to hear such sounds again. I smiled. I was home.

"May I help you?" a gray-haired woman asked. She seemed to have materialized out of nowhere.

"Yes. I'm visiting Sydney for a few days. I'm in the U.S. military now, but last summer I sang with an Australian baritone in Spoleto, Italy. I think his name was Rodney Miller."

"Rodney? You sang with Rodney?" Her accent transformed his name to "Rodnay." She clasped her hands together. "Oh, my goodness! Come with me, please." She bustled across the room and waved to me to follow her.

The Conservatory Office was located at the end of a short hallway leading off the entrance room.

"Lucy," the woman said to another woman behind the desk, "this gentleman sang in Italy with Rodney." She turned toward me. "I'm sorry; I didn't inquire as to your name."

"I'm Ted Bertson."

"Wonderful to meet you," she said, extending her hand. "I'm Clara Wentworth, assistant to the dean." As she spoke, a short, portly man appeared in the doorway of an interior office.

"Clara, what is this commotion? How do you expect me to get any sleep?" he asked in mock sternness.

"And this," Clara said, making a large gesture toward him, "is Dean Wadsworth, whom I have to keep organized. Dean Wadsworth, this is ... I'm *terribly* sorry, but your name has escaped out of the opposite ear that it entered."

"Ted Bertson."

Wadsworth stepped forward and shook my hand. "So, you sang with *Rodnay*?" he inquired.

"Yes, I did, last summer in Spoleto." I had yet to hear if Rodney had been a star or a disgrace to the Conservatory. He had mentioned his studies there but had said little else about it.

"Rodney was one of our favorites, wasn't he, Clara?" Dean Wadsworth asked.

"Of course," Clara answered. "But what brings you to Sydney? Are you performing in the city?"

"I wish I were. I'm in the army now, on R&R from Vietnam."

Their faces dropped. "How awful," Clara blurted out. She brought her hand to her face. "I'm terribly sorry! I meant you being a professional singer and all, having to be in the military, in that dreadful war."

"Clara," Dean Wadsworth interrupted, "perhaps he wanted to be in the service."

"No," I said. "I didn't want to be in the military at all, but Uncle Sam felt otherwise. I had signed a contract to teach at a college, and my wife and I were ready to settle down."

"Oh, dear," Clara said, placing her hand on her ample bosom. "That's dreadful."

"There, there, Clara," Wadsworth said, patting her arm. "Let's not become too upset." Their dialogue reminded me of something out of a 1940s English movie.

Wadsworth turned to me. "Clara is so, so...."

"Empathetic?" I offered.

"Yes, excellent word. Empathetic. Clara is so empathetic that she has been known to hyperventilate out of concern for others."

"I do not hyperventilate," Clara said with a frown.

"Clara, dear, haven't you noticed the small paper bags the students have with them when they attend their peers' recitals? They are for you!" He addressed me then. "I cannot count the number of recitals in which the unintended accompaniment was the crinkling of a paper bag as Clara breathed into it, as she experienced the terrors of performance for the performer."

"Oh, dear," Clara said. She waved her hand in exasperation. "Well, whatever you say, Charles. I'm going for a drink."

She noticed that our eyebrows went up at the thought that she might be imbibing so early in the day. "A drink of *water*," she chortled and waved herself out of the room.

Wadsworth chuckled and clasped his hands together. "Well, what can we do for a visiting star?"

"I wasn't a star," I demurred. "I was just a member of the chorus and assistant conductor. Rodney had a minor role, but at least it had some solo lines."

Wadsworth waved away my objection. "Rodney is one of the few from here who has gone on to the larger world. He's our star, and you sang with him, so we're adding you to our private firmament."

I nodded in thanks. "The primary reason I came today was to find out what is happening, musically. Are there any performances this week? Any music by Australian composers? I don't know any of their work."

"Lovely. Finally, a professional musician who acknowledges that we Aussies might have something to add to the musical pot." A movement by the office door attracted his attention. "Excuse me, just one second," he said and exited the office. I heard him call a name. A few seconds later, Wadsworth appeared again with a young woman in tow.

Wadsworth made the introductions. "Mr. Bertson, this is Cynthia Barstow. Cynthia, Ted Bertson."

As I took her outstretched hand, I realized that hers was the first female hand I had touched in months. She was an attractive young woman with a lively face and a pleasant manner, and I was immediately distracted from what Wadsworth said—something about Rodney, Spoleto, me, Vietnam.

"So, you're a professional singer who happens to be in the army," Cynthia said. "I have a brother in Vietnam, with the Australian military."

"Where is he stationed?" I asked.

"I don't know, now that you ask." She grew serious for a moment. "Somewhere in South Vietnam is all that I know. We all worry about him." She seemed lost in thought for a moment but then brightened. "Well, Dean Wadsworth said you were interested in some new music. Is that correct?"

"Yes, ma'am," I said, slipping into my army-instilled habits when addressing a woman. She smiled at the formality of my reply.

"There is a concert of new choral music by Australian composers tonight that I have thought of attending. If that sounds interesting, perhaps we could meet there. It begins at eight-thirty."

I told her it sounded wonderful.

She jotted down the directions to the concert hall and the time, and then excused herself because she was late to her next class.

I left shortly after, thanking Wadsworth for his time and the information. On the way out, I saw Clara engaging in a conversation with another woman. While she appeared younger than my mother, Clara, in some ways, reminded me of Mom. I felt a twinge of loneliness and wanted to see my folks again. I decided I would write them from Sydney.

Clara saw me and rushed over. "It was wonderful to have met you," she said, shaking my hand. "I hope you enjoy your stay."

"I'm sure I will. Thank you for your warm reception."

Her eyes teared. A linen handkerchief appeared out of nowhere. She dabbed her eyes and grabbed me in a hug, pinning my arms to my sides as her plump hands patted my back.

"God bless you," she said.

I liked that lady. I reckoned she was probably a favorite with many of the students as well.

I strolled through the Royal Botanical Gardens for several hours, admiring the exotic blossoms. Everything, it seemed, was in bloom. I passed young couples, lovers, sitting on the lawn, leaning together under large trees. They were oblivious to the people who passed by, lost as they were in each other.

I had lunch at a restaurant that overlooked the garden. Quietness had settled over me, a feeling of safety from the constant threats that surrounded us in 'Nam.

I walked some more after lunch but less than I might have, due to the chill that was in the spring air. It was quite strange—the early spring in late November. I went up to my room, intent on writing at least one card, but I promptly fell asleep.

At 4:30, I woke with a start. I freshened up, changed into the dressiest clothes I had, and went to find the nearest nice restaurant that I could afford.

I found a small, inexpensive restaurant near the hotel and had a pleasant meal of lamb and a glass of Australian wine. The pleasant time ended abruptly when I looked at my watch and saw that it was 8:00. I moved quickly and was in a taxi at 8:10. At 8:30, the taxi pulled up to the concert hall, I jumped out, bought a ticket, and then waited outside the closed doors of the auditorium. The doors were held shut by a thin, scowling, elderly man whose demeanor said that no etiquette would by breached while he lived. He pointed to a small sign that said "If tardy, admittance ONLY between musical selections." The music stopped, the audience applauded, and I was allowed to enter.

I was hoping to spot Cynthia without too much fuss, but didn't see her. I took the first empty seat I found, near the back of the hall.

In my haste to enter between pieces, I had not picked up a program, so I had no idea what I would be hearing, although what music I was able to hear through the door sounded like it might have been written in the Renaissance. This was rather odd since it was a concert of contemporary music by Australian composers. The conductor had left the stage at the end of the first piece. He returned to the stage to polite applause and began the next section.

My first thought was that the Australians were definitely not innovative. This piece sounded like Monteverdi (an early seventeenth-century Italian composer) might have composed it. The next piece was in a similar style. It finally dawned on me: Cynthia had steered me wrong. I was hearing Renaissance and early Baroque music. She had missed the twentieth century by approximately four hundred years. It didn't matter much; I was happy to hear live music after such a long time.

The choir, a small madrigal group, was quite good, their voices blending and shifting as they moved through Monteverdi's intricate harmonies. As the music unfolded, voices would move together for a moment then break apart, some remained static while others circled through them, enveloping them in changing hues. Ribbons of sound and emotion intertwined. This was food for my ears and my soul.

The group of pieces ended, there was more applause, and then the conductor left the stage. After the applause, as the audience began shifting in their folding chairs, I looked around the hall for the first time. The concert hall had once been a prison. That's why it had struck me as an odd-looking concert site when I had rushed in from the taxi.

The hall was constructed completely of gray, chiseled stone that would probably have been achingly cold in the winter and a steam oven in the summer. The outlines of the cells were still clear on the floor and walls. Holes in which the bars had been anchored were evenly spaced the entire length of the hall floor. One of the holes now served as an umbrella stand for a single umbrella owned by a creative audience member.

Being in a former prison led me to thoughts about Josie's husband, Carl. I wondered if he was alive. I had heard rumors of the hellish conditions that American POWs endured. I doubted his cell would be in a permanent, imposing edifice like this one. I thought of the strangeness of life, that I should be sitting comfortably in a peaceful land while Carl, if he still lived, languished alone.

Once, while in a choral rehearsal at U. of M., the conductor, Maynard Klein, had stopped us. It was a Friday afternoon, around 5:00. Many of us wanted to be on our way to weekend activities and had been singing in a desultory way. Professor Klein looked at us silently for a few seconds and then said, "We are privileged to be here today, singing this music. As we're singing, at this very moment, this very second, some young man is dying in a war thousands of miles from here. What would he give to be able to hear you sing?

"We're in this room, this building that is dedicated to music, dedicated to creating beauty, because that young man and so many others before him have fought and died so we can do this. So we can be *free* to do this." His voice cracked. He stopped, took off his glasses, took out his handkerchief, and wiped his eyes. One hundred fifty choir members sat in that room, but there was not a sound.

He put his glasses on and his handkerchief away, then looked at us and smiled. He said, "The text says we sing with joy; we sing to God. For God's sake, sing it. Sing it like you mean it!

When he gave the next downbeat, the sound of the choir was indescribably beautiful as all of us sang from our hearts. The sounds we made swept us out of ourselves, lifting us to a place of such intense joy that for a moment our mundane worries fell away. Our hearts and breaths became one with each other and the composer; time stopped and expanded. Joy and gratitude for life flowed out of us.

Professor Klein gave the final cutoff. The music ended. Without a word he nodded to us, picked up his music, and walked out of the room. For a few seconds, no one moved. It was as if no one wanted to break the spell we had fallen under. The moment passed and we gathered our belongings to go our separate ways.

I left that room changed in ways I could feel but could not find words for at the time. Only later did I find the right word, a word I had never used before–wonder.

I thought of that moment as the ensemble returned to the stage. The lights lowered, the prison faded into the twilight as the stage lights came up. The conductor appeared and the choir began singing again. The music of William Byrd rose from the ensemble and drifted around the room.

"They that sow with tears shall return again, rejoicing. All who sorrow shall be comforted, the hungry fed, and the prisoners set free."

The concert ended. The applause died, and people stood to leave. I had maneuvered myself near the only exit so I could spot Cynthia. A man stepped out of the crowd and approached me.

"Are you Bertson?" he asked.

"Yes," I replied tentatively.

"I'm Cynthia Barstow's brother David." He was about my height with sandy blonde hair. I had not looked at Cynthia long enough to note if there was a resemblance. "Cynthia had a last-minute rehearsal tonight and couldn't come, so she asked me to come to meet you instead."

"Thank you. That was very thoughtful of her," I said.

"She's a pretty thoughtful young woman. I say that, even though she is my sister," he said. A young woman appeared at his side; she was his wife, Susan.

That was the beginning of a very pleasant series of visits with David and Susan Barstow. They were a couple of years older than me and had a son who had been born in September. I had dinner with them the following evening, and on the next day, Saturday, we went on a tour of the countryside.

My time with them was filled with different emotions as I watched them caring for their son, Peter, and I observed the easy rapport they had with each other. I talked a lot about Karen and Robbie and a little about my experiences in Vietnam.

David and Cynthia's younger brother, Archie, was serving in Vietnam, as Cynthia had mentioned. David would occasionally ask about the war, a concerned brother wondering what his sibling was facing. I had heard that there were two nationalities of soldiers that Charlie did not want to fight: Aussies and Koreans. I did not know if there was any truth to the rumor, but David seemed to find some comfort that his brother was in a "tough" and feared army.

"The bloke doesn't write much, just an occasional letter to Mum and Dad, so we only hear about his exploits secondhand," he said once. "I'm sure Peter will hear plenty about it from Uncle Archie himself, when he gets back."

"I'm sure he will," I said with more confidence than I felt.

Even though David and Susan were wonderful hosts, I spent most of my time in Sydney alone. I enjoyed wandering about, following no particular schedule, sleeping as late as I wished, and eating whenever I felt like it. It felt luxurious to be able to just walk anywhere without running into barriers, to hear English wherever I turned, to be in a city where the air was still clean and clear and did not smell of sewage, like the river did that ran through Saigon. The zoo I visited was filled with uniformed school children, animated and lively as their teachers herded them from exhibit to exhibit, children whose eyes were alive with hope and trust, whose mouths were filled with laughter. These children were so vastly different from the shy, sad-eyed children I visited in the orphanage in Can Tho.

I carried my experiences of Vietnam wherever I went. They sat on me like an invisible weight, reminding me that I would soon return to the dusty embrace of the war. As much as I longed for Karen to be with me, I knew that being with her would have been almost unbearable knowing that I had to go back, that we would, after so short a time, be apart again. My loneliness increased as my R&R progressed.

I thought often of Josie, sometimes allowing myself to fantasize about what it might be like had I found her in Sydney. I wondered if we might have become lovers, two lonely people assuaging their sorrow with each other. At the same time, I experienced pangs of guilt for betraying Karen, even in my fantasies. Being alone was certainly safer, as I obviously could not trust myself with Josie. Besides, I didn't know if Josie was even slightly attracted to me, and I was not sure I wanted to find out. It was true—there was safety in numbers. For me, in Sydney, that number was one.

The morning of my departure from Sydney arrived all too soon. As I rode to the airport, I mused about the pleasant memories I carried with me. I hadn't seen Josie, but that was probably for the best.

From my seat in the back of the taxi, I wished her well on her final day of R&R in Sydney. I would look her up in a few days just to find out what she did and what she saw. That was what I told myself, but deep down I knew that it was really an excuse to see her again.

CHAPTER 34

▼

Just Me and
My Shadow

By the time I arrived at the airport, I was thinking about the long flight and all the rigmarole that would be facing me as I tried to find a flight back to Can Tho. The airport was crowded, just as it had been when I had arrived a week earlier. Droves of eager young men, many with smiling faces, were passing through; new arrivals anticipating their R&R. There were also young men like me, whose demeanor said we were returning to a war zone and were not particularly happy about it.

The first familiar person I saw had a corncob pipe clenched between his teeth and puffs of aromatic tobacco filling the air around him. Colonel Joe Williams, Corncob 6, was heading home, too.

I walked over to him. "Colonel Williams?"

"Ted. Good to see you. Hear any interesting music while you were here?" he asked.

"Yes, sir. I didn't get to hear any new music, but there was a lovely performance of some Renaissance composers. Um, did you have a nice time?"

"Yep. My wife flew down to join me, and we had a good time getting reacquainted. I considered going AWOL to hang out with her, but thought better of it since I probably wouldn't see her much if I were in Leavenworth."

My flight number was called. He clapped me on the shoulder. "Looks like we're on the same flight again, Ted. I'm sitting with some other officers this time, but why don't you stick with me when we land and I'll see to it you're taken care of. What do you say? Seems the least an erstwhile musician can do for a rising star."

"That sounds fine to me, sir. Thanks. I'll look for you when we land."

He gave me a casual salute and went to meet his traveling companions. The boarding line was forming, so I went to take my place.

The flight was uneventful and I slept most of the way. By the time we landed at Long Binh, I felt as if I had become a permanent part of the seat. The hot, humid air of Vietnam enveloped me as soon as I stepped off the plane, so trickles of sweat rolled down my back. At least I wasn't cold anymore.

Colonel Williams and I found each other in the brightly lit holding room where we picked up our luggage. He escorted me past the line of tired, droopy soldiers who were waiting to have their luggage inspected before retiring to the softest berm they could find to sleep on.

We walked quickly from the building to a waiting Huey. "This is Ambassador Harriman's chopper we're using tonight. He's out of the country and didn't need it," Williams said over the wash of the churning blades. The copilot saluted him and received a crisp salute in return. Williams was back in his military mode.

He climbed into the pilot's seat and waved me into the back. The doors were closed, and we flew off into the night.

The city was quite lovely as it flowed beneath us. I was lulled by the sights of brightly lit areas scattered among patches of darkness, and the reflection of the moon on the river that wended its way to the sea.

It was a short flight, lasting only fifteen minutes. We landed smoothly and disembarked. Colonel Williams introduced me to his driver, an E-4 named Lucas, and then told him to take care of me and to be sure to introduce me as his friend. Williams shook my hand and hopped into another jeep driven by a major.

Lucas asked, "So, how do you know the Colonel, sir."

I informed him that I wasn't an officer but merely a Spec 5, and that I had met Williams on my way to Australia.

"A Spec 5? Really?" he exclaimed, chuckling. "I'll be sure to do just what the Colonel ordered: I'll introduce you as his friend. This is going to be fun. You'll get better treatment. Trust me on this, okay?"

We drove to a hooch that was less than half the size of my hooch in Can Tho. "The higher-ranking sergeants live here. You'll stay here tonight," Lucas said as he stepped out of the jeep.

I followed with some trepidation. As I walked into the building, I overheard him saying to the sergeant at the front desk, "... Colonel Williams' friend, Ted Bertson."

The sergeant stood briskly, saluted, then offered his hand. "Sergeant Watkins, sir. Nice to meet you. You can bunk down in Sergeant Royce's bunk. He's Sergeant of the Guard tonight. It's right this way." He stepped around the desk, grabbed my duffel, and proceeded down the hall.

"Are you sure about this?" I muttered to Lucas.

"You're Colonel Williams' friend; you could be anybody—CIA, Intelligence. You'll be well treated," he said, as a big smile covered his face. "I'll pick you up at 7:00. Get some rest." He gave me a snappy salute even though I was in my civvies. His eyes indicated to me that sergeant Watkins was behind me. I returned his salute, although somewhat skeptically. I sure hoped this would work.

The next morning, Lucas drove me to the mess hall for breakfast, then to the building where I picked up my uniform. I told him that we had been told in no uncertain terms that we were not to leave that compound in our civvies.

"You're Colonel Williams' friend, remember?" he said. "Put your uniform in your duffel and come with me. The colonel said to deliver you to headquarters to get you a ride back to your base. You'll get better service in your civvies. Besides, I've already clued in some of my buddies on who you are; you'll brighten their day if we can pull this off."

"Wait a minute. What do you mean 'pull this off'? What happens if we don't pull it off?"

"I don't know. Maybe they'll send us to Vietnam?" he responded much too glibly for my taste. After all, I would be the one serving hard time in Leavenworth.

We arrived at the Brigade Headquarters. It was a large, concrete block building painted stark white. The front entrance was reached by climbing a flight of seven stairs. I climbed out of the jeep, turned to grab my duffel, and noticed that Lucas had a big smile on his face. I turned to see what he was looking at. Standing on the top stair, wearing more braids and metals then I had ever seen, giving a rigid salute, and wearing a big smile was the Command Sergeant Major of the Brigade. He held the rank of E-9, the highest enlisted rank in the army, the general of the sergeants—and he was saluting me. Me, a lowly Spec 5. I wondered if they had Dempsey Dumpsters in the stockade at Leavenworth.

"Good morning, sir. I am Joshua White, the Command Sergeant Major of the 1ˢᵗ Aviation Brigade," he said brightly. He was a large black man, well over six feet, and hefty. I did *not* want to piss him off.

"Good morning, Sergeant Major," I said in return, hoping my voice sounded more confident than my jellied insides felt at the moment.

"Colonel Williams said you would be arriving soon. We have coffee and some donuts. Would you care for something?"

What the hell, I thought. "I'd like a cup of coffee and a cream-filled donut, if you don't mind."

"Cream in your coffee, sir?" he asked.

"Black is fine. Thanks."

"Please come in and make yourself comfortable. I'll have your coffee and donut brought to you. Colonel Williams is in a meeting and will be with you soon."

"Thanks, Sergeant Major," I said. I was starting to like this.

I went into the building and found a large room filled with desks and clerks busy at work. They all wore tan uniforms, like non-combatants working stateside. Every crease was ironed, every shoe polished, all hair cut to regulation length. In short, they were all STRAC, an acronym that stood for Strategic Army Corps. For draftees like me, saying that a soldier was STRAC was saying that he was a rigid, by-the-book, no-nonsense, anal-retentive son of a bitch who would rather lose a testicle than break a rule. It hadn't occurred to me that I could have been assigned to this headquarters and have to look and dress like this. Compared to these guys, I had been living the life of a hippy.

I felt like a spy as I wandered around observing the operation. I was nervous that somehow my cover might be blown. As I passed one desk, a clerk called out my name. I turned and looked at his nametag: Matthews.

"It's Pete. Pete Matthews. From Fort Hamilton. We were in AIT together there."

"Pete, good to see you," I said, recognizing him as he pushed his glasses up the bridge of his nose. It was a nervous gesture I had seen him make whenever Rich was proposing a plan to get us off the base without passes.

Pete came around his desk. "I thought you were a chaplain's assistant," he said under his breath. "Have you gone over to Intelligence or something?"

"No, I'm still an assistant. It's a long story," I said, gesturing to my mode of dress at the moment. "The CO is getting me a ride back to Can Tho."

"I thought so!" he said, being sure to keep his voice down. "I've been telling these guys you're enlisted, like us. No one could figure out who you were. Al, over there, thought you might be Nixon's bastard son on a special mission."

"What are you doing here?" I asked.

"I got assigned to the brigade chaplain. He's a brass-kisser from way back, never goes anywhere, even has me come over here to do morning reports so the big brass think he's working us hard. Sheesh!"

"Here comes the sergeant major. This is great!" Pete said, saluting me with a smirk on his face, then quickly returning to his seat.

The sergeant major told me that the colonel would be tied up in meetings all morning but that his driver, Lucas, would stay with me until I had a ride to Can Tho.

Lucas arrived a few minutes later, told me to hang tight for a while longer, and then disappeared again. The level of activity fell a little as the morning reports were completed, but it didn't stop: The clerks had simply moved into their "look busy" mode. The word of my identity was getting around; more clerks seemed to be smiling as they worked, occasionally catching each other's eye.

I noticed a large, empty space on the wall over the doors at the entrance. I imagined a sign that read:

The stuffed and mounted head on this plaque once belonged to Ted Bertson, a draftee who was discovered impersonating a real person. This exhibit was donated by Command Sergeant Major Joshua White, who will be leaving Leavenworth Prison at the end of his two-week sentence for voluntary manslaughter.

Lucas returned mid-reverie. "I got word to the colonel that you were still waiting for a ride. He's calling the light colonel to order you up a chopper. Let's go; I'll introduce you," he said. I thought I heard him mutter, "This should be rich," but I couldn't be sure.

We walked to a smaller, concrete block building that sat next to Headquarters. The clerk behind the desk, a Spec 3, stood up.

"Joe," Lucas said, "this is Spec 5 Bertson. He's a friend of the colonel's." Joe stuck out his hand. I noticed that they addressed him only as "the colonel." They liked the man.

"Nice to meet a friend of the colonel's," Joe said. "What can we do for you?"

Lucas jumped in: "The colonel sent me here to tell your boss to get us a chopper."

Joe grinned broadly. "Okay!" he said. Then he dropped his voice several degrees. "This guy," he said, indicating the officer, his supervisor, who sat behind the closed door, "is so military, even his shit is STRAC."

Lucas and I snorted. Enlisted personnel, especially draftees, loved to watch the brass take heat. We particularly enjoyed the oft-quoted phrase "officers and men," as that seemed to assign them to some gender other than male.

Joe walked to the door that had a rectangular, black plastic nameplate stamped with white letters: LT. COLONEL ROBERT JOHNSON. He knocked quietly. A voice inside said, "Yes?"

Joe opened the door. "Sir, Colonel Williams' friend to see you."

Lucas led the way. The lieutenant colonel stood up, smiled, and extended his hand. As we shook, Lucas said, "Sir, I would like to introduce you to a friend of Colonel Williams, Specialist 5 Ted Bertson."

We can never be certain what goes on in another person's mind, but Johnson's body language suggested that his entire brain locked up. On hearing my rank, the smile disappeared from his face, his hand that shook mine turned clammy and cold, and his arm seemed to sag. He was touching an enlisted man; he was shaking hands and acting friendly with an enlisted man!

Johnson sat down firmly, his eyes dropping to his desk. What a dilemma: I was Colonel Williams' friend, so he couldn't throw me out, but he would rather pass a kidney stone than deal with an enlisted man, and a low-level enlisted man at that.

Johnson was muttering that it might be a couple of days before there would be anything flying south, and that all the choppers and pilots had other, more important missions. Then the phone rang.

He picked it up. "Johnson." As he listened, his face turned ashen, then red. "Yes, sir … no, sir … yes, sir. Right away." He hung up.

Ignoring us, he shuffled through the paper on his desk. Picking one, he glanced up. At least he remembered we were still there.

"That was Colonel Williams. We'll have a chopper for you within the hour. Please wait outside," he said. We left as he was picking up the phone.

Johnson's clerk was waiting to hear what happened. Lucas flashed him a thumbs-up. "I thought he was going to have a heart attack when he discovered he was shaking hands with enlisted scum," Lucas said.

From inside his office, we heard Johnson's voice begin to rise. Soon, he was yelling. We couldn't make out all the words, but he was, as my Southern relatives would say, mighty piqued. One of Johnson's subordinates was catching flak, and we knew the subordinate's ears would soon be scorched. The thought of the chain of command lighting up was pleasant to us three civilian soldiers.

Lucas told me it was time to change into my uniform. He found a vacant office for me.

I was sitting beside Joe's desk, hoping the sergeant major was far away from this particular building, when a jeep roared up and skidded to a halt. A warrant officer jumped out of the driver's seat and stomped up the stairs to the office.

The WO started first: "Goddamn it, Joe. I'm short. I have two days and a wakeup, and I get this fucking call to come the fuck over here and pick up some VIP friend of the colonel's."

"This is Spec 5 Bertson, Colonel Williams' friend," Joe said blandly.

"You're it? A Spec 5? I'm supposed to fly a Spec 5 to the Delta, and I'm two days short, and—"

Johnson opened his door: "Henderson, come in here."

WO Henderson went into Johnson's office. The office was ominously quiet. We three enlisted personnel didn't say a word. The door opened, and Henderson stepped out.

"Get your baggage," he said curtly and stalked out to the jeep. I shook hands with Lucas and Joe, told Lucas thanks, and mounted the jeep.

The ship was a light observation helicopter (LOH), a chopper that looked like the oversized head of a dragonfly. The pilot and passenger sat side-by-side inside, encircled in Plexiglas. From inside, it was like flying without being in a ship.

Henderson said not a word to me from the time I got into the jeep until we landed at the Can Tho airfield. I stepped out of the chopper, and he was already on the radio, requesting permission to take off. I was barely out of the wash of the ship when he lifted off. He was one pissed pilot.

When I walked into the assistants' office at the chapel, Harry was lounging in his chair, feet up on the desk, reading *Hustler* magazine.

"You're just reading it for the articles, right?" I asked.

Harry sat up and threw the magazine on the desk. "Hey, Ted. Welcome back. Have a good R&R?"

"Yep. The best."

CHAPTER 35

▼

Nobody Knows the Trouble I've Seen

December 8, 1970

Life returned to normal, or what passed for normal in Vietnam. Chaplain Evert took off for another round of visits to other posts, this time taking Harry. Evert had heard the rumors about early DEROS for personnel like me and wanted to make sure Harry knew what to do when I was gone.

The day after they left, word came that we had some new casualties from a chopper accident, and someone needed to go check on them.

I drove to the Field Hospital, thinking that I wanted to see Josie to find out if she had actually made it to Sydney. I found the wounded men, asked them the usual questions, and made the usual offers of assistance, but I found it hard to focus on them. I kept watching for Josie but didn't see her.

After visiting the wounded, I stayed around the ward for several minutes and then decided to give up and head back to the base. I was almost to the exit when she and several other nurses pushed through the swinging doors of the ward.

She seemed to sense I was there before she saw me. She looked at me, gave an enigmatic smile and small wave, and continued on with the nurses.

I felt disappointed. I didn't know what I'd expected (*she runs in slow motion down the hall and flings herself into my arms as the music swells*), but I wished she had just stopped a second to say hello.

Three days passed before I had any reason to return to the hospital. Evert and I drove over to visit two chopper pilots who had been shot down in a firefight.

We entered at the usual door, and I began looking for Josie as discreetly as possible. She wasn't anywhere in sight. We talked to the head nurse and were directed to where the pilots had been taken after the surgery. They were to be transferred to Saigon as soon as the aircraft were available.

We entered the B Ward, and Evert went to the first bed; that pilot was the most seriously injured. I went across the aisle to talk to the other pilot.

The curtains were parted at the foot of the bed, so I could see the thick bandages on his arms which were suspended by wires, elevating them to reduce swelling. IVs were attached, one to each arm.

His head was bandaged, and he was reclining against his pillow when I entered. He heard me and raised his head. It was Bob Perkins.

Bob had attended services sporadically after Skip's death. Then he stopped coming at all. I had not spoken to him since that strange conversation where he had decided that I was the enemy.

The man looking at me from the bed was older and his eyes looked wild. I was looking at fear.

"Bob? It's Ted. Ted Bertson," I said.

"Ted?"

"The chaplain's assistant. Major Riggles' assistant?"

"Oh, Ted. Yeah. Sorry I can't shake your hand. I'm a little tied up here," he said, giggling.

"Are you in much pain?"

"Nope, not much. They have me so doped up that I don't feel a fuckin' thing. Oops, sorry."

This was not the Bob Perkins I knew. Were the drugs talking, or was he on the edge of a breakdown?

"Bob, is there anything the chaplain or I can do for you? Anybody you want us to contact?"

His jaw muscles flexed as he gritted his teeth. He dropped his head back on the pillow and squeezed his eyes closed. He had pain drugs couldn't touch.

Evert came through the curtains. As I introduced them to each other, Bob seemed to withdraw, to shut down as if trying to regain control of himself.

"Sir," he said to Evert, "I appreciate your coming, but would you mind if Bertson and I talked, just the two of us?" His voice was strained and hardly more than a whisper.

Evert looked over at me; I indicated that it would be okay. He patted Bob's leg under the sheet. "Sure. There are a couple of other people I need to see. Ted, I'll meet you by the front door.

"Thanks," I said.

Bob relaxed a bit as Evert left. He blinked several times, as if trying to wake up. He looked at me hard, and then he said: "The only way you can help me is to get me out of here, out of this goddamn country." He hissed the last words angrily.

I was taken aback. "I don't know what—"

"This is the second time I've been shot down. You remember?"

"Sure, I remember."

"These sons-of-bitches will ship me to Saigon, patch me up, then to Japan, then right back to this fucking shithole."

"Wait, calm down—"

"No! I won't calm down. You don't understand; they'll keep sending me back here until the war is over, or until I get shot up so bad that I'm no good to them anymore, or until I get fucking killed. Haven't you figured this out yet? You've been here for a long time; haven't you figured this out yet?" His voice was getting louder.

"Bob, I ..." I stammered. I knew he was right. Chopper pilots were harder to come by as the war continued. Being an officer in the military in a war was like being in the CIA—you never really left.

He'd sat upright during his outburst. Now he fell back onto the pillow, exhausted.

"I'm sorry," he said after several moments. His chest rose and fell rapidly several times. I felt helpless; there was nothing I could do. I put my hand lightly on his chest. "To tell you the truth," he whispered, "I'm afraid." As soon as he spoke, tears ran down his cheeks. I pulled some tissues from a dispenser beside his bed and wiped his face. His chin trembled, and his breathing was uneven as he struggled to speak. "I'm afraid, and I can't be afraid and do my job." Tears were streaming down his face now. "I choked today. I didn't pull up in time and almost got us killed."

"Are you sure it was something you did? Maybe—"

"No. It was me. I should have lost some air speed, but we were taking hits, and I kept thinking that if I got down on the deck quicker ..." He fell silent. His breathing calmed a bit.

"You know, you could talk to the chaplain. He might be able to do something, to talk to someone," I said.

"Thanks, but I'd rather not. He'll say something to my CO, and I'd be hauled up before a disciplinary board in two seconds. It wouldn't help."

"You don't know what the chaplain might be able—"

"*It won't help*," he said. He fell silent again and turned his face away. Then he sighed. "I'm sorry for throwing this shit at you," he said.

"It's okay," I said. "You're in shock and drugged. You need to talk—" I stopped. I was giving him platitudes, weak platitudes at that. There was nothing I could say that would help in any way.

He would be sent to Saigon, then Japan, then to the States for a short leave, then right back here. He was speaking from experience, so who was I to offer advice?

Bob had said he wanted to be a professional pilot when he left the service. If he protested too much, irritated the wrong officers, his records would be forever marked in a way that said he was untrustworthy, unreliable, or couldn't take the pressure. He was faced with a dilemma—keep his dream and risk his life; lose his dream, save his life.

I stayed with him a few minutes longer, but he said little more. He withdrew into himself. The hopeful, confident young lieutenant I had met only months before no longer existed.

As I left the ward, I remembered that our birthdays were in the same month, but that he was a year younger. He had faced death twice now and would probably face it again. He had grown bitter and angry because no one seemed to care. He felt completely alone, without recourse or solace. And he was twenty-four years old.

CHAPTER 36

▼

I'll Be Seeing You

December 10

Around 8:30 in the morning, Evert walked into the chapel and stopped at the assistants' office door.

"Harry in yet?" he asked.

"Harry had to go to the PX to pick up some stuff," I answered.

Evert pulled Harry's chair away from his desk and straddled it, the backrest supporting his arms.

"I have some bad news," he said.

My heart skipped a beat. "Is it Karen or Robbie?"

Evert waved his hand, dismissing my question. "No, nothing like that. It's about Lieutenant Perkins. I knew you were friends, and I wanted you to know. He died last night. The CO told us in the morning briefing."

I wasn't sure I'd heard him correctly. "Died? Bob died? I thought his wounds weren't life-threatening!"

"They don't know what caused his death yet. They'll do an autopsy today to find out."

"Is that usual? An autopsy?"

"No, unless a man dies unexpectedly. They think he had some internal bleeding that went undetected or a blood clot." He stood up. "Anyway, I remembered you spent some time with him at the hospital and that he was a friend of yours. I thought you would want to know."

"Thanks for telling me," I said.

We sat quietly for a few seconds. He stood up. "Well, I have to go to the hospital again today. The jeep's out front. Let's go as soon as Harry comes back." He left the office and went into his.

I had been working on the morning report but couldn't focus after the news of Bob's death. I replayed everything we had said at the hospital and felt even worse than I had then.

On the drive to the hospital, I told Evert what Bob and I had talked about, wanting to know if I should have pressed Bob harder to talk to Evert.

"I'm afraid Bob was right," Evert had said. "I could have tried to intervene with his CO, tried to do something to get him transferred to a non-combat unit, like a training unit, but that's usually seen as the non-combatant chaplain mollycoddling someone who's lost his nerve. The word would have been out, not in writing of course, but by word of mouth. Perkins has cold feet, lost his nerve."

His hands were gripping the wheel harder as he spoke. A nerve had been hit. "In this man's army," he said, emphasizing each word like a title, "if you do your job passably, don't make waves, and go along with the program, you'll do just fine. But raise a question, express a doubt, or even just wonder aloud about the wisdom of our leaders...." He snapped his fingers. "Boom! You're relegated to the hinterlands and forever more passed over for promotion until you get the picture and resign." His voice was vehement. I wondered if he was talking about himself.

He drove for some time, silent, the muscles in his jaw working. Eventually, he sighed. He looked over at me. "I'm sorry about Perkins. It's hard to lose a friend."

I felt drowsy and sweaty as I jostled along in the jeep, almost like I was hung-over. "Thanks." I felt tired and a little disoriented as I walked into the hospital. We went to the nursing station, and Evert got some information about the men we were to see. The nurse behind the desk, Lieutenant Higgens, called me by name, and I nodded and said hello but little else. A thought formed somewhere in my brain that I might run into Josie, but even that didn't cheer me quite the way it usually did.

I went through the motions with Evert as we visited the injured, but I kept having to bring myself back to what the injured soldiers were saying, forcing myself to pay attention. It was like walking in a fog.

We finished talking to the men and headed out of the ward. A nurse I had gotten to know, Lieutenant Joanna Renfeld, was sitting on a bench near the swinging double-doors of Ward B. She was crying. She held her hands over her face as she rocked slowly back and forth.

Evert immediately sat down beside her and put his arm over her shoulders. "Ted, get some tissues, please."

I ducked back into the ward, grabbed a handful from the nearest box, and brought them to him. He stuffed them into her folded hands. They sat like that for several minutes, rocking gently as Evert held her.

A doctor burst out of the double-doors of the intake room at the other end of the corridor and ran by us, tears running down his face. He pushed through front doors and left the hospital. Two more nurses came out after him, supporting each other and crying. Evert and I glanced at each other: Something terrible had happened, but what?

Joanna calmed some. She pulled herself away from Evert and slumped back on the bench, the back of her head against the wall.

"Joanna, what's happened?" Evert asked quietly.

She tried to speak, but the tears started again. She brought her hands to her face as a deep sob emerged from her, as if she had been struck in the stomach.

"Oh, God!" she cried. "They're all dead!"

"Who's dead, Joanna? Who died?" Evert pressed.

"All of them!" she exclaimed, as though she were addressing idiots. Another sob exploded from her as she sought control over the sorrow that was tossing her like a cork in water. Her right arm dropped on her right leg. She began slapping her leg, as if pounding on a drum. "Pete." Slap. "Sharon." Slap. "Earl." Slap. "Dr. Knight." Slap. "Josie." Slap. "Shirley." Slap. Slap. Slap. Her hand turned into a fist as she hit her leg. "All of them. Every fucking goddamn one of them was killed!"

Josie! "Did you say Josie?" I nearly shouted, stepping in front of her. "Did you say Josie?"

Evert looked up at me quizzically.

"Yeah. Josie," she said, looking up at me with swollen eyes.

I don't know how I managed to get outside of the building, but the next thing I remember was leaning on the hot hood of a jeep, vomiting. I stepped away from the disgusting mess on the ground and leaned against the hot cinderblock wall of the hospital. The burning heat felt good.

Evert found me sitting in the passenger seat of the jeep. He climbed in and started the engine. We came to a halt at the Officers Club, and he got out. "Come in, Ted. I'm buying you a drink. Whatever you want," he said as he went to the door.

Inside, the Club was dark as usual. A lone airman sat in one corner, nursing a beer. Evert went to the bar and ordered a Coke for himself and a beer for me. He guided us to a table on one side of the room, away from both the bar and the airman.

For a time, we sipped our drinks without talking. In due time, Evert asked if I wanted to hear any more about what had happened.

I tried to say yes, but what came out was more of a croak than a word. I cleared my throat and tried again. "Yes."

They were on an air force chopper, on the way to Saigon for training in some new medical procedures, he said. There was nothing unusual about that, as the staff rotated through training regularly.

They left early this morning. The chopper was on the outskirts of Saigon when it went off the radar screens in the control tower there. Soon after, an ARVN patrol called in that a chopper had exploded and gone down near them. Army choppers responded and found the debris in a rice paddy, still burning.

"Was she ... was everybody ...?" I struggled to get the words out.

He answered my unfinished question, saying they found all the personnel dead at the scene.

We were silent again. The images of Josie in her fatigues, lying mangled, kept intruding. Or Josie, smiling with the other nurses on her birthday.

I heard Evert's words as if from a distance: "She was a beautiful young woman."

"What?"

"She was a beautiful young woman. Lieutenant O'Malley, Josie," he said. "I really liked her. Wish I had known her better."

"She was very special," I said. "We got to be friends."

We finished our drinks in silence and left. Just before we got up from the table, Evert reached over and put his hand on my shoulder.

"I'm sorry, Ted," he said quietly. Just that and no more.

We pulled up before the chapel. Harry came shuffling out, holding some papers. "Hey, Ted. I got some questions about this report."

I stepped out of the jeep and paused to look at him for a second, then started walking. Harry called after me, and I turned to answer, but Evert said something to him and waved his hand in my direction.

"Go on," Evert said, "we'll cover for you. Go on." Harry looked in my direction, shrugged his shoulders, and followed Evert into the chapel.

I had felt drugged on the ride back from the hospital. But as soon as we stopped, I was full of energy. I felt fidgety, like ants were crawling over my entire body.

My pace was quick as I walked away from the chapel, and it quickened until I was doing an airborne shuffle. My heart kept speeding up; soon I was running. Where was I running? I didn't care.

I was on the dirt road that circled the base. As I ran, images began playing in my head: the night when the grenade exploded in the Enlisted Men's Club and I had run myself to exhaustion on this road; Bob Perkins and I had walked here watching the Cobras land. Now he was dead, and so was Josie.

My ragged breathing became sobs. I stumbled to a stop as a lump rose in my throat and tears started running down my face.

I needed to hit something, scream, howl, something, anything to release the grief that boiled up in me. I pulled my cap off and tore at it, trying to shred it but to no avail. I slapped it against my leg, threw it on the ground, and stepped on it. I kicked it, picked it up, and slammed it down again as hard as I could, all the time screaming obscenities.

I found a rock and hurled it over the concertina wire into the no-man's-land. I threw another and another, yelling with every throw. I found a clot of dirt, sand that had formed itself into a ball the size of a hand. I picked it up and threw it into the wind as I screamed "Fuck!" at the top of my lungs. My hand squeezed it as I released it, so it flew into thousands of tiny bits of sand and dust that blew back at me, into my face. My glasses blocked most of it, but particles managed to get around them and into my eyes, blinding me.

I staggered, my shoulders hunched and my hands covering my eyes, until my tears washed the particles away. A small voice in my head said, *This is what it feels like to lose your mind.*

My breathing slowed and sweat and tears ran down my face, streaking the dust that covered it. I walked on under the hot sun, struggling to understand my loss. *How could she be dead? Why did Skip and Bob ... why did any of us have to die?* There were no answers; there would never be answers.

Three days later, Rich showed up. He walked quietly past the door of the office and shushed me when I started to greet him. He knocked on Father O'Brian's door. O'Brian was seldom in his office because he spent most of his time in the air, flying from post to post. This particular afternoon, Rich was lucky. O'Brian called from within, "Come in."

Rich opened the door: "Hey, Father. Didja hear the news?"

"What news?" O'Brian asked, taking the bait.

"They found the Body."

Rich was leaning against the doorjamb of my office, looking very innocent, by the time O'Brian flung open his door and began his lecture on sacrilege. Rich listened respectfully and said nothing until O'Brian strode back into his office and closed the door forcefully.

"He's going to point his M16 at you someday and pull the trigger," I said, hugging Rich.

"He wouldn't dare kill a Jew. It would set off a Jewish uprising that would make the Crusades pale in comparison," he said with a big smile.

He rummaged through the tiny office refrigerator, and then glanced up at me. "Jesus, Ted. You're not lookin' so good. You have dark circles under your eyes, and you look like you've lost weight." He found a Dr. Pepper and popped it open.

"I'm okay, I guess. I just don't do well when my friends die on me."

Rich stopped mid-drink. "Oh. Hell, I'm sorry, Ted. Anybody I knew?"

My throat squeezed shut, and I couldn't speak. I just shrugged.

Rich looked at me carefully for a moment, then placed a hand on my shoulder.

"You need a good Chanukah party," he said.

I took a deep breath, trying to get myself under control. My eyes had moistened. I wiped them and then asked, "A Chanukah party? What's that?"

He gulped the Dr. Pepper. "I convinced Ira that we should go all over the country, throwing Chanukah parties for all the lonely Jewish personnel who are valiantly serving their god and country, or something to that effect. That includes, of course, any stray goyim who I feel to be worthy of the honor of sharing libations with God's Chosen People. That means you—not the God's Chosen People part, the goyim part!"

We drove to the USO Club that was on the base, where Rich had commandeered the fixings for a party. A Chanukah party, according to Rich, meant scraping together any food that could be made edible and all the booze that he could lay his hands on for the Special Jewish Punch.

Lori, a heavyset, sullen-looking woman who was in charge of the base USO at the time, was already at work, directing her Vietnamese assistants in setting up tables and chairs.

"My *co's* are all off today, probably screwing any GI they can get their legs around, so all I have are *ba's* to help." (*Co* was the Vietnamese term for an unmarried girl; *ba* was the designation for a married or older woman—which in Vietnam meant a woman in her forties.)

"We'll take it from here. Thanks, Lori," Rich said with a little wave. Lori's version of a smile was to raise her upper lip enough to reveal her teeth.

"Did you catch the 'my' part of that?" I asked.

"Yeah. Kind of like some Southerners talk about 'our negroes,' or 'our blacks.' Makes me sick! But I needed her help, and she came through."

"How did you get her to cooperate? She looks like she'd be tough to deal with," I said.

"She wants my body. Of course, most women want my body," he said, sucking his sizable stomach in and raising his chest like a puffer pigeon. Everything fell as he let his breath out. "I led her on, I suppose, but it was for the cause of the Lord." He made the sign of the Star of David on his chest. "To work!" he commanded.

The serving tables for the food were soon readied, and Rich set to work making a Five-Bean Salad as I handed him the ingredients, much like a nurse with a surgeon.

After cheese, crackers, salad, plates, and utensils were set out, bottles of various high-proof alcohol were assembled for the Special Jewish Punch. I discovered that Special Jewish Punch was any and all liquor that Rich could lay his hands on, poured into a large punch bowl over a layer of ice, and stirred. Rich, of course, had many tastes of the concoction to ensure the proper balance of flavors. By the time ten or so Jewish personnel had straggled in, he was in very good spirits.

The party began with a song. Rich's nasal voice rang clear, if not completely true, as he led the singing. The other men were clearly uncomfortable singing, and their muted mutterings provided an accompaniment to Rich's off-key solo.

The food disappeared quickly, as did the first bowl of punch. Within two hours, everyone was gone except for Rich and me. We cleaned up the tables and gave the extra food to the Vietnamese women, and then sat with our chairs tipped against a wall, enjoying the air conditioning and the relaxed feelings brought on by several servings of the Special Jewish Punch.

We were quiet for several minutes, a kind of quietness that can only be between two friends. "So, what's chewing on your soul, my friend?" Rich said eventually. "Out with it. We've both had enough to drink that our tongues should be wagging freely."

I started to talk, but my throat tightened again, warning me that feelings were close to the surface. A little more punch, and I tried again. "You remember the nurse we met sometime ago at the Air Force Field Hospital? The one you assumed I was having an affair with?" I asked.

"Sure. I ran into her a few times after. O'Hara? O'Reilly? Something like that?"

"O'Malley. Josie O'Malley," I corrected.

"Sure. What about her?"

After another sip, I answered. "She was killed when a chopper crashed three days ago."

He didn't say anything at first but shook his head and looked at the floor. "That's terrible. I'm sorry to hear that." He looked at me sideways, waiting. "There's more, isn't there?"

"Yeah. An acquaintance of mine, a chopper pilot, died too. They died almost on the same day, and that nearly did me in. I felt like I was cracking up, you know?

He turned sideways in the chair, draped one arm over the back, and tucked one foot under the other. "This is serious," he said.

I went for more punch. By the time I walked back to my chair next to him, thinking how nice it was to have someone I could talk to, I found him with his cheek resting firmly on the back of his hand, soundly asleep. A thin line of drool ran out of the lower corner of his mouth, and his puffy lips made a very small popping noise as he exhaled through them.

I slumped into the chair; I felt the punch having its effect on me. I smiled fondly at my friend, thinking that he had helped me keep my sanity for the year. I hoped he could say the same for me.

After a time, I rose and shuffled unsteadily across the room and out the door into the heat of the afternoon. I stood on the steps of the USO and squinted into a dark thunderhead of clouds that were being blown to the coast. A small one moved across the sun and, for a minute, it was outlined in silver. For one brief instant, an edge of the cloud looked like the profile of a woman's face. The image disappeared as the wind drove the clouds onward, but in that instant, I knew I had loved Josie in a special way. She had been a lovely, caring woman and a devoted, fiercely loyal wife. I envied the man she'd loved, and I was thankful that I had not sullied the friendship we had.

I raised my plastic glass as I said quietly, "Here's to you, Josie O'Malley. Be with God."

CHAPTER 37

▼

I'll Be Home for Christmas

December 14

The note on my desk was from Harry: "Call for you, 8:00, report to Records Office ASAP." As usual, Harry neglected to write who the note was for or even the date. I could have been looking at a note that was a week old.

This could mean a lot of things, I thought. Leaving a note telling Evert where I had gone—a note with his name and the date and time, of course—I walked over to the white, concrete block, single-story building that housed the personnel records for everyone on base.

At the main desk, a clerk asked for the first letter of my last name; then he directed me to another desk farther back in the room filled with desks. There was a clerk at almost every desk, each one intent on his work.

I stepped up to the desk where I had been directed and waited for the clerk, an E-3, to notice that I was there. It was early in the morning, but he looked frazzled already.

He eventually noticed me and peered at me over the thick black frames of his glasses, the same kind that I wore. In a flat, Midwestern nasality, he asked my name, last name first, birth date, MO, and serial number in a tone that said that I could tell him anything and he would type it.

He was shuffling through piles of papers on his desk. There was perhaps some order to his assemblage, but it escaped my eye. His skinny fingers found my papers, and he pulled them out of a pile with a small grunt—that probably had been his heavy lifting for the day.

He scanned the packet, flipped though the pages, and handed them to me, telling me to take them to the clerk at the first desk in the next room. He pointed to a doorway off to his right. I looked at the top sheet. In the midst of a sea of acronyms, one set jumped out at me: DEROS. I froze in my tracks, searching feverishly for a date and found it—20 December 1970.

I almost ran to the next clerk's desk. He took the papers, removed the bottom sheet, stamped the rest of the sheets, said congratulations, and pointed me to the nearest door.

I ran back to the chapel. Evert was just walking in.

"I'm going home!" I yelled. Evert clapped me on the back, and Harry came strolling out of the office, smiling. The look on his face was probably like the look I had worn so often. It said, *I'm glad you're going home. I wish I was, too.*

"They told me your papers were in, but I wanted it to be a surprise," he said.

Father O'Brian stepped out of his office without a scowl on his face—that was as close as he came to smiling. He shook my hand and disappeared back into the inner sanctum.

Evert said that the first thing I needed to do was write to Karen and get the letter in the day's mail. It would probably just reach her in time for her to make arrangements.

I did that right away, giving her all the information I could decipher about arrival times and flight numbers. I got that in the mail, and then sat down to make a list of what I had to do to get ready to go home. It was a short list: number one—pack; and number two—go home.

The next day I made my last trip to the orphanage. Only two small boxes of children's clothing had arrived from my father's church in the past four months. I was delivering the second.

The sisters were, as usual, effusive in their greetings and, as usual, we could barely understand each other. The children were shy and withdrawn, as always.

I took my camera with me for this final trip. I wanted as many pictures as I could get of them in their innocence, before the world came crashing down on them. Looking at their faces through the camera lens, I felt drawn to them as never before.

My heart was heavy as I said goodbye to the sisters. Outside the compound, I inspected my jeep more carefully than ever; my short-timer nerves were kicking in.

Sure that the jeep had not been booby-trapped, I climbed in and started the engine. Just as I was pulling away, I noticed a small boy standing by the fence. I paused and looked back at the pudgy-cheeked child with his mother's black Asian eyes and his black father's hair and skin color. Then, unexpectedly, he raised his small right hand and waved good-bye.

Something in his gesture stabbed me in the heart. My hand rose to my chest, and my eyes teared. I drove away, feeling ashamed—ashamed for being a part of an invading army, ashamed for the havoc and devastation that we, in our well-intentioned way, had brought to these fair people. This child, this country, would pay a horrible price for our folly for decades, certainly for the rest of his life.

Harry and I were in the office around noon on December 17, thinking about going to lunch, when the chapel shook with a big explosion from the direction of the airfield. We froze and looked at each other. Should we head for a bunker? Seconds passed, but no attack siren sounded.

"I wonder what that was?" I asked.

"I think I'll go snoop around," Harry said, picking up his cap. "See you after lunch." He strolled off in the direction of the explosion.

I finished the paperwork, went to lunch, and was back in the office when Harry appeared, shaking his head. He opened the refrigerator, pulled out a candy bar and a beer, and sat down.

"Well, what happened?" I asked impatiently.

He put his feet up on his desk, leaned back in the chair, and peeled open the candy bar. "Sapper got through the perimeter somehow, or some women managed to sneak plastic in—who knows? Anyway they rigged a Huey so when the door was opened—boom. Pilot, copilot, and a passenger all got it. Bang." He popped the cap of the beer and took a long drink. "Goddammit. They can get you anywhere in this fuckin' country."

My short-timer nerves began tingling. *Much more of this and I'll have to be sedated on the flight out of here*, I thought. *Lord, let me go home.*

Rich arrived the next day. We hugged like long-lost brothers and jumped up and down when I told him my news.

"Your orders should be coming through any time," I said. "We arrived in-country at the same time."

He shook his head. "Nah, I know I won't be going home. I extended for three months."

I couldn't believe it. "Three months? Why the hell did you extend?"

"'Cause then, when I leave this godforsaken country, I'll also leave this godforsaken army. I'll be out—no weekend warrior shit, no meetings, no nothing. Out. Finis. Done. Bye-bye, and kiss my ass, Uncle Sam."

I didn't like the sound of it. Staying in-country one minute longer than necessary seemed crazy, but that was Rich.

He hugged me. "I gotta go," he said.

"You just got here."

"Ira and I are on our way to Vinh Long, and I just wanted to stop to apologize again for being such a schmuck the other afternoon."

"You weren't a schmuck. You were drunk."

"I was a drunk schmuck, okay? I wasn't much of a friend, and I'm sorry. Say 'I forgive you' like a good Christian, and let me go my way."

"All right. I forgive you. Go in the name of the Father, the Son, and the Holy Ghost," I said, making the sign of the Cross.

"Stop. I didn't come to convert; I just wanted to say I'm sorry," he whined.

"Wait. There's some holy water around here somewhere. I'll bet it will burn your hide right off," I said.

"That's it, that's it. I'm taking this Jewish body out of here. You'll be sorry. You won't have Hindeman to kick around anymore."

"That sounds familiar. I think someone's used that line," I said.

"Hey, did I tell you? I received a special commendation," he said.

"What for?"

"I've put together a kosher cookbook that the army can use. Maybe I'll be a kosher chef after the army, cooking in the best kosher restaurants."

"Are there such things as kosher restaurants?" I asked.

"No. Not yet. I guess I'll have to start my own," he said, with a manic gleam in his eyes. He grabbed a piece of paper and scrawled something on it. "Here's my APO address. You better write when you get back to the States, or I'll put a Yiddish curse on your manchild."

"I promise," I said, grabbing him in a hug. "I'll miss you, Rich."

"I'll miss you, too," he said over my shoulder. He stepped back and wiped his eyes. "I gotta go. Ira was bent on converting our pilot to the True Faith. I never knew the Orthodox were evangelical until I met Ira."

"Say hello and good-bye to Ira for me," I said as he hopped into a jeep. I wondered if he had asked permission before he borrowed it.

He turned a corner and was gone. I walked back inside. The walls seemed to move closer together; everything seemed to shrink slightly. I had said good-bye to my friend. I was ready to go.

December 21

We were flying through endless clouds. The fuselage shook occasionally as the high winds buffeted the big plane. I hardly noticed; I was drunk with fatigue.

In Tan San Hut, I had passed through the same open-sided building that I had entered with such trepidation less than one year earlier. This time I was one of the cheering veterans being observed by the scared newbies. We could hardly wait to board that big ungainly bird and head home.

After a long flight, we stopped in Kyoto, Japan, to refuel, and then on to Oakland. In Oakland, we were bussed to a processing area where we turned in our Vietnam uniforms for the heavier, stateside fatigues. I was issued one dress uniform to wear on my flight home. We had papers stamped and re-stamped, and we wandered around in large warehouse-type buildings, waiting to be told where to go next. Thankfully, water was available to drink and bathrooms were plentiful. No food, however, was forthcoming, so by the time we were processed we had not eaten for a day and a half.

I lost track of the time and didn't know if it was day or night, since the sun barely shone through the heavy clouds and drizzle, just as it had been hidden almost a year before. Winter in Oakland. But I didn't care. I was going home. I was on my way.

Within a couple of hours, we were crammed into a bus that dropped about forty of us at the airport in San Francisco. A large wall clock said it was 2:00, but I wasn't sure if it was morning or afternoon. I walked over to a weary civilian clerk behind one of the airline counters and asked him. "2:00 AM" he answered, then yawned.

Everything was closed at the airport in the wee hours of the morning, so most of us drank any soft drinks we could coax out of the vending machines. I had about four of various flavors, as I recall.

I was on the plane bound for Detroit Metro by 7:00 AM and promptly fell asleep. I was vaguely aware that a young woman asked me if I wanted something to drink, and sometime later, something to eat. I roused myself to eat the pasteboard food and then fell immediately back to sleep.

The shaking of the plane as it made its long, windy descent finally woke me. I looked at my watch that I had reset to Detroit time, then at my ticket. Twenty minutes to landing. Nothing but gray clouds outside the window.

My ears told me we were descending, but my eyes said we were in a perpetual fog. Suddenly the plane broke through the fog. We were on the final approach. The ground rose to meet us and we landed with a thump then we taxied to the gate.

There was a strange, unreal quality to the moment. I had been so far from here, from these people, my family. So much had happened. What would it be like to see them again? How could I ever tell them what I had experienced and how I had changed? Had I changed? Had they?

The reflection that looked dimly back at me from the window told me nothing. It was just a vague outline, a pale specter. Who was I?

I had never written Karen or my parents about any of the attacks I had been through—the snipers; the gut-wrenching fear as mortars walked toward me through the darkness; the terror of auto-rotating to a landing when a chopper lost its engine and seeing the ground rising up to destroy us; the sights and smells of the hospital; the deaths I had witnessed. I had not wanted Karen to worry more than she already had, nor my parents. Would their heightened fears have lessened my own?

As far as they could tell from my letters, I had spent a year in a war playing tennis, visiting an orphanage, dining with missionaries, teaching English, and visiting the injured. Now I wished I had told them more.

The man they were meeting was very different from the man they had said good-bye to just eleven months ago. Who was I now? When they embraced me, who would they embrace?

I lay my head back against the seat as a heaviness seeped into my heart. A part of me was lost to these people who knew me so well, these people who loved me and whom I loved. A gap had opened between us; could I ever breach it? Could they? We had been separated for a year, not only by distance but by unshared experiences, events that would cast long shadows on me, and on them, for the rest of our lives.

The plane lurched to a stop; the doors opened. I stepped into the drafty corridor and walked up its slight incline. Heat brushed by me as I stepped into the lights and noise of the busy terminal. My family was there. Karen was holding our child; tears ran down her face.

I paused for a moment and took it in: my mother, wiping her eyes; my father, smiling ear to ear; my younger sister and her husband; Karen's parents and sisters. They were all there, waiting. Waiting for me.

Home. I had come home.

Postlude

Every soldier returning from war has a unique story to tell of battles fought, ordeals endured, friends lost, and the absurdities that are part and parcel of the killing and mayhem that is warfare. Stories to tell—but who will listen?

When I returned home at the end of 1970, the protests and counter-protests, flag waving and burning, tear gassing, rioting, beatings, and exposés had both sensitized and fatigued the country. The very human demands from grieving families to give meaning to the sacrifices of their children, to make them part of a greater cause, had been irresistible to politicians who would make war. So they obliged, and more young men died to honor the deaths of other young men.

The cycle of death-demands for revenge-more death, began when the first American soldiers died. The cycle was repeated fifty-eight thousand times. Officials wrapped themselves in the flag and wept crocodile tears over a war they could have ended years earlier but did not, because they had come to believe their own propaganda. Nixon had fiddled while Vietnam burned. But change was in the air.

Nightly newscasts about the war had become meaningless verbiage. People were tired of hearing about arcane international politics. They were tired of sorting through arguments for and against the war. They were tired of seeing pictures of death and destruction in a far-off country that many could not even find on a map. They were tired of thinking.

With fatigue comes resignation. But with resignation came something else, something unexpected. For too long, people had listened to the voices that spoke of blind, unquestioning patriotism. Now they began paying attention to the voices that called for peace.

Throughout the country, people began questioning their leaders, talking together, whispering that maybe peace was possible. Whispers were becoming murmurs, and murmurs were joining to become a crescendo that even the most ardent supporters of the war could not avoid hearing—enough! The deadly insanity was slowly drawing to an end.

In many ways, my family mirrored the mood of the country—they had been concerned while I was in harm's way, but once I returned, they assumed all our lives would return to normal and forgot that a war still raged. What they did not know, and did not *want* to know, was that the man to who walked into Fort Wayne in August 1969 was not the person who walked off the plane and into their embrace on that bleak December day in 1970. I had a story to tell, but it felt like no one cared to listen. I had been changed, but my family and my country had changed as well.

Even Karen, who had been my best friend and companion, expressed no interest in knowing what had happened to me. She had gone though a pregnancy, a difficult delivery, and the long sleepless nights without me. I felt like she was relieved to have me back not so much as a lover and husband, but rather as a father for Robbie. She had become "Mother," and my expected role was "Father."

For her, "Father" meant loving, kind, a good provider, and not overly emotional. Had our marriage been a play, I would have said that I no longer fit the role that she had cast me in, and she could not change the role that she had cast herself in.

The twenty-one year-old man she married was a non-drinking, non-smoking college student who never used profanity. His emotions were under control, so he was predictable and dependable. The man who came back from Vietnam swore, drank on occasion, smoked a pipe. And he had become irreligious and grown cynical about the war, things military, and politics, in that order.

Those changes didn't seem to bother her. What *did* bother her, something she let me know about in no uncertain terms, was that I got too "emotional" about things. She would find me in tears as I stood beside Robbie's crib, watching him sleep. I could be almost emotionally overwhelmed reading a poem, listening to a symphony, or watching a news story on television about the war. I would flair up in anger when I heard Kissinger growling his way through his arrogant, bloodless, monotone rationales for why more soldiers and civilians (the famous "collateral damage") would probably die so American negotiators would be in a stronger bargaining position.

Everything seemed to evoke a response that was far greater than the cause, she said. Why did hearing politicians simply talking about the war set me off?

She was uncomfortable with strong emotions. The change from my previously low-keyed self, to what seemed to her like hysterical shouting, was scary. I had become unpredictable.

Both of us had been reared in families that kept their emotions under wraps. Neither Karen nor I had role models to help us as we grappled with our own and each other's feelings. When it came to our marriage, arguments, confrontations, and direct, emotional words were out; niceness, politeness, and silence were in. So talk about Vietnam and what had happened to my friends and me was off-limits, because I couldn't talk about it in a calm, unemotional manner.

My response was first to sulk, then to decide that I would revert to my conditioning as a PK and keep everything inside. Years later, a psychologist helped me to understand the obvious: We can't shut down a few of our emotions without shutting them all down. But that is what I did.

Our lives went on, although everything seemed to have a temporary feeling to it. We moved to Louisville, Kentucky, and lived with my sister and her husband while I finished my tour of active duty at Fort Knox. We then moved to Ann Arbor where I enrolled in a doctoral program at the University of Michigan. Then, finally, we moved to my first teaching position in Maine.

We settled into a predictable pattern: She stayed home with Robbie, and I went to work. I would come home and talk about work, and she would talk about Robbie and what she did to keep the household going. It was not long before Robbie and our pre-Robbie history were the only two things that kept us connected.

All of this time, my emotions were under control, or so I thought. If I watched news shows on television, I learned to listen dispassionately. The local paper carried little news of the war, and what did appear in the paper were short summations about the peace talks ("No progress was made in Paris today"), with only a passing mention that another fifty American solders had been killed. I could read that without any emotional reaction because I was numb inside.

Yes, my emotions were under control, but sometimes I would awake in the wee hours of the morning with tears on my face. I would get up as quietly as I could and sit by the window in the living room. I would look out at the night sky in summer or over the deep, white snow in winter. What was I looking for? I couldn't say. Peace? Comfort? If I felt agitated, I chalked it up to anger at the latest machinations of my department chair. But there was always something inside me, something I tried to keep hidden behind a door. Something that kept scratching the door and testing the handle, letting me know that it wanted out.

On January 23, 1973, the agreement to end the conflict was signed in Paris. A cease-fire was declared that would take effect on January 27. The word went out all over the country to every church and public facility—if you have bells, please ring them at 9:00 PM on January 27. Citizens were asked to gather as the bells sounded to mark an end to that senseless, bloody conflict.

At dinner that night, I asked Karen if she would like to go with me to celebrate the end of the war. She thought about it for a moment then said that it was pretty cold out, and it was probably too late to get a sitter to come. Besides, she said, this was more my thing than hers.

In 1973, the town of Orono, where the university was located, had a population of one thousand. There was one main road through the town that led to the university campus. At 8:45, I bundled up, took my pipe, and walked the two blocks down Main Street to the front of the white, clapboard building that housed the Congregational Church. I expected to see a knot of people gathered there in celebration, but I walked into an empty intersection that served as the town square. I assumed people would emerge from their homes as the clock moved toward nine, but no one came.

Precisely at 9:00 PM, a recording of a church bell began playing from the speakers located in the steeple of the church. It played for me alone.

I shook my head at the tackiness of a recording of a bell and was surprised that tears filled my eyes. A solitary car passed slowly through the intersection. The driver glanced toward the church where the bell was ringing and then at me, a lone figure standing on the curb looking up toward the steeple. I watched him shrug his shoulders as he drove through; he was probably wondering what kind of nut would be outside on a cold night in January, listening to a recording of a church bell.

I stepped back from the curb and leaned against a building. I was surprised by the intensity of the waves of grief that washed through me as I thought about all the lives lost and a society destroyed. And for what? It was not a time of celebration but rather a time to grieve.

Worst of all, *worst of all*, the person I loved most in the world was not there with me. For her, the war had been letters, a few cassette tape recordings, a MARS call.

"He didn't have it so bad as a chaplain's assistant," I'd once overheard her saying to another woman at a party. "A lot of other guys had it much worse than he did because he was behind the lines."

I had done my job too well. All my letters about occasionally playing tennis at the air force base, swimming a few times at an American compound, the white lies after attacks ("In case you read something about the base getting hit, it was just a couple of mortar rounds. Not a big deal"), never mentioning my visits to the hospital—all of these had led her to believe that I was on a sort of extended vacation. In my desire to not have her worry, I had created a fantasy.

I had gotten testy with her about what I had overheard. I told her about some of the attacks, some of my friends who had been killed; not everything, but enough, I hoped, to make her aware that it had not been so "cushy." She listened and then said that I hadn't written anything about that, so how was she to know? She had walked away in a huff.

There are no villains in this story. She was not to blame for my misleading her. But standing on that lonely street in Orono, Maine, listening to a recorded bell, I missed her more than I had ever missed her in Vietnam. I felt more isolated, more alone than even on the darkest nights I had spent in that godforsaken country.

That cold January night, I wept not only for me but also for us.

In 1974, we moved from Maine back to Michigan, where I had taken another teaching position. The emotions I tried to ignore would not be ignored, so I became more involved in my teaching and performing. I even took up jogging, trying anything that would dampen the emotional fires that still burned.

That helped a little, but alarm bells finally went off during the fall semester of 1976: whatever lurked behind the closed door was coming out. Outwardly, everything was fine in our marriage (one colleague told me later that other music faculty thought that ours was the perfect marriage). We were cordial, kind to each other, and never argued. In fact, we never talked.

That fall, I realized that I had started to do strange things, like going the wrong way on streets I had driven on a hundred times. I was extremely tired, was having trouble concentrating, and would lose thoughts mid-sentence. I became forgetful of deadlines and meetings, something that was out of character for me.

Once, when a student canceled a lesson, I sat down at my desk to do some paperwork since I had an hour before the next student appeared. I was startled by a knock on my door. The next student appeared, and when I said she was early, she looked at her watch and said, no, she was right on time. She was. I had spent the entire hour staring at the wall.

It grew worse as the semester went on. I was going through the motions, meeting my classes and teaching my voice students, but I was running on automatic. I realized that I was becoming two people—one who went about his work and the other who sat in a control booth, observing, almost as if I were watching myself on television.

I had a student, a woman in her late twenties, who confided that she suffered from a mental disorder that was affecting her studies. As she described her symptoms, I realized that she was describing mine. Hers, however, were much worse, because she had been hospitalized a number of times for attempting suicide.

She would talk about feeling as if she were watching herself get out of bed, walk into the bathroom, take the razor blade, and slowly slit her wrists. She was doing well with her medications, but she wanted to alert me to the fact that the medication had side effects that might impede her singing. When she told me about this, a shiver went up my spine. Maybe I was going crazy.

I went home that night, helped with dinner, played with Matt and Robbie (Matt had been born in Maine, shortly before moving to Michigan), given the boys their baths, and then put them to bed. That had become our nightly ritual. We both loved our two towheads dearly, and I always felt alive when I was with them.

After they were in bed and Karen and I had done the dishes, we went into the living room and sat. I was feeling restless. It was a beautiful, warm autumn evening, so I asked her if she would like to sit outside. She said she would prefer to just watch some television and enjoy the calm.

I stepped outside and immediately felt a weight lift off my chest. But my relief was short lived as a feeling of sorrow bubbled up. Being in her presence was like entering a zone of extra gravity that made me feel heavy and made it hard to move. Worst of all, I realized that I felt nothing for her. The revelation hit me like a brick.

When I thought of her, it was like putting my hand in a bag of cotton and grasping for something firm to hold on to. My eyes brimmed with tears as I realized that the Karen I loved had disappeared while I was in Vietnam. The woman who sat in our living room looked and sounded like Karen, but she seemed remote and withdrawn when she was with me, as if she, too, was just was going through the motions.

I began having trouble breathing. My heart began racing, and it felt like I couldn't take a deep breath. I took a few steps, then half-sat, half-fell onto the lawn. My vision closed in. I felt like I was spiraling out of control, falling into a deep hole. I wondered if I was having a heart attack. I thought of calling out to Karen, but I couldn't. It was as if I would rather die.

The blackness receded; my breathing slowed. I stood up on shaky legs and walked around to the side of the house, away from the road that ran in front of it. With rigid arms, I rested my hands against the house and cried. I tried to cry quietly, and for the most part I succeeded, but I imagine that someone walking along the street would have heard me.

I didn't even know why I was crying, but that didn't stop me. I noticed a movement out of the corner of my eye. I was standing next to our bedroom window, and I discovered that Karen was standing on the inside, watching me. Our eyes met and I saw hers were filled with tears, too. She turned and moved away.

I walked around, drying my eyes and trying to clear my head. I wondered if she would come outside. She didn't.

After a few minutes, I went back into the house. The sky in the west was still light, but the house had grown dark in the shadows. I turned on a lamp in the living room where I had left her, but she wasn't there. I looked down the hall to our bedroom; the door was closed and there was no light in the room.

When I opened the bedroom door, I saw she was under the covers in the bed, her back to the door. I called her name quietly a couple of times, but she made no response. I closed the door, went to the living room and turned on the television: I needed some kind of sound for companionship.

Robbie woke me the next morning. I had fallen asleep in my easy chair in front of the television. Karen emerged from our bedroom and told me to get cleaned up, that she would make breakfast, that it was almost seven o'clock and I had an eight o'clock class, and that I was going to be late. I felt like I was back in the army and she had become my sergeant.

I had trouble focusing the entire day because I kept thinking about the conversation that we might have that evening. I looked forward to it the way a person with a raging toothache anticipates a trip to the dentist—with fear of further pain but hope for relief.

I was greeted by a quiet house when I arrived home that afternoon. Karen met me at the door with a glass of wine for each of us. She had never done this before, so I knew we were in for an interesting conversation.

She had arranged for the boys to spend the night with a neighbor who had children of the same age. She asked me to sit, so I chose the sofa. She remained standing.

"Okay," she said, taking a sip of wine. "I've been thinking about this all day."

"What 'this' do you mean?" I asked.

"Your … your *episode* last night," she said, waving toward the street.

I nodded.

"I need to know, Ted. Are you seeing somebody?"

I was shocked. It had not occurred to me that she might think there was another woman.

"No," I said. "Karen, you've been the only woman in my life, the only woman I've loved since I first kissed you in high school." I felt my hand twitch slightly when I said "loved," because the memory of Josie rose like a tiny balloon out of my memory and flitted across my consciousness.

She sighed and sat down on a footstool. I realized then how tense she must have been. She took another sip of wine, and I noticed her eyes were teary.

After a few moments of silence, we both started to talk at the same time. We chuckled, and she gestured for me to begin.

It was my turn to sip some wine. "I've been having trouble at school," I said.

"Is it George again?" she asked. George, the choral director, had been my nemesis since I had arrived on campus.

"No, nothing like that." Another sip of wine. "I think I'm having some sort of mental breakdown." It was her turn to look shocked. I told her about my peculiar behavior, the memory lapses, and the feeling of being two people. My words tumbled over each other, as I stammered and stuttered my way through what had been happening for the past few months.

"You never told me about this," she said after I had burbled my way to a stop.

"I know. But we never seem to talk about anything other than the boys," I said.

"Or your work," she added.

Silence.

"I think that some of what's happening to me has to do with Vietnam," I said.

Her head dropped. "Then you ought to see a therapist," she said, looking at the floor.

"But you're the one I want to talk to," I said. I felt my eyes watering and blinked several times, hoping to clear them. It didn't help.

She stood up. "You've been different ever since you came back. Maybe things were harder on you than you let me know about. I understand that. But Ted, it's been six years since you were there. Why can't you just get over it?"

"Get over it?" I shouted. I was standing up. "How can I get over what I saw if I can't talk about it with you?"

"But you can't talk about it without going into some kind of *state*. I keep hearing about vets who just go ... go crazy and ... and kill themselves or their families, and ... and it scares me when you're like that. I mean, you're good to the boys and me, but you can be laughing with them one minute, and then you suddenly get all quiet-like, and sometimes you look so … so lost! I don't know what to do when you're like that. I mean, I wonder … I mean, I'm afraid you might hurt—" She stopped. Her eyes went wide.

I was stunned. I felt as if all the breath had been knocked out of me. The room seemed to tilt, and I was looking at a stranger—a stranger who was afraid of me.

"You think I might hurt you or the boys?" I said.

Her face broke apart, and she dropped her wine glass onto the carpet. I took a step toward her, but her hand came up to stop me. Then she covered her face with her hands and cried.

I was helpless with disbelief. I stood with my arms sagging at my sides and watched the woman I loved suffer, and I could not comfort her.

The tears passed and she went to wash her face. I had one of those mundane thoughts that often seem to intrude on moments of great importance—take care of the wine spill. I went into the kitchen to get water. I was looking around for a container to put it in when I heard her voice from the archway that separated the kitchen from the small dining area.

"Club soda," she said.

"What?"

"Don't use water; use club soda. There's some in the pantry."

I found the club soda and turned to her. She had a couple of white towels in her hands.

We went about the process of getting the stain out. It seemed strange that we would be engaged in such a natural, homely moment after what had been said just minutes before.

Our hands touched. She put her hand over mine and held it between hers.

"I'm sorry, Ted," she said.

"Me, too." We were both on our knees. I put my hands on her shoulders, moved to her, and took her in my arms. She kissed me lightly on the lips and put her head on my shoulder.

We stayed like that for several moments. Then I pulled away but held her hands.

"I'm sorry that you felt like I might hurt you or the boys."

"I know you wouldn't intentionally do anything to hurt them or me," she said.

I sat back on my heels.

"'Intentionally'? What do you mean by that? Do you really think I might snap and do something to hurt you or them?"

"Please don't get upset," she said.

I took a deep breath. "I don't know what to say. I feel like I'm damned if I do and damned if I don't. If I let you know how ... how hurt I am that you would even *imagine* that I would harm you or the boys, you'll say I'm getting upset. Maybe I'll explode!" I waved my arms, and she jumped. "If I don't tell you how I feel, which is what I've been trying to do for the past six years," I heard my voice getting louder. She flinched. I stopped and took another breath, trying to calm myself. I began again. "If I talk about my feelings or *don't* talk about my feelings, then I guess I'm either brooding and moody, or about to go into a violent frenzy. Is that right?"

She looked down at the floor. "Maybe," she said.

A half-strangled shout came out of my mouth. I sat back hard on the floor, leaned against the sofa, and folded my arms across my chest. I felt like I was in a straitjacket; I felt like I might explode, literally.

"I'm sorry," she said. She stood up and walked out the front door.

"Shit!" I yelled. "Shit! Shit! Shit!" I shouted as I beat my hands on the carpet.

I was breathing heavily as I stood up. Six years of frustration was oozing up inside me. Maybe she was right; maybe I was having a breakdown. Maybe I would go crazy and take it out on her and the boys. The idea terrified me.

I strode into the bedroom, put on my running shoes, and stormed out of the house. Karen was backing our car out of the driveway. I called her name. She paused for a moment and looked at me. I saw tears, but I also recognized the look on her face behind the tears. I had seen it before in Vietnam: it was fear.

I watched as she drove down the block and disappeared around the corner. I couldn't believe it: Karen was afraid of me.

When these words hit my consciousness, the floodgates opened. *What did I do? What did I say? Why is this happening? Where is she going? Where are the kids?*

The questions tumbled over each other and my heart started racing. I had to move, move or die right there with my heart exploding in my chest.

So I ran. I ran down the block, around a curve, and onto the street that ended at an unpaved country road. I was wearing jeans and a polo shirt, so I was sweating in the cool autumn air in no time. It felt good to sweat, and it felt good to pound the dirt.

I headed north when I reached the road. The sun was setting, and in the dimming light the dirt road blurred as it passed under my feet. Feelings I had tried to keep hidden percolated out, pushing me to run harder, run faster.

My mind was skipping from image to image. *Running on the perimeter road on the base in Can Tho. Screaming into the tropical sun as the sand blew into my eyes. The nurse crying. Bob looking up from the hospital bed. Ryan White holding my hand. Josie's face as I sang for her on her birthday. Karen crying. Karen in the car, looking at me, afraid of me.*

I stumbled, but I didn't stop. I ran on into the growing shadows as images and voices played in my head.

After several miles my stomach began cramping and I staggered to the side of the road and threw up. As I was bent over, my hands on my knees, sucking air, I was afraid I was going insane.

Fear and anger were battling inside me like two cats in a sack: I was afraid that Karen might be right, but also hurt and angry that she would ever doubt me. Suddenly, a new image popped into my head: Robbie and me.

We had been on this very road on a sunny summer day, Robbie on his little bike with the training wheels, peddling away as he accompanied me while I jogged. We would sing and tell stories as I pounded along working up a sweat. As miserable as I felt, I couldn't help but smile at the memory.

I had missed the first three months of his life, but I had loved him from the time he was born because he was *our* son. The thought of Karen and him waiting for me had given me a new reason to fight against the effects of that soul-numbing war. The reality of Robbie and Mattie would give me, give us, strength to work through the problems that had turned our love into a fearful silence. I knew I would die before I hurt her or them.

I straightened, stretched some muscles that were getting stiff, then turned for home. I walked for a while as my stomach settled, then picked up the pace. I needed to see my sons, to see if Karen and I could save our marriage. I needed to go home.

I finally arrived back in front of our house. It was little more than a dark shape in the last of the light that was fleeing over the western horizon. There were no lights on anywhere in the house. I walked around in our yard, mostly to cool down, but I was also reluctant to enter.

When I finally went into the house, I closed the front door but didn't lock it in case Karen had not come back yet. Running usually energized me, but not that night. I felt like I had burned every ounce of energy somewhere along the way and might not even make it to bed.

I walked through the dark house to our bedroom. The door was open, and she was in bed.

I went into the bathroom, peeled off my sweaty clothes, turned on the shower, and then sat in the tub as the water poured over me. My thighs were chaffed from the rough denim of the jeans, so the soap stung, but it felt good to feel something, anything, as I sat under the warm stream hissing from the showerhead. I leaned back and let it wash over me.

The water turned tepid, then cold, and brought me back out of a fatigued reverie. I toweled off, carefully crawled into bed so I wouldn't disturb her, then lay on my back waiting for sleep to come. Karen was on her side, her back to me. A minute passed, then two. She stirred, then turned over and snuggled next to me, her arm across my chest and her head on my shoulder. I inhaled her familiar scent as she kissed me lightly on the lips.

"I am so sorry, Ted," she said. "I've always loved you. I hope you believe that." She put her head on my shoulder again. It was not long before I heard her breathing change and felt her body melt into mine.

"I love you, too," I whispered as I fell asleep.

A tear falling onto my chest woke me. She moved away for a moment; I heard a rustle as she pulled her gown over her head. When she moved back to me, she was naked, like me. Her mouth was soft and sweet as she kissed me, and her tears fell onto my face.

It had been months since we had last made love and years since she had initiated it. Our passion that night was as intense and as sweet as the first night of our honeymoon. It was also the last time we would make love.

When I returned home the next afternoon, she and the boys were gone. There was a note written on her pink stationery.

Dearest Ted;

I am sorry to leave without telling you, but I think it is easier this way. It is 1:00. I'll be at my parents by 5:00. The boys are with me. Please call.

Love,
K

Sometimes love is not enough. Sometimes tears, hopes, dreams and desires are not enough to keep two people together and a family intact. Sometimes the changes that life forces on us make us strangers even to those we love the most.

I had become a stranger to Karen, and she to me. The innocent high school sweetheart she had married had disappeared into a war that no one could justify, and the man who returned to her had seen, felt, and experienced things that had changed him in ways that neither she, nor he, could understand. And what she did not understand, she feared.

So she did what, by her own lights, she had to do to protect herself and our children: she left. In June 1977, we were divorced, and our marriage became another victim of the war in Vietnam.

1986

Karen and I had parted friends, so I had unlimited visitation rights with the boys. About three years after our divorce she married a good man named Brian. He was a mid-level executive at General Motors, so he made a good living and provided the stable home life Karen needed. He also loved the boys as much I did, so Rob and Matt (they preferred their grown-up names) were flourishing.

As for me, I had found a new love right under my nose, more or less. Liz was a pianist who was a member of the music faculty. A pianist and a singer—a combination made in heaven, if they can get along. We got along; we had been living together for several years.

Where Karen had been fearful of my emotions, Liz was fearless. Both of us had talked, yelled, and cried a lot in the first couple of years. It was like we had to clear out a ton of emotional debris in order to make room for our life together. We joked that we were stuck with each other forever since neither of us wanted to go through those two years again. Life was good.

I thought I was done with Vietnam, but like the proverbial bad penny, it turned up again. It happened in May, the end of my twelfth year at the university. The dreaded finals week loomed. This was always a trying time of the school year as music students prepare for the ordeal of performance examinations, and the professors did what they could to help the students succeed. It taxed the patience and energy of both the students and the faculty. In music schools, the performance exams are called "juries," and rightly so.

I was home alone the evening before the first full day of juries. Liz, who had become an associate dean, was out for the evening at one of the many functions administrators had to attend.

I had been doing tedious paperwork and was bored. I opened a bottle of beer, snatched up the remote, and flicked on the boob tube in pursuit of some mindless diversion.

I was flipping through the channels when a news story caught my attention. A reporter was interviewing some guys wearing their Vietnam fatigues. They were giddy with excitement as they spoke of a big parade and a new memorial. There were scenes of men in fatigues embracing each other and weeping, or giving high fives as the reporter announced that there was to be a big homecoming parade for the Vietnam vets the next afternoon. "America is finally saying 'Welcome home' to all these men and women who served in that unpopular war," she said. "It will be broadcast live tomorrow afternoon from New York City."

When she said, "Welcome home," my eyes filled with tears. I turned the television off and sat in the quiet of the living room drinking my beer. I heard Liz come in from the garage and come up the stairs to where I sat. She stepped into the living room, took one look at me, and said, "You saw something about Vietnam, didn't you?"

I wanted to make a quip about her uncanny ability to read my mind, but when I opened my mouth, to my surprise, a sob came out. In no time, she had her arms around me, rocking me as we sat on the sofa, and I bawled into her shoulder. She got up, grabbed some tissues, and came back to the sofa. I was on the fourth tissue before I tried to speak.

"Holy shit! I don't know what brought this on." I blew my nose. "I watched this report about a Vietnam vets parade, and they're saying it's … it's a welcome home …" And off I went again.

I stood up and walked around the living room, into the kitchen, back to the living room, and then out onto the wooden deck, trying to get myself back under control. I needed to move, to feel the cool night air.

Liz came and stood with me on the deck, her hand on my back, saying nothing, just standing close. The storm that had taken me by surprise passed, and we wandered off to bed. I couldn't find a way to tell her what hearing those words meant to me: "Welcome home."

I came wide-awake in the middle of the night. I was lying on my back, and my pillow was wet with tears. I was covered with sweat and shaking, as if I had a fever. The dreams that woke me were strange, jumbled images of dark nights and brilliant sunlight. In my dreams, the faces seemed familiar but indistinct and run together.

My heart was pounding as I slipped out of bed and found my loafers, a sweatshirt, and sweatpants. I left our bedroom, crept to the front door, and moved into the night.

I walked through the quiet neighborhood of darkened houses where our neighbors slept. I breathed in the spring air and shivered in its coolness. All around me, new life was waiting for the sun to touch it. The world, my small world, was serene and ordered, but my emotions felt like small animals inside me trying to get out.

When I crept back into our room, with a sleepy voice, Liz asked me if I was okay.

"Yes," I said, "I'm all right." But I wasn't sure about that.

As I sat in the juries the next morning, I had trouble concentrating on the students' performances. My feelings were so jumbled that hearing even a simple folk song almost brought me to tears.

During the short lunch break, I heard myself announcing to my colleagues that I needed to be elsewhere for a couple of hours in the afternoon. That was all, no explanation. They looked at me with questions, but assured me in their wry manner that they could somehow carry on without me.

When I left the music building, I felt like someone else was in control of me and I could only follow along. I immediately went to the grocery store and bought a six-pack of beer, then went home and made a light lunch. Then I planted myself in front of the television at the time the reporter had said the parade would be broadcast.

I was playing hooky, but didn't care. Liz, the administrator, would be all over my case about unprofessional behavior and irresponsibility. I probably had it coming. What she wouldn't know was that if it had been possible, I would not only have missed the juries, I wouldn't even have been in Michigan. Instead, I would have been in New York, walking in the parade. *That* was where I wanted to be, not in a town where I could only gaze at images on a screen while everyone around me went about their quotidian lives.

So I waited through the usual hype that surrounds televised events and thought about the silence that greeted my return. It had not taken me long to learn that saying "I was in Vietnam," was a guaranteed conversation stopper. The war had been so quickly forgotten that many of the university students I taught in 1972 were not even aware that the war was still being fought.

Sitting in front of the television drinking beer, I began to understand for the first time why veterans of war call each other "brother." The term had sounded hokey to me. I had too many memories of churches where people addressed each other as brother or sister because they shared the same narrow view of the world. I also remembered how easily that cozy familial designation would disappear if anyone dared to disagree or question the dogma.

When our government sent us to Vietnam, we no longer had the luxury of choosing whom we called "brother." The "grunt" in a firefight, the nurse weeping over a child's body, the officer writing letters of condolence, the whacked-out private staring vacantly into the darkness, and even the chaplain's assistant; we were forever bound by the ennui, loneliness, fear, suffering, and rage that form the warp and woof of war. War had made us brothers and sisters, and try as we might, we would not, we could not, forget.

People who had not been there—Karen, my family, my friends, my countrymen—all of them wanted to forget the war. I told myself that people weren't callused and indifferent; how could they care about something they had not experienced, something that was so foreign, so alien? But still, their indifference hurt.

The fact was that two years of my life were MIA—and no one had seemed to care, not as long as I followed the rules, did my job, was not too cynical or bitter, and acted "normal." Fifty-eight thousand had died, and outside of the families who mourned them, few seemed to care. Thousands of vets who had survived wandered our streets, lost in their memories; their hearts were still beating, but inside they were as dead as the bodies of their brothers moldering in their graves. And nobody seemed to care.

That day in May, I discovered how much *I* cared. To my surprise, I discovered I wanted to go stand beside the men and women who would march in the parade—my brothers and sisters, each and every one.

Some of those who marched had endured the opprobrium of the very nation that had sent us to war; others had been scorned by veterans of earlier wars for having "lost" the war. They had survived the war, endured the scorn and criticism, and silently tolerated the communal amnesia that had settled over the nation even before the war had ended.

Now the assembled veterans would walk up Fifth Avenue, showered by confetti as cheers filled their ears. They would walk not as victorious heroes but as ordinary citizens who had done their duty. They were average people who had been put in harm's way for all the wrong reasons, and who had returned not to a joyful national celebration like the veterans of earlier wars, but to an embarrassed silence.

For a few hours on a warm day in May, the silence would end and thousands of veterans would step out of the national shadows and into the light of public recognition that they had been to war and survived. Welcome home? Goddamn it, it was about time.

I watched the parade, drank, and cried. Faces floated through my mind as my memory opened doors that I thought I had welded shut. As the veterans paraded in New York, I saw, and heard, and *felt* the people I had served with: Chaplain

Riggles; quiet, gentle Ira, the rabbi; Wes and Harry, Corncob 6, Skip, and Bob. I saw the face of the tiny, smiling hooch maid, Ba Lin, who swept the chapel almost every day, and I thought about the nuns and the children in the orphanage.

Of course, Rich was with me. His hearty laugh and bon vivant spirit still made me smile, even after sixteen years. And Josie? She was with me too, her tender images like butterflies on a summer day—gossamer, ephemeral, and just beyond my reach.

The parade ended. The confetti scattered in the wind, and the vets wandered away for other celebrations. I went onto the deck and leaned against the railing.

The sky was dark blue and filled with white clouds that glowed in the sunlight. A warm spring breeze played with the budding trees and birds shrieked their beaks off, calling for mates. It felt good to be alive.

I toasted the memory of all those people who had passed through my life in 1970, and told them that I loved them all and wished them well. Minutes passed as I stood in the shadow of the deck, seeing faces, hearing voices, smiling and crying, while all around me life was gathering itself for another summer.

Eventually I dried my eyes, washed my face, and, with a little reluctance, walked back to school.

The breeze was warm, fragrant, and full of promise as I walked to the campus. I felt lighter, and noticed that a calm had settled over me, a feeling I had not had for many years.

The problems and issues of my life that only yesterday felt almost insurmountable, all seemed to shrink in importance. I had been in a war and survived, and today my brothers and sisters were finally welcomed home.

As I approached the side entrance of the music building, I noticed my full-length reflection in the glass door. For an instant, a fraction of a second, I saw a young man looking back at me. Those dumb, black-framed military-issue glasses sat on his nose, and his fatigues hung loosely from his slender body. He carried hymnbooks under his right arm and held an M16 with his left hand. A camera was slung around his neck. He was bareheaded, and his short blonde hair was so light that it glowed in the sunlight. He had an embarrassed grin on his face, as if asking what the hell a musician like him was doing in the army.

I smiled back. "Welcome home, Bertson," I said. "Welcome home."